DESTINY BY CHANCE

MARGARET FERGUSON

Destiny by Chance

A Contemporary Romance Fiction Novel
By
Margaret Ferguson

With special thanks to

_____

Technical Consulation

Bobby Adair and Kat Kramer Adair

Cover Design and Layout

Alex Tsatsos

Editing & Proofreading

Cathy Moeschet

Marcia Rebrovich

eBook and Print Formatting

Kat Kramer

For my mother

So very, very different; yet, so very much the same…
Thank you for all the gifts you've given me, tangible and intangible.
They mean so much… yet never as much as you do.

I love you, Mom.

Preface

I've dreamed of being a published author since I was eighteen years old. Unlike my first two published novels, *Meeting Melissa* and *Letters from Becca*, this story was originally written in the early 1980s. It was the first story that I wrote entirely by hand. It has been thirty years since I've even looked at it. When I turned the first page, it brought back a flood of memories, and before I started rereading and editing, the story unfolded again in my mind. It's a story of loss and love, destruction, deception and passion, faith lost and faith renewed.

Destiny is a combination of several women I know, women who are strong, both in their faith and in their character. Through her, you experience overwhelming pain and loss, anger and hurt. She draws you into her struggles on many levels. You'll champion her as she strives to find her way through.

Bill was born from my perception of the character traits of a particular performer whose career I've followed through the years: personable, approachable, down-to-earth, incredibly charming, and of course, extremely attractive.

In *every* book, one character stands out and takes over the pen, and once again, it's a supporting character. Justine, who started as a minor, annoying character, was initially created to bring a little tension and stir the pot. However, once she took over her part, she became, well, I'll just say, more than I originally intended. I think I had the most fun writing her part because, once again, she became key to the plot and even took the novel in a new direction. And wow! Watch out when you meet her because you never know what she's going to do next!

The places I'll take you in the book are imaginary, but they are real in my mind. I have created the ultimate Bed and Breakfast inn called the Kemper House, in honor of one of the most influential people in my life—a mentor, mother, and one of my dearest friends, Charlotte Kemper Nations. Oh, how I wish I could have shared my stories with you!

Writing *is* my passion, right behind serving God and playing with my grandkids, and I am so excited to be able to share this part of my life with you. I hope you laugh, and I hope you cry. I hope you love the characters in this book as much as I do. I hope you will read to the end because not all of their stories end there.

—Margaret Ferguson, March, 2016

Futility

Crystal rain fell bright and sharp
Leaving scars upon my heart.
These were the tears I shed
To mourn my first love's loss

Futility
Dust in the Wind, 1952
by Marie Sien Halpenny)

Loss

Prologue

IT WAS A BEAUTIFUL DAY. A perfect day by all rights. However, the beauty of the day was overshadowed by the ashen mood of those standing before the dark holes dug into the cold, hard ground. Though surrounded by dozens of family and friends, the green carpet of fake grass and the green manufactured canopy that sheltered them from the sun were a bitter reminder of why they were there—what had to be done.

Brother Bob refused to look down at her as he spoke. *It's God's will,* he repeated over and over in his head. How could he even entertain, much less utter those words ever again? Words that he, as a pastor, now questioned. He stood over them, speaking words of amenity to the mourning crowd. He prayed for strength. For her, for their family. He prayed silently for strength for himself. There were those who heard his words as babbling and would find no value in them. And then there were those that would take comfort in them, finding strength and encouragement in their meaning. His eyes finally looked down at the young widow. What could he possibly say to diminish her grief?

She sat perfectly still, numb from the events of the day. She didn't want to be there. She couldn't believe. It was too much. The words the preacher spoke were jumbled mutterings, falling silent around her. Her eyes rested on the thin embroidered, cotton handkerchief clutched between her fingers, moist with her tears. A hand touched hers, and she looked up, if only for a fraction of a moment. The face seemed oddly familiar, sweat delicately dampening his furrowed brow. His hand squeezed hers gently as he smiled just slightly though it seemed a forced, sad smile. *How could he smile? How could anyone?*

Faces knelt before her, and talked above her, around her. More words; scripted, contrived, formulated, all saying the same thing. Prepared speeches and condolences, spit out over and over, pathetic attempts meant to comfort were simply verbal vomit that made her want to scream. Hands touched her and patted hers, making her feel uncomfortable. She shuddered and wrapped her hands around her arms, hugging herself tightly as she rocked forward.

"Destiny?"

Slowly she raised her head and looked into the eyes of her best friend, one of two people other than her husband she ever truly trusted; now one of the few people she had left in the world.

"Destiny?"

She tilted her head as if trying to understand what was said, as though it would make clearer what she was doing there.

"It's time." Lisa held her friend's face between her hands, nodding slowly. "It's time," she repeated, moving her hands to her friend's, feeling them tremble in her grasp.

Somehow, Destiny couldn't stand. Not because of the air boot that she wore from her broken ankle, suddenly, she just didn't have the strength. Or the will. As if Lisa knew, she stepped back and took one arm as someone else took the other, and they helped Destiny to stand. The sea of strangers and familiar faces before them parted. Destiny looked ahead and gasped. Her knees suddenly buckled but the arms around her caught her, holding her up.

They helped her hobble forward, inch by inch. There was no more talking, no more sounds, except occasional sniffs and soft sobs behind them.

"It's okay," Lisa whispered.

It will never be okay, Destiny screamed in her mind. *It will never be okay again!* She didn't know how she was standing; how she was moving. Tears rolled down her cheeks onto her black polka-dotted widow's dress. They walked, pressed to her side so that she would not falter, holding onto her arms as she arrived at the coffin. Tentatively Destiny reached out and touched the hard surface. Dark cherry wood. Phillip had picked it out himself when they had purchased their plots five years before. Phillip was a planner, always had been. And more than that, he loved a bargain. So when the lady called and told them that they could get their plots for just $150 apiece as long as they paid the small perpetual care fees, he was hooked.

Destiny's hand caressed it, brushing over its detail, carefully touching the etched engraving. As she turned to her brother Andy, who held her other arm, his forehead fell against hers, and he closed his eyes. Destiny thought he looked tired. When he opened his eyes again, they were moist, filled with sadness. Slowly they moved her to the side, away from Phillip's casket, and she suddenly stopped. They urged her forward, but her body refused to move. Gently they pulled her and she shook her head.

"I can't," she muttered, shaking her head more fervently.

"It's okay, Honey," Lisa prodded. "Whenever you're ready." They stopped beside her, patiently waiting. As one they began moving slowly again; stepping purposefully to the right and then stopping. She looked down, the tears momentarily blinding her. Destiny's hand trembled as it reached for the smaller casket that matched Phillip's. All of a sudden she was able to hold it in no more. The sobs came in short gasps, then deeper and louder. Emotions of the past two weeks that she had buried so deeply somehow burst from her throat, and she fell against the small casket, heaving sobs that convulsed her body. A moment later, Andy wrapped himself around his sister, turning her in his arms.

Destiny collapsed against him, crying repeatedly. "Oh, my God!" She held onto him tightly. "This isn't happening," she bawled.

Tears poured down Lisa's face as she rubbed her friend's back. She looked into Andy's eyes, which were brimming with tears as well. Lisa turned to the other friends and family. They averted their eyes, looking down or away. One by one they turned and walked from the graves until only the three of them and Brother Bob were left. When Lisa looked at Andy again, she began to sob, too. But, ever the stoic one, she suddenly drew in several deep calming breaths, then blew them out before facing Destiny. Lisa grasped her hand tighter, looking deeply into her eyes. Destiny stopped just as abruptly as she started, drawing strength from the simple gesture. Drawing courage. Lisa's hands moved to her friend's face, pulling her nearer until they were inches from one another; their gazes locked on one another's. There were no words. None were needed. Lisa nodded.

Destiny drew in a deep breath and began nodding as well. "Okay," she said under her breath, wiping her nose with the handkerchief. "I can do this."

Lisa kept nodding. "Yes, you can, Honey. We're right here with you."

Andy huddled closer to the two women. Destiny turned to her brother once more. Gently he took his sister's face in his hands and wiped her tears with his thumbs. "Whenever you're ready."

Destiny shook her head and sniffed, then nodded and used her handkerchief to wipe her nose again. Stepping toward the coffin again, she slowly released Lisa's and Andy's hands. Destiny stood before her son's coffin and smiled a sad smile, her chin trembling. She unclasped her hand, took his favorite blue Matchbox car from it and set it on the spray of blue flowers. Her fingers delicately traced the copper handle; then she slowly and carefully leaned over and kissed the wood.

"Goodbye, my loves." Destiny stepped to Phillip's coffin and kissed it as well. Then she turned and smiled sadly at her brother, before collapsing into his arms.

Grief

Chapter One

ANDY LOVED PHILLIP LIKE A BROTHER. This loss had been devastating on so many levels. He looked down at his big sister as she slept. Only two years older than him, she had been his best friend all his life. She had watched over him, been his confidant and his sounding board. When their parents both died within a year of each other from separate illnesses, they were suddenly each other's only living relative. Andy was just fifteen. When Destiny married Phillip two years later, it was Andy who walked her down the aisle and gave her away.

Andy brushed back Destiny's dark auburn hair. How could he even begin to comprehend how she was feeling? When he took the call from the Orange County Sherriff's Department that they had been in an accident, he was told they were all still alive. In fact, they were. Phillip, more seriously injured, died just after arriving at the hospital. Rhett, his nephew, alive, but unresponsive, remained on a respirator until Destiny was coherent enough to make the decision to let him go. It had been Andy, when he arrived hours later, who bore the unfathomable burden of telling her, when she awoke, that her husband and only son were both clinically dead.

Andy dropped his head to his hands and wiped his face. Slowly he looked up at the family photo on her bedside table. As he picked it up, he sighed. Andy had been at the hospital when Rhett was born. He could remember when Destiny first set the tiny, swaddled infant into his hands. He had been so nervous, holding a new baby for the first time. Andy remembered how Rhett had felt in his arms, how small and fragile he was. Andy smiled. He remembered cradling him and bouncing him like an old pro. That was eight years, one month and eight days ago.

Phillip, being the ever practical planner, had specified that they harvest his organs. Anything they could use, they took. When Andy asked his sister about harvesting Rhett's organs, she initially told them no. However, just before they disconnected life support, when she looked at his perfect, flawless body, Destiny knew her son would have wanted what his father had wanted: for him to live on in others. Andy was with her when she said goodbye to them both, separately; holding his sister's hand as she let her family go. He returned the picture to the bedside table.

When he stood and turned, Lisa was leaning on the doorjamb, arms crossed, watching him. With a nod of her head and shoulder, she motioned, and he followed her down the long hallway from the master bedroom into the open living and dining area. The house was silent. The guests had long left from sharing a meal after the service. Destiny hadn't made an appearance. Lisa and Andy had brought her in through the back garden, where there was a porch deck entry to the bedroom. They told those who asked about her that she was resting. In fact, the moment they arrived Andy had given her the last of the sedatives her doctor had prescribed two weeks before, the day after the accident. She'd be out for hours.

God, he couldn't believe it had been two weeks. The accident had occurred while Destiny's family was on their annual spring break vacation. This year Rhett had wanted to go to Disneyland in California. Only they never made it. Because the accident was out of state, it took all the different entities involved over a week to release and ship their bodies back to Texas.

When Andy flew out there, he hadn't known what to expect when he arrived. They had told him the extent of her injuries when they called him at work, but he was in such shock, he couldn't remember what they said other than his sister was unconscious, but alive and in stable condition. Her injuries were less severe—thanks to her airbags, than her husband and son's, though she was very bruised and would be sore for weeks. After setting her ankle and running extensive CT scans and other tests to assure there were no internal injuries, she was finally released within three days of the accident. Then Destiny and Andy flew home to make arrangements to receive her family's remains.

Lisa tossed him a towel as he walked into the kitchen. He smiled weakly and set to work drying the dishes she had already washed. Andy leaned on the counter beside her. "You okay?" she asked, looking over at him.

Andy shook his head. "It'll be a while." Then he sluggishly dried the glass in his hands.

"She told me she wants to sell the house," Lisa sighed.

"Yeah, she doesn't think she can stay here."

"I couldn't if I were her." Lisa moved to the liquor cabinet, taking out an almost full bottle of Malibu Rum and holding it up.

Andy drew in a deep breath. "Oh, yeah." Taking the

glass he had just dried and one that was wet, he placed them on the counter.

Lisa handed him the bottle as she moved to the refrigerator and took out two Cokes and a lime. While he poured their drinks, she sliced the lime and squeezed it into each glass as the carbon dioxide bubbles bounced inside of the crystal, like minuscule fireworks on the Fourth of July. His hand raised to hers; they tapped the mismatched glasses together. She smiled sadly before sipping. Andy became pensive as he looked into the amber liquid without drinking. Lisa turned to him and could see the hurt in his eyes, the anger stirring in his heart.

"She's going to be okay," she said determinedly.

Andy took his glass and threw it across the kitchen, and against the rock backsplash, startling her. Lisa cringed and screamed when the crystal exploded into the corner.

"Nothing's ever going to be okay again," he hollered.

She turned to him, startled by his sudden outburst. When Andy dropped his head into his hands, Lisa walked to him and stood before him. It was as though he felt her there, for he turned, moved his head to her shoulder and wept.

Chapter Two

THE SECOND MORNING after burying her son and husband, Destiny woke up to a silent house. It felt like she was in a fog. Usually, the house was bustling at this hour; either Phillip was running on the treadmill or Rhett was playing video games in his room. She looked around, disoriented. The water in the bathroom started running. Then she heard it abruptly stop. *Thank God. It was all a horrible dream.* Destiny smiled slightly, closing her eyes again. *Thank God.* "Phillip," she murmured in a raspy voice. The bed moved around her.

"Good morning."

Destiny opened her eyes, slowly focusing on the voice as she swallowed hard.

Lisa lay on the pillow beside her, facing her. Her delicately colored locks of turquoise, blue and purple made it look like she was laying on a bed of peacock feathers. "Good morning, Dee."

Destiny focused on the person before her as her smile faded.

Lisa brushed her hand over her friend's face, a sad smile on her own. "Hey, Honey."

A single tear slid onto Destiny's pillow.

"You have to get up, Dee," she smiled, brushing the hair from her friend's cheek. "You have to eat."

"I'm not hungry," she replied meekly.

"Either I feed you here, or I haul your butt to the hospital, and we hook you up to an IV," Lisa stated matter-of-factly. "Your choice."

Destiny blinked once. "I'll eat," she whispered.

"Good girl." Lisa raised her eyebrows. "Oatmeal? Biscuits and gravy? Cream of Wheat?"

Destiny nodded.

"Cream of Wheat it is. Now get up. You need to take a shower."

"I don't feel like taking a shower," Destiny moaned.

"It's been three days, Honey. Trust me, you need to take a shower." Lisa rolled off the bed before disappearing into the hallway.

Destiny turned over slowly, then crawled out of bed and dragged to the bathroom. As she stood before the mirror; it was a stranger looking back at her. She didn't recognize herself. Small scratches and cuts on the right side of her face were healing well. Fading remnants of bruising still blotched her cheek and arm. The brown eyes in her reflection blinked back at her. All she saw was an older version of herself. A much sadder version of herself. Destiny moved her hand to her toothbrush and hesitated. Phillip's still stood beside hers in the ceramic holder. Closing her eyes, she took a deep breath, then brushed her teeth and took a shower.

Lisa was just adding the finishing touches of butter and sugar to their bowls when Destiny walked into the room in a t-shirt and sweat pants. She watched her best friend hobble to the table and then set the steaming bowl before her. They sat in silence, Lisa casting glances at Destiny as she ate.

Feeling Lisa's eyes on her, she cut her eyes upward. "I'm eating," she remarked defensively.

"I'll feel better when I know you've put a few pounds back on."

"Only because you want me to stay out of your clothes."

"You look good in my clothes." Lisa rose, carrying her dishes to the sink and rinsing them. She poured herself and Destiny each a cup of coffee before sitting back down beside her. "However, I would like that chic blue cap dress back." Lisa smiled behind her coffee cup. "I have a date Saturday."

"Is this the restaurant guy from Austin or the Dellion-aire from Round Rock?"

Lisa rolled her eyes. "I should be so lucky." She sipped, then set down her coffee. "No, this guy is a marketing exec for a one of the leading-edge tech companies in the world."

Destiny smiled weakly. "Was that his sales pitch?"

Lisa crinkled her brow. "Pretty much."

Destiny stood and carried her bowl to the sink. "Is he cute?"

"Mom seems to think so."

"Your mom met him?"

Lisa walked with Destiny back to the master bedroom. "Yeah, she invited him over to lunch after church and surprisingly, he said yes." Then she plopped herself on the end of her friend's king-sized bed.

"What's his story?" Destiny asked as she disappeared into Phillip's closet. As she looked around at all the reminders of her late husband, she sighed.

"Divorced. Raising his six-year-old daughter on his own while his ex-wife works a hundred hours a week to further her career."

"Role reversal." Destiny carried out a handful of clothes to the bed. "The new family dynamic," she added, placing the clothes on her bed, then turning and going back into the closet for more.

"What's this?" Lisa asked, curiously.

"What does it look like?" Destiny tossed more of Phillip's clothes onto her bed.

Lisa followed her into the closet, moving quickly out of the way as she grabbed more and walked past again. "Are you sure you're ready for this?"

Destiny stopped on the way back to her closet and stared at her friend. "No, I'm not," she confessed, before turning and grabbing another armful. She stopped in front of Lisa again. "So? You going to help me or what?"

Lisa sighed sadly at Destiny before she reached in and grabbed an armful of dress shirts. Within twenty minutes every piece of clothing Phillip had owned lay on or around the bed. Destiny wrinkled her lips and blew them out as she faced the pile before her.

Andy walked up behind them. "Well, that's a mountain of clothes." His face betrayed his confusion. He crossed his arms. "Was there a plan when you started this?" Lisa met him with a shrug when he looked at her before turning to his sister.

"No plan," Destiny exhaled.

"So—" Andy was mystified as he walked around the mound of clothing. "Did it occur to you that your little brother, who I might add, is up to his eyeballs in student loans and can't afford a seersucker suit, has just entered the job market without a dinner jacket in his wardrobe?"

Lisa smiled. "You wear a lab coat."

"Yes," he agreed. "I wear a lab coat. But I anticipate that I will need to have a suit, or two, or three, at some point, in the event," he stumbled over his words, "that I might have a business meeting."

"You're a virologist," Lisa teased

"Or a date," he added quickly.

"Highly unlikely," Lisa quipped.

Destiny dropped to the armchair in the corner, and leaned back, staring at the clothes. As she turned to her brother, he kneeled beside her, his hand on hers. "You sure you're ready for this?"

Destiny drew in a deep breath. "Yes," she replied to Andy before turning to Lisa. "I'm sure." Standing, she walked to their dresser and began taking out the rest of his clothes. "I can't look at his stuff every day. I just can't." Her eyes lowered as did her voice. "I can't."

Lisa and Andy looked at each other, drawing in deep breaths together and then turned back to Destiny.

"I'll go to the store and get some boxes," Lisa offered.

"And I'll pick out my new wardrobe." Andy began lifting hangers of clothes from the pile.

Destiny opened Phillip's tie drawer, and it gave her pause. As her hand lightly brushed over the silky material, she closed her eyes. When she opened them, she picked up his favorite tie and pressed it to her chest. A wry smile grew on her lips. She remembered picking it out for him and giving it to him in the same way that Julia Roberts had given one to Richard Gere in *Pretty Woman*. Of course, she didn't look anything like Julia Roberts, but she always called him her Richard Gere. Phillip had the same incredible eyes, and when he smiled, his whole face smiled. Slender and fit but prematurely gray at thirty-five. And no matter how many times he wanted to, Destiny would never let him dye his hair. She told him it made him look sexy.

Destiny glanced up at her brother as he held suits and shirts in front of himself. After selecting two ties, she held one of them up to the suit and shirt combination he was holding in his hands. Destiny smiled. "He usually wore this tie," she began, having to catch herself, as she placed the tie next to the collar, "with this suit." Destiny looked into his eyes. "He was proud of you, you know."

Andy continued to hold the tie in place as he looked down. The emotions caught in his throat again as he nodded. When his eyes met hers, she smiled again, brushing his cheek with the palm of her hand.

"And, *I'm* so very proud of you." Destiny dropped her forehead to his, nodding until he was nodding with her.

Andy stepped away and sniffed, holding the tie up against the shirt again. "So this works, huh?"

Destiny nodded. "You can have anything you want. The rest I'll donate."

"Really? Anything?"

Destiny smiled. "He would have wanted you to have them."

"Well, I'm not wearing his underwear," he said pointedly. "I don't do tighty whities."

Destiny moved back to the dresser. As she looked down at the ties, then back up to her reflection, the stranger in the mirror smiled back. *You're going to be okay;* it told her. Destiny's smile faded. In her heart, she knew it would never be okay again. Ever.

Chapter Three

DAY THREE. Philip's side of the closet now sat empty, as did his drawers. And yet, he was still there. In every corner of the house. In every room. In the plates, he had personally selected from Pottery Barn. His great-grandma's silverware. His grandmother's crocheted afghans draped over the back of the couch. There wasn't a part of the house in which she didn't feel his presence. Destiny walked past 'his' chair in the living room and each of the plants he had so lovingly tended. In the days to come, she would personally give them all away because she didn't do plants. That was Phillip's thing. Ever since she could remember, she killed plants. She even tried to grow aloe vera and cactus because you weren't supposed to be able to kill them. But they also died.

Destiny hadn't entered Rhett's room since the accident, nor had anyone else. She didn't even open his door. Destiny had covered all their pictures with her black dinner napkins. Anything of Rhett's that she found anywhere in the house she put into a box in the garage, and donated, along with Phillip's clothing, the Monday following the funerals. Lisa and Andy were perplexed, not to mention concerned, by her avoidance, by her calmness. She had gone from devastated to composed in three days' time.

Destiny rolled over in their California king bed, sliding her hand across to the side where Phillip usually slept. She pulled his pillow to her face and breathed in deeply before hugging it to herself. The water was running somewhere else in the house. Destiny expressed her wish to stay in her home, at least until she determined it was time to sell. After much discussion, she agreed, albeit reluctantly, for Andy to move into the guest room, semi-permanently, so that she wouldn't be alone once she was back home. Her house was closer to work than his apartment, so it was a win-win for him. Andy moved in on the day they returned from California.

Destiny hugged the pillow closer to her chest and sighed. When she opened her eyes she could see Phillip beside her; she could feel him there. First, her fingers reached for his, gently teasing his strong, masculine hands. Destiny smiled as her hand traced the firm, strong muscles in his arms and his chest before moving to caress the early morning stubble on his cheeks. Destiny's hands remembered every part of his body, every minor flaw, every perfection, and imperfection. Her mind had memorized years ago, his sounds; the small snorts he made when he rolled over in bed, his murmurs, his snores. Her hand traced his face, every line, every wrinkle. As she brushed back his hair, her fingers played with the softening gray, his light receding hairline. Destiny breathed in the scents on his pillow again. She could stay here forever, and never let him go again. If only... If only.

There was a light tap on the door. Destiny opened her eyes and her heart suddenly sank. It was like waking from a beautiful dream. Her eyes traveled to where her hand had been, on the empty sheets beside her. How long would she remember his smell, the touch of his skin? What would happen when the smell dissipated; when the memories faded? The tap came again. Louder.

"Destiny?"

"I'm awake."

The door slowly opened, and her baby brother peered around the corner. "I was about to make some breakfast." Andy stepped inside and smiled. His sister was still in her pajamas on top of the covers.

"I'm not hungry," she whispered.

Andy walked to the bed and crawled onto it beside her, propped up on his elbow next to her. "You have to eat, Destiny," he insisted. "I'm not going to take no for an answer." His sister didn't move, curled amongst the pillows.

She smiled weakly. "I'll eat. I promise."

Andy reached over and brushed the hair from her face, grabbed a pillow to his chest and lay on it, looking at her. "I thought we could go to the bank today, and the Social Security office," he offered. "And the cemetery. I don't have to go back to work until Monday, so I can go with you."

Destiny reached over and squeezed her brother's hand. "You need to go back to work, Andy. I know you want to take care of me, but, I'll be fine."

"I know you will," he smiled reassuringly. "We're Herings!"

Destiny looked down, still holding his hand. "You know what my biggest fear is?"

Andy leaned lower on the pillow. "I've never known you to be afraid of anything."

Her eyes met his. "I'm afraid that they'll fade with time. That I'll start forgetting," her chin trembled.

Andy crawled from the pillow to her side. "Aw Destiny." His hand lightly brushed across her cheek.

"They'll always be with us. We'll never forget them. Never."

A tear escaped from her eye, but she didn't even have the strength to wipe it away. "It's what everyone says," she said, faintly. "It's what my heart wants." Destiny cried softly. "But it's those precious moments, the seconds of time when we do or say something spontaneous, the funny things Phillip would say, or Rhett's laugh. I close my eyes and I—I'm afraid that if I don't focus on their faces, and think about the things I don't want to forget, that I'll forget those things."

Andy moved closer, wiping her tears. "Destiny," he began. "You'll never forget. I promise."

Destiny looked into his eyes, blinking out more tears as she sniffed.

Andy stroked her hair. "Remember, after Mom and Dad died, how hard it was? I was always afraid of what I'd forget." His eyes focused on the wall behind her, staring at nothing in particular. "I was so sure that since we were so young when they died, we didn't have enough memories to hold us. Do you remember what you told me?"

Destiny shook her head just slightly.

"You told me that as long as we had breath in our bodies, that we'd never forget. That as many stars as there were in the sky, as many moments as there were in time, we'd have that many memories."

"I was trying to help you feel better."

"So you're saying you lied?"

"I told you what you needed to hear. Much like you're doing now."

"You think I'm telling you what I think you want to hear?"

Her eyes averted his gaze.

"Destiny. I'm not lying to you." Andy lifted her chin

with his finger. "Everything you told me was true. You were right. You may not have realized it when you said it, but you were right." When her eyes met his, he nodded. "In fact, there are memories of times with Mom and Dad that just come to me, even now. Sometimes when I want to remember, and other times when I least expect it." Andy smiled. "Remember how Mom used to bake something, like every week?"

She nodded.

"Close your eyes."

Destiny looked at him, perplexed.

"I'm serious." Andy held his hand in front of her eyes. "Close 'em."

Smiling through the tears, she slapped his hand away, then slowly closed her eyes.

"Okay, now remember when Mom would bake those apple pies. Can you smell them?" Andy closed his eyes as well. "I can."

Destiny breathed in and smiled faintly.

"I can smell the oranges when she would zest them for that breakfast casserole she used to make." Andy opened his eyes and looked at his sister. "Do you remember?"

Destiny nodded.

A small smile grew on the corner of his lips. "Do you remember how Dad would never wear a belt, and he'd walk around all day with his jeans slipping? And he'd walk into whatever room we were in, and he'd have the most annoying plumber's crack."

Destiny opened her eyes and grinned.

"And it's like he never even realized it," Andy laughed, remembering. "And he would bend over to do something, and all of our friends would make faces or laugh. He didn't have a clue what we were laughing at," he added.

Destiny chuckled. "And you would shoot tiny pieces of paper at his crack," she shook her head.

Andy laughed out loud. "I wonder if he ever wondered why he had these little pieces of paper in his underwear or if he ever even noticed them."

"Probably not," Destiny laughed. "Or he'd have gotten onto you."

"Me?" he teased. "I remember a couple of times that you tossed some paper down there, too."

"Maybe when I was little," she smiled. "When I was a teenager, it started to become gross."

"Those were good times. Glad he never caught on."

"He would have been so ticked."

""Yeah, he towed the line," Andy remembered, smiling at his sister.

"Thank you," she whispered.

"For what?"

"For everything. For being here."

"I'll always be here for you; you're my favorite sister."

Destiny nestled deeper into her pillow. "Mmm."

Andy smacked her on the bottom. "Now get your butt out of bed. I'm making oatmeal, and you're eating some."

"Oatmeal?"

"I can cook."

"It's not the packaged stuff, is it?"

Andy cut his eyes at her. "Maybe." Then he walked out of the room. "But whatever I make, you're gonna eat, Missy," he yelled from the hallway. "Right?"

"Mmm-hmm," she murmured to herself as she crawled from the bed. Destiny looked at Phillip's side of the bed again, smiled a sad smile, then walked into the bathroom and closed the door.

Chapter Four

THE FINAL STOP on their list of places to go was the cemetery. When Andy parked near the graves, they both sat in the car, quietly pensive. Destiny looked down at her hands, toying with them.

"If you're not ready, we can go."

Destiny sat still for many moments, then nodded as she drew in a deep breath. "I'll be okay."

Her hand tentatively reached for the door handle. Finally, she pulled it and the door released; her heart racing faster and faster as she slowly stepped onto the freshly mowed lawn. Grasped tightly in her hands were two small bouquets of fake flowers that they had just purchased. The Cemetery Association had a firm rule about not leaving real flowers, except those from the funeral.

Destiny looked up. It had been exactly three days since the funeral, and the flowers were still there. Many of the arrangements had fallen over or fallen apart. Beautifully hand-designed displays now lay in disarray on both graves.

Andy walked around her and stopped at Rhett's grave.

He stood the sprays up that had fallen and then collected the wilted and fading roses scattered on the ground. Destiny joined him, kneeling between the graves, picking up the single flowers that were now refuse. When she found several flowers that had not yet ruined, she gathered them into a small bouquet which she set aside. Then she placed the fake flowers at the head of each grave in small vases she had brought. The headstones ordered, including brass vases for the base of each stone, wouldn't arrive for at least a month.

Destiny kneeled between the graves and looked down at her hands. As she closed her eyes, tears rolled down her cheeks. Andy stood behind her, his hand on her shoulder. Her hand moved to his, holding it for many moments. Destiny took a deep breath and stood. She picked up the small bouquet of flowers that she had gathered before turning to her brother. "I'm ready," is all she said, before walking back to the car and getting inside.

They rode in silence the thirty-minute drive home. When they arrived at her house, Destiny put the bouquet into a small vase which she usually kept under the sink. Then she fluffed and trimmed the flowers until they made a beautiful arrangement, adding water before placing it on her kitchen counter, centered perfectly between her coffee maker and her KitchenAid mixer. Satisfied with her work, she turned to her brother and told him she was going to soak in the bath.

Andy offered to rent a movie and pop popcorn, but Destiny insisted on a rain check.

Destiny took a tranquilizer and soaked in a bubble bath until she was pink and pruned, then toweled and changed into her pajamas again before cleansing her face. She wiped the mirror with her hand, then picked up her towel and moved it across the glass in sweeping circular motions, rapid at first, then more slowly as she looked into it, her image disfigured. The more she stared, the faster her heart beat. Her breathing became labored. Destiny rubbed the glass harder, but the distortion became no clearer. The towel dropped to her side as she stared at the fogged reflection. Though she wanted to close her eyes and look away, the stranger before her held her gaze. The mist ran down the glass like rain, making it harder to see. Her breathing quickened.

"Daddy," Rhett asked. "Why can't I have a puppy? Penny Piper has a puppy."

"Penny Piper has a puppy," Phillip repeated with a smile. "Say that fast five times," he laughed.

"Penny Piper has a puppy; Penny puppy has a puppy, Penny Piper's puppy has puppies," Rhett stumbled. "I can't do it," he whined. Then he tried again more slowly. "Penny Piper has a puppy."

"Try Penny Piper has a pink and purple polka-dotted puppy," his father teased.

"Honey," Destiny prodded. "Don't confuse him."

"I'm not trying to confuse him," Phillip reasoned. "It helps with his diction."

Destiny rolled her eyes as her son continued to try and do the tongue twister from the back seat. "Sure you are."

"If I wanted to be mean I'd teach him, 'I slit a sheet, a sheet I slit, and on a slitted sheet, I sit.'"

"You're so bad." Destiny slapped his arm, then glanced out the passenger window. "I wish you'd slow down, Honey. It's really coming down out there, and the roads are slick."

"Yes, Dear," he replied as monotone as he could muster.

Destiny rolled her eyes again. Just then Rhett leaned over her seat.

"Here, Mommy, I made this for you." Rhett proudly handed her a picture he'd created on the drawing pad they kept in the car for road trips.

Destiny turned suddenly. "Rhett Curtis Hering!" she exclaimed. "Buckle yourself up right now, young man. You know you aren't supposed to get out of your seatbelt. It's dangerous."

Phillip turned around to scold his son. "Rhett! Now! You never —" he began.

Destiny turned to look out the windshield just as the car beside them moved over in front of them and immediately stepped on the brakes. "Phillip!" she screamed.

Phillip turned back around, but his reaction time wasn't quick enough to avoid the collision. Instinctively, he slammed on the brakes. The car immediately began to skid. Destiny grabbed the dash to keep from hitting it. The impact was quick; the airbags inflated into their chests upon contact. She remembered how painful it was. She remembered seeing something fly past her on the left as the car stopped only momentarily as they hit the Suburban in front of them. Their car swerved and spun.

Destiny closed her eyes, gasping for breath as she saw and felt it all unfold again in front of her. Then she heard the ominous sound of metal on metal, scraping, and crushing. Her airbag expanded, almost in slow motion, though it only took a fraction of a second. Destiny covered her ears as she heard the airbag explode again—as she heard Rhett scream and her husband moan.

Suddenly, Phillip's side of the car was hit by another vehicle that didn't expect them to be in their lane. Water ran down her face like tears as the rain poured through the shattered windshield. She tried to open her eyes but couldn't. She wanted to cry out for Phillip and Rhett, but she couldn't. Destiny began to shiver as she attempted to free herself. The door was locked. Why couldn't she make the door handle work? Their vehicle seemed misshapen or was it the confusion in her head from hitting the side window?

Destiny tugged on the door, disoriented and in pain. It wasn't moving. She tried to disconnect her seatbelt, but her fingers didn't want to work. She tried pushing the door with her shoulder, but the action was more painful than she could endure. Destiny twisted under the belt trying to free herself. She could move her arms just enough to bang on the glass. Her hands beat harder and harder against the glass as she screamed for help. "Rhett? Phillip?" she called out, to no answer. Destiny closed her eyes as she beat on the window, flat-handed. "Please," she cried, "please help me!"

She hit the glass harder, again and again. When she was just about out of energy, she hit the glass as hard as she could, and it finally broke.

Chapter Five

THE TUESDAY FOLLOWING THE FUNERALS, Lisa finally went back to work. The Salon, *her* salon complete with twelve designer stations, and a full day spa sat in the heart of "hippie town" in Austin. The spa not only catered to the weird but the swanky and the wannabes. After assuring everything was running smoothly, she left early to pick up gourmet pizza from her favorite pizza place in Westlake for dinner and then headed for Destiny's home, nestled close-by in the foothills of Austin.

Destiny's demeanor changed so drastically after the funeral that Lisa had become concerned. Her friend went from grieving widow to removing everything of Phillip's from their bedroom and avoiding going into Rhett's room. They had prepared themselves for her to grieve for months, but not prepared for this.

Andy greeted Lisa with a hug and took the pizza box from her hand. "She's soaking in the bath." He kicked the door closed behind him.

"How did she do today?"

"Not bad. We changed over accounts at the bank and went to the Social Security office, then to the cemetery."

"And?"

"And she did okay."

Lisa shook her head and sighed. "I can't believe we're even having this conversation." Her hand blindly reached into the cabinet and took out the first three cups she found. "It still doesn't feel real." Then she walked to the refrigerator, reached in and took out a Zinfandel wine that Phillip had been saving for their next dinner party. "I need a drink!" she exclaimed. Andy took it from her and poured them each a glass.

"To Phillip." Andy handed Lisa hers and tapped her glass. "A helluva man."

"A helluva man," she agreed, taking a sip. She leaned her glass against her lips, pensive.

"You know she still hasn't even gone into Rhett's room."

Lisa shook her head. "I think that's the moment that will break her. I just hope one of us is here when she is finally ready to go in."

Andy nodded his head, then downed the rest of his glass. He moved to the pizza box and lifted the lid. "Mmm." After reaching in, picking up a piece and taking a bite, he began making yummy sounds as he chewed. "This so hits the spot!"

"Made it myself," she teased.

"You should give up hairdressing." Andy took another bite.

She laughed. "Yeah, except I'd eat up all the profits."

"I'd help," he mumbled, his mouth full of pizza.

Suddenly they heard the sound of glass breaking. They both turned toward the hallway, then back toward each other. Andy dropped the pizza into the box, wiping his hand on his jeans as they raced down the hall.

"Destiny?" Andy called, as he approached the bedroom door.

"Dee?" Lisa shouted. "You okay?" She turned the doorknob, but the door was locked.

"Destiny?" Andy said, louder. "Unlock the door!"

"Dee? Honey, can you hear us? Honey. Open the door!"

Andy wrestled with the doorknob in frustration. Lisa continued to bang harder on the thick wooden door and yelled again for her friend to answer. Andy stepped back and rammed it with his shoulder.

"Ow!" he exclaimed, grabbing his arm. He stepped back, hesitated and began kicking the door repeatedly until he broke it open.

They both rushed in, calling her name. The bed was empty, so they ran to the bathroom door.

"Destiny? Can you hear us, Honey?" When she didn't answer, Lisa turned to Andy. He nodded and Lisa turned the knob. It was unlocked. She pushed it open, but it wouldn't open all the way. There was glass and blood on the floor. "Oh, my God!" Lisa exclaimed. "Call 911!" she screamed. Andy pushed the door as hard as he could to move Destiny's body aside.

"Oh, God!" Andy hurriedly took the phone from his pocket as he helped Lisa push his sister with the door so that they could get in. Blood and glass were everywhere.

"Dee! No, Dee!" Lisa felt her friend's carotid artery for a pulse. Then she grabbed the towels on the floor, carefully placing one under Destiny's head. Her hands searched Destiny's arms and wrists to see where the cuts were. Lisa began to cry.

"We need an ambulance at 605 Oak Knoll Drive. My sister——" Andy began, then started choking on sobs. "She's hurt," he added, trying to speak clearly through the emotion. "My sister, Destiny," he answered. She's bleeding. She's cut."

Lisa turned to him. "There's so much blood!"

"Thank you. Please hurry." The phone slipped from his hands and fell to the floor while the dispatcher was still talking to him. As he lifted Destiny into his arms, Lisa wrapped towels around her wrists. When he picked up his phone, his hands were covered with Destiny's blood. "Yes, I'm here," he sobbed. "Please hurry," Andy cried, holding his only sister's head to his chest.

Chapter Six

DESTINY WOKE, feeling nauseous. It took many moments for her eyes to focus clearly on anything. Nothing was familiar. She sat up slowly and looked around, disoriented. Andy was asleep in the chair beside the bed; Lisa rested on the long sofa against the wall. Destiny glanced down at her forearms, bandaged from her hands to her elbows. Plus, there was a blood pressure cuff on her left arm and an IV in the crook of her right elbow. As she brushed back her hair, she tried to remember what had happened and why she was in a hospital again.

The blood pressure cuff slowly began to inflate, becoming tighter on her arm. It felt like it would never stop, becoming annoyingly painful. She ripped it off before it could complete its process. The alarm on the machine began to beep, causing Andy to stir. Destiny tossed it away from the bed, rubbing her arm. When she looked up, Andy was sitting.

"I gotta pee," she murmured.

"Just go." Andy stepped to her bedside. "You have a catheter."

Destiny sat up and hung her legs over the edge of the bed. Suddenly lightheaded, she took a deep breath, then scooted to the edge of the bed.

Andy reached over with his arm to prevent her from standing. "You have a catheter, Destiny," he repeated.

Destiny sighed, finally comprehending what he was saying, then nodded.

She reached for a cup on her bedside stand. Andy reached over ahead of her and handed it to her.

"I can do it myself," she snapped.

Destiny took a sip of water and lay back, trying to adjust the bed by raising where her head was. When he saw her fumbling with the controls, Andy reached over to help her.

"Thank you," she said more calmly. "How long have I been here?"

"Three days," he replied, looking down and shuffling his feet, arms crossed.

Destiny looked at her forearms again, then ran her fingers gingerly along the bandages, carefully feeling them. There was no pain at the moment, just throbbing. Her heart started to race as she contemplated the seriousness of her injuries, of why she was there. Her eyes were searching his, afraid to ask. Afraid to know. When Destiny opened her mouth to speak, she somehow couldn't find the words, her eyes never leaving his.

The nurse came in to check on her and replace her blood pressure cuff. Lisa sat up when the nurse turned on the overhead light, stretched and then joined Andy at Destiny's bedside.

"Welcome back." The nurse smiled sweetly, as she checked Destiny's IV and glanced at her vitals. "I'll let the doctor know you're awake."

Destiny could feel their eyes on her, making her feel

even more uncomfortable. She pressed the buttons to lower the head of the bed just a little, and she settled uncomfortably. After pulling the covers up to her chest, she turned to face them both. There was an awkward silence as she contemplated what to say.

"So, what do I have to do to get room service around here?" she finally asked.

A small grin grew on Andy's face. "As a matter of fact, I was just about to call down an order before you woke up."

Lisa turned to Andy, mustering a small smile. "I'll fly if you buy."

"Red Robin," Destiny smiled sweetly. "I'd kill for some of those onion strings right now."

Lisa looked at her watch. "You got it." Then she picked up her large purse, carefully pulling it over her head and adjusting it on her shoulder. She fluffed her long colorful locks until they fell delicately around her face.

"Burger all the way," Andy requested. "Cooked medium. Onion strings."

"Double that order."

Lisa winked. "Same for me. Call it in. I'll be back in an hour." Gingerly, she walked out the door, leaving them alone. Andy looked up the number on his cell phone, placed the order and dropped back into the chair beside Destiny's bed.

Destiny looked up at the television as if interested in whatever should be playing on the dark screen. Andy watched her, knowing what he wanted to say, but not quite how to say it. He scooted the chair closer to the bed, leaned over and put his hand on the bed beside hers. Destiny's fingers crossed the short distance to his and enveloped his hand in hers. Her chin began to quiver as she turned to him.

Andy dropped his head onto her hand. When he looked back up at her, tears welled in his eyes. "I can't lose you, too. I can't."

Destiny saw how hurt he was, how scared. His head fell back to her hand, and he kissed it. Slowly her hand moved to his head, gently stroking his soft red hair. His tears continued to wet her hand. Moments later he raised his head and looked at her, again. "I know you are hurting, Destiny. I can't even comprehend how much you are hurting. I don't even dare to say I do." Andy leaned his forehead against hers. "But you have to trust me." His eyes pleaded with her. His heart pleaded. "You have to know that I will do everything, *everything* in my power to see you through this." Her hand lightly brushed his cheek, and he held it there. "Please, Destiny. We can get through this."

A tear slid down the side of her face. She bit her lip and tilted her head.

"Promise me," Andy sobbed. "Promise me you'll never, ever…" he stammered. Overwrought with emotion, he was unable to continue.

Destiny dropped her head to his shoulder as he wrapped his arms around her. "I promise," she whispered. "I promise."

Chapter Seven

DESTINY SAT in her living room feeling as uncomfortable as she ever thought she could feel in her own home. In her hands, she held the grief support information that Brother Bob had just given her. It had been two weeks since she'd seen him, since her unplanned trip back to the hospital, when he had stopped by to check on her. Destiny couldn't face him then, as she couldn't face him now. Not facing him was like her final act of turning her back on God, and that was fine with her.

Destiny hadn't been back to church since the funeral. If she had attended, it would only have been to appease the other mourners. Her church family had been so very kind. They had sent cards and brought food. But if Destiny never set foot in a church again, that would be okay with her. God had taken from her the two most precious people in her life. He had taken away her only son. How could she ever believe in someone who could be that cruel? She had prayed every moment until they began to cut her out of their twisted and broken rented car when she lost consciousness. And when Andy told her Phillip was dead, but Rhett was still in surgery, she had prayed for her son's life.

And yet, Rhett still died.

They sat in awkward silence. Brother Bob had said what he came to say. The donor bank that had harvested her husband's and son's organs had contacted him from California, where the accident had taken place, and subsequently sent him information to give to Destiny. But, she didn't need another reminder that her husband and son were dissected, like animals. It didn't give her any peace knowing that it might have helped someone. The only thing that got her out of bed every morning was her promise to Andy and her absolute anger at God for those she had lost.

Andy walked into the room with two glasses of water. After handing one to the preacher and one to Destiny, he sat beside his sister on the sofa. He picked up the newsletters and information Brother Bob had left on the coffee table from the donor organization, OneLegacy, scanning through them, sensing the tension.

"It was really kind of you to bring this over," Andy offered.

"Although they are in California, they have on-line and phone grief support groups. Don't get me wrong," Brother Bob continued, "we have incredible support groups locally, but since they facilitated the donations and their resources include the recipients, I thought you might want to know. In case you wished to send a letter, or…" He stopped when he saw Destiny shaking her head.

"We appreciate all you've done for the family," Andy said with a sincere smile.

The preacher leaned forward. "My door is always open, Destiny. And for you as well, Andy. I stapled my card to their newsletter again if you might want to come by and visit me, or in case, you would like to call and just talk. The grieving process is a long and painful one, and I want you to know that your church family is here for you."

Destiny nodded in acknowledgment of what he was saying, but still refused to look up at him.

Brother Bob turned to Andy, who shrugged with a sad smile. "Well," he exhaled. "I'll leave you to your packing." The clergyman stood and offered his hand.

Andy nudged his sister, who stood and finally looked up at the man. Gently, she took his hand. Andy followed with a firm handshake, thanked him again for his kindness, then showed him to the door before turning to his sister.

"You know he went out of his way, Destiny. You should have at least been a little more cordial."

Destiny forced a fake smile, before turning and walking back to the kitchen. There was still a list to finish for the movers.

Andy shook his head and looked up. *A little help here*, he mouthed, hands out.

"Did you happen to confirm with the movers this morning?" she asked, changing the subject.

Andy grabbed his hair, pretending to pull it all out, behind her back. She turned, and he quickly brushed it back into place. "Yeah, they'll be here in the morning, first thing." He watched as she nonchalantly looked through drawers and cabinets. Andy stuffed his hands into his pockets as he stepped from the carpet to the cold kitchen tiles. "I thought maybe we would do Rhett's room tonight. You and me. Together."

Destiny stopped and without facing him, shook her head. "I can't."

"Destiny," he prodded.

She turned to face him. "Andy," she said firmly.

"Please. I know you feel you're trying to help, but… please."

"You have to," he began, but she interrupted again.

"Please," she pleaded. "I'm not ready."

Andy walked to her and took her hand. "Okay," he nodded. "Okay." He squeezed it. "Say, are you hungry?"

"Not really," she replied, turning away from him.

Andy didn't release her hand, pulling her back to him, raising his eyebrow in silent reprimand.

Destiny rolled her eyes. "Fine, I'll eat."

"Thank you." Andy smiled. "Lisa said she'd meet us at six."

Destiny narrowed her eyes. "So you were already planning on me going?"

"Of course."

"So… if I refused, what were you going to do?"

"Tie you up and drag you."

"Uh-huh." Destiny turned and raised herself up onto the counter. She looked around and smiled a sad smile. "You know, I thought I was going to die in this house."

"You almost did," he reminded her.

Destiny looked down, embarrassed. "Yeah," she conceded. "I almost did." Leaning forward, she held on tight to the countertop, then looked up at her brother. "I had my whole life planned out, ya know? We were trying to get pregnant before…" she stopped suddenly, looking down. "We wanted to have two more kids. Then I was going to quit teaching and homeschool. We were going to travel the world and introduce our children to different cultures. We were going to teach them and show them things we never experienced when we were kids." Destiny looked down again. "We were going to grow old together. And do all the annoying things old retired people do," she smiled, remembering. "Phillip would talk about spoiling our grandkids, and Rhett wasn't even—" Destiny drew in a deep breath to keep from crying. "He wasn't even nine yet. And we were already talking grandkids," she mused.

Andy leaned against the counter opposite from her, crossing his arms. It was the most they had talked about her family since the accident. "Phillip was *definitely* a planner."

Destiny nodded and smiled, looking down at her feet. "Yeah, he was that." Slowly she began shaking her head. "He always planned for everything. Every scenario. Every outcome. He wanted me to be prepared for everything." She sighed. "He just never prepared me for this."

"For what?"

Destiny hesitated, then looked up at her brother. "Starting over."

Starting Over

Chapter Eight

BILL WOKE with a start when he heard his daughter call out. He threw back the feather comforter (the one his ex-wife had personally selected at Bed Bath and Beyond) and pulled on the L.L Bean bathrobe (that his ex-wife had given him the *only* Christmas they were together). While racing down the hallway to his daughter's room, his little toe caught the corner of the doorframe as he turned the corner. Bill yelped out in pain and fell—more like tumbled, like a sacked football player. Then, he slid ungracefully down the hallway, a result of forward motion, accelerated by the polished wood floor and the expensive fleece robe. When his nose connected with the solid mahogany antique replica of the Captain Davenport's desk (the one his ex-wife had insisted they needed, but then never used) that sat at the end of the wide hallway, the pain in his foot was momentarily forgotten. Then, he cursed, out loud.

Bill limped into the room of his crying daughter, holding his nose, feeling it throb beneath his fingers. He crawled into her bed as she sobbed. She grabbed ahold of him, hanging on tight.

"Shh," he whispered. "It's okay, Sweetie. Daddy's here."

Sydney crawled into his lap and held onto him, tears still running down her cheeks.

"What's wrong this time, Sweetie?" Bill stroked her hair, his nose and toe pulsing with every heartbeat. "Huh?" he asked, taking her face into his hands. "Syd?"

The young girl looked up at him. "There was a mean witch, and she had these things with her. Gargirls."

Bill smiled. "Gargoyles?"

Sydney nodded. "And they were scary, and they were trying to take me away." She pressed herself against his chest again.

"Aw, Sweetie. I'm going to have to stop letting you watch even cartoons if they are going to scare you."

"No," she cried louder and pulled on his arms.

Bill pushed her away and chuckled, brushing the hair from her face. "Daddy just wants you to stop having bad dreams."

Sydney nodded, calming down. As she leaned against him and closed her eyes, she heaved an occasional dramatic sob for effect.

Bill slowly rocked her in his arms, stroking her hair as he hummed. As her sobs subsided he began to sing softly to her. "Hush little baby, don't say a word. Daddy's gonna buy you a mockingbird."

"I miss Mommy," she murmured softly to his chest. She pulled away and looked up at him. "Do you miss Mommy, Daddy?"

"Shh." Bill held her tight and kissed the top of her head. Then he sighed, looking over at the picture of his ex-wife, when she was younger, that his daughter had asked him to place on her bedside table. It was the only picture he had, and Justine's mother had given it to her after the divorce, for Sydney. Bill continued to rock her gently. "And if that mockingbird don't sing, Daddy's gonna buy you a diamond ring…"

Chapter Nine

DESTINY LOVED HER PRINCIPAL. Rita was kind and compassionate. But, she was also a practical joker. There were occasions when staff would come in to find their desk drawers filled with rocks or their desk chairs hanging from the ceiling. Many of the staff tried to one-up her, but that all ended when one of the perpetrators hooked up a bucket of water over the principal's office door and the superintendent (being a man, but not a gentleman), opened the door and walked in ahead of her. He upset the bucket soaking himself from head to toe. Of course, he didn't think it was funny since he was scheduled to shoot a public television segment thirty minutes later and had to drive halfway across Austin in midday traffic to change. Everyone else thought it was hilarious. It had been a long time since Destiny had laughed that hard. And the story never got old, as they retold it at lunch and for many days to come. However, practical jokes ceased at that point forward.

She used to love her job. Destiny was in charge of the gifted and talented program at a high school in the heart of the hills of Austin. After her accident, both her doctors encouraged her to take a full six weeks off to recuperate from her physical injuries and emotional setbacks, before returning to work. Technically, she didn't have to return to work until the following school year. But she wanted to work; *needed* to work. She called Rita, offering to helped during summer school—a time she used to look forward to spending with Rhett—just so that she didn't have to be at home. Alone.

Always the planner, Phillip had purchased hundred-thousand-dollar life insurance policies on himself and Destiny after they were married, plus a smaller one on Rhett after he was born, through Gerber Life. However, he had a second term life insurance policy through his work for a half a million dollars, and a 401K with a good financial investment portfolio, that he contributed to every paycheck. Destiny would never have to work again if she didn't want to. But she didn't have anything else to do. She didn't have any hobbies. There was no more picking up or taking Rhett to school, or any of his extracurricular activities like soccer or Cub Scouts to occupy her long afternoons. No more making dinners for the family, or taking off for mid-day school events.

They owned their home outright, bought with her half of the proceeds from the sale of her parents' home, after their deaths twelve years ago. Within two months of their deaths, their home was put on the market and sold relatively quickly, so she immediately purchased and then moved into a loft overlooking Town Lake. But it wasn't home. It would never be home. It was just a place to sleep and eat and sometimes relax. Coming home used to be something she looked forward to; now she hated going home at all. Her psychiatrist, Dr. Villarreal, encouraged her to get involved somewhere or to find a hobby.

Andy suggested she join a book club or a horseback riding club since she loved both when she was younger. Lisa agreed. Now, the two people she cared for most ganged up on her until she did one or the other. So Destiny did both. She joined a weekly book club at the local library that met one evening a week and found a stable just outside of town where she could ride. Now she rode every weekend.

Brother Bob had called her on two separate occasions over the past two years to visit. Destiny kept the conversations as brief as possible. Her friends in the congregation still sent her occasional notes and cards and called or stopped by her new loft. Destiny was always cordial and polite, but within the first year after the accident, she had cut off her relationship with virtually all of her old friends, except Lisa, and those who worked with her. Andy and Lisa still tried to get her to go to church with one or the other, and yet she always made excuses or just said no. But they never stopped asking her.

Lisa, twenty-nine and perpetually single, worked long hours in her shop, but always made time to do community service activities and *always* invited Destiny to come. Lisa wasn't as understanding as Andy, who accepted excuse upon excuse for Destiny's lack of participation in anything outside of work. In the past six months, Destiny had participated in events from Feast of Sharing for the Homeless, walks for Autism, Heart Association and AIDS, and home builds for Habitat for Humanity. Lisa was involved, both personally and through her business, in at least a dozen charities. Her business, being extremely successful, afforded her the opportunity to serve on many boards and even chair many events. Lisa had twisted Destiny's arm multiple times when Phillip and Rhett were still alive, and sometimes, they had helped or participated as well. Since their deaths, Destiny had been less active, but thanks to Lisa, never inactive.

Lisa had always been like a sister. Besides Andy, Destiny had no family other than distant cousins she'd never met. Phillip's maternal grandparents were still alive but were career missionaries overseas. She'd only met them twice on their visits home. They had wanted desperately to attend the funeral, but Destiny knew the logistics for them to travel would have been detailed and expensive, so had convinced them not to come. In honor of Phillip and his love for them, however bittersweet, she selected their ministry as the beneficiary for anyone who chose not to send flowers to the funeral.

The only *grandpa* she knew was Lisa's by blood though he claimed Destiny as his own. Eighty-seven and feisty as the day was long, he checked up on her regularly as well, always inviting her to be his date for Friday night at the Senior Center. 'I'm not getting any younger,' he would say, insisting every Friday might be her last chance.

Friday nights used to be date night for Destiny and Phillip, so Destiny always tried to schedule something that night. Always alone. Sometimes she would just go window shopping at the mall, or even wait to do her grocery shopping on Friday instead of earlier in the week. And sometimes she went to the movies, always making sure to be home after nine, so she was tired, and wouldn't be tempted to sit around. Time alone was her enemy. It opened the door for her to think. For her to remember all the things she used to be afraid to forget. Quiet times, and moments to herself that she used to treasure, she now dreaded.

One particular Friday night, Lisa invited her (again) to attend the Bingo Night and Fish Fry at the Senior Center. Destiny hadn't played bingo since she was a child, and, since Phillip couldn't stand catfish, she hadn't eaten any since they had started dating almost eleven years ago. So, for the first time in two years, Destiny—without badgering, arm twisting or manipulating involved—agreed to go. Lisa was ecstatic. Destiny assured her friend that she was *only* doing it for Grandpa.

They didn't start until six, and since school let out at three, and Destiny would be out of work by four, she decided to stop by the stable first. She wanted to check on her mentor, Uncle Charlie, as everyone called him who had fallen earlier that week. Destiny had bought him a gift; a little something to keep him busy while he was laid up.

Destiny turned off the paved road onto the gravel and dirt road to the main farmhouse just a hundred feet from the stable. There were three other cars in the driveway that she didn't recognize. Usually, people that came during the week were taking riding lessons and rarely rode free range on the weekends. Destiny, being an experienced rider, could come any time she wanted. Since they didn't allow anyone to take the horses out after dark without escorts on the property, Saturdays and Sundays became her preferred riding days.

Beavis and Butthead, Charlie's beloved beagles, welcomed her with pawing and yipping, excitedly dancing around her even after she accorded them with a head scratch. Before she even reached the steps to the porch, Charlie was standing in the doorway, leaning on one crutch, and holding the screen door open for her with the other.

"What are you doing out of bed?" Destiny scolded him.

"What? Did Jezebel here already warn you to nag me?" Charlie replied with a playful scowl.

"Come on in, Honey." Jessie cut her eyes at her husband. "His bark is worse than his bite." She hugged

Destiny in the doorway, causing Charlie to hobble backward.

"Whatever," he growled, limping past them to the living room, where he proceeded to flop himself into his oversized recliner. He dropped his crutches and finished the root beer sitting beside him on the table.

On the sofa sat a young girl enthralled in the animated movie on the widescreen before them. Jessie caught Destiny looking at the child. "That's our grand-niece, Sydney. We sometimes pick her up in the afternoons after school so she can ride. Tonight is her first time staying over. Sort of a trial run. Her daddy will pick her up in the morning."

"She's adorable." Destiny watched as the child bounced with excitement and sang with the characters on the television.

"Yeah, don't let her hear you say that, or you'll have a friend for life."

Sydney danced and tried to mimic the moves of the animated figures on the screen as she sang.

"Maybe that's not such a bad thing," Destiny smiled.

"So, you come for a quick ride?" Jessie asked. "Charlie is known for his quick rides." Jessie winked as she patted his arm.

Charlie looked up, noting her expression, and scowled. "The hell you say."

Destiny grinned at their sly humor. "No, I just wanted to bring Charlie a little something to occupy his time and maybe keep him out of your hair."

"Oh, my goodness, girl. You can come over every day and bring him anything you want to keep him out of my hair."

"Old woman!" Charlie retorted.

"Better be nice, old man," she teased. "Or you'll be

cookin' your own meals on one leg." She winked again at Destiny.

Destiny handed him his sack. "It's not much. I know every time we've met at Cracker Barrel you always like playing the triangle puzzle, so thought you might want one to play here."

"Why, thank you, Destiny."

"Thank you, Jesus! That will keep him confounded for hours." Jessie grinned.

"Jezebel," he muttered under his breath.

"Scrooge."

"Well, I really should go." Destiny back stepped toward the door.

"Oh, Honey. You have to stay for dinner," Jessie insisted.

"I can't. I'm meeting Lisa at the Senior Citizen Center down the road. We're going to play bingo and eat catfish."

"That the girl with a peacock on her head?" Charlie asked with a smile.

"That would be the one."

"Don't understand young kids today," he added with a shake of the head. "They shave their heads, and if they don't, they go and put every shade of the rainbow in 'em! They even paint themselves with tattoos, and put earrings in their noses and other unmentionable parts of their bodies."

Destiny's grin grew.

"Now, Charlie, that's not a nice thing to say. That's her friend, and she's a nice girl."

"I'm sure she is. Just don't understand it, that's all," he muttered.

"Well, Honey, you don't worry about the unimportant things like what color the girl's hair is and focus on the perplexities of the world that are more important, like how you're going to win that game." Jessie walked with Destiny toward the door.

"Bye, Charlie," Destiny said with a wave. "Bye, Sydney," she added.

The young girl turned and looked at her, perplexed, waved her direction and then went back to watching her movie.

"Hrrmph," Charlie growled, as he took the puzzle out of the bag.

"To him, it's like a Rubik's Cube. It'll keep him stumped for hours," Jessie added.

"I heard that!" Charlie hollered from his chair.

"You ain't heard nothin, old man," she laughed. "Not since your daddy shot off the rifle right by your ear when you was ten."

"Huh?"

"See what I mean. Deaf as he is mean," Jessie added, saying the last part a little louder before glancing his direction.

"What?" Charlie asked.

Destiny turned at the door. "I'll see you in the morning."

"You come on out any time." Jessie reached to hug her.

Destiny welcomed the embrace, closing her eyes. "Thank you." It felt good to be hugged. Daily intimacy was just one of the things that she missed. Throwing a wave over her shoulder, she walked to her car and looked up into the bright, clear sky. The wind blew just slightly and the still warm Texas evening air felt good on her skin. Texas weather was fickle; sometimes the changes were subtle, sometimes more drastic. It could be in the hundreds one day and thirty the next when a cold front blew through. Today was perfect.

As she started her little Sonic, the headlights flashed

on. Phillip was a Chevy man, and after he died, Destiny still felt true to his tastes and his traditions. So, she sold both their cars, and using the remaining money from paying them off, and some of the insurance money, she bought the most practical, energy efficient Chevy on the market. Her cell phone rang in her purse, and she dug to find it before it stopped ringing.

"Hello?"

"You on your way?"

"Leaving now. I'm fifteen minutes away."

"Hurry up!" Lisa insisted. "There's this adorable guy here you just have to meet."

"Not there to meet men," Destiny stated firmly.

"See you in a bit." Before Destiny could respond, Lisa hung up.

Destiny stared at her phone, growling, and dropped it back into her purse. It wasn't the first time her friend had conveniently introduced her to single men she knew. But she wasn't ready. Maybe she'd never be ready. It wasn't something she wanted to think about at this point. Destiny looked at herself in the rearview mirror, hesitating. Then she sighed and backed her car away from the fence, heading back the same way she came, leaving a cloud of dust behind her.

Chapter Ten

THE NEWLYWEDS WALKED up the steps to the porch that wrapped completely around the restored historic house. They arrived at the front door, dragging their luggage behind them, a resounding thud repeating as the wheels traveled from step to step. Bill greeted them at the doorway and took their bags.

"Mr. and Mrs. Walker, I'm so glad you made it. Your room is all ready," he smiled. "I'm William Ireland, the owner. I talked to you on the phone. But you can call me Bill." He shook their hands. "I'll take your bags up to your room if you'd like to go into the library. We've baked some cookies for you. They're still warm."

The couple grinned at each other. "We could smell them when we walked in," the young bride answered excitedly. "I'm Jeannie, and this is Butch."

"Welcome and congratulations on your nuptials," Bill said. "There's a carafe of ice-cold milk and another of iced water to enjoy with your cookies. Please help yourselves."

"Thank you." Butch turned to his wife and with a gentle touch of his hand led her into the library.

Bill dragged the suitcase up the carpeted stairs and into the bridal suite, which was actually the original master bedroom of the ten-bedroom home. He and Sydney occupied the only two bedrooms on the first floor, each with its own bathroom which had been added ten years before he purchased the property. He had originally occupied the second floor but rarely rented out the smaller rooms on the first floor. Most of his inquiries were for the larger rooms upstairs, that had extended views of the gardens, so he thought he would experiment with a room swap to see if it made a difference. Once he traded their residence, he sold out all of his rooms regularly. The relocation worked better for him as well, since he didn't worry as much about Sydney running up and down the stairs several times a day when she was younger. Although, Bill was sure she did it anyhow, only when he wasn't looking.

Bill took great care in pampering his guests. They provided the best soaps, body washes, shampoos and bath salts, all from Austin producers. Every morning their guests dined on exquisite breakfasts, all hand prepared, either by himself, his house manager or a chef they hired on occasion—when overrun with business. And they only purchased from local farmers and purveyors also, to support small businesses.

The Kemper House and Gardens Bed and Breakfast was renowned in Texas and listed as one of the top 20 in the state by *Texas Monthly* and *Texas Highways*. In the eight years since he'd purchased and renovated it, they had been featured in no less than a dozen national travel magazines. Since opening, it had been visited by senators and congressman, stars of television and film, musical performers, and presidential hopefuls. Not to mention twelve seven-year-olds for a slumber party for Sydney's last birthday.

Sydney had requested a princess tea party, complete with makeovers and character costumes. One of the children's parents, a reporter for the *Austin American-Statesman,* thought it would make an excellent article for the Leisure section of the paper one Sunday. Suddenly Bill began getting phone calls inquiring about the availability of the property for other similar parties, such as birthdays, rehearsal dinners, Christmas parties, and even wedding receptions.

The house sat on almost ten acres; it was gated, complete with beautifully manicured gardens and water features that emptied into a one-acre pond. There were paved walking paths that crisscrossed through the property and a gazebo. After that article, they went from being booked every weekend, to being booked almost every day, which made it difficult for Bill to spend the time he wanted to with Sydney. But he refused to be an absentee father. So, he added two other warm bodies that would welcome guests, cook and in general, wait on guests as needed— basically, everything he already did. One of them, Deborah, was allowed to live in an attic room that they renovated but never had success renting out since it was much smaller than all the other rooms.

Within three years of opening he had recovered all his expenses on renovations and was turning a profit. He had been offered over a million dollars on two occasions to sell though he hadn't even listed it. Bill turned them both down. It wasn't that he was holding out for more; it was his home; a home that he shared with strangers, but more than that, a home that he shared with Sydney. It was the only home she'd ever known. She loved meeting new people every week, sometimes, every day. They lived close to her school. It was a safe neighborhood. And Sydney had friends nearby with whom she could play. Of course, they preferred coming to the Kemper House because they could play hide and seek in the gardens or swim in the pool at the base of the waterfall. Bill much preferred that to Sydney sitting in her room playing video games. However, he had to balance the fact that their home was also a place of business and a bunch of screaming seven and eight-year-olds weren't usually what the guests expected when they were visiting.

Deborah peeked her head into the kitchen. "You ready for me to take over?"

"Absolutely." Bill wiped his hands on the apron. He untied it, took it off, and then tossed it into the laundry basket in a corner of the kitchen by the pastel blue wall. "The Walkers just checked in—Butch and Jeannie. I've already taken their bags up. I saw them walking out in the gardens a few minutes ago."

"Beautiful night for a walk," she smiled, putting on her apron. "The rolls rising for morning?" she asked, as she mentally inventoried the prepared items for breakfast. "Everyone else checked in for the night?"

"All checked in," he confirmed. Bill turned to face her.

"Oh, my God! What happened to your nose?"

"Long story," he began. "Let's just say that I'll be using the mahogany desk for kindling come winter."

Deborah snickered into her hand.

"I'm going to go and check on Sydney. Please make sure she doesn't stay up too late, okay?" He narrowed his eyes playfully. "And no late night Coke floats," he added with a wag of the finger. "She was bouncing off the walls when I got home last week."

Deborah smiled, after tasting a finger full of icing from the beaters that she was about to spread on the still-warm chocolate cake. "Yeah," she crinkled her lips. "Sorry about that. Blame that on my blind trust of an eight-year-old with beautiful eyes and an adorable smile."

"You should know better. Even an eight-year-old knows how to work those beautiful eyes and that adorable smile. Trust me, when she's working you, she has an ulterior motive. This comes from someone who's been worked by that same child. Once she wraps you around her little finger, she owns you."

Deborah laughed. "How many for breakfast?"

"Twelve tomorrow and sixteen, Sunday."

"Allergies?"

"One gluten free, one diabetic, one lactose intolerant."

"Right." Deborah turned back to the menu, running her finger over the recipes for the following day. She'd either make the adjustments or use completely new recipes for those with allergies. "Will you be late tonight?"

"Not too late." They walked together toward his living space. "Bingo night again at the Senior Center. If they aren't done and gone by nine, I'd be totally surprised."

"I don't know. I've seen some pretty spry eighty-year-olds. Who knows, maybe they'll catch their second wind and last til midnight."

"God, I hope not," he chuckled. "I'd be a sad sight if they outlasted me."

"I'll take care of everything," she smiled, as she walked up the stairs.

"I know you will," he winked. "Thanks, Deb. For everything."

"No, *thank you*. If it weren't for you, I'd be homeless."

He arrived at Sydney's room. Deborah smiled and walked on up the stairs. Bill peeked into his daughter's room. She was lying in bed, in her Cinderella dress, reading Cinderella. "Hey, Sweetheart. Dressing the part, I see."

Sydney beamed. "Hey, Daddy. You leaving?"

"Yes, Sweetie. But Deborah's here, and she'll get you in bed."

Sydney grinned.

"No Coke floats."

Sydney's smile faded.

"You can have ice cream, though," he countered. "One scoop."

"I guess that's acceptable," she said matter-of-factly as she closed her book.

"Oh, well," he scoffed. "I'm glad that's acceptable."

"Park tomorrow?"

"Park tomorrow," he promised as he kissed her on the head. "Bed by nine."

She rolled her eyes back to her book.

"Nine," he repeated.

She sighed dramatically. "Fine."

Bill narrowed his eyes.

Suddenly a smile grew on her face, and she stood on her bed and jumped into his arms. "Just kidding!"

"You're lucky I love you so much." Bill turned her in his grip, then dropped her back onto her bed.

"And *you're* lucky I love you *so* much."

"Yes." Her father brushed back her straight black hair and kissed her forehead. "Yes, I am."

"Be good." Sydney wagged her finger at him as he turned to leave.

"Always." Bill closed the door and smiled to himself. "Eight going on eighteen," he remarked under his breath with a shake of his head. "God help me."

Chapter Eleven

DESTINY DROVE behind the Senior Center as per Lisa's instructions and parked under a light, as Phillip had always taught her. Growing up in the country, she didn't use to worry about such things. Living in a big city had its perks, and sometimes its pitfalls. Phillip was as overprotective as he was practical. He made sure she had mace in her purse, a key fob with an alarm and even gave her a gift certificate for self-protection classes one Christmas. Though she had rolled her eyes at the time, nine months later she was attacked by a purse snatcher in broad daylight. In class, she was taught to give up her purse. However, she had thousands of dollars of cash and gift cards in her purse for a church fundraiser, and somehow couldn't bear just to let it go. Grateful, at that point, for the classes, she not only managed to keep her purse but gave the perpetrator a bloodied nose. Many of those who witnessed the whole occurrence and rushed to her aid, arrived just after she nailed him in the groin, bringing him to his knees. Some applauded her while the rest sat on the young man until the police arrived.

The parking lot was full. Destiny stepped through the metal door at the back entrance. Tentatively, she walked down the hallway into the bustling hall. The old Senior Center smelled of popcorn and potpourri. The potpourri was to cover the faint smell of cigarettes—a smell that still clung to the insulation and had become a part of the sheetrock—from decades before they implemented a no smoking policy. After being an extrovert most of her life, she had become more introverted since burying her son and husband. So, with every step she took now, she contemplated turning and leaving. But she knew Lisa would only track her down and drag her back. Destiny drew in a deep breath for courage and then entered the main hall.

The bingo caller was rapidly speaking letter and number combinations into a microphone, while men and women sat expectantly in metal chairs around folding tables, poised to stamp in unison once their numbers were confirmed. Some of them had three cards each, their allotted limit for every game. They methodically perused each card in rapid succession to try and stay ahead of the bingo caller as well as the other players. Every fifteen seconds, a new number was called, mostly to assure that they could get in as many games as possible before eight-thirty.

It wasn't hard to spot Lisa. She stood out like a parade float on a city street. She was sitting beside a man in a wheelchair who was breathing with the assistance of an oxygen tank, helping him fill his card. Destiny smiled. Lisa didn't care how differently she dressed, or how much she *looked* like she didn't fit in. Her heart was in the right place. These people welcomed her and talked to her as though she was one of them.

Destiny and Lisa had been best friends since childhood

though their paths through the years had been different. Lisa became an entrepreneur. Destiny, by fate, ended up the head of a household at seventeen. When she wasn't in school, she was working to help make ends meet. Her parents weren't planners like Phillip. They each had purchased just enough life insurance to pay for their funerals. Barely. Destiny and Andy were able to collect Social Security after their parents' deaths. Her brother wanted to go to college and had to depend on scholarships and student loans until they finally sold their family home. Destiny, on the other hand, not only had a full scholarship but applied for enough additional ones to cover the cost of her books and dorm expenses.

Destiny watched Lisa interact with the elderly men on either side of her. Both of them were in wheelchairs. In fact, practically a fourth of those around the tables were in wheelchairs, chuckling and nudging each other in jest. Lisa looked up and spied Destiny. She waved and rushed to Destiny's side. Immediately she grabbed her best friend by the arm and led her to their table. Lisa stood just behind her friends, waiting for someone, anyone to say "bingo." That would give her a fifteen-minute break for introductions. A moment later one of the men sitting beside Lisa yelled: "'Bingo!" Everyone else groaned with disappointment, then immediately stood to either grab something to eat at the concession stand, run outside for a quick smoke, pee, or swap out bingo cards.

"Dee, I would like you to meet my friends, Harry, and Ralph."

Ralph wheeled his chair backward a few inches, holding out his hand, taking deep breaths in between sentences. "Lisa tells me," he began, drawing breath from his portable oxygen tank. "This is your first time here."

Harry, one of the oldest men there, wore a baseball cap

with "American Veteran" sewn across the front, adorned with assorted pins and flags, from various units and states. He also wore a vest with "Veteran of Foreign Wars" embroidered across the back, plus more pins, and several patches. "Can't understand why two lovely young ladies like you would want to hang out with a bunch of old geezers like us rather than going out with some young whippersnappers."

"Ah, Harry," Lisa smiled, kissing his cheek. "You know I like older men." She winked at Destiny. "Besides, with you guys I don't have to worry about anyone hitting on me and then disappointing me."

Destiny grinned.

Ralph laughed, causing himself to cough. "Speak for yourself, Harry," he gasped, then coughed once more. "I, myself, like the attention." He drew in a deep breath. "This is the most action I get all week." He looked at Lisa and tapped his cheek. She obliged him by kissing it.

"You fellas thirsty?"

"I'll take a margarita," Harry grinned.

"Make mine a double," Ralph added.

Lisa narrowed her eyes. "We'll see what we can do." She turned to Destiny and took her by the arm. "Come on, there's someone I want you to meet."

Destiny stopped walking and cringed. "Aww, Lisa."

"Quit whining," she interrupted, tugging her back into motion.

Destiny pursed her lips as she allowed Lisa to drag her to the concession stand.

When they arrived, Lisa refused to release her friend's arm, holding her firmly in place. They stood behind two women with a handful of one-dollar bills, eager to fill their bellies with whatever junk food they could afford. The man behind the counter took their order and glanced just past them. Destiny looked up just as his eyes met hers. They held hers for just a moment before he smiled and looked back to the women in front of her, who were still deciding what they wanted. Destiny felt her face flush. She couldn't remember the last time that a look by any man had brought about that reaction. She quickly looked down at her feet.

"I think you're going to like this guy," Lisa continued. "He's smart, he likes the outdoors, and he's not hard on the eyes."

Destiny looked away, feeling extremely awkward. "By the way, where's Grandpa?"

"Cruise," Lisa answered nonchalantly.

Destiny's mouth hung open as she turned back to her friend. "Cruise?"

"Yeah, didn't I tell you?"

Destiny narrowed her eyes. "No. I guess you forgot that little detail."

Lisa tried to avoid her friend's glare. "Oops," she smiled. "Must have slipped my mind."

"Mmm," Destiny murmured, arms crossed, realizing she'd been tricked.

The women in front of them grabbed their large popcorn, Nestle's Buncha Crunch, hot dogs and large sodas. They squeezed past Destiny and Lisa, their arms overflowing.

"Hey, Lisa," the man behind the counter smiled.

"Hey, Bill." She looked over at her friend nervously. "This, is my best friend, Destiny."

When Destiny's eyes met his again, she blushed. "Nice to meet you," she said, her eyes staying on his only for a moment longer.

"Nice to meet you, too," he replied, offering his hand.

Destiny slowly took it and shook it.

"What happened to the nose?" Lisa motioned with a nod of her head.

"Long story," he sighed.

"I'll bet it's a good one," she teased. "Can't wait to hear it. Two margaritas, please. Make one a double."

"Ralph and Harry?" Bill chuckled.

Lisa nodded.

"Two Seven Ups on the rocks, coming right up."

"Do you want anything?" Lisa asked her friend.

Destiny shook her head. She just wanted to get out of there.

When Bill returned with the sodas, Lisa smiled. "Is Owen around?"

"Owen!" Bill yelled over his shoulder; then he looked at the women. "Sorry," he said more quietly. "Intercom's broken."

Lisa nodded, looking over Bill's shoulder.

A nice looking man, wearing a dress shirt and pressed slacks, looked around the corner and smiled. "Hey, Lisa!"

Owen walked toward them, wiping his hands on a dishrag. Destiny thought he was a little over-dressed for being in such a dive. He smiled at the women before he simply pushed Bill, full-armed, out of the way. A perplexed Bill fell into the wall. It was quite comical. Destiny had to bite her lip to keep from laughing. Lisa showed no restraint and laughed out loud.

Bill recovered after a moment and resumed his duties. "Anything else?"

Lisa looked up at the menu board, then shook her head. "No offense but nothing really looks good."

"None taken." Bill took Lisa's money, his eyes on Destiny.

Owen furrowed his brow. "I take offense. I wrote the menu." He smiled at the women, turning his full attention to Destiny. "So, you're the little lady that Lisa's been talking about all these months?"

Destiny shrugged. He was as nice looking as Lisa had described. However, she kept finding herself casting an occasional glance at Bill as Owen spoke. He looked like he'd been in a prize fight; a swollen nose, dark bruising under his eyes. Despite his injury, he had kind eyes and a friendly smile. Owen walked around the bar counter to get a closer look at Destiny.

"Lisa didn't exaggerate when she said you were adorable."

Destiny blushed again, not sure how to respond.

Owen motioned for her to step away from the counter so that they wouldn't be blocking the line of impatient bingo players anxious to get back to their game. "Why haven't I seen you in here before?"

Destiny looked down as she walked. She shrugged again. "Friday night is usually my night to unwind," she said, hoping it was enough.

"Nothing like unwinding with a bunch of old farts that have nothing better to do." When she didn't say anything else, he added, "Well, I'm glad you finally came. I think you'll see that these guys just want a little company. It's their chance to get out. They get a free, healthy meal. It's kind of like a reverse Meals on Wheels." Owen smiled. "Get it? Reverse Meals on Wheels? They come to us?"

Destiny nodded at his lame attempt at humor. "Got it." She drew in a deep breath and looked around for Lisa, realizing she had conveniently disappeared. "It was really nice meeting you, Owen," she smiled and held up her hands with the cups in them. "I really need to get these to Ralph and Harry."

Owen seemed disappointed, but he pasted a smile on his face. He held out his hand, looked down at hers and realized her hands were full so moved his hand to her elbow and shook it. "I'll check in on you after awhile," he winked.

"See you around." Destiny grinned, then turned and grimaced as she quickly walked away.

Lisa appeared from nowhere and took her arm as they walked to their table together.

"Don't ever do that to me again," Destiny said flatly.

"You didn't like him?"

"He was nice enough," Destiny conceded. "But I told you before, I don't know if I'll ever be ready to date again." She drew in a deep breath. "*Ever.*"

Lisa pulled her to a stop. "Sweetie, I don't care if you ever date again. *Ever,*" she stressed. "Honest. I just want you to meet people."

"I meet people."

"Where? Where do you meet people?"

Destiny hesitated. "The grocery store," she replied, fumbling. "The mall."

Lisa scoffed. "When was the last time you went to a mall?"

Destiny felt cornered. "Umm, just last week?"

Lisa took the cups of soda from her and handed them to Ralph and Harry while cutting her eyes at her friend. "Uh-huh."

"Here's our good luck charm." Harry patted Destiny on the back as she sat down.

Lisa laughed. "What am I now? Chopped liver?"

Ralph patted her arm as she sat. "You're more like filet mignon, Sweetheart," he said with a smile.

Harry sipped his drink. "They forgot the alcohol again."

Lisa snapped her fingers. "I knew we forgot something."

Ralph handed Destiny two of his cards and a stamp. "Make me proud, Sweetie," he grinned.

They played six more games, without another win, and then it was time for everyone to go home. Lisa and Destiny helped wheel Harry and Ralph outside to the bus waiting to take them back to the local Veterans Administration hospital. Ralph made Destiny promise to return the following Friday, and she reluctantly assured him she'd be back.

Lisa and Destiny walked back inside to clean tables and repack the bingo equipment. A little while later, Owen made his way back over to them, to help them clear several tables.

"Sorry you missed the fish," Owen said with a smile. "If you snooze, you lose around here."

"I'll just have to get here earlier next Friday." Destiny cleared the table without looking up at him.

"I'll make sure to hold you a few back if you don't make it in time."

Destiny looked up. Owen was trying so hard she almost felt bad for him. Almost. "Thank you."

Owen drew in a deep breath and glanced at Lisa, who encouraged him with a nod of her head. He turned back to Destiny, nervously. "Hey, would you like to get a drink sometime?"

Destiny continued to wipe down the table she had just cleared, with hot soapy water. "That's sweet, but I'm not really a drinker."

Owen sighed and glanced at Lisa again for encouragement. She motioned with her head for him not to give up. "How about going for a cup of coffee, then?" he asked.

Destiny put on the kindest smile she could muster. "I don't really do coffee, either."

Owen felt himself struggling now. "You do eat, right?"

Destiny glanced at her friend and saw her encouraging Owen. Lisa grinned and shrugged, knowing she was busted. Destiny turned back to Owen, who looked like a little lost puppy. "I've been known to eat. On occasion," she added with a smile.

"So, meet me here, next week, and we'll *talk* about eating," he offered.

Destiny tilted her head, her smile softening. "Sure, we'll talk next week." *What the heck was she thinking?*

"So, it's a date?" he asked coyly, then quickly added, "Unofficially?"

"*Unofficially*," Destiny agreed.

Owen smiled and nodded ever so slightly. "Next week," he added, triumphantly. "See you then." He backed up, turned and ran straight into a table. He nonchalantly looked around, thought no one saw him and walked casually back to the kitchen.

Lisa had to cover her snicker. Destiny didn't even look up, unable to appreciate the humor at the moment. Lisa walked over to her friend. "See. That wasn't so hard."

Destiny glared at her, her stare following her friend as she moved to cleaning the next table.

Bill shook his head and laughed, watching his brother make a fool of himself. Then he turned his attention to the woman with whom Owen had been flirting. Maybe he shouldn't have been so quick to dismiss Lisa when she had told him there was someone she wanted him to meet. When she first walked up to stand in his line, he found he couldn't keep his eyes off her. Destiny was not just pretty, as Lisa had described her, she was drop-dead beautiful— maybe a couple of inches shorter than he was, her hair dark as a moonless night, beautifully framing her delicate features. It had been years since he had even thought of asking another woman out, and now, the only one he would even think of asking was being set up with his brother.

He looked down to recount the money since he couldn't seem to focus. For the fifth time, he counted it again, telling himself not to look up or he'd have to count it over. "Eighteen hundred eighty dollars," he said to himself, then wrote it down on his accounting form.

"Wow," Destiny said, startling him. "Do the concessions always do that well?"

Bill looked up suddenly. She stood before him, holding a bowl of sanitizing water and a cloth. "Um... catfish nights are always good." Bill smiled awkwardly. "It's our best seller."

"Then I definitely need to be here in time next week."

"Yeah," he struggled with what to say.

"Is there anything else you need me to do?" she asked.

"No. No," he stammered. "But thank you."

Destiny smiled. "See you next week."

"I look forward to it," Bill said as she turned and walked away. He watched her and Lisa walk toward the back door. He dropped his head to the refrigerator beside him and banged his head slowly. "You are way out of practice, my friend. *Way* out of practice."

Chapter Twelve

DESTINY PARKED in the same space she had two nights before. There was a slight chill in the air, but it was still and quiet, except for the occasional rooster crowing or the lambs calling for their mamas. The mist hung heavy in the air over the meadows and the ponds on the property. Destiny was usually the first person to arrive on the weekends. She loved riding early. Other riders often began dragging in about ten or eleven. Once the time changed, she could start riding even earlier and undisturbed, for longer. She bridled and saddled Daisy, a beautiful chestnut mare with a star on her forehead.

On her very first visit to the stable, Charlie and Jessie had shown her around the property. She knew instantly that this was where she wanted to ride. Not only were they kind, but it felt like… home. Raised on a small ranch outside of San Antonio, she was taught to handle horses. She'd been riding almost since she was old enough to walk. Until they moved to the city, she lived on a farm. They owned a few milk cows, a couple of hogs, and dozens of goats and chickens. And horses.

Charlie could sense her familiarity with and love for horses immediately. When they arrived at the stable, he had taken her stall by stall to meet them. Destiny had asked which one she would be riding, and he told her it was up to the horse. She teased him about being a horse whisperer. Charlie had laughed and said it was nothing like that. Destiny knew what it was like to love a horse, truly love a horse, the way some people loved their dogs or maybe even their cats. So, she played it his way, walking stall to stall, taking a moment to talk to the horses. It was at the second to last stall that she stopped when the small mare turned from her feed bucket and whinnied softly, snorted and moved to her.

Destiny had held out her hand for the horse to sniff; then the mare gently nibbled on her hand with her muzzle. Slowly, Destiny raised the mare's chin as it sniffed up her arm, arriving at her face. She had been chosen. And she had ridden Daisy every weekend since, for the past eighteen months. It was her favorite part of the week. When they rode, it was just the two of them. There was no past she was trying to forget, no worries about school, no worries about life. It was just them. She would ride for hours some days. Some days Destiny would lead the way, some days she let Daisy lead the way. They had traveled every pathway, every meadow, every deer trail on the farm.

Destiny walked to the mare's stall, bridle in hand, ready for their morning ride. "Hey, Girl," she smiled, first stroking her muzzle and forehead, then her forelock and behind her ears. The mare leaned into the scratch, welcoming it and begging for more with her motions. Destiny laughed. Slowly she bridled her and led her from the paddock.

"Hi," a small voice said.

Destiny turned with a start. "Hi."

"I'm Sydney. I'm eight," she smiled, her arms behind her back. "What's your name?"

Destiny knelt by her side. "I'm Destiny. But you can call me Dee. We met Friday night. Remember?"

Sydney nodded. "That's a pretty name." She studied Destiny for a moment. "Are you going to ride Daisy?"

"Yup," she smiled. "I was just about to saddle her up."

"Can I ride with you?"

Destiny looked around. "Well, I don't know, Sweetie. Where are your parents?"

"My dad had to go out of town. Usually, we go to church on Sundays."

Jessie walked around the corner. "There you are, little miss. I was looking for you. I thought you went to gather eggs."

Sydney took the basket from behind her and held it up. "Here they are."

Destiny looked down. "My, you gathered all those yourself?"

Sydney nodded excitedly.

Jessie took the egg basket and hugged Sydney to her side. "You remember our grand-niece, Sydney?"

"We've officially met," Destiny replied.

"Can I go riding with Dee?" Sydney asked.

"Well, Honey," Jessie said, uncomfortably. "Miss Destiny usually rides alone."

"Has she ridden before?"

"Almost every week," Sydney interrupted.

Destiny looked down at the young girl, then up at Jessie, who nodded. "Surprisingly, she's pretty good," she began. "But, if you would prefer to ride alone, I can take her out after breakfast."

Destiny looked down at Sydney, who pleaded with her eyes, and smiled. "Sure. Why not."

Sydney beamed, calmly walked to the tack room just two stalls away, and took out a bridle. The young girl walked three stalls in the other direction, opened the door, and less than a minute later, walked out with a pony bridled. All under the watchful eye of Destiny and Jessie. Sydney looked at the women.

"Well," Destiny grinned, turning to Jessie. "I guess we'll see you in a little while."

Jessie winked at her and then turned to Sydney. "Little lady, you had better use your manners. Miss Destiny is the senior rider here, so if she gives you any instructions, you listen, you hear me?"

"Yes, ma'am."

"And I want you back by ten. That way Miss Destiny can have some time to herself."

"Yes, ma'am."

"And she has my phone number, so no shenanigans like last time, okay?"

"Yes, Aunt Jessie." Sydney waited patiently for the instructions to end so she could ride.

"You sure about this?" she turned back to Destiny.

"Absolutely," she replied, looking over at Sydney, anxiety brimming in the child's eyes.

Jessie leaned over and kissed her niece on the head. "Best behavior," her aunt whispered, loud enough for Destiny to hear. She stood up and turned to leave. "I'll keep my cell phone on," she said to Destiny, with a glance to Sydney. Jessie patted her coat pocket, then turned and walked toward the main house.

Sydney looked up at Destiny. "You ready?" she asked.

Destiny raised her eyebrows, a little taken aback by the boldness of an eight-year-old. "Sure."

Sydney led, and Destiny followed back to the tack room. Sydney tied her mount, like a pro, to the boards beside her and then slowly ran her hand over his back and flank. Then she slowly picked up each hoof to check for pebbles or rocks. Destiny watched the child carefully look over her mount to assure that he was fit to ride. Then Sydney looked up at the woman expectantly. Destiny slowly tied Daisy beside the pony and checked over her in much the same way. When finished, she walked to the other side of her horse. Sydney had already saddled Peanut and was tightening the cinch.

"Can you please help me make sure it's tight enough?"

"Sure, Honey." She stepped over and checked the cinch, which was perfectly clasped. She moved the saddle back and forth, and it didn't budge. "You're a pro at this."

"Thank you." Sydney untied the reins from the fence.

"What's your pony's name?"

"Peanut," she answered, as she waited patiently for Destiny to saddle Daisy.

"Cute name." Destiny placed the saddle on the blanket and adjusted the cinch on her own mount.

"He's named after Peanut, the companion pony of Exterminator. He won the Kentucky Derby in 1918."

"Really?" Destiny stopped what she was doing to listen.

"Yeah, he wasn't even supposed to run. His owner was going to run Sun Briar, but the horse got hurt, so he ran Exterminator instead, and he won."

"Wow!" Destiny exclaimed, then finished saddling Daisy. "How do you know all this?"

"You can learn anything on the internet." Sydney led Peanut to a feed bucket, turned it over and stood on it to reach the saddle. "Plus it's a book. *Old Bones, The Wonder Horse*. My daddy and I read it last summer. I love horse books," Sydney chattered on as Destiny mounted Daisy. "I have all the *Black Stallion* series. Uncle Charlie and Aunt Jessie gave them to me last year for my birthday."

"I read all the *Black Stallion* series, too, but I was a little older than you." Destiny looked down, adjusting her stirrups.

"So, where do you usually ride?"

"Well, some days I pick. Some days, she does." Destiny clicked her teeth, and Sydney followed suit, with a little kick to get the horses moving. "Do you have any suggestions?"

A small smiled crept up on Sydney's lips. "Yeah, I do." There was mischief in her eyes. She kicked Peanut a little harder, and he started trotting.

Destiny chuckled at the small child bouncing up and down on the pony until he started cantering. Daisy didn't need any encouragement and followed Peanut until she was loping steadily beside them. They took their time riding through the meadow and down to the pond. An hour later they came to the edge of the forest. Then they stopped. Sydney looked over at Destiny and grinned. "My pick?"

Destiny nodded, following as Sydney walked through a dense section of trees. After about sixty feet the woods opened up. The creek that ran through the property and the three ponds on it was much wider through the forest. How had she never seen this before? In the two years she had ridden, she must have been over the property a hundred times, and yet, she had never ventured into the forest, believing it too thick to navigate, the passages too narrow.

It was an incredible sight. The stream ran shallow through the clearing, up to a small rocky ledge, where it split at a larger rock and some brush creating two small waterfalls a few feet apart. The waterfalls poured about three feet or so into a deeper pool just below, which continued to feed the larger ponds further downstream. Sydney dismounted first, followed by Destiny.

"This is my secret hideout," Sydney said. "You have to promise not to tell anyone."

Destiny held her finger to her lips. "Your secret is safe with me."

Sydney walked Peanut to the water, Destiny and Daisy right behind them. They let their mounts drink from the cold, fresh creek.

"They let you come out here by yourself?"

"Sometimes," Sydney replied. "I've been riding since I was little. I used to ride another pony, a Welsh," she continued. "Her name was Nellie. But she died a month ago. Peanut was Nellie's best friend. And of all their ponies, he's the gentlest."

Destiny smiled, giving a little more rein to Daisy so she could munch on the green forest grass. "I got my first pony when I was a young girl."

"Really?" Sydney asked excitedly. "What was its name?"

"Bessie. She was a little dapple gray Welsh pony. She was so sweet and so tame."

"Peanut's a Shetland," Sydney informed her. "I told Daddy I wanted a horse for my birthday."

"A horse? You're still young. And a horse is a big responsibility."

Sydney hung her head. "Yeah, that's what Daddy said."

"I'm betting by the time you're my age that you'll have a lot of other presents that will mean just as much to you."

"Not like a horse," Sydney said, wrapping her arms around Peanut's neck and squeezing. "Nothing would be as amazing as my own horse!"

Destiny looked over at Peanut. "Yeah. I know what you mean. I guess nothing was ever as special as Bessie was." As she watched Sydney with Peanut, she smiled. Ah, to be young and naïve. Then she turned to Daisy. "You're a pretty special lady, too." Destiny scratched the mare's forehead again; then Daisy persisted by using her arm as a scratching post. "Hey, it's about 9:30. We should get you back."

Sydney's face fell, but she didn't complain. She walked to a rock and then mounted Peanut like she'd done it a thousand times. Destiny climbed onto Daisy, the leather squeaking as she rose in the saddle. Silently they rode back to the stable, taking their time, enjoying the morning sounds. They walked past geese on the pond and cattle grazing in the meadow. When they arrived back at the stable Destiny helped Sydney put up the tack and left her brushing Peanut, while she turned Daisy and headed in a different direction along the fence line.

"Dee?" Sydney called after her.

Destiny turned in the saddle.

"Thank you for letting me ride with you."

Destiny smiled. "See you around, Sydney."

Sydney waved, then went back to brushing down Peanut as he munched on oats.

"Cute kid." Destiny grinned to herself as she clicked her teeth and gave Daisy a little kick. Daisy galloped slowly, and then Destiny leaned forward and loosened the reins. "C'mon Girl," she smiled, as they ran faster and faster across the field. Destiny pressed closer to the horse's mane as it whipped against her face, snapping her cheeks like sharp cords; losing herself again like she did when she was a young girl. Embracing the freedom of the fields, the freshness of the morning, the smell of her horse. Soon they were racing across the pasture, her heart suddenly full; feeling better than she had in two years.

Chapter Thirteen

BILL STEPPED into his daughter's domain and found himself surrounded by purples and greens and pinks. Mostly purple, though. Purple was her favorite color. But when she had asked for purple walls, carpet, comforter and furniture, he drew the line. He had the original wood floors stained and sealed, then repainted the walls a soft pink, with white crown molding and baseboards. However, once it was all said and done, and he'd spent $1000 on furniture he painted purple, purple bed sheets, and comforter, and assorted purple accents for her walls, it felt like she got her way. Sydney was only eight. He knew he shouldn't indulge her so much. Bill knew he was overcompensating for her mother's absence from her life, but she was his only child. He had to. He needed to. What else was he to do?

Justine had not only left him after eleven months of marriage but walked away from their child, their beautiful daughter, without ever looking back. Sydney was only four months old when her mother disappeared from their lives. She left without any warning, without any discussion. Bill simply arrived home one day to a note on the mirror. The note was as brief and unremarkable as his marriage had been.

When he first met Justine she was sophisticated and exciting, and he knew he had finally met *the one*. They went out four times in four weeks, and then they slept together. She left the next day with her family on a pre-planned month-long trip through Italy. She teased him with post-cards from exotic ports telling him she was thinking about him and missed him.

However, for three days after she arrived back in the States, she avoided him and his phone calls. The fourth day she showed up on his doorstep, crying and told him she was pregnant. He was surprised, to say the least. But after a moment of letting the news sink in, he was ecstatic. Bill proposed on the spot. They were married the following week at the county courthouse. Before the honeymoon started, the honeymoon was over. Justine had grand plans for them—wanting to travel back to some of the same exotic cities where she had just been so that she could show him the world. But something was just… different. *She* was different. Distant.

Bill shook his head as he picked up Sydney's purple leggings and her purple shirt with a horse outlined with glittery faux jewels, her white tennis shoes with purple hearts and purple shoe laces and her purple and pink polka dotted underwear. Tired of picking up after her, he was going to have to put his foot down. Bill wanted to be the best single dad he could be, but knew he couldn't keep letting her get away with some of her recent behaviors; not cleaning her room, defiance at school. And then there were the nightmares. Plus, lately, she'd been asking about her mother, and she never even knew her. It was all a little overwhelming.

Bill dropped his head into his hands and closed his

eyes. Justine never wanted to be pregnant and was contemplating an abortion, until Bill pleaded with her to reconsider. In her emotional state she acquiesced and kept the baby. Of course, Justine never had the courage to tell him in person that not only did she *not* want children, but she never wanted to be married. When she finally did get the nerve, she left it in a letter, taped to the expensive bureau he never really liked. Then she moved to Italy and filed for divorce, giving him full custody. He hadn't heard from her since.

The front door opened, and he looked up suddenly. He dropped Sydney's clothes onto her bed and walked into the hallway.

"Daddy!" she exclaimed.

And the moment the sound of her voice hit his ears, any thoughts of chores and punishment, simply slipped away. At least, temporarily. His smile broadened with every step she ran toward him. He knelt to receive her hug and fell backward as she jumped into his arms. She kissed him, then furrowed her brow.

"Your nose is still pretty disgusting."

Bill saw his daughter reaching for his nose. He leaned back before her fingers arrived, taking them into his hand and kissing them.

"William Bryan Ireland," his mother exclaimed. "What did you do to your nose?"

"I bumped into the cabinet in the washroom," he lied.

"The cabinet?" she asked, standing over him, hands on hips. "I swear; you never look where you are going." His mother shook her head. "Did you take some ibuprofen?"

"Yes, Mother." Bill hugged Sydney to himself, like a teddy bear or a comforting blanket as he felt a scolding on the horizon.

"Did you put a cold compress on it?"

Bill nodded as he sat back up. Sydney climbed off of him and rushed to her room. "Put your clothes up, Sweetie," he groaned as he stood up in front of his mother.

She looked up at his nose as he moved toward the kitchen, avoiding her glance. "Maybe rub some mentholatum on it before applying moist heat."

"I thought you said a cold compress."

"After the cold compress, dear." She stated this, as though he should have already known that.

Bill grinned as he walked into the kitchen, picked up her purse and headed for the front door, his mother on his heels. When they arrived at the door, she looked up at his six-foot-one frame from her four-foot-six vantage point, tilting her head as she inspected his nose.

"Love you, Mom." Bill leaned over and kissed her forehead. "Thanks for picking up Sydney tonight." He handed her purse to her as he opened the door.

"Sure, Sweetie." She smiled and pulled his arm downward until he leaned closer to her. Then she kissed his cheek. "I'm very proud of you, Son."

His smile grew. "Thank you, Mom."

"You really should ice that schnoz," she added as she walked onto the front porch and pulled her shawl tighter around her.

"I will, Mom. Bye." Bill shivered, shoving his hands into his front jeans pockets, waiting until she was safely in her car.

"Mentholatum, then heat," she repeated over her shoulder.

"Got it, Mom." When she was in her car, he waved and quickly walked back inside. Then Bill dropped his head to the door and banged it gently.

"Syd," he called out. "Bath, now!"

"Aww," he heard from her room.

"And then we'll read whatever you want."

"You'll read, or I'll read?" she asked, as she walked from her room to her bathroom.

"You'll read. Ms. Johnson says you need to practice your reading." Bill rounded the corner as he heard her mumbling. "What'd you say, Sweetie?"

"Nothing," she pouted as her dad started running her a bubble bath. Sydney stepped up onto her purple step stool with white hearts painted all over it and brushed her teeth with her purple toothbrush.

"Ms. Johnson just wants you to be able to read better when you get out of second grade."

Sydney spat into the sink and looked at him in the mirror. "Allie said Ms. Johnson is the book Nazi."

"What?" Bill laughed aloud, as he tested the water, then turned off the faucet.

Sydney took a sip of water and rinsed out her mouth, once, then twice, then swallowed her last sip before putting up her toothbrush in her purple toothbrush holder. "Book Nazi."

Bill helped his daughter undress and then step into the bath. "If you knew what a Nazi was, you would know that's not a nice thing to say."

"Well…" she said as wryly as an eight-year-old could while decorating a Barbie simultaneously with bubbles. "Allie explained that a Nazi is someone who hangs onto something like a bulldog and won't let it go."

Bill shook his head as he bathed his daughter. "Well, she is your teacher. And she's supposed to make you read. So, I guess that's a reasonable explanation but to call her a Nazi, well," he said, as he tried to put it in eight-year-old layman's terms. "That's not only inaccurate but disrespectful and could land you in the principal's office. And if you think old Ms. Johnson's tough, she's probably a piece of cake next to your principal."

"Piece of cake?" Sydney laughed, decorating his head and chin with bubbles. "Where do you come up with these things?"

"Where do *I* come up with these things?" he laughed. "You hit me with book Nazi."

Sydney shrugged. "I call 'em as I see 'em."

Bill poured a large cup of water over his daughter's head. "Me, too," he added. "And I'm warning you, Little Miss." Bill looked at her sternly, shaking his finger at her.

She responded by shaking her long dark hair and soaking him.

Bill dried himself off, then went to check on the rolls for the morning while she finished bathing herself. When he returned fifteen minutes later, she and Barbie were each sporting a bubble beard and tiara. Then he lifted her from the tub, suds and all, and set her onto the bathmat. He knelt beside her and toweled her dry, including her hair. "By the way, I don't want ever to hear those words out of your mouth again, okay?" he said firmly.

Sydney slipped on her purple princess pajamas and then turned for him to spray her conditioner on before combing out her hair.

"Young lady?" he asked again, over her shoulder before turning her around.

Sydney crossed her arms and looked up into the sky. "Yes, sir."

Bill narrowed his eyes and turned her chin with his hand until she was facing him.

"Yes, sir," she repeated more softly.

"Good girl." Bill tapped the end of her nose. "Now put your dirty clothes in the hamper, put up your towel, get a book and then get into bed."

Sydney's shoulders slumped as she did each of the instructed items on his list, then she dragged to her room.

Bill grinned to himself as he watched her complete her tasks before she hurled herself onto her bed. He stood and walked to her room. "One book." Bill held up one finger, then turned on the lamp by her bed and turned off her ceiling light. "One book," he repeated, "then sleep." He walked from the room and closed her door all the way.

"Sleep Nazi," she said under her breath as she turned the page.

Bill stopped in the hallway, tilted his head, thinking he heard something. "Nah." He shook his head, turned off the hallway light and disappeared into the darkness of his room.

Chapter Fourteen

DESTINY DIDN'T mind parent-teacher conferences. It was just that some of the parents were a problem. Some of them were a little pompous, and that rubbed her the wrong way. Many of the children she fostered through the gifted and talented program came from wealth. And a few of those had an entitlement mentality. They were smart. *Very* smart. And manipulative. Then there those who were more than a little arrogant, believing that they deserved the best grade, just for showing up. Sometimes even when they didn't show up.

The year before her accident, she had discovered two of her students were buying their papers online. Destiny immediately removed them from the program. Both of their parents were furious, and after a very lengthy legal battle, the children were allowed to choose whether to stay in the program with a written admission of their guilt added to their school transcript or to drop voluntarily out of the program. Reluctantly, they resigned. The parents of the two boys tried very hard to lobby the school board to get rid of Destiny. However, most of the board were either

her friends, people she'd grown up with, or people she had worked with over the past eight years. They knew her. They knew her reputation, and how much she cared about the kids—even the ones she had suspended from the program. They knew she was an advocate of accountability. Thankfully, her school board had backed her up.

Wally Williamson was the elite of the elite of the film industry in Austin. His son, Frederick, was his protégé. Wally, concerned that his son wasn't performing as well as he could in school, wasn't the overbearing parent who pushed his child to overachieve at all costs. He was the kind of parent Destiny admired; he and his wife came to every school sponsored event that his son participated in and more importantly, every parent-teacher conference. He took her phone calls with concerns, and he or his wife called if they had concerns. She wished all her parents were as invested in their children's lives as he and his wife were. Destiny assured them their son was doing well and that he was trying hard to excel. He was an honest, dedicated young man and Destiny was almost sure Frederick would graduate at the top of his class. Their conference ended with a sincere handshake and a thank you for her dedication.

There was a knock on her classroom door. Destiny looked up. "Winston," she smiled. "How did your meeting go?"

"Not as good as yours," he scoffed. "Your dad was smiling when I passed him in the hall. The dad I just met with, well, let's just say he wasn't smiling."

"At least, he showed up." Destiny walked to her desk and put a handful of files into her briefcase.

"Right," he exhaled, then picked at a paint chip in the doorway. "So, some of us are going out after work, and I was wondering if you wanted to get a drink."

Destiny wrinkled her nose. "Nah. But thanks for asking."

"Maybe some other time, then?"

Destiny looked up at Winston, a substitute teacher who had only been with the school district two-and-a-half years. Originally he had been substituting for one of their older math teachers, Mr. Franklin, who had fallen down the stairs at home, and faced months of rehabbing from multiple injuries and surgeries, a result of his fall. Winston performed so well that the high school administration continued to use him as often as he was available, mostly covering teachers that were out longer stretches of time. Like Destiny. Winston had moved from Seattle just a few months before Destiny's accident and coincidentally subbed in the classroom next to hers. Destiny had taken him under her wing since he was the new kid on the block.

Winston's positive attitude, winning personality, and sexy smile wasn't lost on all the single teachers and moms at the school, not to mention many of the female students. He was fawned over at any school events he attended. Personally, she thought he reveled in the attention. But Winston wasn't her type. Not that she had a type anymore. Attractive with perfect hair and perfect white teeth, he always dressed nicely and was always the perfect gentleman. Maybe that was why she didn't give him a second glance. He was just too... perfect. And to Destiny, that was unnatural. Everyone had flaws, either physical or personality flaws, but he just... didn't.

Winston shoved his hands into his pockets as he walked into the room. "I promise that I'd be a *perfect* gentleman."

Destiny smiled to herself, then looked up him and shrugged noncommittally. "Maybe some other time."

Winston's eyes perked up. "Well, a maybe isn't a no, so I'll take that."

Destiny walked to the door, Winston keeping in stride with her. "So, what do you do for fun?" he asked.

"We're teachers. I didn't think we were allowed to have any fun."

"Sure we are. We just have to get permission slips first," he added, noting a wisp of a smile on her lips at his remark.

Winston talked for both of them as they walked. Destiny could feel his hand at the curve of her back as they turned the corner toward the teachers' lounge. Her body tensed at his touch. It wasn't the first time he had touched her. Sometimes, when he stood beside her, if he were talking to her or telling a joke, he would touch her very lightly; occasionally letting his hand or fingers linger a moment or two. Winston had done it when Phillip was alive, as well. Destiny had confided to her husband that it made her uncomfortable, so Phillip, in Phillip fashion, teased her that Winston was her work fling.

Now that Phillip was gone, Winston tended to do it more. Or was it that she noticed it more or that it simply bothered her more? Destiny would have dismissed him altogether a long time ago if only he weren't so darn charming. Not to mention great with the kids. Destiny found herself relating to him about varied, innovative teaching methods; methods that had changed so much over the past five years alone. Winston had lived in many cities; from Chicago to Portland, New York, and Oklahoma City. When he found it was harder to settle into a full-time teaching position, he immediately offered to substitute teach at the local school district. They had kept him busy ever since.

Within six months of Phillip's death, Winston had begun asking her out in subtle ways, like suggesting a casual cup of coffee or meeting up at a park for the free local entertainment. Destiny had tried being polite in her rejection of his advances, not interested in him or anyone else at this juncture in her life. She couldn't imagine herself ever dating again, much less ever remarrying.

Almost two years since Phillip's and Rhett's deaths, Destiny was much lonelier than she let on. It wasn't just that she missed Phillip's presence, but she missed what his presence had meant. There was no more early morning snuggling and sweet kisses on the back of her neck... surprise romantic back rubs and amazing foot massages. Or random "I love you's," or a quiet smile that spoke the same. All the things that had been a part of her everyday life for ten years were now just a distant memory.

Winston had been hinting at a date for almost fifteen months and here she'd agreed to meet Owen after just one brief conversation. It was as close to a blind date as one could get. And now, thanks to Lisa, she was stuck. Owen... the first man that had successfully asked her out though *unofficially*, in almost a dozen years.

Destiny and Winston each checked their individual teacher mailboxes, rifling through messages as he continued to rattle on about working out after school or a new martial arts movie that was playing. Winston usually chattered on and on about things she knew nothing about or even cared to know. As he turned to leave, he nudged her with his elbow. "See you Monday," he said with a wink.

"Monday," she replied as he walked out the door to the teachers' parking lot.

Destiny turned toward the administration corridor and met a new face smiling up at her from the secretarial desk. "Hi, is Rita still here?"

"I'll see. May I tell her who's asking?"

"Destiny," she smiled.

"What a lovely name. I'm Brenda." She held out her hand.

"Brenda, nice to meet you."

At that moment, the school principal, Rita O'Connor, walked from her office. "Destiny!" she exclaimed. "How were your meetings?"

"They all went well," she replied. "Do you have a second?"

"Sure." Rita turned back toward her office. "Did you meet Brenda?"

Destiny smiled back at Brenda. "I did. Again, pleased to meet you."

Brenda glanced back up from her computer without a break in typing, smiled, and looked back down.

"Where's Ginger?" Destiny asked as she sat across from her boss.

"She quit."

"Quit?" Destiny exclaimed. "Why?"

"Not really sure," she said, the disappointment evident in her voice. "She was acting kind of strange the past two weeks, and then this morning she just didn't show up." Rita nodded toward the door. "Brenda's an intern on loan from the central office until I can find a replacement."

"That's peculiar," Destiny remarked off-handedly. Her eyes met Rita's. "I hate to add to your plate, but I wanted to see about doing a Habitat build with the seniors. They approached me a month ago, and I have to give Habitat an answer by Monday."

"As long as you have all the proper paperwork, I don't see it as a problem."

"Then I'll call Habitat and set up a weekend."

Rita stood and moved to the front of her desk. "That was painless. I wish all the teachers brought me issues with such easy answers."

Destiny stood beside Rita.

"Are you doing okay?" she asked with a compassionate smile.

Destiny smiled sadly and shrugged. "Today's a good day."

Rita's smile grew. "Give yourself time." Rita understood Destiny's pain, having lost her husband ten years before to a massive heart attack. Rita, as Destiny had, threw herself into her work. Her love for the kids was great and helped her deal with the loss. Helped her deal with the pain.

Destiny nodded. "One day at a time," she sighed.

"Look, we're all meeting for drinks at the Oasis in about an hour. You're welcome to join us," she offered, already knowing the answer.

Destiny slowly shook her head. "Thanks for the invite. Winston already invited me."

Rita's smile faded. "Yeah, well, Winston's sweet, but there's something just a little off about him."

Destiny furrowed her brow. "What do you mean by that?"

"Think about it. Why does someone that good looking, who is the perfect gentleman, not have a girlfriend and never been married?"

Destiny shrugged again. "Maybe something happened, and he's nursing a broken heart… or maybe he's…"

"Gay?" Rita finished her question for her, shaking her head. "Not gay," she clarified. "Remember Claire, who transferred to LBJ High last year? Well, she went out with him a few times, I think, just before she transferred. Apparently something happened because she told more than just a few of us that he has a kinky dark side."

Destiny remembered the rumors, simply because she and most of the other females on staff had been skeptical.

Claire was very explicit with those who would listen about her sexual escapades and short-lived relationships. Most of them ended quickly or poorly or both, so no one put any stock in what she had claimed, assuming a date gone very badly.

"I can't go because I promised a friend I would help out at the Senior Center tonight."

"That's so great, Destiny. I'm glad to know you are getting out more."

Destiny picked up her purse and carefully slid it over her shoulder. "I'm trying." She hugged her friend. "Thanks."

Rita winked. "Anytime."

As Destiny walked from her office, Rita held open the door, watching her go. "One day at a time," she sighed to herself, before closing the door behind her.

Chapter Fifteen

WHEN BILL BECAME both mom and dad to his daughter, not only did his family dynamic change, but his job changed, and his housing changed. He went from planning for their family to planning for him and his daughter alone. His entire adult life he had worked for someone else. After Sydney was born, Bill cut working sixty hours a week to forty so he could spend more time with his new family. When Justine left him, his mom offered to babysit. Three months of his mother's daily infant-child-rearing and health remedy advice accelerated his desire to raise his daughter on his own.

Before Sydney's first birthday he sold all his investment stock and his house and bought the bed and breakfast. It was big enough for them to have a place to live and allow them to make a comfortable living. It was a colonial with a full wrap-around porch, including oversized rockers and swings on every side. The older Sydney became, the more interested she became, not only in the workings of a bed and breakfast but the people who stayed there. On many occasions, she would greet the guests with cookies and milk or slip special cards, notes or pictures that she had drawn, under their doors. And the guests loved her. Sydney was simply part of what made their stay so special.

It was Friday night, and after prepping for breakfast the following morning, Bill handed the reins off to Deborah, as his presence was required at the Senior Center. Sydney was staying overnight at a friend's house. It was an eight-year-old's birthday party so he knew they'd be up all night eating cupcakes and popcorn, and watching Disney movies. As long as he wasn't the one dealing with ten eight-year-olds on a sugar high it was all good. Bill wasn't overly strict on Sydney's diet, but because she was a little high-strung, he usually rationed her sweet and soda intake. She was always a little grumpier and less attentive when she over-indulged. He would detox her tomorrow. Tonight he would have enough to handle with two hundred hungry veterans; hungry for fish, hungry for bingo. Hungry for companionship.

Bill loved volunteering at the Senior Center. His father, a veteran of the Army with thirty-seven years of service under his belt, encouraged his three sons to serve their community wherever they could. His father's hope that they would follow his path and join the Army never happened. Bill's oldest brother, Leonard, went into the Marines and served there faithfully for almost twenty years until his death in Afghanistan in 2004. Owen, the middle son, went on to college to study economics and sociology and worked at the VA. Bill, the only one whose career had no military ties, studied economics and finance and worked in banking until he decided to buy a bed and breakfast and raise his daughter on his own. If only his dad could see him now.

Bill remembered his grandfather's stories of World War I and II, and then his father's tales of Korea, and Vietnam.

He used to tell them they should write a book. How many father-son adventures would span five wars? Bill had begun volunteering at the Senior Center after joining Rotary International, through his time in banking. Through Rotary, he had helped bring an end to polio, helped build water wells in impoverished cities around the world and created libraries and schools where there were none. And now, he helped serve veterans every week by feeding them while they played bingo at Veteran's Night at the Senior Center. Bill looked forward to his time with the veterans. He served every week for varied reasons. Now, there was *one* more.

Ever since he first looked into Destiny's eyes, he had thought of nothing else. No *one* else. He found himself distracted, almost to the point of annoyance. Even when he had a million things to do, her face kept coming to mind. And thanks to his stubborn pride, he couldn't even ask her out. Owen, his older brother, had just been through a nasty divorce with his third wife. It didn't seem fair that he had already set his sights on Destiny as the next potential Mrs. Owen Ireland. And they hadn't even had a first date yet. Now he drove to the Senior Center in anticipation of her being there, in the hopes of seeing her there— though part of him hoped she wasn't.

Bill parked under the light as he always did because he was usually the first one there. It was his job to unlock the dumpster and the back door, in preparation of hoards of volunteers arriving shortly after that. It was his responsibility to turn on the lights and the air, or the heat if it was winter. Bill turned on all the equipment and prepared the counter to accept guests in the next hour-and-a-half. Owen walked in almost five minutes later and nodded to his baby brother before starting his own routine. Although inventory was checked each week at the end of their shifts, it was

Owen's responsibility to double-check it before opening the register. It assured that nothing had mysteriously disappeared or was overlooked the week before.

The staff consisted of mostly volunteers, but there were a few paid part-time workers. Owen and Bill were both in their mid-thirties and financially secure. Although offered a small salary for what they did, both rejected their individual offers. They weren't necessarily close. They didn't share a lot of the same characteristics, either physically or traditionally. However, they did have the same core values, mostly based on their father's strict military training and their mother's faith and her belief in making a difference in the world. Combine those two with the perfect alignment of the stars and their life circumstances, and they ended up serving fish and chips to a bunch of veterans on Friday nights at the Senior Center.

"So, did you ask her out?" Bill asked casually, for lack of anything else worthwhile to say.

"Who?"

"Destiny," Bill reminded him.

"Who?"

Bill sighed in annoyance. Owen didn't even remember her name. "The woman Lisa introduced you to last week," he clarified.

"Oh, her," he grinned. "I'll work on her again tonight."

"Wear her down, huh?" Bill said under his breath.

"Whatever works."

"Do you even like her?"

"I just met her," he exhaled. "But, tonight," he grinned mischievously, "I won't take no for an answer."

Bill stopped talking. The conversation only served to discourage him more.

"I think she'd look good," Owen began.

Bill turned to his brother and waited expectantly. Knowing Owen, there was no telling what would come out of his mouth.

"I'll bite, where would she look good?" a voice asked from behind.

Bill turned to see Sheray, the head cook, walk up behind them.

"In my bed," Owen answered slyly.

Sheray rolled her eyes and then began taking food items from the refrigerator to prepare for cooking and serving in the next hour. "You've got to be kidding. Tell me that's not going to be your line."

Bill shook his head. "My guess is it is."

Sheray glanced sideways at him, noting his sarcasm. "Is that how he hooked numbers one through three?"

Owen walked up behind her. "Actually number one started something like this," he began, slowly sliding his arms down hers until his hands were on hers. He then nuzzled against her cheek. "And then I whispered in her ear." He lowered his voice, his lips beside her ear. "Where have you been all my life, Beautiful?"

Sheray moved from his grip. "That actually worked?"

"She fell for it, hook, line, and sinker," Owen grinned proudly, rolling up his sleeves.

"Then she took him for everything—hook, line, and sinker," Bill interjected as he took the cash drawer out of the floor safe.

Sheray walked past Owen, and he grabbed her by the hand, pulling her into his arms, holding her close to his chest. "Number two," he said as he started dancing her around the kitchen. "Number two thought I was suave and sexy and loved my moves," he added in a seductive tone. He twirled her and let her go, and she spun right into Bill's arms.

Bill smiled and shrugged. "And then she realized what he looked like the morning after."

Owen furrowed his brow at his brother.

"And number three?"

Owen wriggled his lips. "Number three wanted more out of the marriage than I did."

"Like what?"

Bill chimed in. "Honesty. Commitment. Monogamy."

"Yeah, well," Owen sighed. "The next one will be different."

"How's that?" Bill asked. He crossed his arms and leaned against the counter attentively.

"You're going to marry for love?" Sheray asked.

"Oh, I loved every one of them," Owen defended.

"Really?" When Owen didn't respond, she shook her head. "When I married Jay, I married him for life." She tossed the bag of hot dogs onto the counter and opened it up, taking one out. "And he believes in honesty and commitment." She set the hot dog on the cutting board and then used the butcher knife to chop it in half. "And monogamy," she added flatly, without smiling, as she looked at Owen.

Owen looked at Bill and made a face. When Bill turned back to Sheray, she winked and grinned before continuing with her tasks. Bill smiled to himself and returned to counting out his cash drawer.

Owen continued, ignoring Sheray's dispensation of the hot dog. "I want someone fun and exotic and patient and—"

"—And won't put up with your crap?" Bill interrupted.

"And won't *mind* my crap," Owen smiled. "She won't mind that I'm a mess and that I don't look especially great in the mornings. That I like to have a beer with the boys and watch football without her ragging on me."

Sheray turned to Bill and mouthed silently, "Is he serious?"

Bill nodded.

"Who won't give me a hard time for not throwing my underwear in the clothes hamper right when I take them off—or when I don't always remember our anniversary or her birthday. Someone who will love me despite all that."

Sheray looked at Bill, who merely shrugged again. "Maybe you should try looking online for one of them Russian brides," she suggested.

Owen looked up and furrowed his brow again as if considering the thought. "Naw. I want her to speak English."

"What about you, Bill? You think you'll ever get married again?"

Bill pursed his lips. The sound of the metal door closing, resounded down the hallway, echoing into the empty room. A moment later Destiny walked from the darkened hallway into the fluorescent-lit room. Her eyes met his. A small smile crept across her lips, and his heart instantly lit up. "Yes," he answered under his breath. "Yes, I do."

Chapter Sixteen

DESTINY ENJOYED WORKING with Lisa and the other volunteers at the Senior Center and had decided that this was going to be her new Friday night routine. It was fun getting to know everyone, hearing their stories. No, it was more than that. Through their expressions and the tone of their voices; through the emotions wrought in their telling, she experienced their stories; learned of loves lost and discovered—felt the pain of death on the battlefield, and of finding God there in the midst of war.

So many stories. So many lives forever changed. She felt she could never listen enough to what they had to say. It was as if this was their one chance to tell their story. It almost made her sad to think how many of the veterans, although surrounded by family and friends every day, had never been asked about their own stories. How many had taken the time actually to listen what these precious veterans wanted to say? Stories that couldn't be told in pictures, pictures that couldn't begin to convey the real horror of what they had experienced. The real history wasn't just the prepared abbreviated messages the media dispensed, but was in the eyes and the very souls of those men and women who had served. Those were the *real* stories. It made Destiny sad to think that so many of these stories would never be heard, never be written down or recorded. Memories lost forever on deaf ears.

"Grandpa!" Destiny exclaimed. Lisa had brought her grandfather with her this week, decked out in baggy shorts and a Hawaiian shirt and sporting a lei; having just spent twenty-one days cruising through the Pacific. "Don't you look like a walking postcard!"

Grandpa lifted and shook the flower lei from his chest and winked. "Had to prove to the fellas that I got leid while I was away."

"Grandpa!" Destiny shook her head at him.

He slowly walked through the room with her on his arm. Every few steps someone would stop him and ask about his trip. Thankfully, Grandpa was a man of few words, unless he found someone special who needed to hear the extended version.

"Good," he'd reply to acquaintances. Or if he knew someone well, he'd respond, "It was unbelievable." He decided to cut Destiny a break, giving her the abbreviated version. "I discovered how much I *don't* want to spend two weeks with my brother and his wife in a confined space." Grandpa held on tight to Destiny's arm, as he pulled her closer and patted it. "It's good to see you out, Girl," he remarked.

Destiny leaned against him as they walked. "It actually feels good to be out," she said sincerely.

"This place is a good start. If you can survive these guys, you're ready for the world." He stopped and looked her in the eyes. "You doing okay?"

Destiny nodded.

Grandpa raised her chin with his finger. "You know. I

think you really are," he smiled. "Your eyes have life in them again. I was starting to worry about you, Child."

Destiny looked down. "Me, too, Grandpa." She looked into his eyes again. "Me, too."

Grandpa kissed her forehead. "I remember when I lost my Betsy. The toughest day of my life. Thought I'd crawl right down into the grave with her." He turned her and walked slowly toward his granddaughter. "And these guys here were a lot of the reason I didn't." He sighed. "Them and my Lisa." He smiled, turning to watch his granddaughter carrying plates of food for those who were unable to carry their own. "If it weren't for them, I wouldn't be here."

"I wish I'd met her."

"My Betsy?"

Destiny nodded.

"Oh, my dear, she would have just loved you. You'd never have met a kinder soul. She never met a stranger, and she would do anything for anybody. My sweet, sweet Bets." He patted Destiny's hand. "You know Lisa's daddy was a hard man. He was military, too. And strict. I raised him to be firm, but never raised him to be unkind. Something happened while he was away, you know?" he stated more than asked. "When he came back from Vietnam, he was a mean SOB. God forgive me for saying that about my own son, but he was outright mean. Was hard on Lisa and her brothers and sisters." He glanced at his granddaughter. "Plain took the spirit out of some of them. Broke poor Betsy's and my hearts to see it, but what could I do? He was a grown man."

Destiny listened intently. It was the first time he'd talked about Lisa's father to her.

"But not Lisa. She has an indomitable spirit. I'm so

glad he never broke her. She's the heart of the family, you know?"

Destiny squeezed his arm. "I can see where she got her character. And I think she'd disagree." He stopped walking and looked down at her. "She's always said that *you* were the heart of your family."

He smiled down at Destiny and whispered against her cheek. "You have that spirit, too, my dear. It has always been there. I've seen it in your eyes."

Destiny leaned against him and smiled sadly.

"Never let that light go out, my dear."

Destiny nodded.

"Promise me," he insisted.

"I promise."

His friends, anxious to hear of his adventures, surrounded them. As Destiny released his arm, he was swallowed by the crowd. She saw him hold up his lei proudly as he began to embellish about his travels through the islands.

There was a tap on her shoulder, and she turned with a start.

"Sorry. I didn't mean to startle you."

"Owen!"

"I promised you dinner."

"You did." She eyed the mound of catfish, French fries and hush puppies he was holding. "It looks delicious."

"Fried it just for you." Owen turned her at her elbow, steered her toward an empty table, then pulled back a chair and sat down before she did.

Destiny sat opposite him. "That was really sweet of you."

"So, like it or not, you're having dinner with me."

"I guess I am."

Owen reached over and took a piece of fish from the

plate, placed it on a napkin and began pulling off pieces to eat as he spoke. "I thought you could use a break. It gives us a chance to get to know each other."

Destiny nibbled nervously on a hush puppy.

"Lisa says you're a teacher?"

Destiny nodded as she chewed.

"You like teaching?"

"Mm-huh," she added, stuffing a fry into her mouth.

"You like the school you work at?"

Destiny nodded again, taking a bite of fish.

"I hated school," he began. "I did what I had to do to get my diploma and then partied all summer until I had to start college." Owen took another bite and talked with his mouth full. "Don't get me wrong, I know high school was important, it just wasn't to me. At the time." He looked expectantly at Destiny. "You want that last hush puppy?"

She shook her head, taking another bite of fish.

Owen popped the hush puppy into his mouth then proceeded to finish his train of thought, talking with his mouth full. "My parents made their expectations clear to me and my brothers. However, I knew what I wanted to do, so I just did it. I didn't graduate at the top of my class, but I still got my degree on the wall, a good paying job, and I didn't have to kill myself to get there."

Destiny pulled a few napkins from the metal holder on the table, wiping her greasy fingers, then her mouth.

"I mean, I think what you do is important and all, but I think some of what they make you learn in high school is worthless. Don't you think?" Owen said, licking his fingers. He grabbed a napkin and wiped them off.

"I believe what I do is relevant."

"Relevant?" he interrupted. "I think it's your job to attempt to educate, and the teenager's job is to set his own path and determine if he's going to go on to college, and if he is, what he needs to do to accomplish his goals."

Destiny glared at him, stupefied. "So, you believe that a child should pick and choose what he thinks is relevant to what his goals are?"

"Absolutely," Owen replied, smugly.

"So, what if he has no goals?"

"Then he'll flip burgers or empty my trashcan at work," he added, confident that his prophetic statement would enlighten her as to her waste of time. "Have you ever read *40 Alternatives to College* by James Altucher?"

Destiny leaned forward as if she was interested in what he was saying. "No, can't say as I have."

"Well, it's simply a reminder of the pressures kids are under to perform and test to standards that are well beyond their abilities. That they are under pressure to graduate at the top of their class and then go to college, where they just incur tens to hundreds of thousands of dollars in debt that's unrealistic to repay. Many of them drop out, don't desire to go into the field in which they have a degree or quite possibly can't find jobs in those fields."

Destiny breathed in slowly, as she thought through what she wanted to say to this man, who was attempting to dispel single-handedly, the notion that everyone wanted to be something more. He would most definitely never be on her list of guest speakers to motivate students.

"Did it ever occur to you that for some students, the teacher is the only positive role model in a child's life? That maybe circumstances, whether it be the family dynamics or learning disabilities or poverty, have caused them not to be able to excel or achieve?"

"That's total BS," Owen said, wrinkling his nose.

"That's simply an excuse. Every child has the same advantages as every other," he proclaimed.

"What hole have you been living in?" Destiny retorted.

Owen leaned closer onto his arms. "I live in reality, Honey. You are just one of the brainwashed who believes that traditional, in any sense, is right. Traditional education, traditional employment, traditional marriage."

Destiny chuckled for a moment, but then realized he was serious. She furrowed her brow and softened her eyes. "Thanks so much for dinner, Owen. It was really sweet of you," she said as she stood up.

Owen sat upright, and, realizing their conversation was over, stood with her. "Well," he stammered. "I enjoyed visiting with you. You've got spunk. I like that in a woman."

Destiny batted her eyes. "It's been enlightening, to say the least."

Owen smiled, feeling confident.

Destiny turned to leave.

"Maybe I can call you sometime," he called after her. "We can talk some more."

"Don't count on it," she said sarcastically to herself, walking as fast as she could in the other direction.

Chapter Seventeen

BINGO ENDED RIGHT ON TIME, with seconds to spare. Lisa left not long after the last game to drive her grandpa home. Destiny insisted Lisa leave. She didn't mind staying to help in any way needed, and knew Lisa still had paperwork to do at her salon. What else did *she* have to do? Destiny wasn't tired, and didn't want to go home. Not just yet. However, to avoid running into Owen again, she worked as far away from the kitchen as possible, cleaning tables and collecting bingo cards. Thankfully, he was busy inventorying for the following week. At one point, when she caught him looking around the room, she ducked down as if picking something up from the floor, peering over the chair until she didn't see him anymore.

"He's gone," a voice said, from behind.

Destiny yelped. "God, you startled me!" she exclaimed, standing, embarrassed that she'd been busted. "What is it about the men around here, sneaking up on people?"

"I wasn't sneaking up on you," he defended.

Destiny picked up a hush puppy from the floor and held it up for him to see as if it proved her intent all along.

Bill nodded wryly. Destiny tossed it into the trashcan and, without another word, moved to the other side of the room. Bill watched her, grinning to himself. He shook his head and returned to the kitchen.

"Hey, Bill," Owen began. "I was just about to leave. You haven't seen Destiny, have you?"

"Destiny?" Bill asked, feigning confusion.

"Yeah, Lisa's friend."

"Oh, yeah, Destiny. No, I haven't seen her," he lied. He turned and dried off the last of the serving utensils. "So, how did your little dinner date go?" Bill mocked.

"Just fine," Owen insisted. "She's not very chatty, though," he replied, almost disappointed.

"Maybe you monopolized the conversation, like usual."

Owen crinkled his lips. "I didn't monopolize the conversation. She was probably so awe-struck by what I had to say that she didn't know what to say, herself."

"Uh-huh."

"Sarcasm," Owen retorted. "I get it. More like misplaced jealousy."

"Jealousy?"

"I see the way you look at her," Owen said, sticking a toothpick between his lips. "But she's not your type."

Bill drew in a deep breath as he turned around, feeling his brother push his buttons, much as he had all his life. "Goodnight, Owen."

Owen made a face, knowing he'd just been dismissed. With a final glance around the room, he overlooked Destiny, who was emptying a trash can. "Well, her loss," Owen said, more to himself than anyone else. "Goodnight," he called to his brother's back, as he strode down the hallway and out the door.

An hour later, after everything was cleaned and locked up, Bill walked with Destiny and three other female volunteers to the back parking lot. They walked Destiny to her car first; then the others walked together until Bill was the only one remaining. After climbing into his top-rated, safest-car-on-the-road-for-families, he started her up. Bill adjusted the temperature and then the radio before looking up. He watched through the windshield, then rolled down his window, listening to Destiny's attempts to crank her car, only it wasn't turning over. Bill sighed and stepped from his own vehicle. Lightly he tapped on her window.

"Jesus!" she exclaimed, as she grabbed her chest. She drew in a breath and rolled down her window.

"Sorry," he said, holding up his hands. "Didn't mean to scare you," he smiled. "Again."

"It's okay." Destiny looked down at her dashboard. "I don't know what's wrong."

"Here, let me give it a try." Bill watched her slender frame slide from the seat so that he could sit down. As she brushed past him, he could smell her shampoo. Coconut Milk. He breathed it in. It was… amazing. When she turned, her eyes were on his. At first, he felt they were making a connection—what kind of connection, he had no clue. It had been a long time since he'd connected with any woman. Then he realized she was waiting, expectantly. Only not for what he was thinking. He stepped aside for her to pass, then sat down.

After several attempts at starting her car, he popped the hood and began jiggling wires and lines, then checked her oil, water, and transmission fluid. Finally, he turned to her and wiped his hands on a rag he had retrieved from his vehicle just moments before. "I'm not a mechanic," he sighed dramatically. "But I'd say, she's not going anywhere anytime soon."

"Great." Destiny exhaled in frustration and took out her cell phone. "I'll call Triple A."

"Whoever they call will charge you extra for this hour of the night," he said. "I only know," he stammered, "because I had car trouble about this time a few months ago." He looked down at his watch. "Look, let me take you home. I can drop you off, and then you can call Triple A. I'll pick you up in the morning and bring you back by here."

"You don't have to go to all that trouble."

"It's no trouble. My daughter is at a slumber party and won't be home until late in the morning."

Destiny dropped her head in defeat and sighed. "I'd argue, but I don't have many alternatives at this point."

"Gee, I'll try and not take that too personally."

"Sorry. Didn't mean it that way."

"It's okay," he sighed. "Lock her up and we'll go."

"Will it be safe here?"

"It will be fine. The lighting is good, and no one has ever been broken into here before."

Destiny took everything from her car that she felt had any value and then hit the key fob several times, to assure it was locked. Then she climbed into the passenger seat of Bill's CR-V.

"Air okay?" he asked, adjusting the temp and the vents.

Destiny nodded.

"Where to?"

Destiny gave him directions, and he keyed them into his GPS computer. Nervously, he ran his hands along the steering wheel as he pulled from the parking lot.

"So, how did your dinner date go?"

"My what?"

"Dinner with Owen," he clarified.

"Oh, that," she said, looking out her window.

"If you haven't already figured it out, Owen..." he began. "Owen is, well, for lack of a better word, weird."

"Oh really!" she exclaimed. "That's putting it mildly," she added under her breath.

"He's always been that way."

"Uh-huh? And you still hang out with him?"

"Well, I'm kinda of stuck. He is my brother."

"Your brother?" she turned to him, surprised.

"Yeah. You didn't know?"

"No, I didn't know."

Bill grimaced. "Well, I have to apologize for him a lot."

"Really? Why? Because he's an idiot?"

Bill laughed. "Yeah. Pretty much."

Destiny chuckled as well.

"Hey!" Bill exclaimed suddenly, as they pulled up to a stoplight. "How about I buy you a cup of coffee?" he asked anxiously. "Like I said, my daughter is at a slumber party. And to tell you the truth, I rarely ever get a chance to steal away. You know, on my own," Bill stumbled over his words.

Destiny looked down at her hands. "Rarely, huh?" She looked up at him.

"Rarely, as in never," he replied. The light changed from green and back to red, and no one noticed.

Destiny hesitated for a moment, then reluctantly said, "Sure, why not?"

"Great. A crappy cup of coffee it is," he exhaled, and then pulled into an all-night fast food restaurant parking lot on the corner.

They were the only ones in the restaurant. It was obvious the staff would have preferred to finish the evening without patrons. Suddenly they had to turn down the loud music, stop joking around and actually work. Destiny and Bill sat in silence in a booth by the window. Many minutes went by before Destiny finally spoke.

"So, you have a daughter?"

"Yeah," he answered nervously.

"How old is she?"

"Eight."

"Eight," she said sadly, looking down at her cup. "My son was eight."

"Yeah, Lisa told me," he winced and sighed. "I can't imagine how devastating it would be to lose a child."

Destiny didn't look up. Couldn't look up.

"I'm so, so sorry," he offered, reaching over and taking her hand.

Destiny slowly slid her hand from the table. "Look, can we talk about something else?"

"We could talk about my brother, the idiot," Bill offered with a smile.

Destiny chuckled. "You know, I really wanted to put him in his place." She shook her head. "But I really felt like…"

"It wouldn't do any good," they said in unison. Then they both laughed.

Bill tilted his head. "It wouldn't." He lowered his voice, as though they could be overheard by the other guests that weren't there. "That being said, he's not a bad guy, all in all. It's just that he dances to the tune of a different drummer," he recited.

"If a man does not keep pace with his companions, perhaps it is because he hears a different drummer. Let him step to the music which he hears, however measured or far away."

"Henry David Thoreau," they said again, together. Destiny leaned forward, her defenses dissolving, feeling more comfortable as they spoke.

"Yeah," he chuckled. "My parents told me that once when I told them… well…" he stammered again. "When I told them I thought he was an idiot."

"You told your parents that?"

"Many times," he said emphatically. "Many, *many*, times." He toyed with his coffee cup and sighed. "But, he was their son," Bill shrugged. "What would I do if someone told me that about my child?"

Destiny pursed her lips, then looked down, suddenly ashamed. "Yeah," was all she could say, understanding how it must feel to hear that about your own flesh and blood. "Yeah."

They sat silently across from each other, quietly pensive. Slowly his hand slid across the table to hers, lightly touching her fingers, teasingly; first two fingers, and then three, then more. When she didn't move her hand away, his hand finally rested on hers. Neither of them looked up as their coffee cooled before them.

After a minute, maybe more, Bill slid his other hand to hers and took her hand tentatively in his. His hands were firm but gentle, his fingers tracing hers, carefully exploring every curve, every crease in her hand. Her skin was delicate and soft; her nails rounded and shiny, and it felt good. At first, she didn't appear to mind, in fact, she seemed to relax in his grip. Bill looked up, opening his mouth as though he wanted to say something, wanted to ask her something. But then he stopped. Her hand still rested in his, the other still exploring, testing her boundaries as it gently brushed her wrist. It had been years since he'd held a woman's hand. Slowly, they embraced hers fully, encompassing it, warming it.

Destiny felt her heart racing. How could something so casual feel so sensual, so intimate? What was she thinking? Who was this man? She didn't know him. They'd hardly spoken. And yet, being here with him felt… right. Nice. Destiny didn't dare look up for fear he'd let go. It had been so long since anyone had held her hand in this way. Years, in fact. Phillip was the love of her life, and yet, she couldn't even remember the last time he had made her feel this way, just by holding her hand. Slowly Destiny closed her eyes. Bill's hand traveled past her wrist, and she suddenly became self-conscious of what he would find. Immediately she pulled her hand from his, and it retreated into her lap.

The manager on duty tapped on their table, breaking the trance. They both looked up at once. The young man that wreaked of stale cooking oil and burgers asked them flatly if they wanted anything else. They looked at each other and then back to the manager and shook their heads. "Great," he responded, before turning and signaling with a circular motion of his finger for his crew to wrap it up. They heard whoops and claps in the kitchen. Destiny and Bill turned back to each other and smiled before bashfully looking away again.

Bill stood and held out his hand for her to take, guiding her through the door, his hand at the curve of her back, as he held it open for her. When he touched her, she didn't tense up, as she did when Winston touched her, or even Owen. Destiny felt herself relax and smile. Actually smile. Bill opened the car door for her, and then closed it after she climbed in. They sat, quietly, after he started his car, then he turned to her, and she to him. Their eyes met, speaking volumes through the silence. His hand sat limply on the gear shift. Destiny slowly moved her hand to his and gently rested it on top, her fingers lightly brushing over his as the music played softly all around them. Bill smiled sadly, and looked away. Then they drove to her loft in silence.

Bill swallowed nervously, as he opened the passenger door. Then he held out his hand once more. Destiny looked up into his eyes, her demeanor softening as she set her hand on his. It was as though, at that very moment, she trusted him. His fingers refused to let hers go as he walked her to her apartment. Their pace slowed, as they neared the point at which he would say goodbye. It was the first time in a lifetime of goodbyes that he didn't want to speak the words. They arrived on the welcome mat at her front door stoop. He didn't release her hand, nor did she pull hers away. He leaned against the door, studying every inch of her face. For many moments, she didn't look up at him.

And then she did.

Destiny felt her heart begin to race as her eyes met his once again. How did she get here? How did this man, this stranger reach into the very depth of her heart when she had so determined to close it off completely after Phillip's death? They had hardly spoken all night, and yet she felt she had known him all his life. His hand still held hers as he leaned against the door nervously.

"Why is it I don't want to leave you?"

"Why is it I don't want you to leave?"

"I have to see you again."

"Have to?" she chuckled.

"Yes," Bill replied emphatically. "Have to." He took a step closer to her.

Destiny nodded as she looked up. She slid her hand from his and moved it to his face. "So, are you going to tell me what happened?" Her hand traced the bruising carefully.

Bill crossed his legs and his arms and exhaled. "Oh." He cringed. "Is it still that obvious?"

Destiny laughed. "You're all black and blue." Her hand brushed his cheek. "Does it hurt? I mean it looks like it should hurt."

"Naw. It doesn't hurt," he sighed, then bit his lip. "Do you ever have one of those days when nothing goes right? Kind of like when things are going bad, and they just start to snowball and then it goes downhill from there?"

Destiny nodded.

Bill wriggled his lips. "Well, this," he made a circular motion around his face with his finger, "was one of those days wrapped up in five minutes."

Destiny smiled, cupping his face with her hands. She leaned up on her toes and kissed his cheek. "Maybe one day," she whispered against it before kissing the other. "Maybe one day you'll tell me your secrets."

Bill suddenly took her face in his hands. "And maybe one day, you'll tell me all of yours." Slowly he leaned in and kissed her ever so gently on her lips.

Destiny closed her eyes and accepted the kiss. It was warm and sweet. And when he pulled back she opened her eyes and gasped. Then she smiled up at him weakly, their eyes locked on one another's.

"What about your car?"

"I'll call them first thing in the morning," she whispered, still reeling from his kiss. "My brother will take me to it. We usually have breakfast on Saturdays."

"I don't mind," he said. "In fact, I was hoping..." he began, drawing in a deep breath, "it would give me an excuse to see you again, sooner."

"I texted him earlier from the car. I didn't want to bother you. But that was before—"

"Before what?" he asked, his fingers gently brushing her cheeks. Destiny looked down, but he tilted her head back up. "Before what?"

She closed her eyes, feeling his breath caressing her lips; welcoming it, wanting it. Slowly his hot breath was against her cheek, kissing it, tracing it to her ear. She felt dizzy. Destiny opened her eyes, looking up into the wood beams. "Before this," she added in a breath.

He stepped away from her, waiting for her to open her door. When she stepped inside, he leaned against the door jamb, just staring at her.

"What?"

"I was just wondering if I should ask you out."

Destiny narrowed her eyes. "You were, were you?" She looked away cryptically. "You don't even have my phone number. How were you planning on asking me out?"

Bill slid the phone from his pocket and keyed in his password. Her hand moved to his, taking his phone, her fingers lightly brushing his palm. Electricity instantly coursed through his body at her slightest touch. A few strokes later she handed the phone back to him. Bill looked at her suspiciously and pressed dial. Destiny's phone rang, and she grinned. When he continued to hold his phone up to his ear, she opened her purse and removed her phone, looking at it.

"Hmmm," she looked at him mischievously. "I usually don't answer strange phone numbers."

Bill looked skyward, patiently, as her phone continued to ring.

Destiny narrowed her eyes and then answered the phone, without saying anything.

Bill held up his finger to excuse himself and stepped away from the doorway, his back to her, as though he was secretive about his phone call.

"Hello?" he cooed.

Destiny decided to play along. "Hello."

"Yes, I was just checking that this was a good number."

"Uh, huh," Destiny murmured.

"You see, there's this amazing woman I met and I was so afraid that when she gave me her number, that maybe she really didn't. You know? Kind of bait and switch."

"Nope. Real number."

"Good. Thank you." Then he hung up.

Destiny took her phone from her ear, then looked at it, perplexed.

"Well, Goodnight," Bill smiled sweetly and nodded cordially. Then he turned and reluctantly walked away, his smile growing with every step.

"Is that it?" Destiny called to his back.

Bill turned instantly and walked back to her, taking her face in his hands anxiously. "God, I hope not," he gasped before kissing her again.

Though his breath was hot and rushed, he showed restraint. His kiss was so sweet, and yet, more than that; it was remarkably... sensual.

Destiny felt weak in his arms, holding the door for support when they parted.

He breathed in a deep breath then slowly exhaled. "Would you go out with me?"

Destiny couldn't speak; her eyes transfixed on his. So she nodded.

"Next Saturday?"

Destiny nodded again.

"Seven o'clock?"

She felt mesmerized as she nodded again.

"I'll pick you up?"

Another nod.

"You're an extremely difficult woman, aren't you?"

Destiny bobbed her head from side to side and wrinkled her nose. A small smile grew on her lips, and she nodded once more.

"Good," he said, leaning over, kissing her again. Softly. "I love a good challenge," he whispered against her lips. Then he gently lowered her head and pressed his lips to her forehead, holding them there for many moments. Bill stepped away, backward, his eyes never leaving hers.

"Goodnight," he sighed. A moment later he was gone from her sight.

Destiny furrowed her brow and smiled to herself. "Goodnight," she replied, under her breath. As she continued to peer through the parted doorway, her heart pounded in her chest. But more than that, her heart smiled again.

And for the first time in a long time; actually, for the first time in a *very* long time, Phillip wasn't the last person on her mind when she closed her eyes and drifted off to sleep.

Chapter Eighteen

SOMETIMES THE MEMORIES came in small discernible pieces—fragmented; snippets of time, forever frozen snapshots in her mind. Sometimes they came like full visions; visions that felt so real she could touch them. Sometimes they came in dreams. Sweet dreams of holding her son, cradling him in her arms, rocking him. She could hear his soft cooing. She could feel him grasping her finger. Dreams so clear that she was there; they were still together. A family. Dreams she never wanted to wake from, dreams she desperately never wanted to forget.

Then there were the nightmares. The accident. Glass shattering. Her son was crying. Her Rhett crying, *"Mommy! Mommy!"* Oh, the blood! Phillip's blood, her own blood mixing with his as rain pelted her cheeks. The door that wouldn't open. The screaming of the saw so close to her face that it was deafening. The sparks flying around her like fireworks as the blade cut through metal.

Destiny sat up with a start, gasping for breath. Her heart was racing, her sheets wet with perspiration. She clutched them to her chest, dropped her head into her hands and sobbed. It had been months since she'd had a nightmare, one so vivid that she woke feeling as though it had all just happened again. As she closed her eyes and wiped away the tears, her arms ached to hold her husband and her young son. Not a day went by that she didn't think of them.

Destiny rolled onto her side, curled into a ball staring ahead at the bare wall. There were no pictures framed around her home. Those were kept in albums, in a cabinet. Hidden. The memories were too painful, and she didn't want or need daily reminders of who was no longer there.

Slowly she reached for her prescription bottle, shakily removing a tablet and washing it down with the water at her bedside. Destiny hated taking any medication, but these helped balance her. Depression no longer consumed her every day. They gave her the will to get out of bed, the will to go to work. The will to live. She drew in a deep breath and lazily crawled out of bed.

An hour and a shower later, she felt somewhat better. Triple-A was sending someone to meet them within the hour. Andy was on his way to pick her up. He agreed, on one condition—a condition he hadn't mentioned the night before. *She* had to buy *him* breakfast.

Andy and Destiny arrived at the same time the mechanic did. The large man with a handlebar mustache readily threw out several suggestions of what the issue could be, all of them expensive to repair. As long as it was a warranty issue, and she didn't have to pay for it, it wouldn't be a problem. In the end, the car had to be towed. Andy consoled her by telling her he'd buy breakfast instead.

"So, why can't you retire, again?" Andy asked, before opening his mouth wide and stuffing it with the giant burrito.

"For the millionth time, I want to work. I need to work." She sliced her burrito into rounds, then each round into quarters, unable to open her mouth wide enough to eat even the small burrito that she had ordered. Then she proceeded to sprinkle a little of the homemade hot sauce onto each quarter.

Andy chuckled at her. "You're so OCD," he teased, watching her repeat the same routine she had practiced inexplicably since childhood, even cutting her hamburgers into quarters.

Destiny glared up at him as she forked the first piece and put it into her mouth.

Andy shook his head, a sly smile on his lips. "I'm going to marry an OCD woman," he informed her. "That way I know that my house will always be clean, and organized and in perfect order."

"And you'll torture her daily like you tortured me?" she retorted, before taking another bite.

"Yeah, but it will be different," he said, holding the burrito next to his face, primed to be consumed.

"How's that?"

"There will be sex involved," he said, lowering his voice. "Lots of sex," he added, his mouth full.

"You're assuming an awful lot," she smiled, then carefully placed the next piece in her mouth, chewing daintily.

Andy chased his bite with a sip of Dr Pepper and, wiped his mouth. "*Lots* of sex," he grinned.

"I hate to remind you, but women aren't built like men are."

"Thank God!" he exclaimed, before taking another bite.

Destiny grinned as she sliced another round of her burrito, then cut it into four equal sized pieces. Feeling his eyes on her, she looked up. Andy was perfectly still, watching her. When she rolled her eyes at him, he finished chewing, a smile plastered on his face.

"I mean," she began, also lowering her voice. "Most women don't just... I mean, won't just," she stammered. "Just don't expect it, like every time you think about it." Destiny took a sip of her root beer.

"What? You mean I won't get laid fifteen times a day?" he asked in a normal voice, drawing stares from all over the room.

Destiny spit out her soda, spewing it all over her food and his, choking.

"Argh! That's disgusting!" he exclaimed, putting down his burrito. He grabbed extra napkins from the holder, blotting his arms, his shirt, plate, and table. Then he chuckled.

Destiny wiped her arms and plate. Embarrassed, she casually looked around, as those who were staring, looked away, one by one.

Andy patted her back. "Didn't think it was that funny." Andy lowered his head to see her face. As she blew her nose, he grinned. "Could have been worse." Her eyes turned to his. "You could have been drinking milk."

Destiny shook her head. "God help the woman you marry."

"Hey, that's not very nice."

"I didn't mean it that way."

"How did you mean it? Andy feigned offense.

"You have a perverted sense of humor. Not everyone would know quite how to take it." She grinned mischievously. "It will take a special kind of woman to appreciate you." Destiny chuckled behind her napkin and shook her head, as Andy crammed his burrito into his mouth—which was much more than would fit. Her cell phone rang, and she held up her finger to her brother while answering. "Hello?" She dabbed her lips with her napkin again. "Oh, hey, Rita." Her voice sounded disappointed. "No, sorry," Destiny said. "It's just my car's not working, so I'm kind of bummed." As she listened, she occasionally glanced at her brother, who was still trying to chew the overabundance of food he had shoved into his mouth. "Tonight?" She closed her eyes for a moment, then opened them again and smiled. "Sure, why not? I don't have a car; so could you possibly pick me up?"

Andy held up his napkin to discreetly wipe the excess food from his mouth that hadn't fit.

"Seven is good. See you then." Destiny hung up her phone. "That was my boss."

"You're going somewhere tonight?" He looked into his sister's eyes and smiled. "Two nights in a row? I'm so glad for you, Dee. You're finally getting out."

"Don't make more of it than it is." Destiny pushed her plate away and looked up, her eyes meeting his. "Please," she added, to end any further discussion.

Andy nodded. "Okay," he sighed, interjecting. "But, I have to say," he continued, to a furrowed brow, "that I'm proud of you. I mean. You've come a long way, Destiny."

Her eyes softened. She looked down at her hands folded in front of her on the table.

Andy put his hand on hers. "You're going to be okay," he smiled. "I was worried for awhile, but, now I know it. You're going to be okay."

Destiny squeezed his hand in return as she dropped her forehead to his. "*We're* going to be okay."

Chapter Nineteen

RITA SHOWED up late to pick up her friend, but the party didn't start until eight, and downtown was only fifteen minutes away. It was a party for one of the teachers from their English department who had worked at the school for fifteen years—a simple going away party with friends from school and their significant others, most of whom she knew. They had planned it weeks ago. Rita and other teachers had invited Destiny multiple times, but she had been adamant that she wasn't ready. As usual, Rita didn't give up, and her phone call was her one last attempt to get her reclusive friend out of the house. After the night before, Destiny felt more confident that she was ready to get out again.

There were delicious passed appetizers and a cash bar before dinner. Winston was the last one to arrive, and he came stag, only to further the rumors that surrounded his personal life. Once he saw Destiny, he stayed glued to her side most of the evening, even sitting by her at dinner.

"Let me, at least, get you ladies a glass of wine," he

offered Rita and Destiny as they all sat down together for their meal.

"Good. I'm tired of drinking alone," Rita insisted, holding up her empty glass.

"Just a half a glass." Destiny smiled, as Winston jumped up, taking Rita's glass. She chuckled at his eagerness to please.

"He's set his sights on you," Rita said flatly.

"Don't be ridiculous," Destiny scoffed. "Besides, he's buying you one, also."

"Yeah, but I'm married."

"Maybe he likes married women."

Rita unfolded her napkin and put it in her lap. "No, I think he prefers them wounded and vulnerable," she added, cutting her eyes at her friend as Winston returned from the bar.

Destiny exhaled dramatically and shook her head. A few moments later, an arm reached around her with a full glass of wine and she sighed. "That's more than half a glass."

"What can I say? They are generous with their portions." Winston smiled, then handed Rita her full glass as well. "Don't complain," he added. "Usually, people think that they get ripped off by the bartenders. For the first time in a long time, I just got my money's worth." He proposed a toast. "To friends," he said, waiting for them to raise their drinks in kind.

They tapped glasses. Rita sniffed her bouquet and sipped some of her wine.

Destiny closed her eyes and sniffed her drink, rolling the dark liquid around in the glass before taking a very slight sip. It was bitter, almost salty and she made a face.

"Too tart?" he asked.

"A little."

"You're just not used to it." Winston downed half of his wine in a few gulps. His eyes stayed on her as she tentatively sipped a little more.

"Thank you." She smiled sweetly.

Uniformed waiters served salads first, and dinner twenty minutes later. Everyone except Destiny was a little tipsy within the hour.

Winston's hand rested on Destiny's chair or close to her hand on the table through most of dinner and dessert. Every so often he would lightly touch it when he spoke, which was most of the time. As talkative as he was before the wine, he was more so after a second glass; going on and on about his prowess in the college football ranks. Winston seemed a little surprised and maybe more hurt when Destiny wasn't aware of his accomplishments. So he spent the better part of twenty minutes filling her in on what the rest of the world already knew and what she, somehow, had missed.

Rita excused herself throughout dinner, disappearing for stretches of time. At first, Destiny was concerned her friend was over-indulging until she realized Rita was running to the bathroom. Rita confided that she didn't feel well. It could have been the mushroom sauce, or maybe the wine; she said, before rushing back to the bathroom only minutes after returning. Fifteen minutes later Rita walked up to them, pale as a ghost.

"We're going to drive you home," Winston and Destiny insisted.

Rita waved them away as she sat down. "I'll be fine she said, before laying her head on the table.

Destiny and Winston retreated, separately, moments later returning, Winston with a ginger ale and Destiny with a cold, wet bar rag. Rita finally agreed to allow Destiny to call her husband, and he arrived fifteen minutes later to take her home.

"Sorry, it must have been something I ate." Rita was weak, hardly able to walk. She held the wet rag to her mouth as Destiny and Winston helped her to the waiting car.

"God, I hope not!" Destiny exclaimed.

"We all had the same thing," Winston concluded, eyebrows raised.

"I'll check on you in the morning," Destiny said as she closed the door and watched them drive away.

Destiny looked around and then motioned for a cab.

"Don't even think about it," Winston said. "I'm driving you home."

"That's not necessary," she insisted as a cab pulled up beside them.

Winston looked hurt. "Please, Destiny. It's the least I can do. You've helped me out more times than I can count; it's my turn to return the favor."

Destiny sighed, then looked up into his eyes.

"I promise I'm okay to drive. And I'll be the perfect gentleman," he said holding up his hand. "I promise."

Destiny's smile softened. "Fine," she conceded.

"Good." Winston motioned to the cab that they'd changed their minds and led her by the elbow toward the parking garage where he'd parked.

"Where do you live?"

"Just a few blocks from here. I would have walked, but my late husband taught me years ago to be practical."

"Practical is good," he offered. "You never talk about him."

Destiny looked down as she walked.

"I'm sorry. I didn't mean to—."

"No, it's okay," she smiled. "Most people don't talk about him because they are afraid they'll upset me. And sometimes I think they are right. Or at least, they used to be."

"Is it easier now?"

"Maybe," she offered. "A little." She yawned. "Sorry. I'm not usually out this late."

"It's okay. Me neither."

"Oh? I thought you were the party animal."

"Not in the least," he chuckled. "I'm usually home in bed by nine."

"Yeah," she smiled. "Me, too."

"I know."

Destiny furrowed her brow.

"You are a teacher, right? Don't we all have a nine o'clock bedtime?"

Destiny smiled and yawned again. They arrived at his sports car. She stopped suddenly, eyeing it from hood to trunk. "Is this…" she began.

"A Jaguar XE," Winston smiled proudly.

"Definitely not a teacher car," she remarked.

"Definitely not a teacher car," he agreed. "How do you think I can afford to work only as a substitute? My family's loaded. I'm a trust fund baby," he added. "And not ashamed to admit it."

Destiny shook her head. Obviously not. That explained the perfect teeth and expensive clothes. And *definitely* explained the expensive car. He opened her door, and she slid down low into the seat. The soft leather cushioned her head and she smiled. Nice. She gave him her address, but when he didn't key it into his GPS, she gave him easy-to-follow driving instructions. Winston parked in her space in the parking garage of her building, insisting that he wasn't going to allow her to walk to her door alone. Destiny was too tired to argue. So Winston walked her to her door, talking all the while about parent-teacher conferences. When she fumbled for and then accidentally dropped her keys, he bent over and gallantly retrieved them, then unlocked her door.

Winston opened the door for her, and before she was completely inside, followed her in. Destiny turned, almost running into him.

"It's late, Winston." She rubbed her eyes, wondering if the wine was making her feel more tired than usual.

He walked right past her into her open living space. "This is incredible." It was as if he didn't hear her. "I always wondered what these looked like inside. Always thought it would be cool to have a loft." Winston dropped her keys on the kitchen counter before moving to and opening her refrigerator.

"Look, Winston…" she began, as she heard him open of one of her caffeine-free Diet Dr Peppers.

"You don't have anything stronger?" he asked, eyebrows raised.

"No," she sighed, watching him fumble through her cabinets until he found two glasses.

Winston poured the bubbling liquid into both of the glasses, turning to face her, holding one of the glasses up to her. When she didn't immediately take it, he shook the glass. "A toast," he insisted.

Destiny rolled her neck to crack it, then took the glass he offered. "A toast. Then you have to go."

"Fine." Winston raised his glass to hers. "To the most kind-hearted teacher I've ever met. And the most beautiful woman I know." He tapped her glass.

"Thank you." Destiny grinned weakly before sipping her drink.

Winston watched her until she finished most of her glass. Then he drank the rest of his soda, gasping as he set it down on the table. "Can I use your bathroom?" he asked, looking around. "Sorry, but it's a long drive home."

Destiny rubbed her eyes again and yawned before pointing down the hallway. "On your right."

"Thanks," he smiled, before walking hurriedly down the hall.

Destiny finished her drink, placing both glasses into the sink. She walked to the wall of windows overlooking the river and leaned forward against the glass. She loved her city, especially at night. The lights shimmered across the still, cold waters of Town Lake. She closed her eyes. Minutes later she heard the bathroom door open. When Winston didn't walk down the hall immediately, she walked toward her living space.

"Winston?" Destiny ambled down the corridor and toward the bathroom. Her feet felt heavy beneath her like she was dragging them behind her. She glanced into the bathroom, but he wasn't there. "Winston?" she moved toward her bedroom, running into the door jamb. When she stepped inside, he was sitting at the end of her bed. "What are you doing in here?" she asked, her words slurring. "This is my bedroom." She stumbled to her nightstand, falling against it. "This is highly inappropriate," she fumbled with the pronunciation.

"You okay?" he asked, standing and walking to her.

Destiny's hand went to her head as she suddenly felt light-headed. "You need to…" she began, then forgot what she was going to say.

"Destiny?" Winston smiled, his hand moving to her face.

She remembered falling against him, and then she remembered nothing more.

The Storm

Chapter Twenty

DESTINY OPENED HER EYES. Her head pounded painfully. Her body ached. She thought for a moment she was dreaming of the accident, again. But she wasn't. Water began to run in the distance. The room was dark except for a thin slice of light coming from somewhere. Destiny tried to focus. It was her bathroom. Her eyes closed tightly, as she tried to remember what had happened. There was a party and then Winston drove her home. Winston was sitting on her bed, and then he was saying her name over and over. *Oh God! No!*

Destiny tried moving, but her whole body felt like a cinder block. Her eyes darted where she could see in the room, to the nightstand. The black handbag was still there where she had dropped it. How long ago was that? She inched toward the nightstand. It couldn't be a foot away, but it might as well have been a mile. Destiny grabbed the sheet, slowly pulling her naked body toward the edge of the bed. Her fingers stretched, but she couldn't reach it. She pulled herself with every ounce of energy she could muster, and yet it didn't seem enough. Moving as slowly as a snail, she wriggled inch by inch across her disheveled bed. The tips of her fingers touched the straps. Destiny drew in a deep breath and made one last exhausting attempt to grasp it. Her fingertips brushed the sequins.

Suddenly the water stopped, and she froze. She heard the shower door close. Destiny wriggled just a little more, and her fingers grasped the strap and pulled it slowly from the night stand. It fell from the table, but her fingers still gripped it tightly, pulling it slowly to the bed. The water began running again. Frantically her fingers pulled the bag onto the mattress. Nothing seemed to work as she tried to open it with one hand, her fingers unable to master the simple task. Gradually, her other hand responded and moved to the clutch, fumbling, opening it just enough to pull her phone from it.

Destiny wanted to cry; she wanted to scream. She was terrified, but she had to remain calm. The water in the bathroom stopped, and she let the purse slip from her fingers. It slid between the bed and nightstand. Maybe he wouldn't notice. Slowly, Destiny slid her phone under her pillow, under her head with both hands. Her eyes closed as she tried to slow her breathing. Though her heart felt like it would beat right out of her chest. The slice of light across the bed grew, and she heard Winston moving through the room. Suddenly the bed moved. A hand slid over her buttocks and her back. And in one fluid motion around her rib cage, under her chest to her breast. She hoped that he wouldn't feel her accelerated heartbeat and breathing. His hand roughly fondled her breast, then let it go and he slid from the bed.

There was jingling, grunting and banging as he moved around. Destiny swallowed hard; her throat was raw. *Please God, make him go away. Make him leave,* her mind screamed out. The bed moved again, and she felt his clad body pressed on top of hers. He kissed her bare shoulder.

"You were good, Babe. Later." And then he walked from the room.

Destiny heard him walking across the hardwood floors to her open living area. His hard soled shoes clopped over the wood throughout the apartment. *Make him go away. Please make him go away.* Her front door slammed, and suddenly her breathing quickened again. Her hand moved to her mouth as she tried to calm herself while continuing to listen. What if he was still here? What if he was testing her to see if she was faking it? A tear ran down her cheek. There were no more sounds, just silence.

Destiny waited what seemed like an hour but was only minutes before taking her cell phone from under her pillow. Destiny started to sob softly into the pillow, trying not to be too loud. Just in case. Each number seemed blurred, as she closed her eyes again, trying to remember the placement of the numbers on her phone. Shakily, she pressed *one.*

"Lisa," she gasped softly. "Lisa?" Destiny sobbed, still afraid he was going to jump on her again. "Can you come? Can you get me? Oh, God? Please, come get me!" Her cries became louder, desperate—no longer caring if he heard. There was a live person on the other end of the phone; no matter what happened now, someone would find her. "Please don't hang up." Her throat burned as she pleaded. "Don't hang up," she gasped, her voice trembling. "Home," she answered in a raspy voice. "I think he's gone," Destiny whispered, "but don't hang up. Just in case." Her eyes felt heavy and closed again. She nodded incoherently to her friend's questions as her breathing slowed.

She felt a hand on her cheek, but she was no longer

afraid. Slowly she opened her eyes. Phillip smiled his amazing smile, his hand brushing across her face. *'My love,'* he said. Destiny smiled back. *'You know it's going to be okay, right?'* he assured her.

"It's never going to be okay again," she cried.

Phillip moved closer to her, his breath on her cheek. *"Shhh… It's going to be okay,"* he promised.

Destiny stopped crying but shook her head.

"Do you trust me?"

Destiny slowly nodded her head. "Phillip, I'm so scared," she whispered.

"You don't have to be afraid ever again," his eyes promised, suddenly easing her fears. His face pressed to hers. *"I promise."*

"Okay," she said, closing her eyes again. "Okay," Destiny whispered as she drifted off to sleep.

Chapter Twenty-One

DESTINY SHIVERED in her paper-thin hospital gown. It was the fifth time they had woken her since she'd arrived. A trail of people had come in and out of her room for the past three hours, collecting evidence; her clothes carefully removed—her body combed, swabbed and photographed. Every sample taken, carefully preserved in bags or envelopes or vials, to be more closely scrutinized later.

Upon her arrival, they had assigned her a Sexual Assault Nurse Examiner and a Sexual Assault Forensic Examiner. But with no outward visible signs of trauma, there were more questions than answers. Had she been drinking? Had she taken any prescription or non-prescription narcotic or recreational drugs? Was there consensual sex involved in the *incident?* When was the last time she had sex before the *incident?* They asked if she had any sexually transmittable diseases. When they suggested she undergo tests for them because of the *incident*, she finally broke down, again, and cried—the very word, *incident*, making it sound accidental. Then the police arrived. And the questions were all repeated.

Lisa stayed by her friend's side, holding her hand through the entire interrogation. Destiny's desperate call at three in the morning had woken her from a dead sleep. And when she realized that Destiny was really in trouble, Lisa, usually the cooler head between them, became hysterical. Although Destiny sounded calmer than Lisa felt, she had quickly thrown on a shirt and sweatpants and raced to her friend's rescue. In the process, she not only broke her own personal rules for driving safety but multiple laws by texting and driving, running red lights and speeding through the streets of Austin. Lisa frantically texted Andy over and over and over, until he finally responded, telling him to meet her at the hospital. She was going to include telling him to call the police, but after five miles traveling down the highway at eighty miles an hour, she had two police cars on her tail, sirens blaring and lights flashing.

It probably didn't help that she was screaming obscenities at them when she arrived at Destiny's apartment and jumped from her car. Once they had her on the ground with her hands behind her back, two of them rushed upstairs to verify her story, while the others stayed with her. Once they broke into the apartment and discovered Destiny in her bedroom, they radioed their colleagues. The two officers guarding Lisa lowered their defenses and allowed her to stand up while they called for an ambulance. Destiny's loft suddenly became a crime scene.

When the officers, nurses, and the examiners were all gone, they brought her blankets, ordered her something to eat and then allowed Andy to come in to see her. He rushed to her side and fell on her shoulder. They wept in each other's arms.

Lisa stepped outside to speak to the female officer that was wrapping up her police incident report.

"What happens now?" she asked, glancing at the officer's name plate. "Officer Torres."

The officer put up her pad and pen. "We'll question the suspect and get his side for the report."

"His side?" Lisa asked angrily.

"Ma'am, I know you're upset."

"You're damn right I'm upset!" she exclaimed, not caring who heard her. "How long does all this take?"

"Ma'am," Officer Torres began calmly.

"Don't ma'am me!" Lisa said, her voice raised. "I want to know when you are going to arrest the SOB that did this to my friend?"

"Look," the officer began again.

"Lisa."

"Look, Lisa. We have a name and description of the suspect. We'll ask other people who were at the same party about what they saw. Every piece of evidence that we collect at her place and that we collected here will be used to put this guy away. I promise you."

Lisa crossed her arms and looked down, feeling angry and ashamed. Her eyes welled with tears.

Officer Torres reassuringly patted Lisa's arm. "If it makes you feel any better, most rape victims that have been drugged don't know they've been raped, and by the time it's reported, the drugs are usually out of their system. Because she called you, and you were able to lead us to her, inadvertently, we got to her early enough to get a urine sample before she peed, and they were able to draw blood. Hopefully, we will find whatever he used on her, in those samples, and if so, we have a much better chance of proving intent." She pursed her lips. "But you have to let us do our jobs. And no matter how emotional this is, it's important that you become a calming voice, for your friend's sake."

Lisa's demeanor softened as she listened.

"Let me give you my best advice, okay, Lisa?"

She nodded.

"First, get your friend to call her family physician and explain what happened. Then get her into counseling. As soon as possible." She looked down into Lisa's eyes. "Is she seeing anyone? A psychiatrist?"

Lisa didn't answer right away.

"I saw her arms, Lisa. When did that happen?"

"Three weeks after her son and husband died in a car accident," she replied flatly.

Officer Torres shook her head slowly. "How long ago was that?"

"Two years."

"If she's not in counseling now, get her back into counseling. Soon. See if you can get her pushed to the front of the appointment schedule. And have her get a restraining order against this creep. More times than not, they don't take kindly to being investigated when they are planning on getting away with it. My guess is he's done this before. He wore a condom. He took a shower. There's a good possibility there are other victims out there. Does she have a safe place to stay?"

Lisa nodded.

"Good. And I'd recommend she doesn't go back to work right away. Until the school district deals with the accusations on their end, she needs to stay as far away from him as possible. That's why the restraining order."

"Thank you. And sorry."

"I understand," she said. "As a woman, I want to castrate the creep. But as an officer, I'm bound by the law. And so are you. So no keying cars or egging houses, or threatening his manhood. Let us do our job. I promise you we'll do everything within our power to make sure he pays for this and doesn't do it again to someone else."

Lisa wanted to hug her but settled for a handshake. "I appreciate what you're doing."

"Not a problem. And oh, uh, sorry for the," she started, motioning at Lisa's face, referring to the scratches she received when the officers forced her to the ground.

"Yeah, well, if I were you, I'd have thought I was high, too."

Officer Torres raised her eyebrow and nodded, then handed her two business cards. "Call if you have any questions or have Ms. Hering call." She smiled, turned and walked away.

Andy walked into the hallway. "She's resting," he murmured. "What did she have to say? Are they going to arrest the guy?"

Lisa drew in a breath for confidence, took Andy's hand and sat him down. She explained everything that Officer Torres had conveyed to her.

Andy dropped his head to his hands. "I can't believe this is happening."

Lisa took both his hands. "She can stay with me," she insisted. Andy raised his head, looked into her eyes, and then slowly nodded. "There's something you need to know," she sighed. "When Destiny was talking to me— God, I don't know how to say this. When she was talking to me, she started talking like she was talking to someone else."

"Who?" he asked, perplexed.

"I think she was talking to Phillip."

"Oh, Christ!" Andy dropped his head into his hands again, then looked back up. "Are you saying she's crazy?"

"I'm going to see if I can talk to her doctor and let her know. She needs to know now. Just in case."

"Just in case what?"

"In case, they feel they need to keep her here. For observation."

"You mean, commit her?"

"I mean that you and I need to agree that *you* have to be prepared to make the tough decisions if she is unable to make rational ones herself."

Andy listened to her and nodded calmly.

"We have to do what's best for Destiny," Lisa reiterated. Then she hugged him.

"What's best for Destiny," he repeated against her cheek. "For Destiny."

Chapter Twenty-Two

THE SHADES WERE DRAWN, though only for appearances since the windows were tinted and little sunlight ever brightened the room, which was lit by a single 25-watt bulb in a shaded lamp she had bought at Goodwill for two dollars. The soft gold walls where Carolyn sat in a comfortable swivel armchair, her feet propped up on the ottoman in her thirty by thirty office, overlooked downtown, Austin. She had studied at the University of North Carolina, a top tier school with a lower tier price. Carolyn graduated with a 4.0, outstanding MCAT scores and a masters in psychiatry. She could have practiced at any hospital or nursing facility that she wanted. But she chose to go into practice for herself.

Carolyn swiveled in her soft, comfortable brown chair and stared over at the matching sofa and ottoman. The woman looked lost, deep in the pillows. Frail. More fragile than when they had first met. Carolyn sighed, then put the end of her fine point pen into her mouth. There was a time when she was the frail woman swallowed in the couch pillows. Sixteen and lost. Only her psychiatrist was a man.

Or rather a hypnotherapy psychiatrist. The things he did to her when she was hypnotized were criminal. But she was a troubled sixteen-year-old, going to a psychiatrist. Those things cast doubt on her claims, and the man went unpunished.

It was at that point that she became determined to be an advocate for those who had experienced sexual trauma in their lives. Many of her clients were rape victims. Destiny had been her client before she was raped. She had already survived unspeakable trauma and now this. Now, sadly, they were starting all over again. But Carolyn felt confident that she could help Destiny work through this because she already knew her medical history. She already knew her story.

Carolyn watched Destiny stare into nothingness. She wasn't going to ask her how she was feeling again. She already knew how Destiny was feeling. She understood how she felt. Carolyn didn't push her patients; she merely guided them through their grief, through what they had lost. And Destiny had lost so much. The woman had literally lost everything. And she had, once again, hidden within herself. Carolyn didn't want her to tuck away the emotions. She needed to bring them out. This was their second session since the rape, and Carolyn felt it was time that Destiny began to deal with her pent-up emotions.

"Destiny?" Carolyn urged. "What are you the angriest about?"

The blank stare was unbroken.

"Destiny?" she asked, a little louder.

Destiny's eyes turned to hers.

"What are you angriest about?"

Destiny slowly wet her lips and drew in a deep breath. "That I didn't listen to my gut."

Carolyn swiveled just slightly, inching back and forth. "And what did your gut tell you?"

"To kick him out." She looked down at her hands that played with a small pillow she gripped in her lap.

"So, why didn't you?"

Destiny felt her heart racing again, as she fought the tears. "I trusted him," she answered, looking up at Carolyn again.

"So you're angry at yourself for trusting him?"

Destiny nodded, tears streaming down her cheeks. "I trusted him. God, I trust everyone." She wiped her tears. "Phillip used to tell me I was too trusting." She shook her head. "I wish I'd listened."

"Trust is not a bad thing, Destiny. It's people that take advantage of trusting people that are the problem. *He* was the problem, Destiny. *He* drugged you. *He* raped you. *He* sodomized you."

"I know what happened. Even if I don't remember, I know what he did," she said, tightly gripping the pillow in her lap. "But *He* let it happen."

Carolyn furrowed her brow. "He who?"

Destiny dropped her head again.

"God?" Carolyn deduced. "Are you angry at God, Destiny?"

Destiny clenched her jaw as she looked away from Carolyn. The woman had just rebuilt the impenetrable wall. Carolyn didn't want to push too hard. It was still too delicate to break down all at once. Her doctor stood and walked to Destiny, kneeling beside her. Her hand moved to Destiny's and squeezed.

"You have every right to be angry, Destiny. Just don't shut down, Honey," she pleaded. "Please."

Tears rolled down Destiny's face.

"You are an amazing, strong woman."

"I don't feel so strong." Destiny wiped her tears.

"So, *be* strong," Carolyn insisted. "*Be* brave," she added. "Today, on your way home, I want you to stop at a grocery store and buy two things."

Destiny rolled her eyes. Carolyn always had exercises to help her every time they met.

"You will choose one of your favorite snacks and cheddar popcorn. Then you will go to a regular lane, not an express lane to purchase your items."

Destiny gave her a perplexed look. Last session all she had to do was stop at a convenience store and buy something. She couldn't cheat and buy gas and pay at the pump. She had to go inside, forcing her to interact with people. Oh, and she had to smile at people.

"Cheddar popcorn?"

"It's my favorite snack." Carolyn grinned as she rose. "You can bring it to our next session. And what else do you have to do?"

Destiny rose and dropped the pillow onto the couch. "I have to smile." She sounded almost annoyed.

Carolyn raised an eyebrow.

Destiny forced a fake smile, then erased it from her face.

"Good girl." Carolyn patted her hand. It wasn't much, but it was progress. Slow, positive progress.

Chapter Twenty-Three

BILL ARRIVED EARLIER than usual to prepare for Catfish Night at the Senior Center. He wanted to be ready early so that when Destiny arrived, he could spend some time with her, without its distracting him from his tasks at hand. She was all he had thought about all week. Bill hadn't thought about any woman in eight years. Sure he noticed women, but none had caught his eye, his heart in such a way that he could think of nothing else. Her eyes had entranced him, her lips enticed him. Walking away last Friday night was the hardest thing he'd done in years. Next to raising an eight-year-old, that is.

Bill was somewhat nervous and a little confused since she hadn't taken or returned any of his phone calls. He had tried to keep them simple; sweet greetings and '*looking forward to seeing you again*,' messages. He had even rehearsed before each call to assure that he didn't come off sounding ridiculous. Or desperate. And yet, he felt ridiculous *and* desperate. Maybe he had scared her. No, that wasn't possible. There was that unforgettable kiss; the way she looked at him after the kiss. Her playfulness. Her own nervousness was actually a little exciting. It felt not unlike… high school. The first kiss. Your first kiss with your first love. But he hadn't talked to her since. It had been a long time, but he was pretty sure he remembered what the laws of attraction were. And yet, now he wasn't sure.

Either way, tonight was the night that he would tell Owen that he wanted to ask her out. Not that he had to ask his permission, since, according to Destiny, he didn't have a chance of dating her. But Owen was his brother, and he owed him honesty. He owed him that much.

Sheray bounced into the building, singing with a song playing on her cell phone, headphones adorning her head. When she saw him, she sang louder and bounced to the music, dancing as if she was on stage. Of course, Bill had to trust that she was singing to the beat. He didn't know any hip hop, and since he couldn't hear any sound, he took her performance at face value. He grinned. When the song was over, she tugged the headphones out of her ears. "Got a new tat," she bragged, lifting the back of her shirt and lowering the back of her jeans to divulge a Chevy logo tattoo centered over her buttocks. "It's my new tramp stamp!" she said excitedly.

Bill shook his head. "Who puts a car logo on their butt?"

"Technically, it's not on my butt." Sheray smiled as she washed her hands and dried them per regulations.

"What were you singing?"

"Eminem, 'Monster.'"

"M and M's 'Monster'?"

"No, Eminem is the singer. 'Monster' is the song."

Bill wrinkled his lips. "Interesting."

Sheray unplugged her headphones, hit replay and turned up the music. Then she began moving with the beat as she took the food from the fridge. When the tune picked up, she danced more dramatically until she was dancing around the kitchen. She bounced next to Bill, motioning him with her head and her hands to join in. Bill slowly began bouncing. Sheray stepped away from the counter, pulling him with her. As he watched her moves he tried to mimic them until he was dancing around the kitchen as well.

"You've got it!"

Bill chuckled. He hadn't danced in years, and *never* to hip-hop. He was actually having fun. "M and M's huh?"

Sheray laughed. "Em-i-nem," she pronounced slowly.

Bill turned as he moved and saw Owen standing, stupefied, in the doorway. "C'mon, Homie," Bill said, with a wave of his hands. "Get down with it."

Sheray laughed harder.

Owen shook his head and smiled. "What have you been smokin'?"

"Homie's in love," Sheray said as the song ended.

Bill stopped dancing and looked at her.

"Nothing makes a man do crazy things like a woman," she observed.

Bill glanced sideways at his brother, who was none the wiser.

Owen began inventorying once again the items they were using and preparing his order for the following week. Bill drew in a deep breath, counted out his cash drawer. A half hour later he walked to his brother's side.

"Hey," he asked. "You got a sec?"

Owen turned to his brother. "Sure, what's up?"

Bill opened his mouth to speak when suddenly the back door closed. He turned expectantly to see Destiny, but Lisa walked in by herself.

"Hey, Lisa," Sheray said.

Lisa nodded once before she walked toward Owen and Bill. "Can I talk to you for a second?" she asked Owen.

"I'm a popular guy tonight," he grinned. "What's up?"

"It's Destiny," she smiled.

"Your friend?"

Lisa nodded.

Bill stepped closer.

"She's not going to be coming back for awhile."

"Oh, okay," he said nonchalantly.

Lisa looked at him expectantly. "And she can't make your date."

"I don't have a date with her," Owen said, a perplexed expression on his face.

"I do," Bill spoke up.

"You do?" Owen asked, a little annoyed.

"Yeah," Bill replied awkwardly. "I asked her out."

"Really? You asked someone out that I was interested in?"

"I was going to tell you."

"When? When you sent out wedding invitations?"

"We'll talk about it later." Bill ignored Owen and turned to Lisa, a look of concern on his face. "What happened? Why am I hearing it from you and not from Destiny?"

Owen moved away in a huff as Lisa took Bill's arm and led him to the side, away from Owen and Sheray. "Something happened last Saturday." Lisa looked down nervously.

Bill's heart sank. "What happened?" he asked. When she didn't answer right away, he grabbed her forearms. "Tell me. What?"

Lisa looked up, surprised by his tone. "She went out with some friends, and one gave her a ride home."

"And?" he asked impatiently.

"He drugged her, and he raped her."

Bill fell against the counter and dropped his head, the words instantly crumbling him. He looked up. "How is she? Is she okay?" He immediately shook his head. "Of course, she's not okay! God. What a stupid question!"

"I'm sorry. I didn't know about you and Destiny." Lisa shook her head. "Look, Bill. She's very depressed."

"I want to see her. I need to see her. I want to talk to her."

Lisa shook her head. "That's not a good idea." She placed her hand on his forearm. "If you care about her, you're going to have to give her some time. After everything—" Lisa's voice began to crack. "After everything she's been through, this is going to be really, *really* difficult."

Bill paced in a circle and brushed back his hair. "I can't believe this." He walked to the metal wall and slammed his fist into it, denting the metal. Sheray and Owen turned suddenly.

"What's his name?"

Lisa shook her head, pulling him further from the kitchen and lowering her voice. "I can't tell you that. There are legal issues involved now."

Bill closed his eyes in frustration and banged his hand on the wall. "I don't care about any damn legal issues. I want to know who did this to her."

Lisa shook her head and frowned. "I can't."

Bill stepped past her, grabbed his jacket and walked out the back door.

"Bill!" she exclaimed, running after him. "Bill!" Lisa caught up with him and took his arm. "Destiny's not at home."

"Where is she?"

"The best I can do is tell you that I will give her your

154

number, and I'm sure she'll call you when she's ready."
Lisa shook her head. "I'm sorry."

"She has my number," Bill said sarcastically, turning
away from her, his hands clasped behind his head. "She
just wasn't answering my calls," he added angrily. As he
paced in a circle and growled, he stopped, dropping his
hands to his knees, taking deep breaths before howling furiously into the night air.

Lisa watched in astonishment. When he calmed down,
she walked up behind him and took his arm in hers. "She'll
get through this one, too," she assured him.

"Tell her," he gasped, fighting the unexpected emotions
that were suddenly overwhelming him. "Tell her that I'm
thinking of her. Tell her we'll be praying for her."

"I will." Lisa kissed his cheek before taking his arm and
walking him back inside.

Chapter Twenty-Four

HER ASSIGNMENT for the week was to do something that she enjoyed doing, something that was part of her usual routine, something that she had stopped doing after the rape. It had been months, and she was just now feeling strong enough to leave the house more regularly. Destiny understood more than she ever imagined she could, the shame and embarrassment one bore, though misplaced, when raped. Although she had no real memory of the rape, what she had experienced was still a brutal, personal assault on her humanity.

They questioned Winston the same day she had reported the assault, and though he refused to submit anything for DNA testing, there was enough evidence in her apartment and on her body to justify issuing a DNA search warrant to do so. What followed was a warrant for his arrest. He made bond that same day. Destiny remembered him telling her he was a trust fund baby, so he was rich enough to hire the best lawyers to see him through a trial. And he did.

Deep pockets.

Taking Officer Torres' advice, Destiny filed for a restraining order the following week. His attorney, in turn, filed for one against her. Her lawyer explained that it wasn't an uncommon move, so as to allow the defense to claim that Destiny was the actual threat and not Winston. Rita didn't know about the assault until she was contacted by the police later the following afternoon at home. She had still been in bed recuperating from the night before. Rita was very helpful in telling them Winston had personally given both her and Destiny drinks. Then she explained how, coincidentally, she had become deathly ill after the first glass that *he* gave her. The police requested she go immediately to the hospital to submit saliva, blood, and urine samples.

There were traces of GHB in Destiny's urine sample, so they had hoped Rita's tests would show similar results. Several more hours had passed since Rita's illness, and if she had also ingested GHB, the chances of it still being in her system were pretty slight. They were skeptical whether she ingested anything else, but a toxicology was run on her just to be sure. Rita also felt it was important to tell them about her two other employees who had quit or transferred after rumored involvement with Winston.

Destiny hadn't been back to her apartment since the assault. She couldn't bear to return. Lisa retrieved much of her clothing that weekend, and Destiny moved into Lisa's guest room that same day. Everything else was boxed up once more by movers, the following week, and put into storage. That same week she listed her loft with a realtor and sold it a few days later for less than market value. Then she shut herself off from the world. Again.

If it weren't for doctor's orders, she would *never* leave the house. Therefore, she was forced to choose. Destiny wasn't about to go back to the Senior Center, and she couldn't face anyone from work yet, so she decided to go to the stable. It was still dark when she left Lisa's house. The possibility of running into anyone while riding this early in the morning was remote. Destiny had even called Charlie and Jessie the night before to assure there were no corporate events or trail rides scheduled and that Daisy was available to ride. They were excited that she was coming and even invited her to lunch. She feigned excitement and then lied about having other plans later that morning. If luck was on her side, she would arrive undetected, have a short ride and then leave without encountering anyone.

The clouds hung heavy in the black morning sky, the sun just beginning to peek out from behind them. Roosters cried out from the treetops as chickens cackled and clucked in the henhouse. Destiny parked closer to the barn than she usually did, anticipating a quick and convenient getaway after her ride. The tack room was on the way to Daisy's stall, so she stopped to pick out her bridle.

"Hey, Girl," she cooed. Daisy turned in her paddock and walked to her, whinnying softly. Destiny stroked her long muzzle. "I missed you, old girl." The gate creaked as she slowly opened it and stepped inside. She whispered as her hands moved along Daisy's recently brushed mane. The mare snorted and shook her head as Destiny slid the bridle over her ears, her fingers working the leather strap through the buckle easily. Daisy followed her obediently from the stall to the tack room where Destiny fed the reins through the fence before selecting a blanket and saddle for her ride. Just as she finished saddling her mount, a familiar face appeared around the corner.

Sydney was swinging a bucket of fresh eggs but stopped when she looked up and saw Destiny. Her face lit up instantly. "Hi, Dee!" she exclaimed, setting down the bucket and running to her. Destiny crouched to accept her hug.

"Hey, Sweetheart." Destiny hugged her tightly.

"You're going riding?"

Destiny nodded.

"Can I ride with you?"

"I don't think so, today, Honey." Suddenly Sydney's face fell and her shoulder's slumped. Destiny drew in a deep breath, looked around, and then exhaled. "Okay, saddle up."

Sydney's smile immediately returned. She ran into the tack room, re-emerging with a bridle seconds later. Within minutes, Peanut was bridled and saddled, and Sydney was standing on a bucket ready to climb onto him.

"Do your aunt and uncle know you're going riding?"

Sydney immediately trotted to the house, the bucket of eggs hanging awkwardly from the saddle horn. She steered Peanut as close to the porch as she could. "Uncle Charlie! Aunt Jessie!" she yelled at the top of her lungs. "I'm going riding with Dee!"

Well, Destiny thought, *that was one way to do it.*

Jessie stepped onto the porch in sweatpants and a man's flannel shirt over a t-shirt, her wavy blonde unkempt hair looking much like dry straw. "Hey, Destiny!"

Destiny waved without moving closer.

"Is it okay?" Jessie yelled from the house.

Destiny nodded, and then listened as Jessie dealt out instructions to which Sydney's head bobbed up and down obediently. Sydney handed her aunt the bucket of eggs, then turned her pony, clicked her teeth, gave a little kick and trotted back to Destiny. "Ready!" Sydney beamed.

"Let's go."

Destiny waved at Jessie, then turned Daisy and waited for Sydney before going through the pasture gate and into the vast fields beyond. The sun was just rising, filling the morning sky with gold, orange, and red hues, to light their way. They took their time this morning, walking through the meadows, at some points even dismounting and letting the horses graze while they walked ahead of their mounts. Sydney seemed to sense Destiny's need for peace and quiet, so she wasn't very talkative. The young girl reminded her of herself so many years ago. Destiny looked down at her. Without her even realizing it, Sydney's presence meant so much to her.

For the first twelve years of her life, Destiny was raised on a ranch. She grew up in the saddle. There was nothing like the power of a horse under her, the grace of the canter, the gentle acceptance of the master's touch. Destiny didn't realize how much she'd missed that until she began riding at Charlie's and Jessie's Farm.

New calves stood warily close to their mothers, in the field beyond. Destiny looked down at Sydney and grinned. As if she knew what Destiny was thinking, a mischievous grin grew upon her lips. Destiny clicked her teeth and then galloped across the small slope of green before her, Sydney not far behind. The cattle, refusing to be herded, moved lazily just feet away to another patch of green clover.

"We're cowboys!" Sydney said excitedly.

"Cowgirls!" Destiny corrected as she changed course. The cattle scattered, then congregated closer to the wooded area.

"Woo-hoo!" Sydney exclaimed, corralling them against the trees.

Destiny stopped and dismounted, slowly walking toward the small herd. The calves moved nervously closer to their mothers. She reached into her pocket and retrieved a handful of apple slices she had brought for Daisy. She sat on the ground and held out her hand. Sydney joined her, looking at her expectantly. Destiny took half the apples and put them into the girl's small hand. The cows all looked at them, stupefied. Whenever Sydney would start to say something, Destiny would put her finger to her lips and shush her.

Daisy nudged Destiny's back, nearly knocking her over. She moved her head over Destiny's shoulder, attempting to steal the apples originally meant for her. Destiny gently shoved Daisy's head away until the mare got the hint and started eating the grass beside her. One of the cows stepped precariously toward them, her calf following close behind. She arrived in front of Sydney and leaned over to sniff the apples.

"Hold them flat-handed," Destiny whispered, demonstrating with her own hand.

Sydney did as Destiny showed her. The cow sniffed before taking the apples, leaving a slobbery mess in Sydney's hand. "Ewww!" she exclaimed, startling the calf, then wiping her hands on her purple jeans.

Destiny laughed as the brown Jersey proceeded to consume the apples she held, slobbering all over her hands as well. She gave a strangely exaggerated look, then wiped her hands on her pants, also. The rest of the cattle, seeing that there were treats involved, slowly made their way toward Destiny and Sydney. Destiny reached up and scratched under the Jersey's neck. The young milk cow stepped closer to Sydney as she stretched her neck further, encouraging Destiny to scratch other parts. Sydney scooted closer to Destiny afraid of getting trampled. The Jersey leaned over and sniffed her head. They both laughed, startling the herd when they stood up. They took Daisy and Peanut by the reins and walked into the woods.

"I didn't expect to see you this morning." Destiny leaned side to side, dodging limbs.

"Yeah, I told my dad I needed some time to myself."

Destiny watched Sydney as she spoke.

"Sometimes there's just so many people coming and going that I can't hear myself think."

Destiny grinned. "How old are you, again?"

"Eight. And then Deborah comes home, and she gets kind of bossy."

"Deborah your sister?"

"No, she lives with Daddy and me."

"Oh," Destiny replied.

"But I don't think she's going to work out, or, at least, that's what Daddy says."

Destiny made a face.

"Yeah, she's nice and all, but just not what he's looking for."

"Your dad told you that?"

Sydney nodded. "We talk about everything."

"Hmm," Destiny said, furrowing her brow as they arrived at the opening in the woods. They released the horses to drink at the spring and sat on a boulder over-looking the water.

"I just hope he can find someone that can make him happy." Sydney turned to Destiny. "Are you married?"

Destiny looked down at the water and shook her head.

"Do you have a boyfriend?"

Destiny shook her head again.

Sydney sat up straight. "Hey, maybe you and my daddy —" she began.

Destiny held up her hand. "Young lady, I know you mean well, but I don't think I'm what your dad is looking for, either."

"How do you know that unless you meet him?"

Destiny looked over at Sydney and brushed her hair away from her face. "The thing is, Sydney, I used to be married, and now I'm not anymore. And it was real hard, after. And, well…" she looked back into the water, "sometimes, I think some people just are meant to be alone."

Sydney leaned against Destiny. "No one should be alone."

Destiny wrapped her arm around Sydney's shoulder. "No," she said sadly. "No one should be alone, but sometimes they just are. And that's not always a bad thing."

"But aren't you sad? Being alone?"

Destiny bit her lip as she released Sydney and started swinging her legs back and forth. "Sometimes," she said, trying not to cry. "But most times, like right now, I'm just glad to have friends, like you, that I can spend time with; then I'm not lonely. Then I'm not sad."

Sydney nudged her with her shoulder. "So you're glad I was here this morning?"

Destiny looked down at the young girl. "I'm *really* glad you were here this morning."

Sydney leaned against Destiny. "Good answer."

Destiny laughed. "Are you sure you're only eight?" She put her arm around Sydney again, pulling her closer to her side. When their laughter died down, they sat quietly, listening to the brook and the birds. The sun burned off the morning mist around them; the cattle settled into a greener meadow to eat, and for these few magical moments, the things of the world that tortured her soul, were forgotten.

Chapter Twenty-Five

ANOTHER FRIDAY NIGHT came and went with Destiny, a no-show at the Senior Center. Bill was beside himself with concern. Though they hardly knew each other, he had become quite fond of her. They had shared such a passionate kiss, with the lingering promise of more just the night before her assault, and he hadn't seen her or even talked to her since. That was months ago. After her prolonged absence at the Senior Center, and still no contact, Bill worked on getting her address from Lisa. Bill promised not to stalk her—unless one considered weekly floral deliveries stalking. How else was she to know that he cared; that he was thinking about her? That he was there for her? After their brief, albeit intimate encounter, Bill couldn't bear to imagine that she was just as suddenly, out of his life forever.

Bill couldn't begin to comprehend what Destiny was going through. The second week after the rape, Lisa confided in him just how devastating the event had been to Destiny. Though in the report, it was recorded as an acquaintance rape, Lisa assured him they weren't on a date. Technically, it was a drug related sexual assault. From the first moment Lisa told him, she saw the tortuous concern in his eyes. She opened up to him about her concern for her friend; the pain Destiny had been going through daily; from the assault to the arrest and potential criminal trial that loomed in the next three to six months.

Winston had not exaggerated when he told Destiny his family was from money. They had gone to great lengths and thrown a lot of money at lawyers to make this one go away. Despite the presence of his seminal fluid in her bed (although there was no presence of a condom, and no presence of seminal fluid on or in her), there were hairs on her bed and in her shower and bathroom that matched his DNA. He, through his lawyers, continued to insist that his sexual advances were encouraged and allowed and that she had willingly accepted the GHB discovered in toxicology reports to enrich her sexual experience. They had spent tens of thousands of dollars to try and wear her down with countless accusations. At many points, Lisa was concerned their tactics were working.

From the day he was told, Bill called Lisa daily to check on Destiny, since Destiny still wasn't answering her phone. And after every conversation, Lisa always promised to convey to Destiny his sincere concern for her well-being. Bill and Lisa had been friends for at least five years, so she trusted him, believing his concern for Destiny was genuine. Lisa knew what he had gone through with Justine and how hard he had worked to be the father Sydney needed him to be, what he had given up. Bill was a good man. He was a kind man. But none of that trumped her caring for and protecting her best friend. So, Lisa didn't press Destiny. Destiny was dealing with her share of emotions and didn't need to be pressured to share them with anyone else if she wasn't ready. And it seemed like she wasn't ready.

The school had stopped using Winston, pending the outcome of the investigation. Their attorneys were in contact with the two previous employees who had rumored involvement with Winston. His attorneys had been busily trying to ensure that those same two women, including two other women whom the school district attorneys weren't aware of, never testified in any way against their client. However, no matter how devastated Destiny was, no matter how hard it was for her just to get out of bed every day, there was one thing and one thing alone driving her— sheer determination that he would never do this again to anyone else.

Within forty-eight hours of the *incident*, as Winston's attorneys still insisted on calling it, they had contacted Destiny, in an attempt to settle out of court. However, at Andy and Lisa's insistence, she retained counsel, and all conversations after that went through her attorney. The defense was working tirelessly to prove consent, talking to Destiny's friends and family, as her attorney had done, to prove *lack* of consent. There wasn't a single person who could besmirch her character. There wasn't a single person who had anything negative to say about her. There wasn't a single person they could find whom she had wronged. Except, Owen.

Of course, Owen, being ignorant of what was transpiring in Destiny's life, wasn't in the least bit suspicious when a random stranger showed up at the Senior Center, casually asking about Destiny. He had no clue when this person struck up a conversation with him and steered the conversation toward the woman who had been absent for a few weeks. Owen had no idea how damaging his statements were when the man suggested to him that Destiny was a tease, and was playing it coy because she was a cougar. Instead, Owen, being Owen, merely played into the other man's hands by agreeing, rather than defending the woman he barely knew; for fear of looking like he'd been played for a fool by her.

So, when Owen's name was on the witness list for the defense, Lisa immediately called Bill. She left him a long message, letting him know she was on her way to pummel his brother. That is until Andy talked her down. It took enormous restraint for Lisa not to drive across Austin and give Owen a piece of her mind; just before killing him. On the other hand, Bill, once Lisa informed him of the subpoena, had no problem letting his brother know just how damaging his pride was to Destiny's case. Then he called him an idiot. Again.

Bill had enough issues of his own. Deborah, who had been such a hard worker for so long, had started seeing someone. Suddenly, her availability wasn't as flexible as before, and she was distracted and not as attentive to the guests. He found himself warning her that he needed someone as committed as she used to be. She agreed that her priorities and goals had changed but assured him that she would be more focused and, for a few weeks, at least, she was.

It had been months since he had come to depend on his aunt and uncle on a weekly basis to help with Sydney on the weekends since those were his busiest times. They didn't seem to mind and welcomed their grand-niece with open arms. But it was hard for him, juggling more responsibility when Deborah wasn't doing her job. If he let her go before replacing her, he'd have to accept fewer bookings to be able to keep up with the paperwork and daily care and feeding of guests. Bill refused to work longer hours versus spending that extra time with his daughter; that's why he had purchased the bed and breakfast in the first place.

It was now the first Saturday in September and unseasonably cool for this time of the year. The Kemper House was full. There was an early Texas Longhorn game, and all of his guests were attending the game and going to an after-party downtown. So after serving an early breakfast, he left everything to Deborah and Patricia and then headed to pick up Sydney from the farm. She'd been bugging him for months to go riding with her, so he thought he'd surprise her by doing just that. Plus, she said she'd made a new friend, Dee, and for months had been begging to invite her over, so that he could meet her. Sydney didn't say much about her except that she was nice. And pretty.

Bill arrived early to surprise his daughter. His Uncle Charlie had invited him to breakfast when he'd called the night before. With an offer of his Aunt Jessica's homemade biscuits and gravy, he promised Charlie he'd be there by eight. Bill pulled through the main gate and drove the mile-long gravel road until he reached the large ranch house. There was a car parked close to the barn, which he couldn't see clearly in the early morning shadows and fog. Bill turned toward the main house and parked beside his uncle's red Ford F250 Super Duty truck. As he stepped from his Honda CR-V, he was immediately accosted by Beavis and Butthead as they excitedly welcomed him.

Uncle Charlie met him at the door with a handshake and a smile. "She's already in the barn," he offered. "Breakfast won't be ready for about an hour. Jezebel just woke up."

Bill grinned at his playfulness. "I think I will ride with her today if that's okay."

"Absolutely. We stalled Beau for you last night after you called, just in case."

"Thanks," he smiled, as he turned and headed for the barn.

"If you don't find them in the barn, they're probably down in the pasture by the herd," he called after him.

Bill waved over his head.

It had been awhile since he'd ridden, so it took him longer than it usually took his daughter to bridle and saddle Beau. Beau, one of the first horses in Charlie's stable, was a beautiful black gelding with a white stripe on his face, from his forelock to his muzzle. He stood sixteen hands tall and was extremely gentle and easy to handle. Sydney had ridden Beau with her father several times when she asked to ride a big horse. Her father would only allow her to ride on him by herself when they were in the corral, where he would stand at the center while she would trot or walk in a large circle around him. In the end, Sydney preferred Peanut, because most days, she could ride without supervision almost anywhere on the property she wanted.

Bill gently kicked Beau, giving him rein. Beau responded instantly, and smoothly galloped through the pasture gate and into the meadow. Bill had forgotten how relaxing riding was, and he allowed himself to unwind, breathing in the cool fall air as he slowed Beau and walked through the pasture to the crest of a small hill. He stopped and gazed across the meadows that surrounded him. The sun was rising, burning off the morning mist that lay low on the land. With a perfect 360-degree view of the entire property, he stopped and gazed across the hills and meadows that surrounded him. There was a herd of horses grazing further away, and scattered herds of goats closer to the barns and main house. In the distance, he spied a larger herd of cattle. He stood in the stirrups and shielded his eyes with his hands as he searched for his daughter close to any of the herds. Suddenly, a large flock of birds flew from the wooded area at the foot of the hill on which they stood. Curiosity alone sent him to see what had spooked them.

Bill leaned back in the saddle as he walked Beau carefully down the thirty-degree incline. It was quiet except for the chirping of the remaining birds, an occasional bawling of a calf for its mother, and Beau, constantly clearing his nostrils. When Bill arrived at the woods, he stopped. Slowly, he led Beau to the edge. Bill hadn't ventured into the wooded area that had grown up around the creek since he was a boy. The trees and underbrush had overgrown so much he didn't think he could enter if he wanted. Bill stopped when he heard something, straining to listen. At first, it sounded like bees buzzing. Then more like talking, or, maybe even laughing. It was coming from deep in the woods. He heeled Beau gently, as they began walking again. Just when he was about to give up on finding a way in, Bill spied a narrow path worn into the ground. The brush was still thick, but as he started down the path, it opened up, and he was no longer scratched or beaten by limbs as he entered the expansive grassy meadow in the center of the woods.

He followed the path, or rather Beau followed it, either because he sensed where he was supposed to go, or he was thirsty and knew where the water was. Either way, Beau walked them slowly upstream where Bill spied two horses, Peanut, and Daisy, their reins hanging loose as they grazed in the meadow by the stream. And on the rock, their backs to him, were Sydney and someone else, whom Bill could only assume was her friend. As he approached, Peanut raised his head and whinnied softly. Sydney turned and a moment later, so did her friend.

"Daddy!" Sydney exclaimed, turning and running to him.

But somehow, he didn't see her or even hear her, because the woman that turned now and looked into his eyes was none other than Destiny.

Chapter Twenty-Six

DESTINY FROZE. There was no escape. How could this happen? How could he possibly have known she was here? Her heart raced. Did Destiny hear her right? Did she say "*Daddy*"? How could he possibly be the man Sydney had been talking endlessly about since they met? She felt foolish. She felt trapped. Destiny had avoided his phone calls for months, simply because she didn't want to talk to him. Then he started sending her cards and having flowers delivered weekly. Destiny had thought about calling him just to ask him to stop. She'd even thought about showing up on a Friday night to tell him in person. But she simply didn't have the nerve. Now here he was and she wasn't ready to see him. Why wouldn't he just leave her alone? Why couldn't everyone just leave her alone?

Destiny slowly turned and then stood on the rocky bank, facing him, her hands nervously shoved into the back pockets of her jeans.

Bill slowly dismounted and embraced his daughter, his eyes never leaving Destiny. When he smiled he very quickly noted that she didn't. His eyes turned to his daughter, her eyes looking up into his, innocently. Excitedly. "Hey, Sweetie. I wanted to surprise you."

"Daddy," Sydney said, pulling him by the arm. "This is my friend, Dee. She's the one I've been telling you about."

Bill slowed and stopped in front of her. Neither of them spoke for many moments. He drew in a deep breath and then nervously spoke first. "Hey," was all he could muster.

"Hey."

"When Syd talked about a new friend, I thought she was talking about one of the riding students," he said awkwardly. "You been riding here long?"

"A couple of years."

Beau tugged at the reins in Bill's hands as he endeavored to move toward the creek. Bill slowly released them, allowing the horse to drink. Beau shook his head, snorted and moved to graze in the forest meadow just feet away.

"So you come here every Saturday?"

Destiny nodded, looking down at her feet. "I usually come early—"

"So as not to run into other people?"

Destiny's gaze met his again. She instantly felt guilty. Bill had been sweet; so very kind. And yet she was doing everything to avoid his eyes. She had done everything to avoid *him*. "I used to ride alone. Until this one here accosted me and asked to go riding with me," she added with a slight smile. Sydney looked at them, stepping to Destiny's side. Destiny reached down, her hand brushing over Sydney's soft hair as she smiled up at her.

"She can be persistent," Bill conceded. "I hope she hasn't been a bother."

Sydney turned to her father, a hurt expression on her face. Destiny pulled the child against her, wrapping her hands around her. She shook her head. "Absolutely not,"

Destiny insisted, looking down at Sydney. "In fact, quite the opposite." Destiny smiled sincerely. "She's been an absolute joy."

"Good," he exhaled dramatically. "I know how she can be."

"Hey! I'm right here. I can hear you," Sydney said, annoyed.

"So, this is a beautiful place," Bill said to his daughter. "I've come out here since I was your age. I don't remember this being anything but an overgrown forest."

"It's our secret hideaway," Sydney beamed.

"Sydney and I come here almost every week and just sit and talk." Destiny shrugged, then looked up at Bill and exhaled deeply. "And sometimes we just sit and take it all in." She smiled a weak smile. "Your daughter's a good listener."

"Oh, really?" he mocked, turning to Sydney. "I'd swear she doesn't hear a word I say when I talk to her."

"Dad," she whined dramatically. "Please!"

As they all chuckled, Destiny relaxed. Bill did likewise.

"So, do you mind if I ride with you?" Bill asked cautiously, his eyes again meeting Destiny's.

She hesitated without smiling for a few moments, looking down at Sydney. "What do you think?"

Sydney shrugged. "I think if we don't let him ride with us, he's just going to follow us, anyhow. So we might as well."

"Hey, I'm right here," he insisted. "I can hear you."

Sydney and Bill laughed. Destiny managed a small smile and looked back down at Sydney. "I think you're right. Might as well," she agreed, facing him again.

Bill shook his head. He looked into her eyes and said, as sincerely as he could, "I don't want to intrude. I'll only come if you're okay with it."

Destiny thought for a moment, but gave in with a smile and turned to Sydney. "Mount up."

Bill walked to the three horses and gathered the reins, ending their free grazing. He handed Sydney Peanut's reins, then turned to Destiny. As he handed her Daisy's reins, his hand lingered a moment longer on hers before releasing them. Just her slightest touch and his heart beat rapidly in his chest. He helped Sydney climb onto Peanut's back, smiled and kissed her head. Tentatively, he turned to Destiny again, then moved to her side. He held the stirrup for her. Destiny hesitated, then slipped her foot into the wooden stirrup encased in engraved leather. She grabbed the saddle horn to pull herself up. Now, for some reason, it seemed too difficult a task. Her legs felt like limp noodles, and she didn't have the energy; it was as though all her strength was suddenly gone.

Bill stepped closer, took her hand and slowly placed it on his shoulder for support. Destiny looked into his eyes, then put her weight against him as he helped elevate her onto Daisy's back. Once she was in the saddle, Bill took her foot and adjusted it in the stirrup. He looked up at her, searching her eyes for what he'd seen when they first met. When they first kissed. Now they only held sadness, and it broke his heart.

Bill sighed as he pulled himself onto Beau's back. He then turned to Sydney and smiled. "You've got the lead." He watched as his daughter kicked Peanut gently. Then they walked back out the way they came, Sydney leading the way.

Chapter Twenty-Seven

THEY WALKED IN RELATIVE SILENCE, not knowing what to say to one another. Quietly distant. Bill sensed it was what Destiny needed or maybe even wanted. Sydney, however, chattered on and on about everything from what book she was reading in school to the astronauts in the space station to how the food chain worked. Every so often Sydney would point out wildlife to them: rabbits, squirrels, geese, and deer. Then she would ask which ones they had eaten before and how they tasted. They traveled the still green meadows, past grazing herds, ponds filled with waterfowl that didn't seem to realize yet it was nearing winter, and to the horse barns.

And then she started singing... every Disney song she knew, all of them dramatically, off-key *and* getting at least a third of the lyrics wrong. If nothing else it made Bill and Destiny smile, which definitely lightened the mood. For the moment.

When they arrived back at the stable Sydney was bursting to show off the many things Destiny had taught her, including how she could coax Peanut to canter and back up. Bill hesitantly stayed at the corral with Sydney, while Destiny rode to the barn. Destiny hurriedly unsaddled Daisy. But she wasn't fast enough. Bill walked into the main corridor of the barn just as she finished brushing the mare down. There was an awkward tension as Bill walked up and stood before her. Sydney bounced into the barn and stood beside her father.

"Syd, why don't you go on in and help your Aunt Jessie with breakfast?"

"Okay, Daddy." Sydney turned to Destiny. "Are you staying for breakfast, too?"

Destiny stumbled for what to say.

Bill could tell she was caught off-guard and intervened. "Honey," he said, petting her hair. "Go on. I'll be there in a little bit after I get the horses undressed."

"Undressed? Daddy, you're so silly."

"That I am." Bill winked at her and patted her bottom. "Go on now."

"Bye, Dee." Sydney threw herself into Destiny's arms.

"Bye, Honey. Thank you for keeping me company."

"Sure. Anytime." She turned, and with a wave of her hand, skipped toward the main house.

Destiny slid her hands nervously into her back pockets. When Bill turned to her, their eyes met. She suddenly dropped her gaze, looking down as she shuffled her feet, stirring the dirt and hay on the concrete floor. When Destiny looked up again, his eyes were still on her. She could see the sadness in them. She could tell he was wrestling with what to say as much as she was. Bill walked past her and tied the horse and the pony to the stall slats. Slowly, he began to unsaddle Peanut and put the saddle and blanket into the tack room. Occasionally he would glance at Destiny, who looked as uncomfortable as she could be. Bill took a brush from the shelf and held it out to her.

"May as well make yourself useful," he grinned, trying to break the tension. When she didn't take it right away, he persisted, shaking it.

Destiny stood numbly in the same place, and looked down at the brush and back up at Bill. Tentatively, her hand moved to accept it. She stepped to Peanut and began to brush him. One hand slowly stroked his thick winter coat, as her other hand followed each motion with the course brush. "Hey, boy," Destiny murmured. Peanut's ears perked up, and he turned his head to her. Then the pony began nibbling on her sleeve. "Stop it, silly!" she exclaimed, tugging her shirt from his mouth.

Bill began unsaddling Beau, his eyes spending more time on Destiny, than on his task at hand. She was a distraction, much like she had been at the Senior Center. After putting everything up, he started brushing the gelding down as well. Bill tried to understand the distance that now hung between them. It was unbearable. Fifteen minutes later they finished brushing both horses, took them to their respective stalls and then met again in the corridor.

Destiny found it hard to look him in the eyes any longer, so she slid her hands into her back pockets, again, and looked away. She wanted to say something, but couldn't find the words. The emotions welled in her heart. In her throat. In her eyes.

"It's been really good seeing you," Bill said, with as much sincerity as he could muster. How does one convey all their emotions into one small awkward sentence? When she didn't look up or respond, he finally turned toward the house. "Well, I guess I'll see you later," he sighed, walking away.

"Thank you."

Bill turned back to her.

"For the cards," she said faintly, "and the flowers." Destiny grinned a crooked grin. "And the messages."

"You're welcome."

Destiny looked down again. "And I'm sorry."

Bill took a step toward her. "You have nothing to apologize for."

Destiny bit her lip to keep it from trembling. "I have *a lot* to apologize for."

Bill saw the tears in her eyes, and his heart broke all over again. He stepped closer to her.

Destiny continued to avert her eyes. "I haven't…" she began.

Bill stood in front of her, watching the tears fall, wetting the dirt and hay at her feet. Slowly, he raised his hand to her cheek, but she flinched, taking a step back.

Bill stepped away immediately, his heart sinking; feeling her pain. He wanted to kill the bastard that had stripped the spirit from her so completely. "Destiny," He reached for her hand. This time, she didn't move away. Bill gently took her fingers into his. "If there's anything—" he began, taking another step to her.

Just the touch of his hand tore down the wall she had so carefully erected for months. Her body suddenly began convulsing with sobs. Destiny shook her head and pulled her hand from his. "I can't!" she cried, as she looked into his eyes once more. "I'm sorry. I can't." Destiny turned and ran from the barn.

Bill took a step to follow but then stopped. When he heard her starting the car, he suddenly raced after her. As she was backing up to turn around, he placed himself in her path, so that she had to stop. She leaned forward on the wheel, staring out the windshield at him, tears streaming down her cheeks. He heard her put the car into park, then turn it off. He could see her chest heaving, wracked with emotion. Destiny dropped her head to the steering wheel. Bill stepped to the passenger door and tried to open it. It was locked. He leaned over and peered into the passenger window, tapping on it with his finger. After a few moments, Destiny glanced at him, then unlocked the doors with the power switch on her door. Bill opened the door and slid into the seat beside her.

Destiny didn't face him. Couldn't face him. She stared numbly at the dials on her dash. God, she hated feeling this way. She just wanted it all to stop. The anger. The desperation. The sadness. She didn't know how much more she could bear. Lisa and Andy had been supportive; trying to help her find the strength, and yet it never came. Her doctor insisted she try and get back into her routine, but now here she was again; exposed and vulnerable. Everyone was sure of what she needed to be doing to heal. At the same time, everyone else was trying to deal with what had happened to her.

They sat there for many minutes in silence. Finally, she wiped her nose on her long sleeve, and, not knowing what else to do, sat back and dropped her hands to her side. She turned to him, her eyes red, her cheeks wet.

Bill smiled a sad smile as he took her hand.

Why was he here? Why did he insist on being so nice to her? He barely knew her. Why did he care? Destiny looked down at their hands, lay her head back against the headrest and stared forward. Why was it that just holding his hand made her want to bare her soul? Destiny closed her eyes, causing the tears that had been welling in them to stream down her cheeks.

"You know, Harry and Ralph never won a game before you showed up that first night. Ever!" he stressed.

Destiny turned to him, perplexed.

"And they haven't won a game since you stopped coming," he said, nonchalantly. Bill's smile grew. "And they insist that it's your fault."

"Do they now?"

"Yup," he grinned, turning sideways in his seat to face her. "And they've told us that if we don't get you back soon, then they are going to boycott the games. And they're working on dozens more guys to join them."

Destiny released his hand to wipe her face. Then she dropped her hands into her lap and looked down at them. "Boycott, huh?"

"Yeah, and those two guys have a lot of pull." Bill shook his head. "You wouldn't want to be responsible for breaking hundreds of guys hearts, would you?" He exaggerated his expression to lighten the mood.

She chuckled quietly to herself. And suddenly, albeit for a few brief moments, she was no longer sad. She was no longer angry. Destiny glanced at him, unable to meet his eyes. "Thank you," she said almost in a whisper.

"For what?" he asked. When she didn't answer right away, Bill's expression became serious. "You don't realize how much pull these guys have. I had to find and tell you before they started picketing the Bingo Hall." He grinned. "How would it look?"

He was trying so hard. And it was working.

"Never underestimate the power of a bunch of veterans carrying signs." He shook his head. "I could see the headlines now, *Destiny or Fate!*" he said, moving his hands above him like a banner.

"Okay," she finally said, placing her hand on his. She smiled slightly. "I got it." She sighed, then looked up into his eyes. "Thank you for trying so hard."

Bill squeezed her hand. "Anytime."

Chapter Twenty-Eight

WHEN THE DISTRICT ATTORNEY and Destiny's attorney had first contacted her about her case, it was one day short of four months after the rape. They felt they had enough evidence to present to a grand jury. There were many factors in the prosecution's favor: sufficient forensic evidence and dozens of character witnesses for Destiny. Her OB-GYN and her psychiatrist offered to testify as well. The District Attorney's office had subpoenaed the two female former employees since it had become apparent after their individual interviews that they had more than likely been assaulted by Winston as well.

The DA had a strong case but stressed that Winston's attorneys were digging in, determined to fight the charges. Destiny's attorney wanted to make sure she was ready for what was to come. Rape trials were notorious for dragging the victim through the mud as much, if not more, than the alleged perpetrator. And although there was virtually nothing they could do to tarnish Destiny's character, they were going to attempt to do just that. They would allude to illicit behavior, assume secretive promiscuity, and even outright lie, if necessary. Anything that would cause reasonable doubt and tilt the scales of justice in their favor would be considered fair game. They were paid for results so that they could call it a win and call it a day.

The lead investigator and prosecutor came up with a strategy which they had proposed to her attorney but needed her permission to implement. So far, the rape had not been publicized. The prosecution wanted to strike first, making the first public announcement that divulged Winston's name. They felt they had enough evidence to call Winston a serial rapist, and felt that if they did so in the papers, there would be others who would recognize him and come forward. But they had to be sure that Destiny was willing to see it through to the end because the press would eventually get her name.

Destiny asked them to give her until Monday for an answer. It was Friday. And it was the first day she was going to attempt to go back to the Senior Center. At least, that was her intent before the call. It had taken her this long to build up the nerve to be around that many people at once —not to mention that it was a last-resort instruction from her psychiatrist.

In the weeks since running into Bill at the farm, she had gone shopping at a mall, and she had gone to a movie by herself. *And* she started taking Bill's phone calls. Only that wasn't on her doctor's list of things to do. Dr. Villarreal told Destiny from the beginning that there were things she should do to heal, things she needed to do to heal, and then there would be things she would want to do on her own. Carolyn commended her for doing that one on her own.

At first, Destiny and Bill didn't talk much when he called. He tried not to overwhelm her all at once, limiting himself to one call a day. At first. Sometimes he would call to tell her good morning or maybe to say goodnight. Sometimes he'd ask her how her day went. Mostly he called just because he wanted to hear her voice. And she had to admit, she started wanting to hear his. Gradually, the calls would last more than a minute or two. They were comforting, and they were becoming comfortable.

Destiny shared with him how, for the first time in years, she wasn't teaching. She had taught in summer school, but somehow she didn't feel she was ready to take on a full class schedule. Rita was disappointed, but understood and supported her decision. However, now Destiny spent so many of her days volunteering and working at the school in a variety of capacities, from organization sponsorships to helping at various school events. Now, she spent almost the same amount of time, if not more, at work daily. So, between that and riding and her book club, she was staying busy. Bill invited her for a crappy cup of coffee once. Destiny turned him down.

She had now done something every week for six months that her doctor had encouraged her to do, and yet, she was apprehensive tonight, walking into the Senior Center. She knew these people. All the other weeks she was going out amongst strangers, mostly. These people were her friends. And other than her few closest friends, she had avoided the rest. Until now.

Destiny chose the timing of her arrival carefully; the after-dinner crowd was now meandering in, which would allow her to avoid the down time before dinner that would make for questions and small talk. She nervously parked under the light, stepping from her car, then locking the door. She took a deep breath, feeling her hands already sweating.

Bill anxiously waited for her at the door. It had been two months since he'd last seen her at the farm. He remembered watching her drive away that morning, never knowing if his words had meant anything to her. Not knowing if he'd ever see her again. The first time she answered the phone after that day, she sounded so fragile; her voice faint, almost a whisper. He was careful not to ask her too many questions, to try and talk as if they were old friends. Bill wanted to give her time; time to adjust. Time to heal.

No matter how hard it was, he didn't show up again to ride when he knew she was there. He did, however, allow Sydney to stay there each weekend. Then he would conveniently arrive earlier than usual to pick her up. He knew it was obvious, but it was lost on her since she had already gone by the time he arrived each week.

When she walked across the parking lot toward him, he smiled. But, more importantly, he saw *her* smile. His heart beat rapidly inside his chest. As she arrived at his side, he opened the door, his hand against the curve of her back. They came to the end of the long hallway at the main hall. He noted her nervousness and stepped in front of her to block anyone's view of her until she was ready.

Just then, Lisa walked up to them and hugged her friend, taking her hand. "Hey, Dee. You look great!" Lisa glanced at Bill and then back at Destiny. "You okay?"

Destiny drew in a deep breath. "No," she shook her head as she exhaled.

Lisa smiled. "Bravery—" she began.

"—is overrated," Destiny finished her friend's statement.

Lisa linked her arm through Destiny's. "There's a few guys more than a little anxious to see you."

Destiny turned to Bill.

"You ready?" Lisa asked

Destiny sighed. "Not really."

Bill lifted her chin with his finger and winked at her. "You'll be fine."

Destiny drew in another deep breath for courage and nodded at Bill, who stepped aside as if on command. They walked forward. Thankfully most people didn't give her a second glance. Others merely smiled or nodded a greeting. She felt herself relax.

"Destiny!" a voice exclaimed from behind. She turned.

"Grandpa!" she said, welcoming his hug and kissing his cheek.

He stepped back from her and looked her up and down. "You're wasting away!" he exclaimed.

Destiny looked down. Her clothes had been a little looser, but she hadn't given it a second thought. She looked back up at him and smiled. "That's why I came back here."

"Nothing like fried fish, French fries, and fried hush puppies to put some meat on your bones, or is it, clog your arteries?" He smiled. "That the only reason you came back?"

Destiny relaxed more as she chuckled. "No. I missed you guys."

Lisa released her friend's arm. "Work calls." She turned to her grandfather. "Behave," she instructed with a wag of her finger.

"Always," he called over his shoulder as he took Destiny's arm. "But if I don't," he whispered to her, "you won't tell, right?"

Destiny grinned. "Absolutely not," she promised.

Someone called out, "Bingo!" from the back of the room, followed by cheers and grumbling all at once.

They weaved a path between tables until they arrived at two men arguing.

"You had a stupid bingo two calls ago, you deaf old fool!" Ralph exclaimed.

"Well, if you hadn't been complainin' in my good ear, I would've heard 'em call it out, you old fart!" Harry rebutted.

Grandpa and Destiny stood behind them, smiling.

"Well, I told you, and you didn't even listen."

"Yeah? I heard you. I was just ignoring you. You were starting to sound like my wife." Harry chuckled.

"That's not nice," Destiny said, causing them both to turn.

"Destiny!" they exclaimed in unison.

She leaned forward, allowing them to each kiss a cheek.

"Our good luck charm is back!" Ralph proclaimed, the excitement showing on his face. He scooted his chair over to allow a third chair to be set between them.

"Hot damn!" Harry said, clapping his hands together and rubbing them. "I feel lucky now."

"You already won, you putz! You just didn't hear 'em call it," Ralph began again.

"Say, why don't I buy you guys a drink?" Destiny interjected.

"Margarita!"

"On the rocks?" Destiny clarified.

"Ah, looks and a perfect memory, too," Ralph grinned.

Destiny looked over at Grandpa, who was ogling at a bosomy young thirty-something volunteer that had just caught his eye. He looked at Destiny and smiled. "Be right back."

"Behave," Destiny said, with one brow raised.

He held his finger to his lips. "Shh." Then he winked and walked away.

Destiny turned from the two bickering veterans and

walked to the concession stand. There was only one person in line ahead of her. She looked past the fully tattooed woman to Bill, who was taking the woman's order. He looked up from the computer, caught Destiny's eye and smiled before looking back to the lady he was serving. Owen walked up behind him, handing him items as he called them out. When he saw Destiny he suddenly froze, quickly averting his eyes, ashamed. Then he turned and quickly walked away. Bill called her order back twice, then looked over his shoulder, realizing that his brother had abandoned his post at the counter.

Destiny's smile faded. She had hoped she wouldn't see Owen, much less have to talk to him. Lisa and Bill had apparently both told him exactly what they thought of his blind ignorance and what it could do to Destiny's case. If he had apologized, that would be one thing. But he merely shrugged as if to say *what did you expect?* "Idiot," Destiny said under her breath before stepping to the counter. When she looked up, she was met by Bill's warm, sincere smile.

"What can I get you?"

"Two margaritas on the rocks."

"Two Seven Ups coming up," he winked. He returned moments later with two drinks and a plate of food for Destiny.

Sheray stepped to the counter and smiled. "Hey, Destiny."

"Hi, Sheray. Nice to see you again."

"Sheray, I'm going to take ten and help Destiny carry this to Ralph and Harry."

"Tell 'em not to blame me for the lack of alcohol," Sheray insisted, as Bill stepped from behind the counter.

Bill walked with Destiny as she made her way back to the table. "How's it goin' so far?"

"Good. It's good."

"Better once you let your guard down?"

Destiny glanced at him. "Yeah."

"I was hoping," he began, nervously, as they arrived at her table. "I was hoping that maybe we could go for a crappy cup of coffee. After, I mean."

Destiny stopped and looked into his eyes. There was the same kindness there, the same tenderness she had seen before. The same tenderness that had touched her heart long weeks ago. But that was before. Everything was *before*. Destiny looked down sadly. She wanted to say yes, but she was afraid. Afraid of being alone with him. Afraid of being expected to bare her very soul. She looked away quickly.

As if he knew what she was thinking, he offered, "Just coffee. We can talk, or, we don't have to talk at all."

Destiny turned to him and slowly found herself nodding. "Okay."

"Okay?" he asked, surprised.

"Okay," she smiled faintly. "After."

Bill set her plate on the table between Ralph and Harry, took the two cups from her hand and placed them before the men.

Harry took a sip first. "Damn. They forgot the alcohol again," he growled.

Ralph looked up at Bill. "Gonna have to register a complaint with the management."

"You go right ahead," Bill replied indifferently. "We check the complaint box every third year and only on February 29th."

Ralph pointed at Destiny's plate. "Why did she get hush puppies? I didn't get any hush puppies!" he growled.

"You did so." Harry shook his head.

"Did not," Ralph insisted.

"Did so. You gave them to me." Harry sat upright in

his chair. "You just forgot. Damned old fool," he added under his breath.

"Putz," Ralph replied.

Bill's eyes bugged out, and he shook his head quickly. "That's my cue." He turned to Destiny. "I leave these two to you."

Destiny ate, listening to the two men banter as they played their cards. By the end of the evening, they had both won at bingo, thus securing her good-luck-charm status.

The last game finished at eight twenty-eight, and by nine, everyone was gone except the volunteers. Owen left early, feigning a headache, though Lisa, Bill, and Destiny knew it was pure cowardice. Soon he was followed by Sheray, and then Lisa, who always went back to the salon on Friday, usually working until early morning. Bill walked Destiny to her car. She was still planning to go for coffee, and he arranged to meet her in an hour, which gave him enough time to go home and check on Sydney. He made sure her car started and followed her from the parking lot. Several moments later, the lights from another vehicle flashed on. Neither of them gave the vehicle a second glance or a second thought, as it pulled out into traffic behind her.

Chapter Twenty-Nine

LISA'S HOME was a vintage seventies Spanish-style ranch house with four bedrooms and three and a half baths that sat in the foothills of Austin overlooking downtown. Lisa never did anything small. When she found the home, she was engaged to and already living with her fiancé of four years. They set a date and started shopping for a home together. The engagement ended abruptly when she found him in bed with his Pilates instructor. *And* her best friend. Lisa dumped the fiancé, bought the house and never looked back.

The home was filled with shabby décor to match Lisa's unique taste, mostly bought at yard sales and thrift stores. An eclectic mix of modern and rustic that only Lisa could pull off. Her parents had given her the deposit and co-signed the note. Once her business took off, she refinanced and ended up paying it off early. It was more house than she needed, so she had converted one of the rooms to an art studio, another one into a yoga and dance studio. Her only guest room was where Destiny stayed.

Destiny walked into the expansive chef's kitchen and

dropped her keys onto the granite countertop. Her phone rang suddenly, startling her. Although she didn't recognize the phone number, she accepted the call. When no one spoke, she hung up. It rang several more times. She answered politely every time, with the same result. Finally, she turned off the ringer and set it on the counter beside her keys.

The thought of driving around for an hour hadn't appealed to her, so she opted for going back to Lisa's to shower and change clothes before meeting Bill. Destiny didn't know if she felt like talking; she just knew she wanted to see him. Now she found herself looking forward to his calls, his kind notes and even the flowers that made her sneeze. As hard as it was to admit, Destiny missed him. Bill had been so sweet... and patient. For weeks she had tried, to no avail, putting all of it out of her mind—the way he held her. His touch. The kiss. She didn't know if she was ready. Or *what* she was ready for. But after all this time, she *did* know she was ready to see what might happen if she gave him a chance.

Destiny stepped out onto the deck Lisa had added two years ago and past the pool she'd added the year before that. It was a still, cloudless autumn night. The water had the appearance of a flat sheet of glass, flowing down the side of the cliff beyond, on which Lisa lived. The moon shone over the city, reflecting on the water. It was time to think about moving. Destiny hadn't discussed it with anyone yet but had already made the decision. Lisa assured Destiny she could stay as long as she wanted. Andy, of course, offered his apartment as well. But it was time. She was ready. Winston's case was expected to go before a grand jury within weeks. And when talking to her attorney that morning, she had approved the process of filing a civil suit against Winston, with the stipulations that any settlement proceeds go to the Rape Crisis Center. Winston had bragged about deep pockets, so she was determined to hit him where he would feel it most and use those resources to help other victims.

Destiny stepped back inside and looked at her watch. She suddenly remembered to call Andy. He usually stopped by on Fridays early in the evening. They would pull up a movie from NetFlix, eat popcorn and drink Barqs root beer until one or the other fell asleep. Because Destiny had gone to the Senior Center, they had made plans for later that evening. She needed to call him before he left, to tell him she had since made other plans. She picked up her phone to dial him, but it went to voice mail.

"Andy, taking a rain check on tonight. Hope you didn't leave yet. Will explain when you call me back." She hung up, then slid her phone into her pocket, and walked the length of the hallway to her room to shower. Twenty minutes later, she felt refreshed and awake. With fifteen minutes to spare, she decided to make herself a cup of hot tea. A cool breeze blew as she walked into the living area, and she turned. The patio door was wide open, the colorful curtains blowing in the wind. She stopped for a moment and tilted her head. She could have sworn she had closed and locked it. Destiny shrugged to herself. She forgot things all the time nowadays. The door to the garage opened and closed. She looked at the clock on the microwave. Lisa must have finished early.

Destiny walked into the kitchen. "You're early," she called out to her friend. "Or did you forget something?" When there was no answer, she walked toward the garage. The hallway was dark. And empty. Panic struck, and she froze. Slowly she removed her phone from the front pocket of her jeans. She reached to dial 911 and Andy's number flashed on the screen. Her finger moved to accept the call as she was turning. Then she looked up as something caught her eye. Destiny yelped with a start, her phone falling from her hand and crashing to the floor. Winston was standing perfectly still beside the granite island.

She grabbed her chest as dread filled her instantly. Destiny knew she was in trouble; Winston was dressed all in black. *And* he was wearing gloves. Destiny's heart felt like it would beat out of her chest as she assessed her options. Her first inclination was to run, but common sense told her that he was bigger and stronger, and probably faster. And, to where would she run?

"What are you doing here, Winston?" she asked aloud, hoping Andy could hear her.

"I missed you," he said, stepping toward her.

Destiny took a step back. "You shouldn't be here. You need to leave," she demanded firmly.

He took another step toward her. "What if I don't want to leave?" he asked calmly.

Destiny continued to step backward until her back pressed against the freezer side of the refrigerator.

Winston stopped a foot away but leaned his hand onto the fridge, his arm next to her head, his breath on her face.

"What do you want?" she asked, allowing her fear to turn to rage. She knew he wasn't there to intimidate her; he was there to hurt her. If he knew how terrified she was, he'd win. Rage would be her only defense now.

Winston reached his other hand to her face, but she batted it away.

"Don't touch me," she yelled. "Don't you ever touch me again."

Winston grabbed her chin. Destiny felt his gloved hand tighten its grip on her face. Then he smiled, released her and patted her cheek before leaning back. He grabbed the door handle and opened the fridge. Winston rooted around and took out a bottle of wine. He stepped away from her and inspected the bottle. He pursed his lips. "Not my favorite year, but it'll do." Winston turned his back to her as he reached above the granite counter and took down two wine glasses that hung over him. He slowly opened the wine and poured a little into each glass. Then he added something else to hers.

Destiny glanced down and saw her phone still lit up, but it was hard to see if Andy was on the line or trying to call her back. If only she could reach it. Her eyes darted quickly around the room. Lisa was a clean freak—everything was organized and put in its place. No knives on the counter. No meat thermometers. Nothing close-by to defend herself if needed. Not even a damn rolling pin or pan to hit him with! Destiny closed her eyes and drew in a deep breath. And for the first time in a long time, she asked God for strength. She asked God for courage.

Winston turned to her and held out a wine glass with little in it.

"If you think I'm drinking that, you're mistaken." Though her body trembled, there was defiance in her voice.

"No one should drink alone." Winston picked up his glass and sipped from it. He continued to hold out the other one to her.

"You raped me, Winston," Destiny snapped defensively. "You drugged me, and you raped me."

Winston narrowed his eyes and set his glass down. "Baby," he smiled, as he stepped to her again. "I remember everything," he whispered in her ear. "You enjoyed every minute of our time together. Besides," he added, his finger curling in her hair. "I'd never hurt you." He reached to brush her cheek.

Destiny turned her face away before his hand arrived,

then looked back at him. "But you did hurt me, Winston. I thought we were friends."

"We *are* friends."

"Friends don't do what you did to me."

Winston leaned his hand against the refrigerator again and held the glass to her lips. "Just one sip."

Her eyes challenged him, refusing to look away. Slowly her hand moved to the glass and took it from him. As she closed her eyes for only a moment, she lowered the glass and poured it out onto the stained concrete floor.

Winston smiled smugly. "We can do this all night, Babe." He took it from her hand and moved to refill the wine glass. "Your friend always comes home late on Fridays. I heard you cancel with your brother." He turned and held out the glass to her again. "It's just you and me."

"Why are you wearing gloves, Winston?"

Winston's smile grew.

Destiny shook her head, stepped away from the refrigerator and toward him. She looked down at the glass he held out to her. Guardedly, she took it from him, holding it up to her nose, sniffing it, then swirling it around. Destiny slowly raised the glass to her lips as if she was going to sip it, her eyes never leaving his. Then, just as slowly, she lowered the glass, holding it in her hands as she stepped past him. He turned with her, their eyes never leaving one another's. Destiny asked him faintly, "Why, Winston?"

He tilted his head, a perplexed look on his face. "There is no reason. There's no explanation for us, except that I could." Winston stepped toward her again. "And now, this has all gone on long enough. It's time to end it." He set his glass on the counter behind them.

"End it?"

"The others didn't care. Anyone can be bought." He walked in a circle around her, sipping his wine. "Some people put more value on their *issues* than others. But ultimately, *everyone* can be bought."

"Not me, Winston."

"Yeah," he said, shaking his head. "That's why I thought we needed to talk. Ten million dollars, Destiny? Really?" he laughed. "When my lawyers called me today I couldn't help but laugh."

"It's not for me."

"It doesn't matter who it's for; it'll never happen."

"How do you think you'll get around it, Winston? You can't be that arrogant." Destiny placed the glass next to his on the counter. She sighed, then looked into his eyes and softened her voice, speaking tenderly. "I liked you, Winston. I really did."

Winston reached for her face, and she closed her eyes. He caressed her cheek gently. Unexpectedly, her face relaxed against his palm. He felt a tingle of excitement at her acceptance. Winston took his hand away, removed his glove, then touched Destiny's cheek again. She didn't pull away, allowing him to caress her cheek, then her hair. Her hand moved to his, then slid tenderly down his arm. Destiny evened out her breathing, as she opened her eyes, meeting his gaze. Slowly he leaned toward her.

Suddenly she turned, taking his arm with her, bending and lowering her body at the same time, twisting his arm and turning it backward in an arm lock. Winston screamed out in pain, unable to break her grip or strike back from that angle. Then quickly, she threw two elbow punches to his nose. As he fell against her, he grabbed for anything to stay up—the anything being her hair. Winston hung on, disoriented, one arm hanging uselessly at his side. Destiny screamed out as he began to fall, pulling her with him. Desperately, she tried to crawl away; only he still had her hair, which he used to drag her back to him. Immediately, she turned over, and heel palmed him in his nose, his fingers relinquishing their grip on her, causing them both to fall against the island cabinets.

Shakily, Destiny reached up for the countertop. When Winston attempted to pull himself up, one-armed, she took a single step away from him and side-kicked him as hard as she could on the inside of his knee. Winston howled and cursed as he dropped like a sack of potatoes back to the concrete floor. Then he groaned and whimpered as he tried to stand. Only he couldn't. Winston furiously reached for her, making broad sweeps with his good hand; his breathing labored as he spewed snot and spit and blood across the floor, mixed with random obscenities hurled directly at her.

As she anxiously attempted to reach across the counter for her keys, he lunged and managed to grasp her ankle. Trembling with fear, she desperately tried to shake and kick herself free of his grip. But he wouldn't let go. His restraint on her ankle tightened as he used his hold on her to pull himself nearer. In one final attempt to free herself, Destiny stepped back once more and prepared to kick him like she was kicking a field goal, as hard as she could. Only he pulled her leg from under her, and she fell flat on her back, knocking the wind out of her. Winston now dragged her toward himself, still using her ankle as leverage. Destiny, momentarily shaken, felt him grasp her calf. Drawing in another breath, she desperately kicked out repeatedly, with all her might, with her free foot, making contact, but not knowing where. Slowly his hand slid from her ankle. Destiny crawled backward away from him until she ran into the refrigerator, which she used to upright herself. Winston was lying on his side, holding his nose, fresh blood dripping through his fingers, what seemed to be the result of her last efforts. Destiny stared down at him and then finished what she started, before he pulled her over, kicking him as hard as she could. Right in his groin. Winston's hand slid from his nose as he seemed to go limp. He didn't yell or cry out. In fact; he barely moved—his body gradually curling into itself, like a clam shell closing in slow motion. Finally, she drew in a deep breath, reached over the last few inches of granite and grabbed her keys. Immediately she pressed the car alarm, and it began bleating, echoing loudly in the garage, just mere yards away. Destiny ran from the kitchen, leaving the man no more than a pathetic lump on the floor, wheezing, and gasping in semi-conscious pain.

Tears blinded her as she raced into the garage. Once she locked herself in the car, she hit the garage's door opener, but then accidentally dropped her keys. Destiny closed her eyes and pressed on the horn—the alarm and the horn awakening every family in the quiet mountain cul de sac. Suddenly there was banging on the driver's side window. Destiny refused to open her eyes, exerting all her force onto the horn, screaming, "Leave me alone! Leave me alone!"

The banging moved to the windshield, startling her. She looked up, terrified. Only it was Andy looking down at her. She gasped, released the horn and quickly, shakily fumbled to unlock the door. Destiny fell into her brother's arms, sobbing. Within two minutes sirens and flashing colored lights further interrupted the stillness of the peaceful neighborhood. But Destiny didn't see or hear them through her sobs and Andy's consolation.

"It's over," Andy said, stroking her head. "It's over, Destiny."

"It'll never be over," she sobbed against his chest. "Never." She cried softly, holding on tightly, afraid to ever let go again.

Chapter Thirty

BY THE TIME the police arrived Winston had somehow managed to drag himself to the back patio door. The police found him there, struggling to open it. They weren't very compassionate about his pleas for help, nor his sobs of pain. They simply rolled him over and handcuffed him with a knee in his back, as he lay on the ground, in his own blood and spit and snot.

"She attacked me," Winston whined.

"Sure she did," one of the officers said.

"I want her arrested for assault," he gasped.

"We'll get right on that," the second one retorted, sarcastically.

"I need a doctor."

"Yeah, EMS is on the way," the first one replied. "We told 'em a girl just kicked your ass."

The second officer chuckled.

Andy walked into the kitchen and straight toward Winston. Both officers grabbed Andy by his arms to prevent him from doing anything to their suspect though their first inclination was to turn their backs and allow him to beat the ever-loving snot out of him. They knew who he was and what he had been accused of doing. However, they were bound by the law and had to trust that the justice system would do its job.

Andy had, in fact, heard her after she dropped the phone, and immediately merged calls as he dialed 911. Then he texted Lisa, as he sped to her house, praying that he wasn't too late. Lisa arrived just minutes after the police. Destiny was still shaking and sobbing, distraught beyond consolation. The first EMTs who arrived assessed her, and though she had no visible injuries, she was transported immediately to the hospital.

Lisa asked her next door neighbor, Beth, who was woken from a dead sleep by the sirens and lights, to stay with the police until the crime scene had been worked, so that she could ride with Destiny to the hospital. Beth and her husband, David, were more than willing to help, as much out of kindness as of sheer morbid curiosity. Lisa rode in the ambulance with Destiny, if only for her own peace of mind. Andy followed the ambulance in his car, matching its speed all the way.

The paramedics weren't overly sensitive to Winston's plight since he insisted on verbally assaulting them with obscenities and threats upon their arrival. They finally assessed him, determining that his knee and nose probably needed further attention. None of his injuries were life-threatening, but they felt a trip to the emergency room was warranted first. Though none of them would have minded if he remained in some pain for the near future. Regardless of his rants of police brutality or his threats of suing them and having their badges, they temporarily braced his leg, loaded him into the back of their ambulance and drove—within the speed limit—all the way to the hospital.

Upon Destiny's arrival at the hospital, emergency room

personnel immediately interviewed her again, to determine whether she had physical injuries. Her psychological trauma was apparent. She had become withdrawn and quiet. After reviewing her chart and talking to Lisa and Andy privately in the hallway, a doctor immediately administered a sedative so that Destiny could relax. Andy and Lisa stayed by her side until she fell asleep. Then Andy, stoic for his sister's sake, broke down and cried at her bedside. Lisa wrapped herself around him as she contemplated what to do with her friend now.

Destiny had sold her loft after the rape. How could she ever go back to Lisa's house after this? Her phone vibrated in her pocket repeatedly, unanswered.

"Why don't we get some coffee?"

"I don't want any coffee," Andy said, wiping his eyes. "I want to drive over to the police station, wait until they release him and then kill the bastard!"

"And then what?" Lisa asked, tugging him up from the bed.

Andy stared at her for many moments, as if in a daze, before looking away.

"Look, I'll take first shift." Lisa pulled him toward the door. "Then I'll call you if there's any change in the morning."

"I'm not leaving," he said emphatically.

"Look, there's no way I can go back home yet. And I'm too wired from all this. I need to get my head wrapped around what we're going to do with her now." Lisa smiled faintly. "One of us needs to go home and get some rest."

Andy looked down and nodded, lacking the strength to argue.

"Then break out the air mattresses," she sighed. "She's running out of places to go."

Andy turned to Lisa. "You know, if it weren't for you

being so levelheaded, he'd be in the morgue right now, and I'd be the one behind bars."

"Yeah? I was just about to tell you the same thing," she grinned and kissed him on the lips. "Now, get the hell out of here."

"Ooh. I love a woman who takes charge." Andy smiled weakly.

"You couldn't handle me."

Andy stared into her eyes for a moment, feeling them revive his strength, feeling them somehow encourage him when he felt so discouraged. He finally nodded, and then without saying a word, walked away.

Lisa retreated to a chair in the waiting room and fell into it, her body exhaling at the same time as the vinyl cushions. She dropped her head into her hands in utter exhaustion. Her phone vibrated again in her pocket, and she took it out. Bill's phone number scrolled across the screen.

"Bill?" she asked, surprised. "Yeah, I'm with her right now." Bill explained that they were supposed to meet hours ago for coffee. Since she wasn't answering her phone, he had become concerned. "Bill," Lisa sighed, initially reluctant to say anything. Then she dropped her head and closed her eyes. "We're at the hospital." She listened for a moment as he spoke, then gave him the abbreviated version of what had happened. "She's sleeping now." Lisa smiled at a passing nurse. She told him which hospital when he asked. "Bill, I don't think it's a good idea. Bill?" Lisa then took the phone from her ear and looked at it before placing it beside her ear again. "Hello?" Only, he was no longer there.

Chapter Thirty-One

THE HOSPITAL WAS EERILY QUIET. The eleven to seven shift was making their rounds throughout their floors, entering the results of their visits to each room into their computers. Nights allowed for more one-on-one time with each patient, not that many of them were awake at that hour. But there were no doctors or family members in the hallways, conversing with them, distracting the staff from their regular duties. Some found it hard to adapt to overnight hours and to sleep during the day, but after a few days of the routine, their bodies usually adjusted, albeit with a little more caffeine to help them through; using whatever was needed to trick their circadian clocks into resetting to a new schedule.

Marji had been in nursing for almost twelve years, with her last four being as a night duty nurse. When her husband, Mike, was offered more money for the midnight shift at a local factory, he encouraged her to switch to an overnight shift as well. Their kids had all grown up and moved out. Marji was a night owl, anyhow. That way they'd both be on the same schedule.

In his first week of overnights, however, the factory record was reset from no injuries at work to two. Mike's best friend, Jorge, stepped too close to one of the floor machines and his vest became caught in the gears. Mike was working desperately to free Jorge when his own arm became caught in the machinery. He bled to death before they could rescue him but not before he'd saved his friend. Margie, also on the late shift, was on duty when she got the call. She met him for the last time at the emergency room entrance.

Marji quietly entered Destiny's room to check the few monitors and the IV they had inserted as a precaution to ensure Destiny was taking in enough fluids since she wasn't drinking anything and refused to eat. Marji looked over at Destiny and gently pulled the blanket over her frail body until it covered her completely. She had read the chart, and she had heard the gossip by the nurses from the emergency room. The poor woman had been through so much. It only served to remind her that when she was missing Mike, feeling like no one could understand her pain or her loss, there was always someone who had gone through worse, who had suffered more pain, who had suffered more loss. She put her hand on Destiny's arm, lowered her head and prayed for her.

It was not something she'd always done. In fact, before Mike died, she'd never prayed with her patients. Not because it was awkward or for fear of someone reprimanding her. It just never occurred to her to do so. When they had brought her husband in, his arm shredded, his body contorted, Jorge was still holding Mike's other hand, and he was praying for him, even though he had died an hour before. After the funeral, friends from the factory had told her that once Jorge was free and Mike was dragged into the machine, they were finally able to turn it off. Mike was crying in pain, knowing he wouldn't get out, and that he didn't have much time. While many worked to free him, a few of his co-workers stood around him, laid their hands on him and prayed over him. And even when he died, Jorge wouldn't let go of him.

That's why she prayed over other people's mothers now, other people's fathers. And their children, and their husbands—because someone had prayed over hers.

Destiny stirred, and Marji stepped back. The things for which she prayed for Destiny others had prayed for her after Mike's death—that she not give up, that she not be so angry at God that she would lose her peace. Marji knew she was still alive because of those prayers; she knew it deep in her heart. Marji smiled weakly and wiped a tear from her face. So many people in pain every night. So much sorrow. It used to be a job, just a job. And it used to break her heart. But now she looked at it differently. It was an opportunity to make a difference, to say a prayer or hold a hand or even help loved ones say that last goodbye, something she wasn't able to do in her own life.

She looked up when she saw the light from beyond the door creep into the room. She didn't recognize the man, so she walked toward him. He stood just inside the doorway; his hands stuffed deep into his jeans pockets. She put her finger to her lips as she stepped around the bed. "Can I help you, sir?"

He looked at her with pained eyes. "I know it's not visiting hours, but…" he whispered. "She's been through a lot. I just needed to see her, to see that she's okay."

Destiny opened her eyes, letting them adjust to the darkness around her. She moved her arm to rub her eyes and realized that she had an IV in the crook of her arm. She held her arm up and looked at it with narrowed eyes, contemplating it. She glanced over at Lisa, who was asleep on the fold-down chair in the corner. She turned her head just slightly to see two people talking in the shadows at the end of her bed.

"She's resting. And since you know she's been through a lot, she really shouldn't be disturbed," Marji said, as quietly as possible.

"It's okay," Destiny said weakly, causing them both to turn.

Marji smiled and patted Destiny's foot. "Just a few minutes, okay? You need your rest."

Destiny nodded against her pillow.

Marji turned to Bill. "Keep it brief," she instructed firmly, patting his arm before leaving, pulling the door mostly closed behind her.

Bill stepped closer to the bed and crouched beside it, rocking on the balls of his feet. "Hey."

"Hey," she said, softly. And then there was silence. Unbearable silence. It was dark, but not so dark that she couldn't see his eyes. "You shouldn't have come."

"I know," he sighed. "But I had to. You know?"

Destiny nodded slightly, a single tear slipping from her eye and running across the bridge of her nose to the other side of her face.

Bill reached in and wiped it away. "Don't cry," he whispered sweetly.

Destiny curled tighter against her pillow. "I can't do this anymore," she whispered back.

Bill reached through the railing on the bed and took her hand, squeezing it. "Yes, you can," he said emphatically. "You have so many people that are here for you, that love you." He stopped suddenly, then smiled. "Sydney, my little girl. She's nuts about you. She's got a birthday party in two weeks and all she talks about is making sure that you're there." He leaned in closer, feeling as though he was looking through jail cell bars. "You wouldn't want to break an eight-year-old's heart, would you?"

Destiny let go of his hand as she sniffed and wiped away her tears.

"Well?"

Destiny barely moved, but he saw she was shaking her head. He rocked on his feet and scratched his head before reaching his hand back through the railing. He brushed her cheek with the back of his finger. He wanted so much to tell her that his daughter wasn't the only one who was nuts about her, but he knew this wasn't the time. There would be a right time, just not now. The room became brighter as Marji opened the door slightly.

"I've got to go," he sighed. "Before they throw me out."

Destiny shook her head slightly, and held his hand tighter, her eyes conveying her fear.

"You know I have to go." Bill motioned with his head toward the door. The warmth in his smile was immeasurable, reassuring, and she was no longer fearful. Bill pulled her hand to his mouth and kissed it gently. "But I'll see you soon."

"Promise?"

"I promise." He kissed her hand again. As he stood he heard Lisa move and glanced over to see her sitting up, still wrapped in a hospital blanket. He nodded slightly to her, then Bill turned back to Destiny, releasing her hand. He leaned over the side railing and gently brushed her cheek again. "I promise." He pulled the blanket up over her shoulders, turning to Lisa as she slowly stood. He looked down at Destiny as he hesitantly backed away. The light from the hallway filled the room for a few moments, disappearing again, taking him with it.

Lisa walked to her friend's bedside, crouching by where Bill had just stood. "I think he's sweet on you."

Destiny looked up at her, slowly moving closer to the side, pulling the blanket with her. Lisa stood, and walked around the bed before lowering the railing on the other side. Then Lisa crawled into bed with her, wrapping her arms around her friend, much as she had done when they were children, and again when they were in high school right after Destiny and Andy's parents died. Destiny didn't care what people thought, or what people might say. She felt safe in her friend's embrace.

"You know I love you, Dee."

Destiny nodded.

"You know you're going to be okay, right?"

Destiny closed her eyes and tried to think about nothing as she slowly drifted back to sleep.

Chapter Thirty-Two

MARJI WALKED into Destiny's room and turned on the lights at about six-thirty. Lisa wasn't there, but Andy was; sitting in the dark, checking e-mails on his cell phone. Destiny slowly opened, then rubbed her eyes as she sat upright.

"Good morning, Sleepyhead." He smiled.

"Where's Lisa?"

"No idea," he replied. "She was gone when I got here. She texted that she had to go home, but to call her when they released you."

"I wish you'd quit worrying about me."

Marji lingered at the monitors, deliberately taking her time.

"Really?" he looked at her, aghast. "After last night? Really?"

Destiny glanced at Marji, then back at her brother. "I have to pee," she said flatly.

Marji smiled and moved the IV pole toward her. "When the doctor does his rounds, we'll see if we can disconnect you. I know he wanted to see you before releasing you. Until then—" she said, rolling the pole into Destiny's hand. She took the blood pressure cuff off Destiny's arm and the oxygen clip from her finger.

Destiny rolled her eyes and growled. "I just need to get out of here," she said over her shoulder as she walked toward the bathroom.

"And go where?" Andy called after her. He turned to see Marji watching their exchange. He forced a smile. "Where do I have to go to get some coffee?"

Marji grinned and motioned with her head for him to follow. In the hallway, she pointed toward a small kitchenette specifically for the families of patients, just past the nurses' station. Then she stepped back into the room.

"I don't care where we go," Destiny called from the bathroom. "I'll check into a hotel. There's no way I'm going back to Lisa's. I don't even know how *Lisa* can go back to Lisa's." She flushed the toilet and walked into the sink area to wash her hands. "Maybe I'll just camp out at your place." Finding no paper towels, she walked back into the bathroom and grabbed a hand towel. "I think all I needed was a little sleep," she called louder. She stood upright as if she had an epiphany. "In fact, I feel… okay. Considering." She shook her head in amazement. "I mean, somehow, I feel… empowered." She tossed the towel onto the floor and dragged her IV pole with her as she walked back into her room. "I don't know how to explain it. Suddenly, it's like a weight has been lifted from my shoulders." She instantly stopped when she looked up and realized she was talking to herself. Or rather talking to herself while her nurse was standing there.

Destiny walked back to the side of the bed, and Marji motioned for her to sit down. She sat obediently, looking up as her nurse gently wrapped the blood pressure monitor cuff around her arm again and pressed the button. Marji looked into Destiny's eyes as the cuff inflated.

"One more time," she said, with a comforting smile.

She could feel the pulsing of blood through her artery as the kindly woman gently began removing the tape around the IV on her. Destiny looked at her, confused. Marji smiled as she carefully removed the IV and then placed a cotton ball in the crook of Destiny's arm and folded it. She tilted her head, as she moved Destiny's arm up in the air.

"Hold it there for just a few more seconds, dear."

"I thought the doctor had to see me, first."

Marji grinned at her, patting her knee. "I have a feeling he's going to release you."

Destiny watched her work.

"Anyone can see you are doing so much better than you were when you arrived late last night." She watched as Destiny averted her eyes. "I was here when they brought you up to my floor."

"You were here?" Destiny asked, lowering her arm.

Marji nodded as she removed the blood pressure cuff and wrapped it around itself before setting it on top of the monitor. "You seem better." Then she carefully registered the systolic and diastolic numbers into her handheld computer and turned off the machine.

"Yeah," Destiny said, with a dismissive shake of the head. "Can't explain it."

Marji patted her on the leg, again. "Dear heart, some things aren't meant to be explained."

Andy walked into the room with a cup of coffee in his hand and Lisa on his heels. "Hey, Dee. They release you yet?"

Destiny turned to her friend and brother. "No, the doctor hasn't been in yet."

Marji smiled as she walked toward the door. "I'll let him know you're doing better and are anxious to get out of here."

Destiny smiled in return. "Thank you," she said as Marji turned and walked from the room.

Lisa hugged her friend. "I've already packed you a bag. So when they let you go, we're out of here."

"Where are we going?" she queried, looking at them.

"Where are *you* going?" Lisa repeated back to her.

Destiny focused her attention on Lisa. "You're staying in *that* house?" She suddenly felt uncomfortable. "After what happened?" she asked, her voice raised.

Lisa and Andy looked at each other.

"I don't understand."

Lisa sat beside her best friend. "It's going to be weird and awkward, but I'm not going to move just because that jerk…"

"That *jerk* was going to drug me and hurt me again. Maybe even kill me!" Destiny barked.

"Now, Destiny…" Andy replied evenly, in an attempt to calm his sister.

"No!" she declared, standing up and stepping away from them. "Don't patronize me."

Lisa shook her head and sighed. "Dee——" she began but was interrupted as the doctor walked into the room.

"Good morning." A small row of white teeth appeared through his thick gray beard.

Destiny stared at Lisa, who looked at Andy, who glanced around the room before focusing on the bird outside the window.

The doctor sensed the tension and looked down at the chart. "Well," he exhaled dramatically. "Everything looks good. How do you feel?"

Destiny pulled her glare from Lisa and looked at the

doctor, who motioned for her to sit on the bed. She frowned and reluctantly dropped onto it, her shoulders slumped. He glanced at the chart, pulled up a chair beside the bed and sat. He looked expectantly, at Lisa and Andy, who took the hint and walked into the hallway.

"You had to tell her now?" Andy asked in a loud whisper, waving his arms dramatically to emphasize his concern once they were outside the room.

Lisa closed her eyes and rolled her head to relieve the tension that was building. She drew in a deep breath and slowly blew it out. "Just…" she began, then looked into his eyes, noting his frustration. "I need you to trust me. Just let me handle this, okay?"

Andy pursed his lips and thought for a minute. Without answering, he threw up his arms in frustration and walked away.

"That went well." Lisa looked up at the ceiling. "A little help here."

Destiny sat, looking down at her hands. The doctor reached toward her, slowly took her hands and turned them over. He inspected the scars on her wrists. When she realized what he was doing, she quickly jerked her hands away and wrapped her arms around her stomach, without looking up.

"Destiny? Can I call you Destiny?"

She met his eyes. He had kind eyes. Her demeanor softened. Destiny nodded.

"I've read your chart from front to back. Twice, mostly because I couldn't believe what I was reading."

Destiny looked back down, her hands dropping to her lap again.

"Then I called and spoke to Dr. Villarreal. She's a remarkable woman. Remarkable," he repeated. He reached over and took her hands again, holding them gently, loosely—the simple act revealing to her that she could pull them away at any time. Slowly, he dragged them forward and turned them over again. "And she thinks you're pretty remarkable, too." He studied her arms. "You are obviously a very courageous woman," he said, meeting her gaze.

"I don't feel so courageous."

"Courage comes in many forms." He set her arms back onto her lap. "Sometimes it comes in great deeds, standing up for what you believe, much like you did last night."

Destiny stared at him.

"Courage is sometimes as simple as leaving the house, or even getting out of bed in the morning after life knocks you down."

Tears welled in her eyes.

He released her hands, but she didn't pull them away, as she couldn't take her eyes from his. "Courage is staying here. In the here and now, even when giving up is easier." He searched her eyes. "You have nothing to be embarrassed about or ashamed of, Destiny," he added, nodding toward her arms. "Absolutely nothing."

The tears streamed down Destiny's cheeks. She didn't even have the inclination to wipe them away. She felt numb.

Her doctor pushed the chair back and stood up, looking down again at the file. "When the police and the paramedics are calling you a hero for fighting back, well, I would say what you did was courageous." He tilted his head as he spoke. "People talk."

A small smile crept onto the corner of her lips.

"Two quotes that come to mind," he grinned. "'Courage is grace under pressure.'"

"Ernest Hemmingway."

He nodded. "Yes," he repeated. "Ernest Hemmingway.

And the other, is 'He will never leave you or forsake you. Do not be afraid; do not be discouraged.'"

Destiny shrugged.

"Deuteronomy 31:8."

Destiny looked down.

"I'm releasing you, with the condition you'll see Dr. Villarreal as soon as possible. She's already reworking her schedule to try and see you this afternoon. And I was going to prescribe you a strong antidepressant and anti-anxiety cocktail, but somehow I feel like you won't need them. If I gave you a prescription, would you fill it?" he asked, cryptically. "Well," he sighed. "I'll let you and Dr. Villarreal discuss that. I've also put my personal cell phone number on your release papers. I want you to call me if you need anything."

Destiny met his glance once more. "Thank you."

"No, *thank you*," he said with a small smile. "Courage," he repeated as he walked toward the door, then turned. "From now on, whenever I think of that word, Destiny, I'll think of you," he said, winking at her again. "Take care."

Destiny looked down at her arms and then slowly clasped her hands together. About ten minutes later, Lisa and Andy and Marji walked into the room as one. Marji walked to her and handed her the large stack of papers that meant the hospital officially considered her checked out. She went over the prescriptions and the doctor's instructions, which included rest for at least a week, finally, confirming her appointment with Dr. Villarreal that afternoon at three.

Destiny nodded.

"Ready?" Andy asked. Destiny's lips turned up slightly into a wisp of a smile, which made his own smile grow. "Good!" he exclaimed. "Then let's get the heck out of here. Hospitals are depressing."

Marji looked at him strangely.

"No offense."

"None taken," she said, opening the door for them. "Now scoot." She turned to Destiny. "I was supposed to leave thirty minutes ago, but wanted to make sure that they let you out."

"Thank you," Destiny said, looking into the woman's eyes. Then she leaned in and hugged her, surprising everyone, including herself. Lisa and Andy looked at each other again.

"You are welcome, dear child," Marji said, hugging her and brushing her hand over Destiny's hair.

Lisa hooked her friend's arm, then leaned over and looked at Andy. "Fine," he said rolling his eyes playfully, before grabbing Destiny's other arm. He leaned back over again and smiled. "We aren't going to do the *Wizard of Oz* thing like we did in school, are we?"

Lisa leaned her head forward and narrowed her eyes. "Really?"

"Hey!" he exclaimed. "I never know what you two are going to come up with."

Lisa held Destiny closer and said to her cheek, "You ready?"

"Yeah," Destiny drew in a deep breath. "I think I am."

Softly, Andy began whistling "We're Off to See the Wizard." By the time they were in the elevator, they were all stepping in time, softly humming the song.

Marji's smile grew as she watched them walk away together. She glanced upward, her hands folded, and winked. "Thank you," she said, before turning back to her computer, in no hurry to leave after all.

Chapter Thirty-Three

DESTINY STEPPED from Lisa's blue 2000 Honda Insight onto the curb facing the Kemper House Bed and Breakfast. Andy pulled up behind them in Destiny's car and parked. Lisa told her friend she'd booked accommodations for her indefinitely until she determined what she wanted to do next. Lisa wanted Destiny around people. Not just people she could trust, but people who would help lift her spirits. Lisa just failed to convey one little detail to Destiny.

"I didn't even know this place existed," Destiny said, in awe, looking at the wrap-around porch and at the small orchard on the side of the house that led to the extensive gardens beyond.

Andy picked up two of four bags of Destiny's belongings that Lisa had packed and carried them up the wooden steps. "Wow," he said, admiring the woodwork. "The detail is incredible."

"Yeah, it *is* kind of cool," Lisa said, carrying a third bag.

"This place must be a hundred years old," Destiny said as she stepped onto the front porch, carrying her last bag.

"A hundred and twenty, to be exact," Bill said as he stood in the decorated entryway.

Destiny looked at him, shocked, and turned abruptly to Lisa and Andy.

Bill opened the front door and held his hand out with a sweeping motion. Everyone walked in but Destiny. Bill stood there, returning Destiny's gaze. "I'd do this forever, but it costs a small fortune to cool this old place, and it's warm out here," he smiled wryly.

Destiny hesitated and walked inside. Bill closed the door behind her as she set her bag down and turned to him. She opened her mouth to say something, but the words wouldn't come.

"When Lisa called me and said you needed a place to stay…" he began. After a moment, noting that her expression hadn't changed, he stated in a louder voice, "Usually we have milk and cookies waiting for all our guests!"

At that moment Sydney walked backward into the room through the butler doorway, and turned. In one hand she held a plate of fresh baked cookies, in the other, a carafe of ice-cold milk. She placed the plate carefully upon a table in the library, and stood stoically beside it, holding out her hand as if making a presentation.

Andy dropped the bags and walked to the tray, taking a cookie in each hand. "Don't mind if I do."

Destiny's eyes followed the young girl as she walked through the room. She looked back at Bill, who smiled with pride.

"If you don't, at least, try one, she'll be heartbroken," he mouthed to Destiny and Lisa, so that Sydney couldn't see.

Lisa stepped into the library first, followed by Destiny, then Bill. They all proceeded to take a cookie.

"Milk?" Sydney asked politely, poised to pour.

"Absolutely," Lisa said, as they each took a bite of cookie.

Destiny nodded as Sydney poured four glasses of milk and, one by one, handed each of her guests a glass and a napkin. Destiny's demeanor softened as she looked down at Sydney, who proudly beamed. "These are good."

Sydney grinned. "I made them myself. Just for you," she added, looking at Destiny.

Lisa nudged Andy, and they stepped casually toward the enormous Christmas tree that took up the front corner of the room.

Sydney turned to her dad. "Can I show Dee my room?"

"Sure," he nodded. "I hope it's presentable."

Sydney grabbed Destiny's hand and dragged her from the room. "Be right back," Destiny called over her shoulder to Lisa, her brow furrowed. "We need to talk."

Lisa ignored her friend's reprimand and turned to Bill. "Thanks so much for doing this."

Bill nodded. "It's the least I can do. And I promise we have the best security, or I wouldn't have offered. She'll be safe here."

Andy stepped forward and held out his hand. "I don't know what to say, except thank you."

"My pleasure," Bill assured him, shaking his hand.

Andy took two more cookies and headed for the door, disappearing with a wave of his hand. Lisa walked up and threw her arms around Bill. "You're unbelievable." She gave him a peck on the lips.

"Anything for you, Lisa, you know that."

"And anything for Destiny?"

Bill looked down, shuffling his feet before looking back up at her. "Yeah, I'd do anything for Destiny," he replied. Bill walked her to the front door and onto the porch. After they had driven away, he walked back inside, through the garland-and-candle-lit hallway, to his daughter's room. Sydney was still showing Destiny around, picking up random things and explaining where she got them and why they were important to her. He smiled at Destiny when she glanced his way, walked back to the entryway, picked up two of her bags at a time and carried them to his room. They were already completely booked for the next sixty days. And yet, when Lisa called him at four that morning, he didn't hesitate to make room for Destiny. After cooking for and serving his guests, Bill spent the rest of his morning moving his personal belongings into a small office/workroom on the same floor. Then he drove to Academy and bought an air mattress to place in Sydney's room temporarily for himself, as he prepared to take on an additional, unexpected guest.

Bill looked through his drawers for the last time, checked his bathroom, and lastly his shower, finding things he missed in his earlier rushed search. As he rounded the corner to Sydney's bathroom, he ran into Destiny, literally, and dropped the few shaving items in his arms. They both knelt to pick them up. When she looked up at him, he was smiling, causing her to smile. They stood together.

"Where are Andy and Lisa?"

"They, um…"

"They ditched me, didn't they?"

First Bill shrugged, and then he nodded.

"Figures," she said, shaking her head as she handed him his razor. "Bill—" she began, but he interrupted.

"Look, I know what you are going to say. You're going to say this isn't a good idea and that you can't stay here. Well," he began, nervously. "I think you *should* stay here. The Kemper House is a great place; it's safe, and we would love to have you as our guest."

"Bill, I—" Destiny tried to interject.

"We serve breakfast every day, and I always make sure we eat dinner as a family. There's always someone around, but we won't be underfoot. You can have a space of your own," he rambled. "And you can come and go as you please. I'll give you the house code."

"Bill—" she said in exasperation.

"And I promise that we'll respect your privacy, and—" he continued until she put her fingers to his lips.

"Bill!" When he stopped talking, she took her hand away. "Could you possibly show me to a bathroom?"

Bill felt his face flush as he pointed over his shoulder toward his room. "In there."

"Thank you." Destiny walked past him into the bedroom, noting her bags on the bed. She found the bathroom and locked the door behind her.

Bill heard the timer go off in the kitchen. He had left the dough to rise that needed to be punched down and kneaded again before its last rise. Bill was making cinnamon rolls for breakfast. He dropped his shaving items onto the kitchen table before turning off the timer. As he worked his way through the room, he stopped to wash his hands, put on his chef's apron, then he floured the granite counter and began again. Minutes later Destiny walked up behind him, watching him work. Bill sensed her presence, as he continued his prep. Guests would begin arriving within the next couple of hours, and there were things to prepare before they arrived. His morning had been spent moving rooms and cleaning, so now his focus was on receiving eight more couples before evening came.

"You look like you know what you're doing."

"Well, I've had to learn my way around a kitchen, something I never imagined I'd be doing with a masters in finance. I cooked when Sydney was growing up, but we ate a lot of spaghetti and sloppy joes if you know what I mean." He grinned over his shoulder as he finished spreading the filling over the dough.

"So, where do you get all your recipes?" she asked, as she leaned against the counter.

"Well, my mom gave me her old Better Homes and Gardens cookbook, and I started there. Then I began looking for recipes online, mostly allrecipes.com. Finally, I discovered Pinterest," he added slyly.

Destiny chuckled to herself. "Pinterest?"

"Yeah. Who knew? Now I'm making eggs Benedict and Belgian waffles while my mom is still cutting recipes from the backs of boxes and can wrappers."

Destiny stuffed her hands into the back pockets of her jeans, as she slowly perused the room. Bill glanced at her occasionally as she was familiarizing herself with her surroundings. "Did your mom cook?" he asked.

Destiny smiled sadly. "Yeah. She was a pretty good cook." Her hand delicately traced the restored wood on the original cabinets. "But my dad was better. He was the barbecue king in our neighborhood. He would spend hours concocting all kinds of barbecue sauce recipes and matching them perfectly with the right meats."

"Yeah? My dad did that, too. 'If it can be killed, it can be grilled' was his motto."

Destiny chuckled, remembering. "And he had to use a particular wood when he cooked."

"Mine, too!" Bill exclaimed as he sliced the perfectly seasoned log of cinnamon, sugar, and dough. "I remember this one time when my dad caught his pit on fire at a cook-off. And not just the pit, but the ribs, the wood that was stored underneath it and *everything* within five feet of it. He went into our motorhome for just a few minutes, came back out and the whole thing was on fire." Bill chuckled, placing the rolls in a pan carefully, leaving equal spacing between each piece. "Which included the pit of the guy a few feet away. Who was pretty peeved, since he had his heart set on the prize money." He shook his head, placing the pan close to the oven. "I think he was trying some new-fangled lighting fluid." He looked at her. "So, what do you say?"

Destiny looked at him, confused.

"About staying here?"

Destiny looked down at her hands as they toyed with a placemat on the table. "I don't know," she answered faintly.

Sydney stopped in the doorway. "You're not staying?"

"I didn't say that Sweetie," Destiny clarified. "I have a lot of decisions to make over the next few days, one of them being where I'm going to land permanently."

Sydney ran up to her and grabbed her arm. "Please!" she begged. "Stay with us."

Bill turned to Destiny expectantly, suddenly wanting to beg her himself. He could see the pain in her eyes. She was hurt and confused and putting up a good front. Bill looked down at his daughter, who was now tugging on Destiny's hand. "Sweetie, why don't you help make the salad for dinner? And then you were going to make some more cookies for our guests. They'll be arriving in the next couple of hours. You know the routine," he added, his eyes firmly set on hers.

Sydney dropped her shoulders. "Yes, sir."

"Good girl. Now, salad first, then cookies, then book report."

"Dad, it's not due until Friday!"

He held his eyes on hers.

Her face fell to match her stooped shoulders, in utter defeat. "Yes, sir," she said as she dragged across the kitchen, to get the ingredients she needed to finish the tasks he'd assigned to her.

Bill looked to Destiny and made an anxious face, causing her to grin.

"I'll tell you what," she began. "I have a doctor's appointment in about an hour, and when I get back, I'll decide. Deal?"

"Deal," Sydney replied, unconvinced. "Daddy, when is Deborah coming home?"

He looked at his watch. "She should be here anytime." As if on cue, the back door flew open, and Deborah breezed through it.

"Greetings, family!" she exclaimed, looking at Sydney and Bill.

"Deborah!" Sydney squealed, running into her arms. She kissed and hugged her before returning to making the salad for dinner.

Deborah walked up to Bill and hugged him. Then she kissed him on the cheek, her arm still around him. Bill turned immediately to Destiny. "Deborah, I'd like you to meet Destiny. It's possible she's going to be staying with us awhile."

"Destiny," Deborah said, excitedly, releasing Bill to shake her hand. "It's good to meet you."

Destiny felt flush, fidgeting awkwardly, already feeling her mood darkening. She looked at Deborah and then Bill, then back to Deborah. "Nice to meet you," she replied, forcing a smile. "Look," she began, suddenly looking down. "I'm going to go." She pointed toward the other room. "I have that thing that I have to do." Destiny edged her way from the room. Her heart beat rapidly in her chest as she hurried to the room where Bill had placed her luggage.

Destiny looked at her watch. There was no time to load

everything now. She'd worry about that when she got back. How could she possibly stay here now? Everything that Sydney had said about Deborah came back to her, and suddenly she felt so foolish. And angry. Destiny rubbed her brow with her fingers. Not only was she going to be late, but now she was getting a headache. She grabbed her keys and her purse and rushed out the front door, suddenly wanting just to disappear.

Chapter Thirty-Four

SINCE DESTINY HAD BEGUN THERAPY, it had been difficult to get her to talk much at all. But suddenly, it was though she had been fed a truth serum. And a triple shot of espresso. She paced while chattering away, almost from the moment she arrived. And yet, Dr. Villarreal, who had rescheduled a week's worth of appointments to fit Destiny in today, had only touched briefly on the traumatic incident from the night before. No, she was ranting about the owner of a bed and breakfast, who had kissed her, but was involved with someone else. It was all so muddled. The doctor finally had to make Destiny sit and explain everything from the beginning so that she could understand what the distraught woman was talking about.

When Destiny had finally unburdened herself, she sat perfectly still and stared at her psychiatrist, who merely smiled back at her. "How can you smile, Carolyn? Didn't you hear what I said?"

Dr. Villarreal nodded slowly. "Yes, dear. Did *you* hear what you said?"

Destiny furrowed her brow and tilted her head, confused.

She drew in a deep breath, leaned back and crossed her legs, rolling the pen between her fingers. "You spent the night in the hospital, and yet you have spent the majority of our session talking about Bill and his daughter, Cyndi, is it?"

"Sydney," she corrected her. Destiny sat quietly, staring ahead, realizing that she *hadn't* talked much about last night, except that Bill had come to see her, and how good it had made her feel. She drew in a deep breath. How was it possible that just seeing him, had helped her to forget about Winston if only for a day? And now, knowing he had a lover under the same roof made her so angry that she wanted to scream. She wanted to cry. Was it possible that she was falling for him? She never meant to. She never intended to. And yet… how could she have misunderstood that kiss? The way he looked at her? In the end, had he merely made a fool of her?

Dr. Villarreal clicked her pen annoyingly as she spoke. "Destiny, you've come a long way. You're experiencing emotions brought on by post traumatic stress. But be careful that you don't transfer all of your anger and frustration at Winston onto Bill. I think that could be very destructive, especially if things aren't as they appear."

Destiny was aghast. "Things are *exactly* as they appear." She stood and shook her head. "And I'm going to go back there, give him a piece of my mind and then check into a hotel." Destiny looked around for her purse. "Or maybe I'll check into a spa for a week." She slid into her jacket. "I can afford it. God knows I need it."

"Destiny?"

She turned to her doctor, poised to receive her words of wisdom.

"Be careful," she warned. "Don't push away someone who has unexpectedly been there for you. If he's able to bring out these types of emotions; if you are that passionate about being angry with him, then there's something else you need to deal with first, before you confront him about anything else."

"Yeah, what's that?"

"How you *really* feel about him."

Destiny stared at her, then turned and walked out the door.

Dr. Villarreal looked down at her watch. "Well, that was a record," she sighed to herself. Her first speed-therapy session, she thought, as she closed the door behind her last patient for the day.

Destiny contemplated not driving back to the Kemper House and just checking into a hotel, then sending for her things later. How could Lisa have put her into that situation? Surely she knew about Bill and Deborah. Or maybe she didn't. Destiny hadn't told her about the kiss. Too many things had transpired since then, and it simply hadn't come up. She sat at the light, at a crossroads of whether to turn left and drive five blocks to the bed and breakfast or go five blocks the other direction and check into one of a dozen hotels downtown. Destiny glanced up at the light, and the left turn arrow flashed above her.

"There ya go," she said, taking it as a sign, turning left and heading for the Kemper House. She pulled into the long, wide driveway beside a dozen other cars. Great! She forgot there would be other guests. That would deter her plans. Only slightly.

When she walked in the back door, she could hear people talking in the library. So, she walked straight into the room where her belongings were, only her suitcases weren't there. As she looked around, she opened the drawers, and sighed. Someone had unpacked her things. *That's just great!* she thought sarcastically. Destiny turned suddenly to find Sydney standing directly in her path. She grabbed her chest.

"Sydney!" she exclaimed. "You startled me."

"Sorry," she grinned. "You're just in time." Sydney took her hand and began dragging her down the hallway.

Destiny didn't know what to say. She wasn't about to cause a scene in front of Sydney. Now she was regretting letting a left turn signal determine her fate for the evening.

Sydney led her into the kitchen and to a small dining table by the window. There were four places set with china, silver, crystal and a small ornate floral arrangement in the center of the table. Sydney walked to the refrigerator, taking out a salad and Greek dressing. As she set them on the table, Bill walked into the room, smiling as big as Sydney was.

"You're back."

Destiny nodded, no smile on her face.

Bill ignored her mood and walked to the oven where he took out several Corning dishes. As he set them down, he carefully described their meal, emphasizing key ingredients that made each dish special. There was parmesan encrusted chicken, seasoned green beans, and garlic mashed potatoes. He set them each on thick pads to protect the antique table from the heat, as he turned and pulled out a chair for her.

Destiny hesitated and drew in a deep breath before sitting. Bill sat beside her. Sydney sat opposite her. As she put her linen napkin onto her lap, she looked down. "Someone put my things away."

"That would be Deborah. She's quite industrious. She'd already done it before I told her you might not stay."

"Now you have to stay," Sydney explained.

Destiny slowly looked up at Sydney. "I can't. I'm sorry."

Sydney slumped in her chair.

Bill's smile faded, as he put his napkin on his lap before motioning Sydney to do the same. "Well," he sighed, "at least, we get to serve you a nice dinner before you leave."

Destiny glanced over at Sydney and then pasted a small smile on her face. "It's nice, thank you."

Sydney reached for her father's hand and then Destiny's. Destiny hesitated a moment as she looked from daughter to father. Destiny felt her face flush and her heart beating faster in her chest again.

"Do you mind if we bless the food?"

Tentatively she reached and took Sydney's hand and his. They bowed their heads, although she silently refused to. She watched them as her heart raced. When they finished, she quickly pulled her hands from theirs.

They ate in silence, only occasionally looking at each other. Destiny glanced at the extra place setting and felt herself getting angry again. "Deborah isn't joining us?" she asked.

"I asked her to handle the guests so that we could enjoy dinner together," he smiled. "She usually handles the guests' nighttime requests."

"Mmm," she murmured as she chewed her food.

"She pretty much does whatever I ask her to do." Bill smiled.

Destiny shook her head slightly, then pushed herself back from the table and dropped her napkin onto her barely-touched food. Suddenly she felt like she was going to be sick. "Look, this was all very nice, but I have to go." Destiny looked at them. "Please excuse me," she added, as she rose and walked hurriedly from the room.

Bill looked at his daughter, who shrugged, and he, too,

placed his napkin on his plate. "Finish your dinner and clear the table," he instructed, ensuring Sydney would be busy for a while. Then he went to find Destiny.

Destiny walked through the small throng of people that mingled in the hallway and sundeck, looking down and smiling at no one as she excused herself over and over. She rushed into Bill's room and immediately started pulling her clothes out of the chest of drawers. She felt the hurt returning, her eyes brimming with tears. Bill arrived moments later to find her unpacking the drawers that Deborah had just filled.

"Look, I'm really sorry if we were too pushy. We just wanted you to feel at home," he said as she stood with her back to him.

Destiny scoffed, turning to confront him as quietly as she could with people just yards away. "Really? How could I feel at home, when *she's* just in the other room?" She looked at him with disdain in her eyes. "You're just like all the rest. I don't know why I ever trusted you." Tears rolled down her cheeks.

Bill shook his head. "Whoa! Did I miss something? What in the world are you talking about?"

"Where are my suitcases?" she demanded.

"Destiny? If I did something to offend you, I'm sorry."

Destiny shook her head and gave him an exaggerated, sarcastic look. "Yeah, you did. And I just need to get out of here."

"Destiny?" Sydney said, standing by her dad's side.

Destiny turned away so that Sydney wouldn't see her crying.

"Did you finish your dinner?"

"Yes, sir."

"Dishes?"

"Not yet, but—."

"Syd, please. Dishes. Then go to your room and work on your book report."

"But, Daddy," she moaned, as Destiny continued to unpack the drawers.

"Sydney Ellen Ireland, now!" he said, firmly but gently.

"Yes, sir," she said, grumbling as she walked away.

Bill stepped into the room and closed the door behind him. "So, you want to explain what I did to upset you?"

"No," she began, then turned. "Yes. You embarrassed me by leading me on and then bringing me here, flaunting me in front of *her*," she motioned with her arm.

"Her, who?" he asked, utterly confused. "Sydney?"

"No, not Sydney," she replied, angrily wiping her tears. "Deborah." She shook her head as she moved to the closet and found the suitcases she was seeking. "I don't know what kind of family dynamic you have going on here, but I'm not interested."

"What does Deborah have to do with anything?"

"She has *everything* to do with it. Your daughter already told me you and she weren't working out. And you bring me in here while she's still around?"

Bill looked at her, perplexed, but suddenly smiled. "Oh, you think… me and Deb?" He began to laugh. "No wonder."

Destiny felt her face getting hotter. She pushed past him with the suitcase.

Bill took her arm as she passed and turned her to face him. "Deb and I aren't an item. We were never an item. She works for me. That's all. She lives upstairs."

Destiny stopped where she was like the breath had been knocked out of her. "But Sydney—" she began and stopped. "Then you and she aren't…?" she continued.

Bill chuckled softly. "She needed a place to live and a job, and I desperately needed someone to help with guests.

She's not working out because she has a boyfriend now, and she's been pretty much useless since he came into the picture."

Destiny fell to the upholstered bench at the end of the bed and dropped her head into her hands. Dr. Villarreal had been right. And she had been so very, *very* wrong. She looked up apologetically. Bill stopped chuckling and sat beside her on the bench.

"Look Destiny," he exhaled. "I hope you'll reconsider and stay. We hardly know each other, and I'd be lying if I said I wasn't hoping to get to know you better. But that's not the main reason I would like you to stay. If you're here, I know you're safe."

Destiny looked down at her hands. She was so ashamed. She wanted to crawl under a rock right at that moment.

"But I don't want you to feel pressured to stay. I want you to stay because you want to. No pressure." Bill held up his hand. "I Promise." He smiled. "Except for Sydney, I can't guarantee that she won't pressure you. She's persistent."

A small smile grew on the side of her lips. "I have a feeling she gets that from her father."

Bill nudged her with his shoulder. "I'd like to think it's one of my finer qualities."

"That and forgiveness," Destiny added meekly.

"Nothing to forgive." Bill stood and faced her.

Destiny looked up at him. He held out his hand for her to take. "C'mon." Bill motioned with his head. "There's an eight-year-old in there that could probably use a hug right now."

"Yeah, well, there's a thirty-year-old in here that needs a hug, too."

Bill pulled her to him. "Thought you'd never ask." Bill

brushed back her straight dark hair from her face with both hands. Her brown eyes were mesmerizing. At that moment, he wanted so badly to kiss her. So he lowered her head and kissed her forehead before pulling her against him.

"Thank you," Destiny smiled against his chest. "I really needed this."

"Anytime," he promised. "Anytime."

Chapter Thirty-Five

FOR THE FIRST time in years, Destiny not only slept through the night, but she slept late. She was usually up by five every morning when she was teaching, and her body clock usually had her up by six-thirty, without an alarm on days when she wasn't. When she finally rolled over and looked at the clock from where she nestled, deep in the soft sheets under the goose feather comforter in the four-poster bed, it was noon. She grinned to herself. There were voices from the other room, faint and echoing across the wood flooring and under her door. She heard Christmas music playing softly as well.

But she didn't rise, not just yet. She stared out the glass French doors that overlooked the gardens beyond the porch. What an amazing sight to wake up to! It was like waking in a dream rather than the nightmare of the past six months. She was sure that by tomorrow her attorney would have received her message. She was hoping, because praying was still a distant thought, that there was enough evidence to keep Winston in jail until a trial. Hoping there were certain things that money *couldn't* buy. She pulled the pillow to her chest, closed her eyes and smiled.

Last night, after her meltdown, Bill had invited her to join Sydney and any guests who wanted to participate in singing Christmas carols on the porch. During the last five weeks until Christmas, several streets in the subdivision were closed off evenings, allowing foot traffic to enjoy the decorations and lights of the historic neighborhood. Some of the guests sang while Sydney served hot cocoa, and individually-wrapped Christmas cookies with business cards tied with dainty bows, to passersby who came to enjoy the music. Destiny played bystander for the first few songs, but then Sydney and several guests coaxed her into joining them. It was the most fun she remembered having in years.

Bill had been right. She felt safe. She couldn't explain it. Somehow, knowing Winston was behind bars gave her peace. She wasn't looking over her shoulder, fearful that he might appear again. Marji had suggested it was God, but considering everything she had been through, she wasn't quite ready to accept that, not just yet.

Destiny rose and made her bed before showering and washing her hair. She finally exited her room about two in the afternoon.

Sydney met her at the foot of the stairs, just sitting there, expectantly. "Bout time!" she exclaimed, throwing herself into Destiny's arms. "You missed church *and* Dad's famous cinnamon rolls."

Destiny grinned. "I'll bet he'll make them again." She allowed Sydney to drag her into the kitchen.

"Good morning, er, uh, I mean afternoon," Bill said, looking down at his daughter. "Can you please check on the rest of the rooms and see if our guests want their beds made or if they need fresh towels?"

"I'm on it," Sydney replied, rushing through the butler door.

"Coffee?"

"I would love some," she purred.

"Regular or decaf?"

"Decaf," she replied, the smell of cinnamon still lingering in the air.

Bill took out a decorative holiday cup and filled it, then held out a basket of assorted creamers and sweeteners. "She's been planted on those stairs since we got back from church, just waiting for you."

Destiny smiled as she doctored her coffee and moved to the table where she sat close to the window. She rubbed her eyes with her fingers. "I can't believe I slept that late."

"It's a comfortable bed," Bill remarked, sipping his coffee. "There's been many a morning I haven't wanted to crawl out of it, either."

"That's your room?" she asked, surprised.

He held up his hand. "Before you start making arguments, it was either give up mine or Sydney's, and I don't think you could have handled waking up to a sea of purple every morning."

"I like purple," she replied meekly. "Thank you," she finally said, accepting his gesture of kindness.

"Besides, I think everyone deserves a view like that when they wake up," he added, his voice trailing off as he sipped his coffee. "And after everything you've been through, you definitely needed it more than I did."

"It *was* incredible waking up to that. It reminded me..." she began, and then hid her mouth behind her cup. Destiny tentatively sipped her coffee, smiling against the cup as she remembered. She glanced up at him.

Bill looked at her expectantly, waiting for her to finish her story.

Drawing in a deep breath, she set down her cup. "It reminded me of Casa Laguna in Laguna Beach." Destiny looked down at the table as she reminisced. "It was our second anniversary. Phillip wanted to take me to the beach. I'd never been to the Pacific Ocean." She looked up at him, her eyes glistening. "He surprised me. Literally. He was always so spontaneous." She relished the familiar sensation as if talking to an old friend. "Spontaneous from my point of view, but he always planned everything out. He loved to shower me with presents, and trips he'd put together for the weekend. But this place was—it was so... so...," she turned to him again. "Perfect."

"Phillip sounds like he was very special." Bill watched her as she spoke, knowing the memories must be painful.

Destiny smiled sweetly. "He was." She propped her elbows on the table, her chin on her hands. "He used to get up early and make *me* breakfast. Of course, it was usually French toast." Her smile grew. "I always hated French toast, but it was just so sweet that I didn't have the nerve to tell him." Destiny looked up at him. "I miss his French toast," she cooed to herself, as she lowered her eyes.

Bill sat beside her and reached for her hand. Her eyes met his. "That's the first time I've talked about him," she added, a little surprised by her admission. "All this time, I've not talked about him. Or Rhett. To *anyone*, except my inner circle. Lisa. Andy. Dr. Villarreal."

Bill didn't know what to say, so he merely listened.

"It's been more than two years, and I don't think I've even talked about him much to my psychiatrist until just now. I mean, I've talked around him. Around them. But I haven't said his name again, until just now." Destiny looked up in astonishment. "And I mean, *no one*," she reiterated. She started breathing faster, excited. "I've tried to forget everything. Block it out, you know? Then waking up here,

looking out into the gardens; remembering was suddenly…
peaceful. All the things that I tried to forget, the things I
miss. They're still here," she said, tapping her chest. The
tears escaped from her eyes and slid down her cheeks. "But
suddenly, it's okay to remember. Somehow, it doesn't hurt
as bad."

Bill leaned in until their foreheads met. They both
closed their eyes.

"Thank you," she whispered.

"I didn't do anything," he whispered back.

Destiny moved her arms back just slightly, and Bill
matched her motion, their eyes locked on each other.
Slowly her hand moved to his cheek. "You've been so kind.
You hardly know me, and you've been a really good
friend."

"A friend," he said in a breath.

Destiny could see he was maybe a little hurt by her
statement. "Right now, I really need you to be my friend,"
she smiled sadly.

Bill kissed her hand. "I can do friend," he sighed reluctantly. Then he stood and pulled her up to him. "Okay,
Friend," Bill said, pulling her with him. "Time for the
formal tour." Bill dragged her to the stairs.

Destiny stopped, his hand still attached to hers, jerking
him to a stop as well. "On one condition."

"What's that?"

"That you promise if you need my help, you'll ask."

Bill opened his mouth to argue.

Destiny held up her hand to stop him. "No arguments.
I will only stay on the condition that you allow me to pull
my weight. I'm off until after New Year's, so I have time on
my hands." Bill started to say something, and she stopped
him again. "And when I have something to do, to keep

busy, it gives me less time to think about things. You know?"

Bill looked into her eyes and nodded. "Sure." He took a step up, stopping and Destiny ran into him. "Be careful what you ask for." He squeezed her hand and then kept walking up the stairs. "You may be regretting your offer as soon as tomorrow."

Chapter Thirty-Six

WHEN TOMORROW CAME, Bill was *more* than glad that Destiny had made the offer she had the day before. Deborah arrived with the exciting news that she was engaged, announced her wedding date and told them they were both invited, after which, she quit. Well, at least, she gave two week's notice, which meant that the week after Thanksgiving was her last week. Bill gritted his teeth and smiled. Then he excused himself, walked into the kitchen and panicked. When he returned, he hoped no one was the wiser to his concern.

Destiny could tell that he was shaken though he tried well to hide it. After Deborah had taken over the duties in the kitchen for the evening, Destiny cornered Bill to invite him and Sydney to dinner. All the guests were checked in, afternoon snacks served, and beds turned down, so he could leave. Bill was more than ready to get away, especially after Deborah's news. Destiny suggested that Sydney should choose the restaurant. So that way, everyone was happy.

Sydney chose the Twisted Root since they had a mini golf course and an Amy's Ice Cream right next door. Had it been twenty degrees colder, one or both of them might have hesitated, but since it was still in the seventies, Bill agreed. Destiny had never been there, so she was excited about trying something new.

They played a round of golf after they ordered, and enjoyed fresh-brewed root beer and burgers made to order. Bill allowed Sydney to watch the other golfers, permitting Destiny and he time to talk on their own. They sat in a back corner booth, appealing to Destiny's sense of separateness. Just because she was willing to go out in public, didn't mean she liked being around people—it was still uncomfortable for her. One of her psychiatrist's suggestions was to go to a new place with strangers all around, without actually interacting with any of them. Now she could mentally check that one off her list. Bill was obviously distracted, but then, so was she. They both had much on their minds.

The hearing for the new restraining order had been that morning. Destiny checked her cell phone regularly until her attorney texted her that he was out of court, and she could call. The conversation was brief. There was enough evidence to issue the order. He had spoken to the Assistant District Attorney as well. They were now seeking an indictment on burglary of a habitation and possession of a narcotic with malicious intent, not to mention breach of a restraining order. And, because Winston was in possession of 10 grams of GHB when he was apprehended at Lisa's, which was also a felony, he would potentially be facing other charges as well. He had given them plenty of ammunition to amend the original charges against himself —the virtual shooting of oneself in the foot. These charges were solely related to Destiny's case, with other possible charges pending, once they finished interviewing the other potential victims. If the grand jury handed down an indictment, then a trial could begin as early as the following month or as far out as next year. Winston's attorneys had already made several motions in an attempt to have the evidence disallowed. All of the motions were denied, which had his criminal attorneys scrambling to try to undermine the case. The problem was that although none of Winston's fingerprints were on anything in Lisa's house, he left DNA on the wine glass when he sipped, not to mention *he* was still in the house when Andy and the police showed up. His attorneys had a hard time getting around that one.

The defense stuck to their story that Winston was an invited guest and that he wore gloves because he used them to drive. It wasn't cold enough to use that as an excuse, so they had to come up with something reasonably plausible. Her attorney told her Winston had even arrived to court in a wheelchair, to further his claims of bodily injury by the supposed victim. Destiny had not only kicked him hard enough with her heel to break his nose, but the angle of the kick to his knee had torn ligaments and tendons as well. Meaning, she'd done some serious damage that would possibly stay with him for the rest of his life, even with surgery. Never in her life had she meant to hurt anyone. And now he wanted to sue her for trying to defend herself? However, looking back, defending herself had probably saved her life. The fact that she'd hurt him so badly, actually gave Destiny no joy, even considering what he'd done to her. The defense was dug in, but the District Attorney wasn't flinching at this point, so it looked like there was a strong possibility of going to trial.

Her anxiety all morning had been apparent, but Bill didn't press her for details. She'd discuss it when she was ready. Most of the dinner conversation was about what was next for the Kemper House. Bill had put an ad on Craigslist immediately after Deborah had given her two weeks' notice that afternoon. Sandy, his other house manager, was interested in taking on more hours, but had a house of her own and a family, so living on premises wasn't an option. Patricia, one of his part-time house manager's had another job that paid very well. She wasn't looking at increasing her hours by any means. Bill still needed someone to handle things when he wasn't there. It was like they were starting from scratch.

Destiny could sense his frustration. But Bill didn't want to burden her with his problems. She had enough concerns of her own. From Thanksgiving through Valentine's Day was their busiest time of year. And besides the Kemper House, there was a cottage two lots over in the extensive gardens that could accommodate up to fifty people, which he rented throughout the year for all types of parties. And during the holidays, it was booked every night.

It was now Destiny that took his hand. "I have a suggestion."

"Does it include temporarily sabotaging an engagement?"

Destiny chuckled. "You think she's distracted now? Do that and you'll have a slobbering, crying mess on your hands."

"You're probably right," he sighed. "What's your suggestion?"

"I'll move into her room, at least until you find a suitable replacement, and stay at least through the new year to help you out. That way you don't have to stress through the holidays. Plus, you don't have to interview during your busiest season. *And* you get your bed back."

Bill chewed on the inside of his cheek, a habit he

hated, not to mention that it was painful, but was something he did every time he had some heavy thinking to do. What she proposed was quite appealing, only it still implied that she would be leaving at some point. The longer he was around her, the more he wanted her to stay. It would definitely take the stress off him for the next few weeks and allow him time to look for someone reasonably qualified whom he hopefully, could count on for years to come.

Destiny could see that he was actually contemplating her proposal, so she decided to sweeten the deal. "I will only consider doing this if you do *not* pay me." She could see that he was about to balk at that, but she held up her hand again. "I want to do this for you. I need to keep busy, and I'm taking off the rest of the school year, anyhow. So I could stay until after New Year's Day, if you needed me to.

Bill bit his cheek again, wincing as he bit too hard. He could taste the blood in his mouth.

"And did I mention," she began, lowering her voice, "that Phillip planned very well in case he died." She watched as Bill pondered her statement. She lowered her voice as she leaned forward to reiterate. "*Very* well." She leaned back again. "So, I will only do this with the stipulation that it's in exchange for room and board."

Bill looked around and leaned forward. "Breakfast, lunch and dinner included," he added to the negotiation. "But you stay in my room until after New Year's Day." She started to say no, and he held up his hand. "We really don't have time to switch before then."

She contemplated for a moment. "Fine, but only breakfast and dinner," she counter-offered.

"Good, so far. And, you have to come to Sydney's birthday party next weekend."

"That's a given," she smiled. "Last condition. Your daughter continues to rave about those cinnamon rolls, but by the time I wake up, they are gone. I want one."

"Done," he agreed. "Can you cook?"

"Can *I* cook?" she grinned.

"Yes, we have a reputation to uphold, and I have to know that you can do more than boil water."

"I make a mean boiled egg," she teased. Noting that he was serious, she added, "Absolutely. I can follow a recipe."

Bill contemplated another moment and extended his hand across the table. Destiny slowly moved her hand to his and shook. "It's a deal then." He held her hand for just a moment longer and smiled. "Thank you," he said sincerely. Slowly, he released his grip. "Seems we need each other, after all," he murmured, looking down and drawing imaginary circles on the table with his finger.

"Seems that way." Destiny leaned forward, causing him to look up at her. Her smile put him at ease. "It's the least I can do. You rescued me, right? It's my turn." Destiny turned to look for Sydney, who was still watching young golfers compete.

Bill held his gaze on Destiny, unable to look away. How could he ever look away? She was more beautiful than the first time he saw her. Every time he was with her, every time he looked at her, he tried to memorize everything about her. Lips so perfect and pink that they begged to be kissed. Dark eyes, entrancing him, daring him to look into them forever.

She had a smile that lit any room she stood in. A smile that that brightened his heart, stirred every desire within him, and yet could put him at ease. Every time he was with her he wanted to bring it out of her. Bill wanted to wake up to that smile every morning. And now she would be living in his house? When Destiny caught him looking at her, Bill felt his face become hot. Sweetly she smiled, her eyes taunting him; mesmerizing him once again. His palms started to sweat, and his thoughts became muddled. He rubbed his temples in frustration. What the hell had he gotten himself into?

Chapter Thirty-Seven

THE KEMPER HOUSE had a phenomenal reputation. Bill worked hard to ensure meeting the needs of each guest, from the oldest to the youngest. The expensive Egyptian cotton sheets and Turkish cotton towels, the European goose down comforters and fresh flowers in every room when new guests arrived, terrycloth bathrobes in the shared and private ensuites and mints on every pillow were all meticulously prepared for the guests. Age and gender specifically tailored welcome baskets waited for guests in every room. The Kemper House made the top ten in national travel publications in 2007, 2008 and 2009, and though it was on the upper end of the price range, those who knew of the guest house's reputation had no problem paying for the lavish perks and the extra attention. Kemper House's rooms were always full and *never* discounted.

Bill had gone to tremendous expense to add three new cottages on the closest of the two large vacant lots he'd purchased the year after he bought the bed and breakfast. He extended the gardens, for those who wanted more private settings on the grounds, or for those needing handicap accessibility or pet-friendly accommodations. The cottages were small, but comfortable, with every amenity they could squeeze into them without looking baroque, including wood burning stoves, pillow top mattresses, whirlpool bathtubs and porch swings that each faced a different part of the garden, for ultimate privacy. Separate wheelchair user accessible paths led to each of the cottages. Since he'd taken the first floor rooms for himself and his daughter, he wanted to build something that was handicap accessible. For what it would have cost him to install an elevator and upgrade all the upstairs rooms to handicap accessibility, he built the three small cottages and upgraded the first and second-floor bathrooms to appease the state requirements.

Bill had sealed all the doors onto the balcony when he moved in. Structurally, it needed more support before he could allow guests to walk onto it. There was enough money left from other projects, to rebuild and strengthen the porch that stretched the entire back length of the house, which overlooked the gardens. Then they opened the sealed doors, painted the porch and filled it with conversation tables and outdoor furniture. He knew he had made the right move when it was part of a spread on best bed and breakfasts in Texas Monthly the following month.

Bill took great pride in the Kemper House. And it showed in everything he did, from taking his time showing Destiny how he preferred things, to how he carefully attended to every detail. Bill was pleased, but not so very surprised by how confident and competent she was. Though she knew how to make a bed, he taught her how to triple sheet the beds—and after a couple of tries, Destiny was a master. She learned how to launder the expensive towels and sheets, and where they stored all the luxurious bed and bath amenities. Sydney helped her put together welcome baskets and the specialty baskets for each of the rooms and the baths. Everything was precisely placed and correctly aligned to assure aesthetic perfection. Destiny was amazed at what it took to run their ten-room inn.

Two small Asian women, who barely spoke English but were efficient and affordable, hand-pressed the luxury sheets and pillowcases. Local vendors provided all bath and bedroom products. Subcontractors provided Kemper House's other services, from pedicures and manicures to full body massages. A local cleaning service cleaned and reset the reception cottage, to exact specifications, daily or weekly as needed.

However, Bill showed Destiny where everything was; from cleaning supplies to utilities. Bill had built a fantastic rapport with other local vendors to assure that nothing was left undone. In the seven years he'd owned it, he'd only had one complaint—when a coyote ate one of their guest's toy terriers. That cost him five hundred dollars and spurred him to add to his contract the stipulation, *"not responsible for any pets on premises."*

Destiny was exhausted after her first full day, but happy to have something to do again. Lisa and Andy checked in on her daily, thereafter, even popping in twice a day, some days, after abandoning her there that first morning. Mere days after Destiny's release from the hospital, Lisa had stopped by for breakfast. She arrived to find Bill teaching Destiny how to make his famous cinnamon rolls. Lisa was excited to see them working so intently together, but she was even more excited to be able to eat the only roll left from that morning's breakfast.

Sydney, still in pajamas, bounced into the kitchen and right into Lisa's lap.

"Good morning, Beautiful."

"Good morning, Lisa," Sydney beamed as she leaned back against her chest and looked up. "I love your hair." She looked back at Bill. "Daddy, can I get hair like Lisa's?"

Bill gave an exaggerated shudder as he looked from Lisa to Sydney and back. "Not unless you want never to leave your room."

"I'd be okay with that," she grinned. "I have enough books to keep me busy for years. And I'll grow my lavender and green and blue hair out until it's as long as Rapunzel's."

"And the prince will climb your hair to the third story balcony and sweep you off your feet and ride away," Lisa continued.

"On his amazing purple horse," Sydney finished.

Bill furrowed his brow.

"My story, my pick on the color." Sydney batted her eyes playfully.

"You can have any color horse you want," Bill began, taking the leftover cinnamon roll from the microwave and serving it to Lisa. "But as long as you live in *this* house, your hair color is natural, and there'll be no climbing through any windows by anyone of the male persuasion now or any time before you're thirty years old."

"Oh, Daddy." Sydney rolled her eyes.

Lisa smiled and whispered into her ears, "You'd look beautiful in lavender hair."

"I heard that," Bill said sternly. "Don't encourage her."

Destiny watched their playfulness. It reminded her so much of her own family dynamic. Phillip had been the instigator in their family, taking advantage of every moment to start something in the household. Whether it was putting sugar in Rhett's bed and then pointing accusingly, secretly, at her when he didn't think she was looking, or tying Rhett's doorknob to the one across the hall so that he couldn't get out of his room. Phillip did that only once since Rhett tore the screen out of his window to get out of his room, just to prove to his dad that he could. Then there were the soaker gun fights. One never knew from where they would be attacked. Destiny smiled, both at what she was watching, but also at what she remembered.

"Are you coming to my party Saturday?" asked Sydney.

"I wouldn't miss it for the world!" Lisa replied, tearing off a piece of the warm roll and savoring it.

"We're riding horses."

"Yeah, you ride. I'll watch." She looked at Bill. "I don't do horses."

"Destiny does!" Sydney exclaimed, proudly.

"Good for Destiny. Lisa will watch you and Destiny ride while she sips margaritas by the pool." Lisa eyed her friend.

"There's no pool, silly," Sydney chided.

"And no margaritas," Bill added.

Lisa snapped her fingers. "Darn it. What kind of party is this, anyway?"

"A nine-year-old's birthday party," he reminded her.

"I remember your ninth birthday party." Destiny smiled wryly.

"Yeah, we won't talk about that." Lisa shoved more cinnamon roll into her mouth.

Bill leaned onto the small mobile wooden island in the center of the room. "Do tell."

Destiny grinned. "Well, let's just say it involved a missing bikini top and twelve euphoric nine-year-old boys."

Everyone started giggling, except Lisa. "Yeah, and one naughty little seven-year-old. Your baby brother, who thought it would be funny to remove it."

"You had a bikini when you were nine?" Sydney asked, enviously.

"Don't even think about it, young lady! You're lucky I don't put you in one of those bathing suits from a century ago; that go all the way down your legs and your arms."

Sydney rolled her eyes, the action not missed by her father.

"Yeah, you only think I'm kidding. Why don't you play or read or better yet, clean your room?"

"Why do I have to? I want to stay and talk to you guys," she pouted.

"Okay, I guess we'll just not discuss planning your party, then," Bill sighed dramatically.

Sydney leaped from Lisa's lap and hugged her, then rushed from the room.

"What are you giving her for her birthday?" Lisa asked.

Bill glanced around the corner, ensuring his daughter wasn't standing in the hallway, listening. "I bought Peanut, the pony she rides at the farm," he said in a lower voice,

"Oh, Bill! She's going to be so excited."

"You're such a pushover." Lisa stood and wrapped her arm through his. "But, you're a good dad. I mean, you'd do *anything* for that sweet little girl in there. Wouldn't you?" she asked slyly.

"What are you getting at, Lisa?" Bill eyed her questioningly. "What do you have up your sleeve?"

"I want to do something special for her birthday if you'll let me." She watched him lean back on the counter and cross his arms. "Don't you trust me?" she asked, a Cheshire Cat grin on her face.

He narrowed his eyes, pensive, as he turned to Destiny. "What do you think? Should I trust her?"

Destiny crossed her arms as well, playfully scrutinizing her friend. "I don't know."

Lisa looked at Destiny. "Traitor!" She took her jacket

off the back of the chair. "That's fine." Lisa batted her eyes at Destiny then hugged her before turning and kissing Bill on the lips. "I'll see you next Saturday." She grinned mischievously before walking out the door.

Bill shook his head and smirked. "Why do I think she's going to hijack our party?"

Destiny smiled, pouring herself a cup of orange juice. "I've known her for twenty-two years. I guarantee you she's going to hijack your party."

Bill shook his head nervously.

"Relax." Destiny wrapped her arm through his. "Don't worry."

"Relax, she says," he exhaled.

Destiny casually leaned her head against his arm, and suddenly he did relax. And he forgot about Lisa and Sydney and the party. He forgot about work. He forgot about everything else in the world.

Chapter Thirty-Eight

BILL STOOD in the shadows watching his daughter as she slept. She was the most precious thing in his life, and she was growing up so fast. He stroked her head, much like when she was tiny and fragile in his arms. He remembered her first birthday. Her soft auburn curls had danced around her face as she stood in the chair beside the table. The economy was shaky. He had just gone out on a limb and sunk every penny he had into his purchase of the Kemper House and the two lots next to it. Justine had just served him with divorce papers, or rather, her attorney had them served. Justine had already been out of the picture for months. He hadn't talked to her or heard from her at all. She had simply disappeared from their lives. She had even taken the pictures. All he had left was Sydney.

Bill had bought her a small birthday cake at Walmart. It was just Sydney, his mother and him. It was quaint and sweet, and he would remember it for as long as his mind would allow him to remember. Sydney had no clue what all the hoopla was about. All she knew was that there was something in front of her that flickered. Sydney had been mesmerized by the candle and cried when they helped her blow it out. So, they lit it repeatedly and let it burn down before blowing it out again. They went through three candles until she realized that what was under the candle was even more exciting. His daughter put her hand smack into the middle of the cake and grabbed, mashing cake and icing through her fingers. She continued until she realized it was food, and it was sweet. He remembered what a mess she was, and how neither he nor his mother were interested in eating the cake after that. Sydney had managed to demolish it in a matter of minutes, like she was playing with a bucket of mud, wearing more of it than she had eaten.

Bill reached over and kissed her on the head before leaving her room, carefully closing the door so as not to wake her. He and Destiny had bowed out of serving at the senior center that evening since tomorrow was such a big day and they would be heading to the farm early to set up. Bill smiled to himself—his little girl was about to be nine years old! Suddenly, as he turned the corner, he ran right into Destiny, who was carrying a lemon meringue tart that he had made as a snack for the guests that afternoon. After running into Bill, she was now wearing it. Bill apologized, at the same time trying very hard not to laugh. Destiny immediately walked back into the kitchen and set the plate in the sink, leaning over it so that the contents, which she now wore, landed in the sink as well. Bill followed her silently, then stood beside her as she tried to figure out the best course of action. He turned on the water, leaned over her and extended the sprayer. As the hose extended, it became twisted. Attempting to straighten it, he accidentally sprayed Destiny square in the face. She screamed, more from shock than from the cold water.

"Oh, God," he laughed. "I'm so sorry."

"You did that on purpose." Destiny grabbed the sprayer from his hand, pretending like she was going to squirt him. Then she narrowed her eyes to reprimand him, as she turned back to the sink. Stretching her shirt over the sink, she sprayed the meringue, crust and lemon curd from the front of it.

"You know, I do have a washing machine," he reminded her, grabbing a hand towel.

"Yeah, but this one needed a garbage disposal." Destiny continued to lean over the sink.

"Why don't you let me help?" he asked as he dabbed her face and neck with the towel.

"I think you've helped enough."

He tossed the towel onto the counter, unbuttoning his flannel shirt as he spoke.

"What are you doing?" she asked, as he undressed.

"Here, put this on."

"I can't wear that."

"Put it on. Please. I'd rather you don't walk through the house soaking wet." He turned his back to her, holding his hand backward with the shirt in it, shaking it.

Destiny stood leaning over the sink, her entire shirt soaked. She felt her skin bristling as it became chilled. Slowly, she pulled her long sleeved shirt over her head and dropped it into the sink.

When she didn't take the shirt right away, he glanced around slightly and saw her standing there in her bra. He turned back suddenly, embarrassed as she grabbed the shirt from his hand and slid it over her slender frame. A few moments later she said, "You can turn around now."

Bill turned, and Destiny sprayed him right in the chest. Bill jumped back, startled, staring at her in disbelief. "I can't believe you just did that!"

"Really," she laughed. "Like you accidentally sprayed me?"

"I did!" he exclaimed, as he tried to dry his soaked undershirt with the small dish towel. He looked at her. "Can I borrow your shirt?"

Destiny chuckled. "Not a chance," she replied. "I'm sorry, but I'm not as gallant as you are."

"It's okay." Bill pulled his undershirt off and then dried himself with the small dishtowel.

Destiny stopped chuckling as she watched him mop his well-defined chest with the towel. Her heart began to race. She found herself looking at him, checking him out, as Lisa would say. Though her mind told her to stop looking, her eyes wandered, from the wisp of hair above his jeans to the soft matting of hair across his broad, muscular chest. Slowly her eyes traveled to his. When she found him looking at her as well, she quickly averted her stare.

"Sorry," she said, wrapping her arms around her stomach, the sleeves of his shirt hanging loosely over her small hands.

Bill stepped toward her, his hands on her shoulder, traveling down her arms until arriving in her hands. He took one in his, their eyes meeting again as he rolled back the cuff of the sleeve, once, and then twice. Bill raised her hand to his lips, turning it over. Destiny suddenly blushed, pulled her arms away and looked down as she wrapped them around herself again. Gently he unwrapped her arms, raising one to his lips, kissing her palm, then the heel of her hand—his kisses moving up her wrist to the straight scar across it. At first, she tensed, but then he felt her relax in his grip as he completed buttoning her cuff.

Tentatively Bill took her other hand in his, kissing it tenderly, as he had the first. As she allowed him to unfold her hand, he brought it to his lips, kissing it sweetly. Destiny looked up into his eyes.

"So much pain," he whispered as he kissed the scar on her other arm, before also folding the cuff and buttoning it. Bill kissed her hand again. "If only I could kiss away all your pain," he cooed.

Destiny smiled sadly. *If only*, she thought.

Slowly his fingers slid back up her arms to her shoulders where they straightened her collar, before roaming her arms again. He shook his head as he drew in a deep breath. "How is it you look better in that shirt than I ever could?"

Destiny turned from his grasp back to the sink and then wrung out her shirt, setting it into the dish drain as she pushed the remnants of her late-night snack into the garbage disposal. "That was the last tart, too," she whined.

"You like lemon meringue pies?"

"They are my favorite," she pouted.

"I'll make you another one."

"You don't have to do that."

He stepped to the sink, crowding her, as he wrung out his shirt and set it beside hers. "I'd love to…" he began, nervously, "do that for you," he finished.

Destiny glanced up at him. His eyes were so kind—warm and inviting.

His hand slowly slid across the sink and found hers. As it covered hers, he squeezed.

"Bill," she began, looking down at his hand on hers. "You've been so good to me."

Bill waited for the "but." It never came.

Destiny smiled faintly. "And so patient."

Bill turned without releasing her hand.

He was so close she felt his warm stomach against her hand. Destiny found herself tempted to look at his beautiful chest again—to touch it. She smiled sweetly, blushing at the thought. Only she couldn't pull her eyes from his. Bill raised her hand to his lips, gently kissing it, holding it there.

"Bill," she began again, only his other hand moved to her mouth, pressed against her moist lips.

"I know what you're going to say."

"How is it you always seem to know what I'm going to say?"

"You're going to say that you're not ready yet." He watched her eyes, as they averted his stare. "And that no matter how hard it is to resist my amazing powers at juggling parenthood and owning my own business, my great culinary prowess, my incredible ability to triple sheet a bed…"

Destiny giggled as she looked up again.

Bill sucked in his stomach and stood up straight. "Not to mention my svelte, perfect form," he said, stepping back and releasing her hand, modeling for her.

Destiny laughed, shaking her head.

"Alas. I regress. I will wait." He stepped away from her, taking her hand with him. "Pa-tient-ly," he said, dramatically, drawing the word out. Destiny didn't move, and he was now at arm's length. He raised her hand to his lips, his eyes once more holding hers, entranced. "Somehow," he inhaled, alternating hands to kiss. "I'm betting you're worth it."

Destiny swallowed hard. His lips brushed against her skin lightly. The goose bumps traveled her arms under his flannel shirt, making her shiver. As his grip on her hand loosened, hers tightened. His eyes showed confusion as she slowly pulled him closer until he was pressed against her, as she was looking up into his eyes. Just a few inches taller than she, she didn't have far to reach.

Bill slowly leaned down to her, meeting her halfway. His lips brushed against hers, ever so gently, teasingly. Electricity coursed through his body. Suddenly he was tingling in places he hadn't tingled in years. He moved his hands from hers and took her face in his hands.

Sydney walked in and stopped suddenly. She grinned ear to ear. "*Al-right, Dad!*" she said dramatically with a nod, breaking the magic.

Bill and Destiny both turned abruptly. Bill gave his daughter a stern look. "You're supposed to be in bed, Sweetie."

Sydney rubbed her eyes. "I'm too excited 'bout my party tomorrow."

Bill stepped away from Destiny, her hand slowly releasing his. He knelt beside his daughter. "You have to get some rest, Honey." He turned her around and patted her bottom. "Off to bed with you," he said playfully, but firmly. He stepped into the hallway and watched her turn the corner to her room.

Destiny stood by the sink and looked out the window at the colorful lights that lit the paths and walkways and the street beyond. It was almost Christmas, and though she was a little sad, her heart felt more alive than it had in a very, very long time. Bill stepped to her and stood behind her, slowly pressing himself against her. His hands traveled her arms until they rested on top of her hands on the counter. "So, what happens now?" he whispered in her ear, his hot breath exciting her.

Destiny dropped her head. "I don't know," she sighed. "Do you have any suggestions?" she asked, turning in his arms.

"I have a few," he smiled, his hands moving to her face. "But they are all R-rated."

"Just R?" she quipped with a mischievous smile.

Bill looked up and away. "Maybe some PG."

"PG?" Destiny laughed.

"I've got an eight-year-old daughter. I'm lucky when I make it past G-ratings." He eyed her cautiously. "Besides, anything else only keeps me up nights."

"Hmm," she murmured.

"Where we go from here, depends on you."

"Me?"

Bill's body pinned hers against the counter.

Bill swept back her hair. "I don't want to make things more… complicated. You still have a lot going on in your life."

"Yeah," she scoffed.

"But I want you to know that you're welcome to stay as long as you need to. No pressure. No expectations."

"None?" she asked, furrowing her brow.

"Okay." Bill grinned slyly. "Maybe a few."

Destiny leaned against his shoulder. "Good," she smiled. "Me, too."

Bill hugged her close. She turned back around in his arms, and he continued to embrace her, his chin resting on her shoulder, his arms wrapped tightly around her. They looked out the window, enjoying the beauty of the lights. And for a breath of a moment, they enjoyed the warmth of something neither of them had experienced for a very long time—the warmth of someone else in their arms, enjoying the season together.

Chapter Thirty-Nine

THE FENCE LINING the farm property had balloons placed at every fencepost, leading to the rustic farmhouse. There were three acres just behind the house that were flat and mowed, and perfect for the horseshoes, washer throws, and even for croquet, just in case any of the adults had an inclination. The weather was perfect, seventy degrees and sunny. The weather forecasts had been for rain. Actually for storms, bringing with them colder weather. However, the front never reached this far south, allowing all the party guests to stay outside, versus in the barn—a last minute back-up in case the weather didn't cooperate. Their neighbors to the north received torrential rains and flooding and even tornados. Go figure, December in Texas!

Jessie and Charlie had offered Bill the use of their property every year since Sydney was one. However, now that Sydney was older, and was riding horses, it seemed more appropriate. They owned several ponies and had stalled them all overnight, so that they could give all the kids rides in the corral, providing the weather held. There were eight girls and four boys that attended, all excited to be able to go to a birthday party on a farm.

Jessie and Charlie had gone all out, with a small menagerie of animals for the kids to pet: a piglet, three goats, two calves, a foal, baby chicks, rabbits and even a young llama. They had hooked up a flatbed trailer with two-foot sides to the tractor and loaded it with hay. They took the kids on a hayride through the fields. Bill's mother made Sydney's favorites: strawberry cake with a butter-cream frosting, served with a bowl of fresh locally-grown strawberries, on the side. *Plus,* a pitcher of ice-cold cow's milk to wash it all down. The kids ate things many of them had never tried before, like freshly made gut summer sausage, deviled eggs, and goat cheese quesadillas, all made with the help of animals on the farm.

Lisa didn't disappoint, as she showed up with two of her staff, not only giving the girls manicures or pedicures if they wanted but the parents as well. None of her staff minded since they made more from that party in tips alone than they had all week. But the hit of the party was Lisa's collection of wash-out hair chalk. Even the boys and a few of the moms took advantage of the opportunity to change the color of their hair for a day or two. Destiny wasn't in line for the treatment, but when Sydney pouted dramati-cally, Destiny acquiesced, and allowed Lisa to have her way with her hair. Lisa took great joy in the number of times she had to assure Bill that it *would* wash out with the first shampoo. What resulted was a colorful blend of children and adults that made for some great pics for YouTube, Facebook and screen savers for their personal devices and phones.

Then there were presents and cake and homemade ice cream. Strawberry, of course. Destiny sat on the steps of the porch watching Sydney open her gifts. Sydney's birthday party was the first child's celebration she had attended since Rhett's death. Destiny had wrestled with staying home, but she would have broken a nine-year-old girl's heart. Dr. Villarreal had built her up and encouraged her, reminding her that she was strong enough to go. Destiny smiled as Sydney opened present after present. Then Sydney came to Destiny's present, the biggest box on the table. All the kids helped her rip off the paper. Sydney squealed with delight at the purple and black leather saddle with a purple seat and purple crystal trim.

"My own saddle!" she excitedly exclaimed, throwing herself into Destiny's arms and hugging her neck. "This is the best present ever!" Sydney ran to her father. "Can I put it on Peanut?"

"Well, let's see." Bill turned to Charlie. "Is Peanut still in the barn?"

Charlie rubbed his gray stubble chin. "Hmm. I'll check."

"Finish opening your other gifts, Sweetie," Bill encouraged her. "Your friends are all leaving soon."

Sydney eagerly opened her last few presents, thanking each child and his or her parent politely before moving on to the next one. Jessie and Destiny busied themselves picking up the rest of the torn paper from the picnic tables. One of the children pointed, and Sydney turned, looking at her father questioningly. Charlie led Peanut toward them, with a gigantic purple bow tied around his neck.

"Go ahead, Syd. Unwrap your last present," her father smiled.

"Oh, Daddy. Is he mine?" she asked, unable to believe it.

Bill nodded his head and knelt beside her. "Happy Birthday, Pumpkin."

Sydney ran to her pony, followed by the remaining children and began to pet his nose.

Lisa moved to the stairs and sat beside Destiny, who discreetly wiped a tear. "How ya' doing?" She asked, nudging her gently with her shoulder.

Destiny smiled. "Fine. I'm fine," she replied softly. "I thought it would be harder, but I'm okay," she said, as convincingly as possible.

Lisa took her hand and squeezed. "I'm so proud of you. You're one of the bravest women I know."

Destiny shook her head slightly. "It gets easier, day by day," she sighed.

"I'm not talking about that, Honey," Lisa grinned, glancing upward. "I'm talking about that awful hair color they put in your hair."

Destiny laughed, and Lisa joined in.

"You told me, 'never in a million years' once, remember?" Lisa beamed in triumph.

"You cheated—using a nine-year-old's birthday party to trick me into coloring my hair."

Lisa shoved her again. "Tricked?" she scoffed. "I don't think so. I saw you two. You went willingly."

"Like a lamb to the slaughter." Destiny conceded.

Lisa chuckled. "No, actually, it looks good on you. I think you should wear it like that all the time." She looked around and saw Bill walking toward them. She turned to Destiny and added teasingly, "Just wait until he finds out that his daughter's color *won't* come out for several washings." A stunned Bill stood before her, as she sat with as straight a face as she could. "Oh, hi."

Destiny bit her lips to keep from smiling.

Finally, Lisa could contain her laughter no longer, and it burst forth from her mouth. "Just kidding." Lisa slapped his arm playfully.

Bill exhaled dramatically. "Thank God," he gasped, relieved. "That wasn't nice," he added, glancing at Destiny.

"Told you she was trouble," Destiny said, nonchalantly. "But you wouldn't listen. You said you wanted to invite her." She stood, stretched, and walked down the stairs.

Lisa watched as Bill walked with Destiny, his hand at her back. "Hmm," she hummed to herself before turning back to watch Sydney nuzzling with her pony. Most of the kids had walked off, joined by their parents as they collected their goody bags and other belongings. Lisa watched the children and parents thank Bill and Destiny, as though they were a couple.

When the last of the families had left, Sydney moved to the presents and asked her father to put her new saddle on her pony. The purple saddle looked perfect on him. And Sydney, dressed in purple as well, with hair almost the exact color as Lisa's, sat astride him, proud and tickled... well... purple. Bill and Destiny began picking up party remnants while Jessie and Charlie collected their yard games to put into the barn, in the event the distant storm took a projected turn. Lisa gathered the rest of her hair and nail products—her staff long gone before Sydney opened her presents. She stored them in the back of her car, then helped the others before collapsing into one of two swings on the extended outdoor covered porch.

Jessie and Charlie walked by her and stopped.

"You look tired," Jessie remarked, a bag of trash in her hand.

"I forgot how exhausting a child's birthday party can be," she replied. "I'll just sit here for awhile if that's okay with you."

"How about a drink?" Charlie offered her, opening the door for his wife.

"On the other hand, I think I can make it a few more steps." Lisa jumped from the swing. She stopped momentarily, watching Bill and Destiny as they helped Sydney with her new pony. She smiled to herself and followed them inside.

Chapter Forty

SYDNEY DIDN'T HAVE to beg to take Peanut out. The sun was still out, mostly, and though the storm looked like it was turning their direction, it was far off in the distance. Bill set her new watch and told her to be back in an hour and to stay where he could see her. She took off like an old pro, breaking in her new saddle until she was on the other side of the gate, galloping through the pasture.

Bill turned, Destiny by his side, traveling the length of the road; Bill untying balloon strings and handing them to her as they walked the fence line. They didn't speak; the only sound was the crunching of the ground beneath them or the occasional breeze through the trees. They arrived at the end of the dirt and grass pathway, where it emptied onto the paved road that split to a neighboring farm. They turned left and continued, collecting the last of the balloons on the fence that fronted the house.

"Are you okay?" Bill asked, breaking the silence.

"Yeah," Destiny smiled faintly. "I am."

"Thank you for coming."

Destiny furrowed her brow. "Of course, I was going to come."

"Well, you know, you really didn't have a choice," he added. "Considering how Syndey would have made your life miserable if you hadn't."

Destiny looked down at her boots.

"What I meant to say, was," he stumbled, "it was very courageous of you."

"You going to tell me it was brave of me to color my hair blue, also?"

Bill grinned. "Actually, I like the teal look. It's kind of sexy," he teased.

Destiny kicked a larger rock across the road.

"No, I mean, I know it couldn't have been easy. Coming to a kid's birthday party," he continued, nervously.

Destiny took another balloon and then looked back down. "I was scared to death," she admitted.

"You did a good job of hiding it," he observed. Bill cast a glance over his shoulder to assure Sydney was still visible, before turning to untie the last balloon. As he did, he handed it to Destiny, his hand sliding down the ribbon, touching hers; holding it for just a moment longer until she faced him again. Suddenly, he looked away and then blew out two breaths nervously. "I think you are incredible and exciting, you are unimaginably beautiful, and you are absolutely the most courageous—"

"Stop," Destiny insisted, looking down, embarrassed. "I'm none of those things." Slowly she lifted her eyes until their eyes met and she blushed. She kicked pebbles awkwardly, then turned to walk back to the farmhouse.

Bill took her arm, stopping her. "You're *all* of those things," he said, stepping closer to her. Destiny looked down again, but he lifted her chin with his finger until she was looking him in the eyes, balloons bouncing around their heads. "Ever since the first time I saw you," he began, brushing her cheek with the back of his hand. "I knew."

"You knew what?" she asked faintly.

"I knew I had to meet you. I knew I wanted to get to know you. I knew I wanted to…" he stopped suddenly, taking her face in his hands. Then he kissed her sweetly, gently. Much like he did the first time he had kissed her. His hands moved from her face to her shoulders and down her arms and to her back. They parted only for a moment, and then he kissed her harder, deeper, his tongue pressing past her lips, her teeth, exploring hungrily—her mouth still sweet from cake and ice cream. Minutes later they parted again, each wiping their mouths.

Destiny looked down, and he pulled her to his chest. She closed her eyes, welcoming the beating of his heart against her ear. When he released her, and she looked up again, he leaned in to kiss her, but the balloons blew in between them, pounding their faces as the wind picked up. They both laughed as she moved the strings from one hand to the other. Bill kissed her forehead, then wrapped his arm around her. They took their time walking down the fence line, retracing their steps from before. Eventually, they turned the corner, where the gravel ended, and the dirt road began. She slowly moved her hand to his back, holding onto him by his belt loops. They could hear Peanut running up beside the fence but couldn't see clearly for the balloons blowing behind them. As the pony trotted past them, they both turned and stopped suddenly. Sydney wasn't in the saddle.

They released each other immediately, and Bill jumped the fence, running to Peanut. He grabbed the pony's reins as he frantically called his daughter's name. Destiny looked around, not seeing Sydney anywhere. She let go of the balloons, the wind tossing them carelessly into the sky, and raced up the path to the barn. Bill ran inside the fence, calling Sydney's name over and over, pulling the pony behind him. He ran straight to the house, tied Peanut to the post outside and rushed inside.

Destiny raced into the barn, to the first stall that had a horse in it. Thankfully, it was Daisy. She grabbed the lead and hurriedly pulled her to the tack room, where she bridled and saddled her in record time. Bill, Lisa, Jessie and Charlie arrived as she climbed into the saddle. "I'll start looking for her." She looked at Bill's face. She knew that look. She knew that feeling. "I'll find her," she said, before turning Daisy and heeling her harder than she ever had before. The mare responded, bolting into a gallop from the start as if released from a chute at the rodeo.

"I'll get the truck," Charlie said, moving as fast as he could. When Bill rushed passed him, he whistled at him. Bill turned and caught the keys he threw in midair, and ran for the old farm truck on the other side of the house.

Jessie looked up at the sky. "Storm's turning this direction." She pointed upward. "Come with me," she said to Lisa, turning toward the house. "We'll make some phone calls and see if we can't get some help to find her."

"Do you think she's okay?"

"Sure she is," Jessie assured her. "She probably just got bucked off and is nursing a sore butt or sore pride."

"I hope you're right." The worry showed on Lisa's face.

"Me, too," Jessie agreed, as she hobbled toward the house. Bill pulled alongside them, and Jessie told him her plans to recruit their neighbors. Bill nodded and moved on to pick up Charlie, who hadn't made it much past where they left him.

When the women arrived at the door, Lisa looked up at

the sky and out over the pasture. "Please God, let her be okay." She hurriedly walked back inside, closing the door behind her.

Chapter Forty-One

DESTINY RACED Daisy as fast as she would go along the fence line from where Peanut had come, and then over each of the small hills, scattering herds of goats, and horses and cattle as she ran. She stopped every so often and called out Sydney's name, sitting high in the saddle, her eyes searching carefully for a purple lump in the field somewhere. They had told Sydney not to go too far, but Destiny knew that every so often the young girl would push the limits and go a little further. She arrived at the last summit that was visible from the house and looked down at the field and the forest beyond. Jessie had warned Sydney to stay away from the creek because the flooding upstream would soon reach their property. Destiny looked up and saw the wall of rain just miles away. She could smell the rain that hung in the air. Suddenly Destiny felt a wave of panic. She kicked Daisy hard and galloped down the hill to the woods.

A small herd of cattle was grazing by the path where they usually entered the forest. They scattered as Destiny raced toward them. When she arrived at the entrance, she walked Daisy through. It was something she had to navigate carefully; she could be unseated and even scratched and cut by the branches. She called Sydney's name, again and again, waiting for an answer, but all she heard was the rushing water just a hundred yards away. She thought she heard a faint voice call back. She listened again, ducking and dodging and trying to navigate her way through the branches into the clearing just feet away. When she finally broke through, she clicked her teeth and galloped the last hundred yards to the fork in the creek.

Immediately she saw Sydney, standing in the middle of the island that was now surrounded by water on both sides. Beside her was a brown Jersey and a brand new calf that couldn't have been more than hours old.

"Sydney!" she screamed.

"Destiny!"

"Don't move!" Destiny looked around to get her bearings and assess the situation.

"The water's getting higher!"

Destiny reached for her phone in her pocket, but it was gone. Crap! It must have worked itself out during her search. She paced in a circle for a moment, and then drew in a deep breath and moved to where she remembered the shallowest crossing. Then she heeled Daisy repeatedly. The mare hesitated to enter the rushing, rising water, but she finally obeyed and cautiously walked into it. After a few feet in, the water was up to the mare's knees. Destiny drew in a deep breath. She hoped she hadn't misjudged the depth of the water or the length from the shore to the island.

. . .

B ill drove as fast as he could, carefully navigating the bumps and the hills, so as not to run into a bewildered herd. They, as Destiny had, drove the fence line first, then with no luck, turned and drove into the pasture. Ten minutes of driving frantically through the fields felt like hours. Charlie looked over at Bill and could tell he was beginning to panic.

"Where the heck is she?" Bill exclaimed, slapping the wheel.

"I don't see Destiny, either," Charlie remarked. "Where could they possibly have gone? It's like they disappeared."

Bill sat upright as he crested the summit of the hill overlooking the forest. Raindrops began to fall on the truck, and he fumbled around trying to find the window wipers. "I know where they are," Bill said, hitting the gas and sending dirt and grass flying behind them. He raced down the hill toward the forest. "They are in there," he said definitively.

"What the hell are they doing in there?"

"It's like their secret hideout."

"Yeah? Look!" Charlie said pointing at the creek below. What was usually a peaceful brook now ran over its banks, and he could see white water and debris in it. "Creek's up. If they're down there, it's a dangerous place to be right now," he said, worry now showing on his face as well.

Bill pressed the gas pedal harder.

D estiny arrived on the island and jumped down, holding the reins in her hand. She hugged Sydney to herself and looked her up and down. "Are you okay?"

Sydney nodded confidently.

Destiny shook her shoulders as she snapped at her.

"What were you thinking? Your dad is scared to death? *I* was scared," she said, tears filling her eyes.

Sydney started to cry. "They got stuck on the island, and I just wanted to try and help them get off, but they wouldn't come, and then the creek got higher," she sobbed. "I'm sorry."

Destiny pulled her to her chest again and held her tight. "I'm sorry, Sweetie." Destiny stood and looked around. The water was still rising. She felt a raindrop on her head and looked up. "We've got to get out of here, now!" Destiny said, taking Sydney's hand.

Sydney stood firm. "We can't leave them here! They'll drown."

Destiny looked at the cow and its calf and then back to Sydney. She drew in a deep breath and knelt before her. Destiny shook her head and then gently took Sydney's shoulders. "Okay," she agreed. "But first, I'm getting you out of here. Then I'll come back for them."

Sydney glanced at the cow and her new baby, and then back at Destiny.

"Do you trust me?"

Sydney hesitated, then nodded. "You promise?"

"I promise. But we have to move fast. We're running out of time." She moved Sydney to Daisy's side and then lifted until the girl's feet reached the stirrup to climb onto Daisy. "Sit forward, Sweetie," she instructed, as she climbed behind the saddle, holding Sydney from behind. Once more she had to coax Daisy into the water. The water was now at her mount's forearms, just beneath the stirrups. "Doin' good, Girl," she said, praising the mare as they proceeded through the rushing water. Once they arrived on the other side, Destiny quickly dismounted and helped Sydney down.

. . .

As they neared the wooded area, Charlie looked over at Bill. "You know there's no way in there by truck."

"I know," Bill said. "But they have a path they travel. I've seen it."

"For what it's worth, this old thing has been through the ringer. That bein' said it's just an old farm truck. Why Jessie's always kept full coverage on it is a mystery to me." Charlie turned to his nephew.

Bill looked at him, understanding his meaning fully. He accelerated. "Hold on!"

The moment the truck hit the brush on the opposite side of the woods where it was less dense, Destiny and Sydney turned and yelped. The explosion of trees and brush and rocks startled them all, including Daisy. She reared, but Destiny held firm to the reins. The truck crashed into a large tree about a hundred feet away. Destiny immediately climbed onto Daisy and looked down at Sydney. "Stay here," she ordered her as she raced to the truck. She jumped off the mare and quickly tied her to a branch, then ran the rest of the way.

"Bill!" she screamed, when she saw him in the driver's seat, his head against the steering wheel, blood splattered on it. She screamed his name again and rushed to his door, trying to tug it open. "Oh, God, no!" she cried.

Slowly, Bill raised his head, a small cut on his temple oozing blood down his cheek. "I'm okay." He looked around, disoriented. "Sydney?"

"I found her."

"Daddy!" Sydney screamed at that very moment and ran to him, climbing through the brush and the door and onto his lap.

Destiny gasped and sobbed, with relief. Then she

looked over at Charlie. "Charlie?" she yelled, climbing through rubble to the other side of the truck.

Charlie moved his neck, side to side. "I'm gonna feel this tomorrow," he moaned. "Did you find her?"

Destiny pulled his door open, and he slowly stepped out. "Yes. She's okay."

At that moment, the cow bawled as the water neared their feet.

Destiny looked around and then glanced into the back of the truck. She saw tools and tack. And rope. She reached in, grabbed the rope, raced back to Daisy, untied her and climbed back into the saddle.

"Where do you think you're going?"

Destiny turned Daisy, glancing back at Charlie. "To keep a promise."

Bill climbed from the truck, his daughter wrapped around him, slowly walking after Destiny.

"Fool girl," Charlie called after her. "Don't risk your life for a damn cow!"

Sydney gave Charlie a hurtful look, watching as Destiny and Daisy moved laboriously across the water, which was now up to Daisy's belly. When on the other side, she immediately looped a noose around the Jersey's horns and began pulling her. The bovine refused to budge, so Destiny edged Daisy closer and whipped her with the other end of the rope and kicked her with her foot. She repeated this several times until the cow finally started moving. She wrapped the lasso around the saddle horn several times, literally dragging the reluctant cow into the water. The calf tried following but wasn't nearly as brave.

Just then, six men, plus Lisa and Jessie, ran into the forest where the truck had made a path. They looked inside the truck and raced to where a bleeding Bill and injured Charlie stood. Several of them moved closer to the water and even stepped into it up to the tops of their boots. When Destiny was halfway across the steadily rising water, she motioned to the men and then tossed the other end of the rope to them. When one of them caught it, she unwrapped the end from the horn. The new recruits immediately all grabbed the rope and began to drag the cow to safety. The fearful calf stood, water covering his hooves, bawling for its mother, who was now safe on the other bank of the growing river. Destiny turned Daisy and headed back to the island.

"Leave it," several of them yelled after her. Destiny turned in the saddle and watched them all wave to her. Sydney stood there looking at her, pitifully. She heeled Daisy; the motion slowed by the water at her knees. When Destiny arrived at the island, she dismounted, one last time and approached the calf, lifting it carefully in her arms. As awkward and challenging as it was, somehow she found the strength to straddle the little beast over the saddle. She climbed back onto the mare, readjusting the calf so that it was in the saddle with her. She could feel its heart beating rapidly in its chest. She pinned the calf against the saddle and horn with her hips, and she started her last trip through what was now raging waters.

The men had waded in almost waist deep from the shore to help her since the water was still rising. It was now at the bottom of the saddle, and it was harder for her to maneuver. Just yards from the shore Daisy jerked suddenly as a snake wriggled through the water just a foot from her head. The mare twisted, unable to rear. She fearfully tried turning, lost her footing and suddenly all three of them disappeared into the swollen creek.

Lisa screamed the instant she saw Destiny go under the water. Two of the men held a rope, the other end securely tied to a tree, ensuring that they didn't get dragged into the growing river as well. They both jumped into the water in an attempt to save Destiny. The others ran downstream to try and get ahead of her. Bill handed Sydney to Jessie, who shielded the girl's eyes in case it didn't end well. A few yards downstream Destiny surfaced, the calf in her arms. The water carried her a few more feet until one of the neighboring farmhands grabbed her and pulled her from the water, her arms still wrapped around the small, terrified creature. Daisy surfaced beyond them, found her footing and climbed from the water, shaking immediately to try and remove all that encumbered her.

They dragged Destiny to the shore where she finally released the calf, which ran immediately to its mother's side. Everyone else ran to Destiny, surrounding her. Bill pushed through them and grabbed her tightly to himself. She wrapped her arms around his neck and began to cry. Gently, he lifted her into his arms and carried her out of the woods to the waiting trucks beyond.

Chapter Forty-Two

DESTINY AND SYDNEY showered and changed into some of Jessie's clothes before huddling under blankets, each with a cup of hot cocoa in their hands. A roaring fire in the massive fireplace warmed them. Bill hosed himself off outside to remove the mud and blood. Then he stripped and finished his cold shower outside before toweling off. Bill pulled one of Charlie's undershirts over his chilled body before covering it with an old flannel shirt. He slid on a pair of Charlie's jeans, holding them up with his hands, in need of a belt. He finished just before the storm rolled in.

Three men who had volunteered to bring Daisy, the calf, and its mother back walked into the barn five minutes before the storm front blew in. Jessie and Charlie offered coffee and hot cocoa to those who had helped, but everyone wanted to get home before the storm let loose in all its fury. And when it did hit, it hit hard, blowing a cold front in along with high winds and cold rains.

Bill walked into the massive open living room, his bare feet slapping the natural hardwood floors as he moved across it. He crouched beside Sydney and brushed back her damp hair, kissing the top of her head as she silently sipped her cocoa. He looked over at Destiny. "You okay?"

Destiny nodded.

"Can I get you anything?"

Destiny shook her head, then looked back into her cup. Bill leaned over and kissed her head as well. He closed his eyes and held her head to his lips for many moments, trying not to think about how close he had come to losing his daughter. To losing Destiny. When he stood, he turned to Lisa and Charlie. "Thank you so much," he said sincerely. To Charlie, he said, "I owe you my life."

"Nope, you just owe me a truck." Charlie smiled wryly.

Bill smiled in return. "Heck if I know how I'm going to explain this one to the insurance company."

"Durn brakes. I've meant to take that old thing in and have them looked at." Charlie offered, with a grin. "Sorry about that. Should have told you." Charlie tried to look as disappointed as possible.

Bill grinned back. "I'll call the insurance company first thing in the morning."

Jessie walked from the hallway just in time for Bill's grateful hug. "Well, I made up all the rooms and put fresh towels in the bathrooms."

Bill opened his mouth to argue, but Charlie held up his hand. "Now what kind of host would I be if I let you go out in this weather? 'Sides that, I don't think you should take those two anywhere for awhile." Charlie nodded toward Destiny and Sydney.

Lisa rose and picked up her purse.

"That goes for you, too," Charlie said firmly. "We have plenty of rooms, plenty of food. No need for anyone to take any more chances tonight. Right?"

Bill looked at his daughter, turned to Charlie and

nodded. "I'll call Sandy and make sure she's got everything covered." He pulled his cell phone from his pocket and excused himself. Sandy had already graciously offered to stay the night since it was Sydney's birthday so that he didn't need to rush home.

"I'll just go." Lisa slowly side-stepped toward the door.

"Don't even think about it, young lady. We've got a room for you, too."

"I hate to be an imposition.,

"Sweetheart, you're never an imposition."

Lisa nodded and followed Jessie down the hall to choose a room.

Destiny set her cup down, and Sydney matched the motion before crawling into Destiny's lap. She held Sydney close; her arms wrapped lovingly around the young girl.

"Thank you, Dee," a tiny voice said from under the blanket.

"A promise is a promise." Destiny brushed back the girl's hair.

Bill walked back into the room and straight to Sydney, crouching again before her. "Your Uncle Charlie and Aunt Jessie offered to have us stay here tonight. Would you like that?" When she hesitated, he added. "Maybe if the weather lets up, you can check on Peanut in the morning."

Sydney instantly perked up. "Can I ride him?"

"We'll see. No promises. C'mon," he groaned, as he picked her up. The man's t-shirt Sydney wore, fit her like a dress. As he gathered her into his arms, she wrapped herself around him. He carried her and her blanket to the only room with a bunk bed in it.

Destiny rose, carrying the two empty mugs to the kitchen. As she began to wash them out, Jessie gently pushed her away. "I'll take care of that," she insisted. Destiny gave Jessie a hug and a thank you, before shuffling across the floor to the enclosed porch. She nestled into the swing by one of four other wood-burning stoves in their home and stared out the wall of glass windows into the night sky.

Charlie moved to the counter across from Lisa and uncapped a bottle of whiskey with one twist. After pouring two shots, he handed one to her. She raised her glass, tapped it to his, downed it and gasped. Charlie poured them another as Bill walked back into the room. "Pour you one?"

Bill shook his head.

"Is she asleep?" Jessie asked.

"Yeah, she fell right off," he replied. "Where did Destiny go?"

Jessie nodded toward the porch, then turned and walked to Charlie. Without alerting him, she reached in front of him, and slowly she started unbuckling his belt.

"Woman, this isn't the time or the place." Charlie looked at his wife, perplexed, as she bent down at his waist.

"In your dreams," she said, pulling the belt quickly through his loops. With a satisfied grin, she turned, walked back to Bill and handed the belt to him.

"And what am I supposed to do about keeping my *pants up*?" Charlie inquired.

Jessie grinned. "Not to worry. Between your belly and your butt, honey, you have nothing to fear."

Lisa chuckled at their playfulness.

"Jezebel," he grumbled, as he downed another shot.

"Scrooge," she muttered under her breath, flashing Lisa a wink.

Bill stepped through the door and onto the extended porch. Destiny was curled up in one corner of the swing, laying against one of the comfortable pillows Jessie had used to decorate. Awkwardly, he sat on the other end.

Destiny glanced over at him and reversed her position, nuzzling under his arm and laying against him. The wind howled and whistled through the cracks, the occasional flashes of lightning outlining the trees as they blew in grand motion, even the branches on the heaviest of them swaying slightly in the massive storm.

"How's Syd?"

"Sleeping," he replied, slowly rocking them back and forth with his foot. "You okay?" He leaned his head until he could see her face. She didn't move, but he saw her discreetly wipe away a tear. He turned, causing her to stir. "Destiny?"

"I'm okay. Really." She wiped away another tear and lay flat in his lap. He leaned back again, petting her head, the wood squeaking against the metal with each swaying motion. "I was just so scared," she finally said, "when I couldn't find her." Destiny slowly sat up on her arm, looking into his eyes. "When I thought," she began. She took a deep breath. "When I thought you…" she suddenly started to sob.

Bill immediately pulled her to his chest. "I'm fine," he assured her. She pulled away. "But when I thought that you were…" she began again, unable to say the words. "I was so scared." She sniffed and her hands moved to the scratches on his face. "I can't lose you, too," she added sadly.

Bill smiled sweetly and pulled her closer to him, kissing her forehead and pressing her against his chest. They rocked for many moments in silence before she slowly pulled away. She looked up into his dark eyes, searching them, memorizing them. Tentatively her hand traced his face, his cheek, his hair. He dropped his forehead to hers, and she closed her eyes.

Destiny leaned back against his chest. You know when

Dr. Villarreal asked me what I was the angriest about, after…" her voice trailed off. "After Winston…" Somehow she couldn't mouth the words. "And I couldn't tell her? Maybe it was because there were so many things I was angry about and I was afraid if I spoke them out loud that they would be real. So, I just… didn't."

Bill gently rubbed her arm as she spoke, allowing her to talk through overwhelming emotions.

"I was angry about Phillip. I was angry about Rhett. At first, I was angry that I didn't die with them."

Bill closed his eyes, her words breaking his heart.

"I was angry about what Winston did, that I trusted him. I was angry with myself for being so stupid." She bit her lip nervously. "I was angry because he stole more than just my trust. He stole something so much more personal."

Bill looked down as he continued to rub her arm.

"Phillip is the only man I've ever been with," she cried softly. "And when he died, I swore I'd never…" Destiny caught herself as the tears streamed from her eyes. "That I'd never get close to anyone again. That I'd never fall in love again."

Bill's hand moved to her head, stroking her auburn hair.

"And then I met you," she sniffed. "And suddenly, I thought—" She bit her lip again to keep from sobbing uncontrollably. "I thought that maybe I *could*… be with someone else. But he stole that from me, too," she concluded with another sniff. She sat up suddenly and looked him in the eyes.

His heart broke, seeing her tear-soaked face. He reached to wipe the tears away.

"He took away my choice. He ripped away that precious thing that we give of ourselves to one another." She looked deep into Bill's eyes. How could he ever understand? "I wanted it to be you," she said almost in a whisper. "And he took that away," she cried. "Now, I don't know…"

Bill pulled her with all his might until she was sitting on his lap. "I can't begin to know how you feel, but know that it doesn't matter," he said, wiping away her tears.

She wiped her nose with the blanket.

Bill raised her chin with his finger. "It doesn't matter." He smiled sincerely. "And I hope that you come to a place where you don't allow him to have another moment of your day by giving him the satisfaction of thinking that he stole *anything* from you." He held her face within his palms. "He was a coward and took what he couldn't get by any other means." He brushed back her hair. "But it will never change how I feel about you, or how I look at you, or, when you're ready, how much I want to be with you. Make love to you. And I do," he said, pulling her face closer until their foreheads kissed. "It won't be any less special because of him. I won't give him the satisfaction."

Destiny closed her eyes and felt his cold kiss on the tip of her nose. She smiled and dropped her head to his shoulder again as he rocked her in his arms, feeling spent, emotionally. "I didn't mean to fall in love with you," she whispered.

"I didn't mean to fall in love with you, either," he replied, opening his eyes. "In fact, if this is all we *ever* do, I'll be happy—just holding you in my arms."

Destiny sniffed. "How is it you always seem to know the perfect thing to say?"

"I used to write Hallmark cards."

Destiny chuckled. "Yeah, so why did you stop?" she asked playfully, with a sniff.

"Well," he sighed dramatically. "I didn't have anyone around to inspire me."

"So, what happens now?"

Bill drew in a deep breath. "Well, *first*, I'm going to take *another really* cold shower." He felt her chuckle under his arm. "And then I'm going to crawl into a bunk bed, which, by the way, I haven't slept in since I was fourteen. And then, I *hope* that I can fall asleep."

Destiny felt her eyes getting heavy as she smiled against his chest.

"Then I'm going to wake up, call the insurance company and see what we can do about Charlie's truck."

"And then?" she said in a breath.

"And then," Bill hugged her tighter, "I'm going to take my family home."

Destiny's smile softened. There were no more words spoken. No more words were needed, as they rocked quietly until she fell asleep in his arms.

The Past

Chapter Forty-Three

JUSTINE STEPPED from the luxurious executive room ensuite and finished packing her Luis Vuitton monogrammed bags. She would never have to use faux anything again. Uri lavished her with every extravagance a wife could ever want. There was even an expense account, in which he kept, at least, ten thousand dollars at all times, so she was never in want of anything. Mostly. They'd been together for almost nine years now. Ten if one counted the time that she was pregnant when she mysteriously disappeared from his life. The moment they met, there was an instant spark between them. An intense spark, at that.

They met in Italy during her family vacation in 2000. Uri sought her out within minutes of seeing her at his vineyard, one of his many businesses, and spent the rest of the time she was in Italy wooing and then bedding her. He probably wouldn't even have cared that she was already involved with someone if she had bothered to tell him. Uri promised her the moon and gave her more. He begged her to stay. Justine promised she'd be back after she wrapped up her affairs stateside.

Except that, the day she returned to the States, she started getting sick, attributing it to the rough flight home. After two days, she suspected it was food poisoning or the flu. Her physician assured her it was none of the above. When Justine found out she was pregnant, she panicked—not something she would usually do. She blamed her emotional state on her hormones, went home, composed herself and contemplated what to do next.

Bill was a nice guy, and he was sweet, but Uri was well-dressed and virile. Though he was ten years her senior, he was fit and athletic, not to mention he had a commanding presence. There was a sophistication about him; Uri was so sure of himself; self-confident. Only now, she knew he was also full of himself. Most importantly, he was loaded.

Bill was a jeans-and-flannel-shirt kind of guy, who worked a boring job in a boring city. For Justine, in the end, it was a no-brainer. The timing of the pregnancy, however, was going to be a problem—simply because she had told Uri she was a virgin, and she was pretty sure the child was Bill's. Justine considered herself a pretty good actress and felt her performance with Uri their first time in bed made a believer out of him, not that she had to overact since he had another excellent attribute: Uri was *very* well-endowed.

She explained her need to stay in the States once she was back home, telling Uri she was now expected to be the caretaker of her ailing grandmother, who was actually long deceased. When her mother realized her plight, she insisted Justine marry immediately or give up the child for adoption. Justine started contemplating all her options and plotting her eventual outcome. She knew she didn't want to be married; she certainly didn't want to be married to Bill, but she didn't want to be a single mom living on food stamps and child support, either.

Being an adopted child herself, she refused to have her

child grow up in the system. And though she didn't practice her Catholic faith, she could hear the nuns screaming
into her ear that she couldn't have an abortion. So she
went crying to Bill, mostly because she was genuinely
heartbroken that he was her last resort. And he took her in,
as she knew he would. He proposed. She accepted. Her
mother was thrilled. But Justine was miserable.

Bill had tried to be a good husband, and he was a good
father. His attentiveness was well-intended. He would bring
her soup if she felt sick, massage her feet when they hurt
and put pillows under her knees when her back hurt.
Justine actually felt a little sorry for him because he
sincerely had no clue as to the fact that she never had any
intention of staying. She contemplated, albeit not for long,
that she might take Sydney with her. However, in all her
scenarios, showing up at Uri's door with a child that more
than likely wasn't his wouldn't have ended well. When she
would finally show up at his door, she knew that he also
would have soup brought to her, but hand-prepared by his
personal chef. And if her feet hurt, he would hire a
masseuse to massage any part of her that hurt, at a
moment's notice. And the pillows he would place under
her knees would be covered in the best milled Egyptian
cotton and stuffed with the finest goose-feathers. There was
no comparison.

When she left, she took everything with her, including
the pictures. Then she burned them all. There needed to
be no proof of their life together that could ever come
back to haunt her. When she left, she quietly walked out of
the door, hailed a cab, and took the first flight to Florence.
She was on Uri's doorstep within two days and in his bed
the night after that.

Throughout her pregnancy, she had used expensive
lotions and oils to help her skin's elasticity, in the hopes of

not having any daily reminders of ever giving birth. Justine prided herself on being able to explain her way out of anything, and up to now that had served her well. Stretch marks? She explained how she had shamefully gained weight while acting as her grandmother's caregiver. Thankfully, she was able to lose most of the weight, though she feigned disappointment. And as for Uri's calls? Taking care of a seventy-eight-year-old Alzheimer's patient had taken such a toll on her. It had been difficult for her. After all, he was on the other side of the world. Uri's letters? She had conveniently routed those to a secret post office box. The lies only became easier and easier with time.

Justine was becoming skilled at deception. She had an answer for everything. In the end, it was Uri who ended up apologizing, for ever questioning her. They were married in a private ceremony two months later. None of her relatives were in attendance. Only because Justine had disposed of their wedding invitations instead of mailing them. Although Uri offered to pay for their flights, she made plausible excuses for their absences, after which he showered her with more gifts to help her overcome her sorrow at her family's lack of consideration.

But now the clock was ticking. Literally. Uri was getting impatient for a child, an heir. He wanted a son but would settle for a girl. She no longer trusted birth control pills since she'd been on them when she got pregnant. After Sydney's birth, Justine got the Implanon implanted to ensure that she couldn't get pregnant again, covering the incision with a beautiful tattoo. Poor Uri. After several years with no results, he had gone through every conceivable test to assure that he wasn't shooting blanks. Of course, anytime Uri suggested Justine get tested. she would conveniently fly back to the states to see her personal physician, rather than one, of his choosing, in Florence.

However, instead of seeing a doctor, she would spend the weekend at a spa, working on her story for when she returned. It was on Justine's last trip to the States before the new year when her excuses were getting as thin as Uri's patience that she decided to make a little side trip.

Justine drove the streets that she hadn't driven on in over ten years. So many things had changed, so many never would. As she drew close to her destination, she slowed. She glanced out the window to her left as she drove past. It was called the Kemper House. She was simply amazed at what he had done with the place. Justine remembered the day they drove by the old run-down building years ago. Bill had offhandedly remarked that someone should buy that old place and turn it into something amazing. He had done just that. When she had called her mother to announce her marriage to Uri, her mother told her he had bought it. She laughed. He must have gone off the deep end after she left him. She was sure he'd end up bankrupt.

Now, as she drove by the manicured property, she narrowed her eyes slightly. He had actually made something of himself. Justine turned the corner, made the block and slowly drove by again. Her mother had felt obligated over the first few years to update her on Bill and Sydney's lives. She would send Justine articles she clipped when national magazines featured the Kemper House. And sometimes she would send her daughter pictures of Sydney that Bill sent her at Christmas. Justine disposed of them all immediately. Thankfully, her mother had moved away within two years of Sydney's birth, so her updates were less frequent, albeit still occasional. Then when they stopped altogether, she was grateful, until she realized her adopted mother had died. Then she was sad. But like everything else in her life, she got over it.

Justine was hoping to get maybe just a glance of Sydney, if only out of curiosity. She pulled to the street corner across from the famous bed and breakfast and then stepped from her rented BMW. She took out her cell phone and pretended to snap pictures of the beautiful house, but was hoping Sydney would appear. It was afternoon, about the time school let out, and carpools and school buses would be delivering children to their rural, ordinary lives.

As if on cue, a blue Honda CR-V slowed and pulled into the wide white rock drive and stopped. Justine sidestepped casually, her phone still close to her eyes. Then she saw her. The dark-haired child jumped from the back of the car and rushed eagerly down the driveway right toward her. Justine froze. Sydney looked into the mailbox and pulled out the large stack of mail, rooting through it. After a moment, Sydney glanced across the street, right at her. Justine felt her face flush. Sydney looked at her for a moment after which she smiled and waved.

"Hi," she called across the street.

Justine slowly raised her gloved hand and waved back. "Hi." She watched her daughter turn and walk back to the side of the house. A dark-haired woman put her arm around the child and walked with her inside.

Justine slowly lowered her phone, stepped to her car and climbed back in. She sat in the seat, staring straight ahead, her heart racing, her breathing accelerated. Slowly, Justine pulled off her gloves, lifted the phone and began to look at the pictures she had just taken. There were dozens of the young girl as she walked away; every angle that Sydney had turned, Justine tried to capture, until the moment she had disappeared inside the large house. Her fingers pushed the arrow forward and then back until she found the picture she sought. Her heart stopped. Sydney had his chin and his eyes. Her hair was jet black; she had an olive complexion. A horn honked and she looked up suddenly with a start, only to find a woman who had become annoyed with an older couple driving too slowly, so she had mashed on her horn, just before shooting them the finger. Justine looked back down at the phone, refreshing the screen and enlarging the picture. She couldn't believe it. After all this time. Was it possible? She looked at the house and back at the picture, certain she was looking at Uri's daughter.

Chapter Forty-Four

SYDNEY THREW her backpack on the kitchen island, dropped her jacket and kicked off her shoes.

"Whoa, young lady," Destiny said. "Your father would have my hide if I let you slack off while he's away."

"Really?" she pouted.

"Really," Destiny replied firmly, handing her the backpack and standing over her.

"Fine," Sydney growled dramatically, throwing her head back and picking up all her belongings before heading for her room.

"And he also said——"

"I know. Book report first!" Sydney called from the hallway. "You do realize I'm on Christmas vacation," she added, before shutting her door.

Destiny smiled to herself. The front doorbell rang, and she walked through the kitchen and into the hallway still decorated for Christmas, arriving just as it rang again. There before her stood a beautiful woman in a colorful Missoni dress, a stunning ankle-length cashmere belted coat, and calf-length leather boots. Destiny smiled and invited her in. "You must be Mrs. Watson," she said, reaching to shake her hand. "We've been expecting you."

The woman took her hand tentatively as her eyes took in her surroundings first and then slowly settled back on Destiny. Without removing her expensive Persol sunglasses, she shoved her hands into her coat pockets. "Is Mr. Ireland here?"

Destiny narrowed her brow at the tone of her request. "No, I'm sorry, he's out of town for a few days. But I can help you. I'm Destiny, his house manager."

Justine stepped past her as she looked around, walking into the library and looking side to side. She didn't say anything until she turned back to Destiny. "Destiny, what a lovely name."

"Thank you." Destiny was a little curious at the woman's cryptic demeanor. "Are you not Mrs. Watson?"

The woman didn't' answer, but her smug smile spoke volumes, as did how she carried herself. She had an air of superiority, and it was more than slightly irritating.

"Was Bill expecting you?"

"Bill?" she asked coyly, her smile growing.

"Mr. Ireland?" Destiny was now getting mildly annoyed. "I'd be happy to take down your name, or if you'd like to leave him a card, I'd be glad to give it to him."

"I'll bet you would, Honey." Justine held onto the banister, leaning around it to look upstairs.

Just then Sydney emerged from her room. "Cookie time!" she exclaimed. She stopped when she saw the woman before her.

"Hi." Justine's demeanor softened. It was like looking at a picture of herself twenty years ago. Only Sydney's face was that of a happy child, not one whose childhood was wrought with abuse—physical and emotional—by the hand of those who conceived her. She had the face of someone who was loved, not one of fear of and resentment toward those whose blood coursed through her veins. "What's *your* name?"

"Sydney." The girl reached out her hand, as her father had taught her.

Justine bent at the waist, taking the small hand gently into her gloved hand and holding it for just a moment longer before releasing it. Of course she knew the name. She had named her daughter the day of her birth, after her grandfather on her mother's side. A man she had adored. The only person who had stood up to his own son when he found he was sexually abusing his granddaughter. Not that it did any good. His son had simply taken his wife and his two daughters and moved to another city, where no one seemed to care much about such things. As she rested her hands on her knees, she looked into the young girl's face. "My, you are beautiful," she said, tapping her on the chin. "You have your father's eyes."

Destiny reached over and put her arms around Sydney's chest, pulling her backward to herself. "I didn't catch your name," she said as sweetly as she could muster.

"That's because I didn't give it to you, Dear." Justine looked around once more, then added. "I'll come back next week. What day did you say he'd be back?" she asked.

"I didn't," Destiny replied flatly.

Justine looked at her for a moment then smiled wryly. A worthy competitor. She bent slightly at the waist again and smiled at Sydney. "Nice to meet you, Sydney."

Destiny stepped back, taking Sydney with her. She stepped around the woman and opened the door, the simple act speaking volumes. Justine stood there for a moment, smiling defiantly for effect, slid her hands back into her coat pockets and walked out without another word. Destiny closed the door behind her and locked it before peeking through the sheer curtains. She watched as the woman got into her car and drove away. "Well, that was weird," she muttered to herself.

"Who was that?"

"Beats me," Destiny replied, walking to the kitchen.

"You know? I saw her outside."

"When?"

"Before, when I went to get the mail. She was taking pictures of the house. I thought she was a tourist," Sydney replied, as she rooted through the refrigerator.

"You didn't talk to her did you?"

"I just said 'hi,'" she offered.

"Did she say anything back?"

"She said 'hi,'" Sydney grinned.

Destiny pursed her lips. "Hmm. Interesting." She glanced at the clock. "Three-thirty, Syd. Cookie time." Nervously, she glanced out the kitchen window at the street.

"Gotcha," Sydney said, taking out the cookie pans and the dough that Destiny had made that morning. "Can we do pizza for dinner?"

"That's an excellent idea!" Destiny seemed relieved that she didn't have to cook or clean up. "You call it in after we check in all our guests and tell them to have it here by five thirty. Sound good?"

Sydney hugged Destiny. "I'm so glad you're here."

Destiny smiled, stole a ball of cookie dough from the pan and popped it into her mouth.

"Hey!" Sydney exclaimed. "Omah says that'll give you worms."

"Then I'm sure my belly is full of slimy, slithery, wiggly worms by now," she said, leaning over and tickling Sydney's stomach. "Because I've been eating dough all my life."

"That's disgusting." Sydney made a face.

"No, disgusting is that new sauce recipe your dad tried for the chicken the other night," Destiny remarked, glancing toward the street through the curtains again.

"Um. I'm going to tell him you said something he made was disgusting."

Destiny grabbed Sydney and tickled her again, not letting her go. "I seem to remember that you scraped all yours off and didn't eat much chicken, either."

Sydney wriggled and laughed. "That's because it was disgusting," she finally conceded.

Destiny released her. "Uh-huh." She pointed at the fridge with the knife she used to cut the dough. "I think it's time we accidentally pour that sauce down the garbage disposal."

Sydney smiled. "I'm with ya!" she exclaimed, moving to the refrigerator and taking the sauce out. She popped the lid and poured it into the sink.

"Aww," Destiny whined dramatically. "What a waste."

Sydney giggled and walked past Destiny, who grabbed her and swung her around the kitchen several times before releasing her. Had she looked out the window once more she would have seen the same steel gray BMW that had driven past the house several times pass by once more.

Chapter Forty-Five

BILL SMILED TO HIMSELF. He remembered lifting Destiny from the swing and carrying her to the room Jessie had prepared for her. It was directly across from his. He remembered thinking she would be too close to resist, much like at home. He remembered how as he lay her on the bed that Destiny took his hand and held him then pulled him down next to her. Bill laid beside her, his breathing quickening as she rolled against him and wriggled under his arm. Destiny snuggled against his chest; her arm draped over him. He remembered how good she felt against him. Bill could feel Destiny's heart beating, her soft, steady breathing against his side. He could feel her unbound breasts through the thin shirt she wore, pressing against him.

He remembered how hard it was to be so close to her and not be able to kiss her—to undress her. To make love to her. Bill hadn't been with anyone since Justine. He loved Justine, once, or, at least, he thought he did. He thought she was *the one*. Justine was the second woman he'd ever slept with; only he couldn't remember sleeping much when he was with her. Everything about Justine was exotic, and Bill had instantly fallen for her. She had broken his heart and soured him from ever wanting to be in love again. The only love in his life from that point on had been Sydney. His whole life had been her. Well, her and the Kemper House.

Until now. Destiny changed all that. From the moment he first saw her across the concession counter ordering margaritas for two silly old men, he felt his heart come alive again, alive in a way that he didn't even believe possible. And then, when she spoke, her velvet voice reached his ears and touched his very soul.

He remembered leaning over and kissing her forehead as she nestled closer into his arms. He reached over and held her hand, his fingers toying with hers; so small and so cold, soft to his touch. His hands slowly explored them, gently embracing them, then moving over the long sleeves of the t-shirt she wore. Destiny stirred just slightly.

Bill jerked awake suddenly as the plane shook. The turbulence through the whole flight had been rough. Thankfully, he wasn't one of those who suffered from motion sickness. He glanced at his seatmate, an eighteen-year-old Boston student heading home for the holidays. He looked out the window and checked his watch. Another hour. He would never have considered leaving during their busiest time of the year, but he had heard about an old B&B in Canada that had closed years ago. It was a run down property that had deteriorated and was on the auction block, an opportunity he just couldn't pass up. Bill leaned back in his seat again and closed his eyes, resting on his trusty self-inflatable Brookstone travel pillow. His breathing steadily slowed and within minutes, he was back asleep and dreaming of Destiny.

No, this time, Bill was going to do it right. He was

going to wait. He wasn't going to rush her; wasn't going to push her. He knew Destiny would be worth waiting for; and then he was going to propose to her. And then he was going to marry her, and they were going to have children together. Destiny would be his "happily ever after."

Bill remembered opening his eyes, but Destiny's were closed, her breathing steady. She slept peacefully. He smiled sweetly, then kissed the end of her nose before reluctantly sliding from the bed, knowing he couldn't stay —knowing that he shouldn't…

His eyes never left her as he rose. Only suddenly she was no longer asleep. The moon beyond the windows reflected in her eyes, the light entrancing him, pleading for him to stay, to hold her, to touch her… and more. Her arms reached for him and pulled him back to her side where she pressed herself against him. Slowly she slid her hand under his shirt, discovering the treasure trail of hair from his jeans and following it upwards to the matting of brown hair that adorned his chest. She touched and toyed with his chest, her fingers tracing his nipples, then moving upward to his neck, where they lingered, delicately dancing against his late evening stubble. They caressed his cheek on their way to his mouth. His lips.

Tentatively, her fingers brushed over his lips, the simple gesture taunting him. Destiny raised onto her elbow, leaning more on his chest. He closed his eyes as he felt her firm breasts pressed against him. Though there were two layers of shirts between them, in his mind there were none. Her fingers continued to toy with his lips, then she kissed his cheek, turning his head toward her. He opened his eyes, her eyes still on him as she leaned further onto him. Her lips parted just enough that when she gently kissed him, he felt the moist heat of her mouth. Of her breath. They traveled along the side of his mouth and his cheek; her tongue darted about, daring his to join hers. Then she kissed him again, and again, never fully kissing his lips. His heart fluttered, his skin tingling at her slightest touch. God, it was unbearable.

"*I never meant to fall in love with you,*" she said, *without him seeing her mouth move.*

"*I didn't mean to fall in love with you,*" he whispered, *without opening his mouth.*

Destiny leaned against him, her warm breath teasing him, driving him mad. She brushed her lips over his once, then again. When her tongue flitted across them, he could bear it no more. Bill grabbed her hair and pulled her forcefully to himself, kissing her hard, kissing her deeply, with such passion that he thought he would explode. Suddenly she leaned back, breathlessly, gasping for air. Her hands moved to his shirt and frantically removed it. Bill lay there expectantly, his heart feeling like it was going to beat out of his chest. She slowly crossed her arms on her stomach and began to remove her shirt. He watched as the gray material slowly revealed her bare midriff. It felt like she was moving in slow motion, so he rose to help her. Then she smacked him square in the nose with her elbow.

Bill sat up with a start.

"Sorry, buddy," the young man in the seat next to him said, as he picked his backpack up off Bill's lap and handed him a Kleenex.

Bill looked at the tissue in his hand as blood dripped onto it, suddenly realizing his nose was bleeding.

"You were really in a deep sleep. Must have been some dream," he said with a smirk, motioning with his eyes at Bill's lap.

Bill looked down and quickly jerked his travel pillow into his lap and looked back up, red-faced.

The young man leaned over the seat next to him and held out his fist. "Fist bump, dude! Guy your age! Way to go!"

Bill, still disoriented, stared at the fist and then the rugged teen. He balled a fist and hit the young man's hand.

"Way to go," he repeated with a shake of his head as

he tossed his backpack over his shoulder and then joined those deplaning.

Bill glanced around to see if anyone else noted the exchange or the reason for it. He held the Kleenex to his nose as he looked out the window. Maybe it was a good thing Bill *didn't* finish the dream, or he could have been *way* more embarrassed than he was at that very moment. As he stared out the window, he chuckled to himself. *A guy your age?* He shook his head, and slowly a smile crept up the side of his lips. He casually balled his fist, and discreetly fist bumped his reflection in the window. "Way to go, old man," he murmured to himself, as passersby grumbled and talked to themselves, anxious to get to their next flight or to their final destination, oblivious to the proud moment Bill was sharing with himself.

Chapter Forty-Six

SYDNEY RAN INTO HIS ARMS, her usual greeting, whether he was gone an hour or a day. She was getting bigger and heavier, but he didn't care. He dreaded the day when she would come to the realization that it was no longer cool to hang with her dad. Until then, he would savor these special homecomings as long as he could.

"I missed you, Daddy!" she exclaimed.

"I missed you too, Sweetie." Bill gave his daughter a multitude of kisses. He glanced up at Destiny, and blushed; his heart still holding his fantasy that he had dreamed while on the plane. "Hey."

"Hey," she smiled sweetly, her hands stuffed into the back pockets of her jeans.

Sydney went to check on the cookies she was baking for their afternoon arrivals.

Bill slowly walked up to Destiny, gently slid his hands through her arms and hugged her to himself. He gave her a small kiss as well. On the cheek. "Ouch!" he exclaimed, touching his nose.

"What's wrong?"

"I was attacked by a rogue backpack." Bill grinned and then kissed her on her cheek, more carefully, just catching the side of her lips. Reluctantly, he released her, picked up his bag and carried it down the hallway.

Destiny followed him. "How was your flight?"

"Rough."

"Really?"

You have no idea; he sighed to himself.

She followed him into Sydney's room. He suddenly stopped before turning to Destiny. "Where's my bed?"

With a motion of her head, she begged him to follow her. So he did, to his room, where she opened his drawers and held out her hand. He looked at her, perplexed. His things were in their original places, and hers were no longer there.

"Deborah's gone, so it didn't seem fair that you had to keep sleeping on an air mattress," she said, with a slight shrug of her shoulders.

"Oh." Bill's face fell, his voice expressing his disappointed. "You didn't have to do that."

"Sure, I did. Isn't that where your house manager stays?"

His face brightened just slightly. "What are you saying?"

"I'm saying that if you need me, I'll stay. That is unless I don't work out." Destiny shuffled her feet. "Or you get tired of me."

Bill dropped his bags and went to her, taking her into his arms. "I'll never get tired of you." He kissed her again, ever so gently.

Destiny lowered her head, wiped her lips and stepped back. "I don't want this to be awkward, Bill."

"Why should it be awkward?" he asked, brushing back her hair.

"I mean, if this… if we…" She hesitated, looking into his eyes. "If we don't work out."

"Oh," he said, almost hurt, turning away. He put his suitcases on the bed and began to unpack.

"It's just," she bit her lip. "There've been some extraordinary circumstances surrounding you and me." Destiny brushed the floor with her house slipper. "I just don't want you feeling like if things change," she stammered, "you have to keep me. I don't want you to feel obligated."

"Are you kidding?" Bill turned back to her, taking her hands into his. "I'm in love with you." Destiny looked up into his eyes as he spoke. "That's never going to change. *Never*," he whispered. Bill leaned over and kissed her forehead, holding it to his lips.

Destiny smiled at his touch, at his words. Only, the doorbell broke their moment, the silence.

"I got it," Sydney chimed from the kitchen.

Bill smiled against her forehead, never wanting to let her go.

"Daddy, it's for you!"

Bill raised her face with his hands. "Be right back," he smiled, kissing her again. Destiny watched him disappear around the corner before she began unpacking his things. She sorted his clean clothes from his dirty ones and slowly put the clean ones back into his dresser. As Destiny placed his ties onto the felt-lined wood, she suddenly stopped and smiled. Her hand gently brushed across the fabric. It had been so long since she'd cared for someone else's clothes. Another man's clothes. Well, there were her brother's, during her brief stay at his place, but that didn't count. There was something unattractive about doing your adult brother's skid-marked underwear when he was in his twenties and still single.

When Destiny had removed her clothes from his drawers earlier that morning, she had yearned for a day when they would lie together with Bill's, when she would lie side by side with him, in his bed—*their* bed. She looked up at herself in the mirror. How can someone be so ready and not ready all at the same time? Destiny saw the hope that grew on Bill's face when she walked him back into his room, saw it dashed when he saw that her clothes were no longer there. She took his folded undershirts and placed them neatly into the cedar drawer.

Destiny sighed as she moved to hanging up the dress shirts he didn't use, and then his suit. She wanted to share with him her news of the hearing, but she was nervous. Three more women had come forward since Winston's picture was flashed across the news. However, two of the women had apparently settled their civil suits already, out of court, and had somehow disappeared. The District Attorney's office was having a hard time tracking them down to subpoena them to testify.

Deep pockets.

She shook her head. Destiny's was the largest civil suit by far, and though, through her attorney, he'd offered to settle, Destiny refused to back down. Sure, ten million was a ridiculous amount, but it wasn't for her. And the Rape Crisis Center would probably never see even half of that, but her intention was to hurt him in his pocketbook and to make a statement all at once. That's why he had shown up that night at Lisa's, a night that seemed like forever ago, but which, in reality, was only a few short weeks in the past.

Destiny walked from Bill's room and met a downcast Sydney. "What's wrong, Syd?"

"Daddy told me to go to my room."

"Why? What did you do?"

"*Nothing,*" she replied, upset. "He just got a letter and then got all weird and told me to go to my room."

"Okay, Sweetie." Destiny kissed her on the top of her head. "I'll check on him. It'll be fine," she added. "Just give us a few minutes."

"Fine," Sydney said emphatically, closing the door behind her.

Destiny walked to the kitchen. Bill was sitting at the kitchen table, his head hanging down. She stepped around him. He was reading a legal document, so she poured herself a cup of water from the kettle and selected a blackberry tea. The teabag popped up and down as Destiny steeped it. She cast occasional glances in Bill's direction as she took her time doctoring her tea with Stevia, honey, and a little lemon. Returning to the table, she sat beside him, blowing silently on the steaming liquid as she watched him read. He carefully read every word, turning to the last page. Finally, Bill leaned back in the chair and sighed.

Destiny leaned forward and put her hand on his arm. "Is everything okay?"

Bill shook his head. Frustrated, he brushed back his hair with both hands, and then clasped them behind his head.

Destiny waited patiently, watching as he stared at nothing. Something was wrong, but she couldn't imagine what had him so distracted and distant. She set her cup down and stood, moving behind him and holding his hands. He accepted her gesture and held tightly to them. Suddenly, he took his hands away and dropped his face into them. Destiny sat back down. "Bill," she pleaded. "Please talk to me."

When he removed his hands from his face, his eyes were wet.

"Bill?"

"Justine wants to see Sydney." He was hardly able to get the words out.

"What?"

"She wants to amend the divorce decree and get shared custody." Bill turned to her, still in shock.

"I thought you said she left when Sydney was a baby."

"She did," he replied. He stood and turned, wiping his eyes discreetly. "And she never once has tried to see her."

"Why now?"

"I don't know," Bill snapped, then softened his gaze. "I'm sorry," he added, shaking his head. "It's just… I never in a million years could have expected this." He hugged her.

The phone rang, and Destiny moved to answer it. "Kemper House Bed and Breakfast." She listened for a moment and turned to Bill. "It's your attorney. He said he's been trying to reach you on your cell phone."

"Darn it." Bill pulled it from his pocket. It was still in airplane mode. Bill sighed and then took the phone from her. "Hey, Dale." Bill began to pace.

Destiny sat by her tea and slowly sipped on it. Poor Bill. After all this time. As she sipped her tea, she furrowed her brow. She thought of the elegantly dressed woman who had appeared in their doorway the week before. Could the two incidents possibly be related?

"Yeah, I understand." Bill ended the call, looking down at the phone.

"What did he say?" Destiny asked as she turned. "Bill?"

But he didn't look at her. He just stared at the phone oddly. Then suddenly, inexplicably, with all his might, Bill threw it across the room, sending it crashing into the wall where it shattered into dozens of pieces, startling her. When he turned to her, there was so much pain in his eyes, so much anger. Without a word, he turned and walked from the kitchen. A few moments later, the house shook as he slammed the door to his room. At that instant, the buzzer on the stove sounded, and she rose quickly to check on the cookies Sydney had started. Once they were on the cooling rack, Destiny turned off the oven and placed the dirty pan and spatula into the sink to be dealt with later.

The doorbell rang, and Destiny quickly slid off her slippers and into her shoes. She smiled and opened the door to welcome their guests. Four couples were traveling together for their two-night stay. Destiny asked them to sign-in as she pulled their paperwork from a folder and handed each of them their receipts and their policies to review and sign. Behind her, she heard the door swing open. A moment later, Sydney was standing there with a plate of cookies and a carafe of milk. Destiny smiled and winked at her. She carried the tray of treats carefully to the library as everyone "oohed" in awe of her presentation. Destiny stepped beside her and whispered down to her, "I'm going to get your dad."

"He's gone," Sydney whispered back. "He was just in the kitchen, and then he left."

Destiny pursed her lips. "Did he say anything?"

"Nope. Hey, what happened to the phone?"

Destiny kissed her head and then turned back to their guests. "We'll show you to your rooms whenever you're ready," she offered. Then she left them with Sydney in the library and walked into the kitchen. She contemplated before taking her phone out and calling him. Bill's phone went straight to voicemail. She wriggled her lips. Something was wrong. Something was very wrong. Destiny sighed, put on her best face, and went to show their guests to their rooms.

Chapter Forty-Seven

JESSIE OPENED the door and smiled. "William! What a pleasant surprise. Come on in."

"Sorry to bother you like this. Bill anxiously stepped through the doorway; his hands shoved into his front jeans pocket. "Is Charlie around?"

She walked ahead of him and waved her hand, pointing toward the recliner. "He's on his throne, as usual."

Charlie looked up, saw it was Bill and smiled.

"Can I take you up on that drink now?"

Charlie turned off the television with his remote and sat up, slowly adjusting the old recliner to an upright position. Carefully he rose, his neck still in a brace from the accident just days before. He cast a glance at his wife, who took the hint. She leaned over and kissed Bill's cheek before walking back to their bedroom and closing the door. Charlie walked into the kitchen, reached into the cabinet and took down the half-full bottle of Weller and two shot glasses. "What are we celebrating?" Charlie quipped, noting the seriousness in his nephew's eyes. He couldn't remember the last time he'd actually had a drink with him.

Bill rested his hands on the counter as he contemplated what to say, how to say it. Then he sat, his eyes on the small glass between his fingers.

"Just say it, Son," Charlie encouraged him. "Get it off your chest."

"Dad said that you couldn't ever talk about what you did for a living because of *what* you did for a living," he began, looking up at the unshaven man.

Charlie narrowed his eyes. "You're not going to ask me to kill somebody are you?"

Bill toyed with his glass and chuckled. The thought momentarily sounded good. *Momentarily.* He looked up at Charlie. "I want to know how to disappear." The words hung in the air, as he downed the entire glass of whiskey. He gasped, made a face and set it down hard next to the bottle.

Charlie furrowed his brow, looking into Bill's eyes. "You almost sound serious."

Bill sighed and looked the old man in his eyes. "I was served today. Justine wants joint custody with Sydney."

"How's that possible? She's not been around since she was, what, six months?"

"Four." Bill rubbed his temples. "Then I got a call from my attorney. She's also requested a blood test, claiming that Sydney's not—" his voice cracked, then he dropped his head to his arms suddenly and wept.

Charlie didn't know what to do. Since 9/11, he'd never seen another man cry. Slowly, he downed a second glass, then walked around the counter and patted Bill on the back. Bill raised his head and wiped his tears, drawing in a deep breath. He downed the small glass of whiskey, slamming the glass on the counter by the bottle.

"This won't help, Son."

Since Bill's father had passed away almost ten years

ago from a massive heart attack, Charlie and Jessie were his only family besides his mother. He and Charlie had been extremely close. His father's sudden death had been devastating for all of them. Now he was coming to his uncle, as he would have gone to his father. Bill looked into his eyes. "I don't know what to do."

"Running away won't help, either," Charlie insisted, as he poured less into Bill's glass and pushed it to him. "I'm sorry to ask this, but is it possible?"

Bill took the glass and looked into it again. "After we…" he began. "She went to Italy for a month with her mom and her Aunt Jean so that she could have…" he struggled to say the words. Then he looked into Charlie's eyes again. "I know she's mine," he said emphatically. "I know it, with all my heart."

"Then you have nothing to worry about." Charlie held the glass up to his nephew, then knocked back the glassful.

"But how do I tell her? How do I tell Sydney, after all this time, her mother wants to see her? And then I have to explain that they have to take her blood. How am I going to explain *that*?"

"Do you have to?"

Bill stood and began to pace. "She's nine. She'll figure it out," he added sarcastically.

Charlie didn't take offense to his outburst. "So, you go home, and you talk to her. You said it yourself. She's a smart girl. She'll figure it out. If Sydney were still just a baby, then I'd say the gloves go off and go for the throat. But she's nine." "How you handle this will not only be a testament to your role as a father, but a testament of your faith." He put the cap back on the whiskey bottle. "You fight, but you do it silently, behind the scenes, so to speak. Like the *Wizard of Oz*. '*Don't pay attention to the man behind the curtain.*' You can go crazy pulling the knobs and levers. Talk to the attorneys and judges, whatever you have to do. But on the outside, keep it calm, and *she'll* be fine."

"I'm worried about *me*," he chuckled, as he sat back down. "What if I…" he began again, his eyes moist. "I can't," he mused, struggling to finish. Bill shook his head. "I can't lose her."

Charlie reached over and put his arm on Bill's. "You're not gonna lose her son," he reassured him empathetically. "You fight like hell for her. For *her*, son. She's *your* daughter. You know what's best for her. You fight for *her*," he encouraged his nephew.

Bill pushed the shot glass back to Charlie, as he stood. Charlie walked around the counter and put his arm on his back as he walked him to the door. "You'll do the right thing. I know you will. You're a good man."

"I don't feel like a good person right now." Bill shoved his hands into his pockets again. "Right now, I want to kill my ex-wife."

"Understandable emotion," Charlie agreed. "But then, Justine wins. And none of us wants that."

Bill shook his head, then looked into Charlie's worn face. "Thank you, Uncle Charlie." Bill forced a small smile.

Charlie clapped his hand on his nephew's shoulder and squeezed it. "You'll be okay, Son," he promised with a sigh. "And if you need anything, you know you can come by or call anytime. We're here for you."

Bill nodded. "Thank you."

"Anytime, Son." Charlie pulled his brother's youngest son to his chest, as he had done when he was a young man. Charlie watched Bill walk away, waving to him as he climbed into his car.

His wife joined him at the door, her hand on his shoulder as she looked around him. "He gonna be okay?"

Charlie exhaled. "I hope so. For that little angel's sake, I certainly hope so."

Chapter Forty-Eight

DESTINY WALKED down the stairs carefully, so as not to slip on the wooden steps or the carpet that ran down the middle of the staircases. Her hand slid down the polished wooden banister that curled at the bottom of each floor. She didn't remember setting the alarm, and she didn't mind the exercise, but she wasn't looking forward to three flights of steps up and down this late at night. All the guests were already asleep. More importantly, Sydney was asleep. Sydney had become worried when her father wasn't answering his phone and worked herself into a sobbing mess, concerned that something had happened to him.

There was a light on in the kitchen that she didn't remember leaving on. Many times guests came down to help themselves to drinks or snacks that were left out, and, most times, they were less conscious of turning the lights off. Destiny walked to the porch and turned on the light. She narrowed her eyes but didn't see Bill's CR-V in the driveway with all the other cars there. She checked the alarm, and it indicated there was a door open. She turned off the porch and kitchen lights and began checking all the doors in the house. When she was sure that they were all closed and locked, she checked the alarm again. *Hmm.*

She hesitated, then, slowly walked to Bill's room. She drew in a deep breath and knocked softly. She waited a moment and put her ear to the door. She started to knock, but instead turned the knob and opened the door. She knocked lightly again, as she stepped inside. "Bill?" She listened. There were no sounds beyond the door. Destiny stepped into his room and shivered from the cold. There was no lump on the bed. She drew her robe tighter around her and walked to his outside door. It was unlocked and open. She looked out over the moonlit gardens, the light fully revealing the beautifully landscaped and manicured lawns. She turned and a shape startled her.

"Jesus Christ!! You scared me." Slowly, quietly Bill emerged from the shadows. "What are you doing out here? It's freezing."

Bill stepped to her and she could see his eyes shimmering through the darkness.

"Are you okay?"

Bill reached forward, to her face.

She gasped at his touch. "Your hands are like ice!"

Bill cupped his hands and blew into them and then rubbed them together before moving his hands to her face again, taking her cheeks with them, brushing them with his thumbs. Destiny felt her face drop into his grip. Bill took another step toward her and held her face in both his hands. His eyes beckoned her, pleaded with hers. Destiny stepped to him, her eyes locked onto his. Slowly he pulled her against him and kissed her gently. Then harder. She could taste the alcohol on his breath, but she didn't care. Bill's hands slid from her side to the curve of her back as he held her tighter. Overcome by the passion of the moment, Destiny felt herself melt into his arms, but he held her up. He hungrily pulled her nearer, his mouth wide, his tongue exploring, savoring.

Destiny stepped back, breathless and gasped, her gaze still on him. She pressed herself against him again, her hands taking his face, pulling him to her. When they parted again, Bill looked down at her. Her robe had loosened in the fray and hung open. Under it, she wore a thin night-shirt and cotton night pants. He looked down at Destiny, her body visible through the thin white material in the moonlight. He felt like the wind had been knocked out of him. She was stunning. She was perfect. Bill could see her bosom rising and falling with every breath. He closed his eyes and kissed her again, his hands moving inside her robe, squeezing her to himself. It was all too much to bear. Her mouth moved to his neck, nibbling on it. Bill dropped his head back.

Destiny side-stepped slowly, pulling Bill with her as they kissed frantically. She felt her robe fall from her shoulders. Or was he pulling it off? She didn't know. She didn't care. She just knew that she wanted him to make love to her, to hold her and never let her go. Destiny looked down, her hands moving to his soft flannel shirt, unbuttoning it as fast as she could manage. As they stepped inside the door, Bill pulled it closed behind him, his lips never leaving hers. They neared the bed, her robe now in a heap on the floor. He turned, tripping over it and they both fell together onto the bed, laughing. They lay on the bed, looking at each other, their laughter dying down. Bill wriggled onto the bed beside her, his body pressed against hers.

Suddenly, he wanted to take his time. His hand moved slowly over her shirt and up to her face. He slowly leaned over and kissed her, ever so gently, his lips traveling down her chin, then her neck. His hand tentatively made its way back to her stomach, his hand sliding inside her shirt. Bill felt Destiny's warm skin tremble at his touch. His hand traced her stomach and around to her bare back, pulling her closer. His kisses became more passionate as his hand moved to her shoulder. He pulled her as close as he could, squeezing her tightly. He looked up, just for a moment—a mere fraction of a moment. Only it was a moment too long, as his eyes rested on the framed photo at his bedside. Bill stopped suddenly, his forehead dropping to hers, his breath hot and hurried against her face. "I can't," Bill said in frustration. "I'm sorry."

Destiny lay there, her breathing quickening with each beat of her heart. She looked up at him, confused.

Bill slowly pulled away and sat up on the side of the bed and dropped his head into his hands. "I'm sorry."

Destiny felt her fortitude fail, and she quickly slid from the bed. She softly sobbed as she slipped back into her slippers and grabbed her robe.

"Destiny!" Bill grabbed for her arm.

But she was already rushing down the hallway, pulling her robe on as she went. Destiny tried to maneuver the stairs, her tears blinding her. She slowed, her chest heaving with her sobs, as she tried not to cry out loud and wake the guests. She held her hand over her mouth as she climbed the third flight and rushed into her room. Then she fell onto her bed and sobbed profusely. She felt embarrassed. Humiliated.

Suddenly, there was a light knock. Maybe if she ignored him, he would go away. The tap came again. The door creaked open, and she realized in her haste, she failed to lock it. "Go away," she managed to whimper. Then she felt him lean on the bed beside her.

"Destiny," Bill grabbed for her arm.

She rolled away from his touch.

"Destiny, please," he pleaded. "It's not you."

Destiny rolled over and glared at him, reached behind him, grabbed a handful of tissues, blew her nose, and wiped her face. She finally stood and looked down at him. "I knew this was a mistake. I'm sorry."

Bill gently took her hand. "Destiny, please," he begged, until she sat beside him on the bed, sniffing.

"I want to explain something to you." Bill slid to his knees before her to ensure she was looking at him, still holding her hands in his. "I want you more than you know," he said. "Maybe more than I should," he continued, as she finally faced him. And I didn't want to stop. I *wouldn't* have stopped," Bill assured her.

"Then why did you?" she asked, mystified. "We're two consenting adults. And I *was* consenting," she said, blowing her nose. "I put myself out there; I trusted you."

"That's exactly right. You trusted me," he reiterated. "And you have to trust me now. I want you more than I've ever wanted any woman. I love you more than I've loved any woman."

"But?"

"But suddenly, I saw Sydney." Bill climbed from his knees and sat beside her again. "And I was suddenly ashamed. How would I want someone to treat my little girl?" He tilted his head toward her. "Would I want some guy to treat her the way I was treating you?" He looked away, embarrassed, shaking his head. "God, the fact that I'm even thinking about that already is disturbing on so many different levels." He turned back to her and drew in a deep breath. "Point is if I want that for my daughter—if I want someone to respect her and love her and wait for her until he marries her, shouldn't I do the same?"

Destiny wiped her eyes once more, chewing on what he said. "So, it wasn't me?"

Bill chuckled. "Oh, God, no," he assured her, turning and

hugging her. "I love you. I *want* you. Some things are obvious," he added, looking down at his lap. She followed his stare, then looked back up at him, blushing, a small smile crossing her lips. "I can hide some things, but…" he said, shrugging; eyebrows raised. "So, it's *definitely* not you. It's all me."

Destiny fell back onto her bed, and Bill fell back beside her. "I guess snuggling is out of the question."

"Snuggling, kissing, petting, being in the same room." Bill turned to smile at her. Slowly, his fingers reached across and gently took her fingers. As he glanced down at their hands, he added, "Holding hands is permitted."

"Oh, thank God!" she exclaimed. "I was starting to think we were going to have to have sex without actually touching at all."

He looked up at the ceiling. "Somehow, this is going to be harder than I ever thought it would be."

"So, what happens now?" she asked, rolling onto her side, and leaning on her elbow.

"If we get married tomorrow, Sydney will be in bed by nine, ten at the latest. We can finish this conversation tomorrow night, at say," he looked at his watch. "Ten-o-one."

Destiny smiled down at him. "There's a hearing on my civil suit tomorrow."

"Darn it!" He rolled back onto his side, and leaned on his elbow as well, looking at her like he had an epiphany. "If there's court, there's a judge, right? We can ask for an adjournment and then he can marry us in chambers. We'll ask him to excuse us for, say," he looked at his watch again. "Five minutes."

Destiny laughed. "Five minutes?"

Bill raised his eyebrows and looked up. "It *has* been, uh, how old is Sydney, and then add six months?"

Destiny laughed again and took his hand. "So, is this you proposing?"

"Just proposing a means to an end," he sighed, looking into her eyes. "No, this is not me proposing. When I propose, it's going to be right. It's going to be perfect." He sweetly smiled, reaching for her shirt.

Destiny immediately held up her hand to create a barrier.

Bill narrowed his eyes. "You're going to make me pay for this, aren't you?"

Destiny grinned. "Absolutely."

Bill rolled onto his back again, staring upward. He sighed. "Why does life have to be so complicated?"

"Life is messy," she agreed.

"Justine requested a blood test, saying Sydney might not be mine," he said weakly before looking over at her.

"Oh, Bill! No!"

"Yeah. How am I supposed to tell Syd?"

"Do you have to?"

"Well, they want to do a blood test on her and me."

"No, Bill." Destiny was pensive for a moment. "You can fight it."

"Yeah. Dale said I could, but then I'd be in default of a court order and could be arrested. And then what would happen to Sydney?" he asked looking at her. "And in the end, he said, I'd still have to do it."

Destiny thought for a moment. "Tell her that she has to have it for school."

"Lie?"

"Absolutely," she insisted. "Then she'll never have to know why."

"Unless…" he began.

Destiny's hand moved to his chest, then to his face, and

she turned him to face her. "She'll never have to know," she smiled sweetly.

Bill looked down at her hand. "What happened to the protective barrier?"

"Pity touch," she grinned.

Bill rolled back to his side, his hand moving to hers. "*And* she has a sense of humor, too."

"It's part of the chastity training."

Bill's smile grew. "I love you."

"I love you, too."

He stood and looked down at her, eyeing her from head to toe and back. He contemplated what he was walking away from and shook his head.

"Good night," he said, walking to the door. He opened it and stepped outside, then reached in and checked the doorknob and the lock. He looked back up at her. "I suggest you lock this."

"I'll be fine," she offered. "I trust you."

"Lock the door," he reiterated. "*I* don't trust me." He disappeared through the door and pulled it closed behind him, wriggling the doorknob for effect.

Destiny smiled to herself, pulling the pillow to her chest and hugging it. She could feel his hands all over her, his tongue in her mouth, his breath on her neck. Suddenly, she heard the doorknob rattle again, and her eyes popped open. She slid off the bed and walked to the door. It rattled again.

"You there?" Bill whispered against the door.

"Right here."

"I needed to tell you..." he murmured, hesitating. "I *am* going to propose to you, Destiny. In a way that you deserve." Destiny's hand went to the knob. "And I'm going to spend the rest of my life showing you how much you mean to me. Showing you that I love you more than life itself."

"I love you, too," she said through the door. She felt the knob turn slightly in her hand. If she let him in, she knew she wouldn't let him leave. She heard him sigh, and then he wiggled the doorknob one more time.

"Just testing," he said. "Good night."

Destiny grinned to herself and dropped her cheek to the door. "Good night," she whispered to the locked door, knowing it was as close as they would get tonight.

Chapter Forty-Nine

THE PRELIMINARY HEARING STARTED LATE. It would be the first time she would have to face Winston since he showed up at Lisa's, and considering what she'd been through, her attorney wasn't sure it was a good idea. The prosecutor, however, was thrilled. He thought if Winston knew that his victims weren't afraid of showing up in court, he would be intimidated. Dr. Villarreal was on the fence about the whole appearance, ultimately leaving it up to her and not trying to persuade her one way or the other. The civil case was to make a point, and to drive that point home. Winston's failed attempt to do harm to Destiny and remove her from the equation only strengthened the prosecutors and Destiny's case against him. The DA's goal was still wanted to try him to the fullest extent of the law, and make an example of him. Destiny was their star witness, but, not their only witness.

She looked around the room, noting two other women there who sat solemnly on their own. One of them, Ginger, Rita's former secretary, sat at the end of her row, closest to the wall. Destiny stood and made her way toward her. When Ginger saw her, she rose and nodded. Destiny hugged her and squeezed her hand. "You okay?" she asked.

Ginger nodded.

Immediately a man from her legal team came over and stood beside them. "You two can't be talking," he said, taking Destiny by the arm and leading her away. She looked over her shoulder and smiled at Ginger, who smiled faintly in return.

Destiny sat back down. Suddenly, she felt someone standing next to her.

"Mind if I join you?"

Destiny looked up and smiled. "What are you doing here?"

"There's no way I'm going to let you do this on your own," Bill said, smiling down at her. She moved over as he sat beside her. He looked around the courtroom before looking back at her and taking her hand. "Hand holding allowed, remember," he winked.

Destiny smiled as she looked forward. When Winston entered the room, her smile faded. She stared at him until his eyes met hers. He smiled at her. The gesture alone made her ill, but she held his stare, refusing to look away. Destiny felt Bill squeeze her hand tighter, and it gave her confidence.

The bailiff announced the judge as he entered, and the court was in session. He listened to motions by the defense, which were all denied. Both attorneys approached and haggled over legal details that no one else could hear. Every so often Winston would look her way, but she averted her eyes. She didn't want to face him again. It only disgusted her more. Destiny could hear the attorneys arguing, and the defense attorney pointed in her direction. She felt her face get hot. A moment later her attorney walked over to her and said that the judge wanted to talk to her. He told her not to worry. It was simply intimidation by the defense. Was she okay with talking to him? Destiny swallowed hard and then nodded.

The walk to the front of the room felt so lonely and long. She had to walk right past Winston and his smug airs. Destiny was determined not to look at him at all if she was able to avoid it. She sat quietly until the bailiff asked her to raise her right hand. She raised her hand and swore to tell the truth, the whole truth and nothing but the truth.

The defense attorney asked her name and where she worked, then pointed to Ginger and asked if Destiny knew her. Destiny said that she did. He asked if she had spoken to Ginger since the case had begun, before today. She said she hadn't. Then they asked her if she'd spoken to her today, asked her what they talked about and why she approached her. When Destiny had answered all their questions, they reworded them, twisting them in a more divisive manner. They accused her of approaching Ginger deliberately to discuss the case and sway her testimony. They asked her the same question almost ten different ways. Her attorney continued to object, stating that the questions had been asked and answered. The more they repeated their questions, the more melodramatic the defense attorney behaved. Finally, Winston's lawyer stated he was through with the witness and allowed Destiny to return to her seat.

Bill took her hand and squeezed. "You did good," he whispered from the side of his lips.

Destiny smiled.

"Hey, while you were up there, did you ask the judge

about what we talked about last night?" he whispered again. Destiny elbowed him in the side, fighting a smile.

The lawyers approached the bench again, argued some more, and then the judge called for a short recess. Winston lowered his head as his attorney spoke into his ear, and he cast a glance Destiny's direction. Only, this time, he wasn't smiling. She held his gaze again, refusing to look away first. He turned away quickly. Destiny could tell he was rattled, by his demeanor. She glanced to the end of her row, and Ginger was no longer there. Destiny hoped she hadn't been deterred by what had happened. The defense's tactics were meant not only to intimidate her but also any of the other witnesses in the room.

The judge clapped his gavel, and her attorney stood immediately and came to her. He leaned over and patted her hand. "You did great."

"How does it look right now?" she asked.

"His attorney requested a meeting, so we'll see."

"So, is this guy going to do hard time?" Bill asked, concerned for Destiny if he got out.

"Oh, yeah, that's a no-brainer at this point," the balding man assured him. "It's just a matter of how long, and that all depends on this little lady here and the other witnesses."

"And the evidence?" Destiny asked.

"And the evidence," he concurred. "Look, don't stress yourself out over a trial until we get past the grand jury."

Destiny smiled slightly and nodded.

"Thank you," Bill offered, somewhat relieved. Then he turned to Destiny. "How about lunch?" His phone rang at that instant. He looked at it and then quickly answered it.

"That would be nice," she replied flatly, as Bill held up his hand to quiet her. She turned to pick up her jacket and dropped her phone, which fell over the first bench and by the railing that separated the front of the court from the back. The attorneys conferred at their tables, while Winston sat, his head hanging at the defense's table. Bill was still on his phone, so she stepped around him, moved to the railing and leaned over to pick up her phone. Only, a hand picked it up before she arrived and held it out to her. Destiny found herself looking into Winston's eyes, just inches from hers.

"Hi, Destiny," Winston cooed softly.

Destiny froze. She felt her skin crawl at just the sound of his voice.

"Miss me?" he whispered.

Destiny could feel her heart racing, and she couldn't move. Somehow she couldn't hold his stare this time.

A moment later Bill stepped up beside her and grabbed her arm, pulling her away from Winston. He could feel her shaking. Bill glared hatefully into Winston's eyes, looked down and saw Destiny's phone in the man's hand.

Destiny's attorney turned and instantly saw that Winston was interacting with Destiny and Bill. He turned to the bailiff, who was speaking to the judge. "Bailiff!" he yelled, pointing toward Winston.

Winston held out the phone to Bill, a smug smile on his face. As Bill reached for it, Winston leaned toward him and said, "She's a sweet piece. I hope you're enjoying it as much as I did."

Winston's attorneys turned the moment Bill took the phone and realized from Bill's face that something was about to happen. They lunged to grab their client, but they weren't fast enough.

Bill tried not to react to Winston's taunting gaze, but it was too late. All the anger and frustration of the past few months had culminated at this point, and all reason, all sanity left him. He dropped his coat and in one swift motion punched Winston in his not-so-completely-healed nose, breaking it again. He was about to jump over the barrier when her attorney, the bailiff and one of the other men in the audience grabbed his arms to prevent him from reaching over the banister and pummeling the man.

"Dammit!" Winston screamed, in apparent pain; his new $3000 suit ruined. Not to mention he would need a reasonable repair of his nose, again, at county expense. "I want him arrested."

Destiny, who had fallen on the first bench in the melee, reached up and grabbed Bill's arm. She tried to get him to face her while everyone else had their hands on him, pulling him in other directions. She looked at him perplexed. "What are you doing?"

The bailiff held Bill back. "What just happened?" he asked.

"He baited me," Bill defended, as they walked Winston from the courtroom, his hands and face bloodied.

"What did he say?" he asked.

Bill took Destiny into his arms and exhaled loudly. "Doesn't matter."

"Yes, it does, Son. You just assaulted another man in front of witnesses. In a courtroom."

Destiny stood by Bill and took his hand. "What does that mean?"

"It means, that they are going to arrest him."

"Arrest him?"

Bill realized his stupidity. He dropped his head and then handed his phone and his coat, his ring, his watch and everything in his pockets to Destiny. He gave her his phone password. "Call Dale and ask him to meet me at the jail." He looked down, ashamed. "I'm sorry. Please don't tell Sydney," he pleaded.

Destiny nodded.

A moment later, an officer walked over and began talking to her attorney, the bailiff, other witnesses, and finally, Bill.

And then they arrested him.

Chapter Fifty

CONSUELO SLID over in the California king bed and kissed her shoulder multiple times, the simple act bringing goose bumps to the surface of her soft skin. His hand slid down her arm to her naked, shapely hip, her buttocks and back. He usually traveled with her when she was in the States. Sometimes even when she wasn't, depending on how bored he was. He always kept it exciting, surprising her when she least expected it. Tonight, he ordered room service in, after which he massaged her with exotic oils, teasing her with every touch before he made love to her on the bedroom floor.

They were traveling in first class when they met, only because anything else, other than a private jet, was beneath her. He had dark, penetrating eyes. Eyes that stripped her bare, undressing her to her very soul, seeing her in a way she never felt anyone had seen her before. They shared a glass of wine; they shared dreams and fantasies. Five hours later, they shared a bed. Both were married, so they kept their affair discreet. It was a casual thing. But to Justine, he was like a drug. Consuelo was like the piece of candy or the cookie you were forbidden to eat when you were a child—the one you would sneak and hide away before slowly savoring it. Sleeping with Uri was still good, but there were things you just couldn't do with your husband.

So, they saw each other when they could, mostly meeting in countries other than their own, to ensure utmost discretion. Like her, his spouse was the one with all the money. They both had prenups with lots of conditions and deadlines, the first of hers looming by their tenth anniversary—a child. She had just had her Implanon removed the day after she had arrived in Austin, knowing that she had to be pregnant by the end of the year. Her arm was still sore. But now, she had a dilemma; maybe she *wouldn't* have to be pregnant again.

Timing was everything, and she was quickly running out of it. Once she'd met Sydney, she knew. She was certain Uri was the father. That's why she had paid extra to have her personal attorney attend to the legal matters at an expedited rate. Within hours of his arrival home, Bill had been served and notified of the blood test requirement. Of course, the paperwork had to be manipulated only slightly, since Uri was technically not American. Not to mention he knew nothing about it. If luck were on her side, she'd have his daughter, at least legally, before the deadline. Justine had already laid the preliminary groundwork. And if Uri believed the story she was weaving—and he *always* believed her stories—then she knew he'd fight like a badger for his daughter. And he had the money and the inclination to do so. Bill wouldn't have a chance.

Justine was a noise person. She didn't watch television; she usually just liked having it on so that she didn't feel so alone when she was alone. Only it wasn't Justine who turned it on today. Consuelo, Connie to his closest friends, and to her, was already up making Justine his famous nutritious breakfast smoothie. She walked into the kitchen and grabbed a bagel from a bag on the counter. Justine cut her eyes at him. Connie talked healthily but indulged in crap. Justine had asked him not to bring junk food into any of the places where they stayed. She had a hard time resisting it herself, so it irritated her when he ignored her wishes.

When she heard Bill's name, she turned suddenly, walked back into the room, and hit rewind on the cable remote. She dropped into the comfortable chair in shock, and when the report was over, a small smile crept onto her lips. Justine couldn't have been more pleased. She picked up the phone and called her private investigator, who had been following Bill since she arrived in Austin. Why hadn't he called her with the news about which she had inquired? Justine ignored his lame excuse until he explained that he was at the courthouse, where he had been digging up information as to why Bill and his mistress were there. She instructed him to continue digging and then she dialed her attorney. She crossed her long, tanned legs and that Cheshire Cat grin appeared, pasted across her smug face. "I couldn't have scripted this better myself."

Chapter Fifty-One

BILL WAS out on bail by dinner. Because it was a public hearing there had been plenty of witnesses, *and* there had been plenty of press because of Winston's family name. So, like it or not, he made the news. Sydney wasn't allowed to watch the news, but her friends' parents did. Within five minutes of the report, there were four phone calls in a row on her cell phone, asking her if her dad was okay. Bill had to break down and tell her what he'd done. She took it well. In fact, she told him she was proud of him for standing up for Destiny. That was little consolation for the attorney's fees he was about to incur, not to mention his bond, the publicity, and a civil suit that Winston would probably file at some point.

During dinner Destiny was quiet, pensive. The press had already been calling the house. She was concerned about Bill, about Sydney, and about his business. For the first time since taking on her new job, she let all the calls to the Kemper House go straight to voice mail so that she could screen them. Later, when she heard one of the female guests discussing Bill's arrest with her husband,

Destiny could stand the innuendo no more. Discreetly, she took the woman aside and explained what had happened and why they were court in the first place. There was no more gossip from that point on.

Andy and Lisa both showed up at almost the same time, talking over each other until Destiny assured them that Bill's and her attorney were taking care of everything. Destiny pulled her brother aside, told him about the blood tests the following morning and then asked Andy if he knew anyone at the testing facility. He did and promised that the lab had a top notch reputation. If anyone could get the information before the attorneys did, he would, but he told her not to hold her breath. Not only was it confidential information, but it was a crime to attempt even to get it. He kissed her and made her promise to have dinner with him on Christmas, as they'd done since her family's death. She promised she would, but they'd talk about the time later.

Lisa wasn't as easily appeased. When dinner was over, and the guests were all checked in, Bill took Sydney aside to talk to her about the blood tests the following morning, while Destiny filled her friend in on the past week. She told her about Justine's pop-in visit, Bill's meltdown with the phone, and finished up with the blow-by-blow details from the courtroom.

"Wow!"

"Which part?" Destiny asked, cryptically.

"All of it!" Lisa exclaimed. "And you stayed here because you thought it would make your life *less* complicated?"

"Uh, if you remember correctly, *you* brought me here. And then *you* abandoned me."

"*You* have a car, and *you* could have left anytime *you* wanted to."

Destiny looked down at her hands, then replied meekly. "I stayed here to help Bill."

"Uh-huh. Is there something I'm missing here? Something you're leaving out," her friend asked coyly.

Destiny averted her eyes.

Lisa looked at her questioningly, then sighed. "Okay, I'm guessing there's a *lot* you're leaving out."

"There's a lot I'm leaving out." Destiny finally faced her. She held up her hand to prevent Lisa from grilling her further. "But I'm asking you to give me some space… for now. I'm feeling a little overwhelmed."

"A little?"

"Okay, a lot overwhelmed."

Lisa pouted but hugged Destiny anyway. "He never gives you more than you can handle."

Destiny looked down sadly, wringing her hands in her lap, a tear sliding down her cheek. "Really? With everything I just told you and everything that's happened, you can *still* say that?"

"Honey, you're still missing the big picture."

Destiny wiped her tear. "I wish I knew what the big picture *was*. I wish I knew what I was supposed to do."

"Dee, Honey, you have all these people giving you advice. But, you're asking the wrong people. You need to ask the one with the answers."

Destiny looked up at her.

"There's only one reason you're still standing," she raised her eyebrows, pointing upward. "It's called prayer."

"I stopped praying a long time ago."

"Who said I was talking about you?" Lisa smiled sweetly. She took her friend's hand and leaned forward. "Do you trust me?"

Destiny looked at her, tears in her eyes. After a moment, she nodded slightly and leaned toward her friend.

"Trust *Him*," she whispered.

Destiny shook her head and shrugged. She glanced toward the library where Bill was talking with Sydney. He sat beside his precious daughter, his arm wrapped around her. She looked a little sad. But she nodded and hugged her dad, wrapping herself around his neck. Bill held his daughter tight and closed his eyes. Destiny watched them together and smiled sadly.

For the first time in a long time, she thought of Phillip and Rhett. She could see them together, Phillip holding his son. Her son. Tears filled her eyes. She had spent so many days… so many nights, trying to forget because it was too painful to remember. It had been so long since she had been able to picture them. Putting them out of her mind had been easier, but they were never really out of her mind, or out of her heart. Oh, how her heart ached for Phillip's wisdom. Oh, how her arms ached to hold her son, just one more time.

Suddenly, she looked back up at Bill and Sydney. They weren't her family. But she wanted them to be. Bill looked despondent. Gradually his eyes lifted and met hers. Her heart beat faster in her chest. Those eyes spoke to her, calling to her, somehow breaking through the impenetrable barrier of the circumstances under which they met and the distance between them that now was just a matter of yards. Bill smiled and for a brief moment, she felt like she was home.

Chapter Fifty-Two

BILL HADN'T BEEN himself since the arrest. There's something about being fingerprinted and put into a jail cell that simply humbles a person. His attorney assured him he would work through the details and that he'd try to bargain for community service as a plea deal. Bill would more than likely have to pay a fine as well. No one discussed a civil suit, but they were sure that would come. Not to mention that looming heavily on his mind were the paternity test results. And on top of everything, there was still the press hovering and hounding him. And this was just the first day! When he felt the pressure getting to him, he finally called Charlie, not just for advice, but for help. He had three requests of his uncle.

Uncle Charlie was an ex-United States Marshall and worked specifically with WITSEC, or the Witness Protection Program. He had plenty of connections; *deep* connections, deeper connections than Winston had deep pockets. Within an hour, there were armed off duty plain clothes police officers watching the bed and breakfast on a twenty-four-hour rotation, compliments of Charlie—who was calling in lots of favors. The second request Charlie had taken care of before Bill even asked. After Bill's visit to the farm, Charlie had hired several private investigators to check Justine out. *Extensively.*

Bill's third request was the first thing he had asked when they had talked previously at the farm. Bill was seriously concerned that the paternity tests might not come back in his favor. If that were the case, he wanted to disappear. He and Sydney *and* Destiny. Charlie reluctantly promised to help if needed, though he reiterated that he thought that was a bad idea. Bill gave him the address of a place in Canada where he wanted to go. Charlie explained to him that it usually didn't work that way.

Then Bill made one last phone call. He called his attorney and told him to set up a meeting with Justine. Dale spent the better part of an hour laying out an incredible defense and trying to talk his client out of such a meeting. In the end, Bill simply told him to do it. He didn't tell Destiny; she would only try to talk him out of it as well. He thought it best not to tell Charlie, either. Bill needed to do this on his own. Although he didn't care if he ever saw her again, she was Sydney's mother, and he felt they needed to talk face to face.

After he'd made all his phone calls and the guests were all in their rooms, he tucked Sydney into bed and peeked out the front door. It was close to midnight, and the streets were mostly clear. There were only a few late night strollers wandering through the decorated streets. He put on his jacket and stepped onto the porch, blowing his breath into the air in front of him. He shoved his hands into his pockets for warmth. It had taken so many years and so much work to make the Kemper House what it was. But in the end, it was only a house. What he'd made it was a home. But that would be wherever he and his family were, and that could be anywhere.

The door opened behind him, and he stepped out of the way. Destiny smiled as she walked over to him. "Wanted a little privacy, eh?" she asked, pulling on her gloves.

He smiled and reached for her hand, pulling her to his side. "Nah," he replied. Bill clapped his hands together and rubbed, and blew on them, cupping them against his mouth. "I haven't really had a chance to enjoy all this," he said, waving his hand. He turned to her. "Want to take a walk?"

Destiny grinned. "Sure." She wrapped her scarf around her face and took his hand as they walked down the stairs together. The Kemper House and its properties cornered the street, so they walked across the street and took a left. "I've never been down this street when it's been all lit up," she commented, her voice muffled by her scarf as she looked around.

"Yeah, we started all this," he said, with pride. "We went all out decorating the first year we opened. And slowly everyone else on the block followed suit. Then the next street, then the next. A lot of older houses on these three streets were bought, then converted to businesses. So when traffic started backing up and there were some major traffic jams, not to mention heavy foot traffic, the city decided it was time to close things off and now..." Bill held his hands out wide.

"You *should* be proud of everything you've done here."

"I am," he replied a little sadly. "But I didn't do it by myself. The community, the business owners, and home-owners all came together. We all did it together." Bill sighed. "I just hate to think that after everything, I could have ruined all this, that I could have hurt what we've built here."

Destiny slid her arm through his. "Oh, I don't think that could ever happen, Bill."

He looked down, at her arm, then up to her. "Relaxing the boundaries?" He could see the smile in her eyes.

"It's cold. I call exception for cold weather."

"Ah," he smiled back. "Why not?" he added looking back down at his feet, shuffling as he walked. They arrived at the end of the street and crossed it before taking a left and walking back toward the house. They walked in silence for the rest of the trip, making the block back to the wrought iron gate at the front of the walkway. Bill turned to her and took her hands. He looked into her eyes and opened his mouth as if to say something, but then changed his mind; drawing in a deep breath. Destiny smiled as he turned and offered his arm to her. They walked back up the stairs and sat on the top step.

After a few moments of silence, he stared straight ahead. "I'm sorry about today," he said. "I hope I didn't make things worse, but I'm so afraid I did."

"Bill…" she began.

"No, please, let me finish." He rubbed his hands together again and blew into them to defrost them. "I will make everything right. By you and by Sydney." He opened his arms wide and added, "By all these fine folks," he said aloud to the quiet neighborhood. Sincerely, he turned to her. "I promise." He nudged her.

Destiny smiled behind her scarf. After a moment, she nudged him back.

"Had enough?" he asked, stuffing his hands into his pockets.

Destiny laughed. "Yup. Freezing."

They jumped up and walked hurriedly to the door.

Once inside, they hung their jackets on the antique over-sized coat rack. Bill took her hand. "Walk you home?"

Destiny smiled, motioning with her head for him to follow. They walked up the stairs quietly, occasionally glancing at each other. When they arrived at her door, they stood facing each other. "This is me."

Bill glanced inside. "Nice room. Looks more like a broom closet."

"Yeah," she replied with a sigh. "Came with the job. What can I say, it was this or the pool house."

"Pool house, huh?" he wrinkled his lips. "Man, your employer sounds cheap."

Destiny tilted her head. "No, actually, he's a pretty cool guy."

"Cool?" he chuckled. "I don't think anyone has referred to me as cool since high school. Especially not my eight-year-old daughter."

"Nine-year-old," she corrected him.

"That's right," he smiled, his finger to his chin. "I do think I remember something about a birthday party. I think I saw you there. Your hair was a different color."

Destiny smiled.

"I love it when you smile," he said, stepping toward her.

"Really?" she grinned. "What else do you like about me?"

Bill took another step toward her. "I love the way you make me feel when I'm around you."

"And?"

Bill took one last step to her, leaning toward her as he took a deep breath. "I love the way you smell." His hand moved to her hair, and he brushed it with his fingers. After toying with her hair, they moved to her cheeks. "I love the way you feel." He took her face carefully into his hands, leaned in, and kissed her. "And I definitely love the way you taste." He kissed her once more.

Destiny closed her eyes and felt herself melt into his arms again as they wrapped around her. When they parted, she held up her finger. "I think I should go," she gasped, pointing inside.

Bill drew in a deep breath. "Good idea." He exhaled. "I don't think I could handle another night like last night."

Destiny stepped inside her door. "Thank you for walking me to my room."

"Not a problem. Didn't want anything to happen to you." He looked around and lowered his voice. "You never know who might be lurking around the corners."

Destiny dropped her head, cutting her eyes at him. "Good night."

"Good night." He tapped on the door knob. "Don't forget." Destiny closed the door, slowly separating them once more. He reached down and wriggled the door knob. It was locked. He grinned to himself, as he spoke to the door, "Just testing."

Chapter Fifty-Three

THE FOLLOWING MORNING, they prepared breakfast as usual for their guests. And yet everyone seemed to be distracted, their smiles forced. Bill and Sydney were supposed to report to the lab by noon. As the time neared, Bill didn't know if he could follow through. He'd awoken that morning determined to fight the court order, but a last minute call to Dale was sobering. They talked through his options, and together they agreed his choices were limited. Then Bill reminded him he wanted to see Justine. Her attorney hadn't returned Dale's call, but Dale promised to call Bill as soon as he did. Bill stressed that he wanted to see her *before* the paternity test results were released; his attorney stressed once more that he still didn't think it was a good idea.

Although the court order specified they arrive by noon, Dale had instructed Bill to wait until just before five o'clock. It was Friday, and from his experience, that alone would delay the test by three more days since the labs didn't work on the weekend, which would buy Dale and his client extra time to determine how best to fight

Justine. At four fifty-nine, Bill, and his daughter walked into the lab. Sydney repeatedly insisted that she didn't remember any paperwork requiring lab work for school. But in the end, she reluctantly gave in, on the condition that Destiny come with her and hold her hand throughout the process. Destiny said she'd be honored to do so.

Afterward, they went to Twisted Root again. Though it was too cold for mini golf, they played anyway—a specific condition of Sydney's agreement to give up her blood. Then they went home and spent the rest of the evening baking and decorating Christmas cookies to hand out when they caroled on the porch again that weekend. Christmas was just days away, and yet, all of a sudden, there were so many other things distracting them from doing what he and Sydney had come to consider part of their family tradition.

Bill wanted as much normal as possible for his daughter. He looked at their tree. They had decorated it together. This year she had picked purple, again, since for the past four years that was *her* color. So there were white and purple round glass ornaments, with a scattering of silver. There were ribbons and lights, and a beautiful angel adorning the top. There were also a variety of ornaments that didn't match anything, ones she had made over the years, and ones they had bought together that were dated, representing every year since Sydney was born.

There was so much more he wanted for his daughter, now and for her future. He wanted her to go to college, to get married and have children. In that order, of course. He wanted to be a part of her story as long as he was alive. There were dozens of presents under the tree, all for Sydney. He still had one more thing to get, but now, he wasn't sure. If he could just see the results early, he would know what to do. And what if they showed that he wasn't…? How could he tell her? *What* would he tell her?

Bill had already begun to work the details out in his head. He only needed a day to disappear. He would clean out his bank accounts, all of them. Charlie had enough contacts to get them all new identifications, and Bill would pay whatever it took. He hadn't changed his will since Sydney was born, so he had asked Dale to amend it that morning. These were details no father wants to think about, but it was his responsibility to protect his daughter's interests. Bill dropped his head into his hands. He couldn't believe he even had to consider such things. How could everything have fallen apart so fast?

Bill stepped to the tree, his hand reaching for a small unique ornament. It was one Sydney had made in kindergarten—a clear ornament with white confetti, a little fake sprig of a pine tree with a berry, and her picture inside. He smiled fondly at the image. She had a toothless, forced grin, her bangs hanging down to her eyebrows, her hair pulled back by some elastic twisty-thingy, as she used to call it. He shook it slightly so that the fake snow settled perfectly around the picture. He hung it back onto the tree and smiled sadly. His daughter was the most precious thing in his life. He couldn't lose her. He wouldn't lose her.

And what about Destiny? He wanted to ask her to marry him. Now was he going to ask her just to disappear with him and his daughter? How reasonable was that? Bill rubbed his forehead. And what happened if she said no? He felt a headache coming on. How could he leave her now? He was madly in love with her.

Bill looked at his watch. Owen, Sheray, and the rest of the crew would be serving fish about now. This made two weeks in a row he hadn't gone to the senior center. Because he was a creature of habit, somehow, not going, made his life feel out of kilter. He missed the routine; the normalcy of going every Friday night and serving the Veterans and what it meant.

His phone rang suddenly, and he hurriedly pulled it from his pocket. Dale's personal cell phone number scrolled across the screen. Bill listened while Dale talked. Justine had agreed to meet. They were supposed to meet in an hour at what he assumed was her hotel's bar. Dale reiterated that he didn't think it was a good idea. When Bill refused to take his advice, Dale suggested that he take someone else, just in case something went wrong. When Dale finally hung up, Bill merely stared at the phone and sighed before sliding it back into his pocket. He looked at his watch and walked back to the kitchen where Sydney and Destiny were finishing the last of the cookies.

"Hey, Daddy," Sydney said, excitedly, flecks of blue, green, red and yellow icing on her face and in her hair.

"Hey, Sweetie," he said, kissing the top of her head. "Wow, those are some beautiful cookies. You're an excellent decorator."

Sydney brushed back her hair with her gloved wrist, swiping another streak of yellow icing through her black hair. "Actually, Destiny did that one. These are mine," she said, pointing to two dozen that weren't as professionally iced.

"Those are the ones I was talking about, Sweetie!" he insisted. He looked at Destiny. "I've got to run an errand." He reached over and stroked Sydney's hair. "I might be awhile." "Can you hold down the fort until I get back?" Bill forced a smile.

"Everything okay?"

"Of course," he insisted, looking away, hoping she couldn't read his eyes.

"I'll bet Daddy's going shopping." Sydney smiled slyly, without looking up from the cookie she was decorating.

"You don't think I have enough presents under the tree?"

"There can *never* be enough presents under the tree," she beamed, brushing back her hair again.

Bill leaned over and kissed her on the head. "I fear, my child, that I have done what I promised myself I would never do."

"What's that?"

"Spoil you rotten."

"Oh, Daddy. I'm not spoiled."

"Of course not." Bill rolled his eyes and smiled at Destiny. He then motioned with his head for her to follow. He kissed his daughter once on her cheek. "Love you, Syd."

"Love you, too, Daddy."

"Be right back." Destiny took off her apron and washed her hands, before walking him to the front door.

Bill slid on his coat. "I don't know how long I'll be," he added. "Look, if anything…" he began, then looked down, his fingers fumbling with the zipper. "With everything going on, I left a list of phone numbers on the dresser. Just in case."

Destiny narrowed her brow. "In case of what?"

Bill zipped his jacket. "I don't know. Just in case." He forced a reassuring smile. "And I gave Dale and Uncle Charlie your number, in the event they can't reach me. I hope that's alright."

Destiny searched his face. "Are you sure you're okay?"

"I'm fine." Bill was finding it harder to lie to her than he thought it would be. He took her face into his hands and leaned in, kissing her gently. "God, I love you."

Destiny smiled. "I love you, too."

Bill dropped his forehead to hers. "See you in a little bit.

"I'll wait up," she grinned, mischievously.

Bill kissed her once more before he walked out the front door. Destiny watched him through the antique lace curtains, after which she returned to her kitchen duties.

"I think Daddy likes you," Sydney remarked as she piped white icing onto a green Christmas tree.

"Do you?" Destiny asked, putting her apron back on. "Well, I kind of like him, too." As she slid on her gloves, she asked, "Has he said anything to you?"

"No," Sydney said, casually. "But a girl can tell these things."

"Really?" she asked, drawing out her response. "So, how would you feel about that? If he did… like me?"

"I'd tell him, 'it's about time!'" she beamed.

"Yeah. About time." She grinned to herself as she decorated the back of Sydney's hand with yellow icing.

"Hey!" Sydney exclaimed, turning and piping icing onto the back of Destiny's hand.

A small icing war began. Ten minutes later, when an armistice agreement was declared, there was icing all over their faces, arms, and hands; not to mention the floor and the countertop. All of a sudden, Destiny grabbed Sydney from behind and lifted her up, holding down her arms so that she couldn't ice her anymore.

"I love you," Destiny whispered into her ear.

Sydney turned in her arms. "I love you, too," she said excitedly, hugging her neck. She slid from her arms and started decorating another cookie. "Why don't you have any pictures of your family in your room?"

Destiny froze, the question so random and so unexpected.

"Don't you miss them?" Sydney asked. Her innocent eyes tried to hold Destiny's, but she kept looking away.

Destiny felt her eyes welling with tears. She swallowed hard, her heart racing. "Yes," she said weakly. "I do miss them." She didn't even feel the words leave her mouth, but she heard herself say them, and then the tears fell. She turned as she wiped them away.

"I miss my mom, and I haven't even met her," Sydney said. "I have her picture in my room, next to my bed, so that I'll never forget her."

Destiny sniffed, wiped her cheeks and turned back to the young girl as she put her arms around her, watching her as she decorated another cookie. "I've seen that picture, Sweetie. Your mom is quite lovely."

"Do you think she thinks about me?" Sydney asked, looking up at her. "I mean do you think she misses me?"

Destiny smiled down at her. "I know she does," she said. "I'll bet she misses you every day, too," she added, squeezing her harder, before kissing her on the forehead. Sydney turned and hugged her again. Suddenly Destiny felt Sydney's hands on her head.

"You just put icing on my hair, didn't you?" she asked, reaching behind her head. Blue icing colored her hand when she brought it forward.

Sydney shrugged and giggled.

Destiny pulled off her gloves backward over her hands, causing them to snap against her skin. She grabbed Sydney and smeared yellow icing on her face. What ensued was another playful icing fight that could only be remedied by a bubble bath and lots of shampoo. Destiny tickled Sydney and swung her around in her arms, finding a perfect kinship that she had been missing for a very, very long time.

Chapter Fifty-Four

BILL ALMOST DIDN'T RECOGNIZE her at first, in her sun hat and expensive Italian dress, looking so refined, so sophisticated, beautiful. But she was always beautiful. Somehow, as he looked closer, she still looked like she did ten years ago. Bill often wondered how he'd feel if he ever saw her again, whether he'd be angry or hurt or maybe even if he would have other feelings toward her like he used to. But he felt nothing. No, that wasn't true. He felt sadness, grief for the time she'd missed with Sydney. Sadness that Justine didn't even know her daughter, and that her daughter didn't know her.

Justine turned and smiled when she saw him, but it wasn't a good-to-see-you smile. It was more a smile of arrogance, with an air of nobility, as though she were looking down on him. Bill sat on the bar stool beside her and turned to face the bartender. He didn't usually drink, but he felt today, *especially* now, he needed one. The bartender poured him a shot of Weller, as he turned to his ex-wife.

"I don't think I've ever seen you drink," Justine said, sipping on her stinger.

Bill didn't want to appear weak. She always told him he was weak. "I don't. Usually."

"I was surprised when you asked to see me." Justine turned toward him and crossed her legs, her skirt sliding to the top of her well-toned thighs. She put a slender cigarette between her lips and sat there, waiting for someone else to light it. After only a moment, the bartender reached over and lit it for her. She didn't even acknowledge him as if he was expected to attend to her, so she didn't owe him anything. She blew the smoke away from Bill. "She's beautiful," Justine remarked off-handedly, glancing at her nails.

"She is." Bill toyed with his drink, as though waiting until the moment he would need it for courage. "And she's smart, one of the brightest in her class."

"I was never really that good in school." Justine sighed, then slowly sipped her drink. "So, she couldn't have gotten her smarts from me."

"Why are you here, Justine?"

"I'm here to see my daughter. To let her know how much I love her and miss her. And to introduce her to her *real* father."

Bill knocked back the drink and slid the glass toward the bartender. "I'm her father," Bill stated emphatically.

Justine motioned to the bartender for another drink. "That's yet to be determined," she replied, facing away from him.

"You left her, remember? You walked away and never looked back."

"You're wounded, so this is you striking back."

Bill shook his head. "This isn't about me. It's about Sydney. *Our* daughter."

"*My* daughter needs her mother."

Bill shook his head as his fingers traced the rim of the shot glass. "You've always been welcome here, Justine." Bill spoke as calmly as he could. "So, why now? Did you just wake up one morning and realize that you missed your daughter? What is this? I'd like to understand what's going on here."

Justine turned to him. "What's going on is that I knew deep in my heart that leaving all those years ago was the best thing for my daughter. Our relationship was illusory, and it wasn't the best thing for my child. Or for me."

"And yet you left her here."

"Let's go upstairs where we can talk." Justine slid off the chair, "Somewhere more private."

Bill hesitated, then downed his second shot before standing. It was probably best to relocate since he was beginning to get angry and didn't want to cause a scene. Justine didn't wait for him to answer, she just sashayed with graceful elegance toward the elevator. Bill tossed enough cash onto the counter to pay for both of their drinks and followed her. He wasn't surprised at all when she pressed the top floor button. He'd heard she married money. After Justine had left he never tried to find her, he didn't go after her. For a few years, her mother would call or come by, and casually mention how well Justine was doing. She had married an Italian, and they lived in Venice. But he never inquired further. It was too painful to think she had moved on so easily, to think that she could walk away. Not just from him, but especially her daughter. And *never* look back.

When they arrived at her suite, Justine stepped off first, removing her sun hat and tossing it onto the cream sofa. She fluffed her hair before turning and smiling at him. "Be a dear and pour me a drink." Justine turned away, moving toward the expansive windows that overlooked the city.

Bill glanced around the room until he spied what looked like a gold Faberge egg with an eagle on top, sitting on a golden tray on the wood and glass coffee table, two glasses beside it. He pulled the gold-plated stopper and poured them each a drink. He hesitated only for a moment before carrying it to her, holding it out for her to take.

She looked at him indifferently, but smiled as she reached for the glass, her hand deliberately touching his. Tentatively, she took the glass from him and sipped from it. "Have you ever had Imperial before?" she asked, holding up her glass. "It's one of the best vodkas on the market. Twenty-five hundred a bottle." She looked back out the window. "Only the best."

"Justine, I—" he began.

"Don't you think she deserves the best, Bill?" Justine licked her lips.

"She has the best."

"Yes, but in Italy, she'll have the best schools."

"Her school *is* the best," he reiterated.

"Do they teach her two languages?"

"She's learning Spanish."

Justine scoffed. "You mean Mexican, the language of laborers. True Castilian Spanish is a finer language. But Italian, and Latin… those are languages that she can do something with."

"You do realize that Central American Spanish originated from Spain," he replied, annoyed.

Justine turned dismissively, moving away from him and waving him off with her hand as she moved gracefully to the sofa. She sat, then patted the place beside her. Bill sighed, as he walked to the couch facing her, on the other side of the table. Her smile was sly, her eyes twinkling with mischief. "I won't bite, Bill."

"Why are you doing this, Justine?" he asked, wringing his hands. "After all this time? Why now?"

"Why not?" she casually answered, as if it was her right. "You make it sound like I have an agenda."

"Don't you?" he said, matter-of-factly. "I knew you long enough to know that you didn't do anything without having a plan in place."

Justine stood and paced slowly, her red Christian Louboutin stilettos moving stealthily across the plush white carpet. "Let me play devil's advocate, here. Any court here will never deny a mother's plea to be with her daughter," she said, her back to him as she looked out the window again.

"You abandoned her."

"Mental duress," she said dramatically. "It happens all the time. Mental anguish."

Bill shook his head. "Mental anguish?" he scoffed. "Really? You expect anyone to believe that?"

Justine turned. "Not anyone, Bill. Just the judge," she replied coyly, her finger to her lip, while holding her glass. She could see he was hurt and confused. She walked to him and sat beside him, setting her glass on the table by his. Delicately, she put her hand on his knee. "Now, Bill, I know you want what's best for Sydney. You've had your time with her," she said, nonchalantly. "Now it's my turn."

Bill looked at her in shock. "Your turn? She's not a puppy, Justine." He shook his head and stood up. "You're welcome to see her anytime you want. You've always been welcome." He looked defiantly into her eyes. "But she's staying with me. She's my daughter."

"Is she?" Justine asked, standing next to him, her stilettos making her eye level with him. "That's yet to be determined," she said, her eyes narrowing with a hateful stare.

"She's mine."

"Now, who's acting like she's a puppy," she said smugly. He began to turn, and she put her hand on his arm. "Bill, if you haven't figured it out yet, I *always* get my way. All you're going to do is bankrupt yourself trying to fight Uri and me, and we'll still win."

Bill turned and grabbed her by her forearms. "Now let *me* tell *you* something. I don't care if it bankrupts me or if it kills me, if you think I'm just going to let her go without a fight, you're very mistaken. You may think you'll win because you have money, but you're not going to win this one."

Suddenly, Justine had fear in her eyes. "Ow!" she exclaimed, as the defiance returned. "Let go of me this instant."

Bill pushed her away as he released her so that she fell back onto the couch. If only his voice could evoke every emotion inside of him, he would scream at her. But he looked down at her and held her gaze. "You're not going to win!" Bill barked angrily. He turned and left the suite.

Justine stewed for a moment, watching him get onto the elevator. He stared at her determinedly, and she could only smile just as determinedly in return. After he had left, she rubbed her arms where he held her. Justine rose calmly and lit another cigarette as she walked back to the window. "Stupid little piss-ant. We'll see who wins." She walked to the counter, took out her cell phone, and dialed with her smoking hand. She tapped her shoe impatiently until he responded. "What do you have from the courthouse?" She waited for an answer, annoyed that he was giving her the long version.

She sighed dramatically. "Fine. Stay on it. I'm paying you for answers. So find me some," Justine snapped, and then punched the button to hang up the phone. As she paced back and forth, the elevator dinged, and she set her phone down. She stepped to the window and smiled to herself. Justine closed her eyes and imagined Connie's hands all over her, pleasuring her in ways no other man could. She felt the tentative kisses on her neck, and then she suddenly stood upright. She turned, stunned, but transforming her shock into a seductive smile as he stepped back.

"Uri!"

Chapter Fifty-Five

BILL BRUSHED BACK his daughter's hair, remembering. He didn't know what real love was until the nurse placed Sydney in his arms. There were tears in his eyes, stinging them. Bill couldn't believe that he wasn't her father. *Wouldn't* believe. It wasn't possible. And even if it was, he didn't care. He would steal her away, and they would live in Canada or somewhere else. They would start over. As long as there was breath in his body, he would never let her go.

The light from the hallway brightened as the door opened wider. He wiped his eyes and sniffed before turning. Destiny stood against the doorframe, arms crossed.

"I thought it was you." She smiled until she saw his tear-stained face. Her smiled faded. "I was getting worried," she whispered. Bill walked past her, down the hallway and into his room. She followed him to the doorway and sat sideways on the bench at the end of his bed. "Do you want to talk about it?"

Bill pulled out his suitcase and began taking clothes from his drawers and filling it.

"Are you going somewhere?"

"Yes, I am," he retorted. "I'm taking Sydney, and we're getting out of here."

Destiny felt like she'd just been punched. She rolled forward onto her hands in total shock.

"Justine's not going to give up. I could see it in her eyes."

"You went to see her?"

"Yeah," he sighed, resignedly. "I know I shouldn't have, but I thought if I could just reason with her… I should have remembered; there's no reasoning with Justine." He angrily stuffed everything he could fit into the case. "She has money and a powerful husband, and she's made it clear that she's not going to quit. It's not just about joint custody. She wants Sydney."

Destiny grabbed her head. "How can you just walk away?" Her heart was in her throat.

"Owen can run the Kemper House, or he can sell it. I don't really care."

Destiny bent over, feeling like she was going to be sick. Bill stopped packing and saw her rocking. He exhaled before going to her, kneeling before her. "Destiny, I want you to come with us." Bill took her hands in his, speaking as earnestly as he could. "We can start over. Together."

She looked at him, perplexed.

"I already talked to Charlie about it. He can get us new identifications, and we can start over."

Destiny couldn't believe what he was saying. The thought of losing them now was too much to bear. "You can't do this, Bill." Destiny pulled her hands from his. "If you run, they'll find you, and then what? They'll take her away from you because you'll be in jail."

"I have to try!"

"This is wrong." Destiny tried to be the voice of reason.

Bill threw his overnight bag across the room. "Then, what the hell am I supposed to do? Just stay here and let her take Sydney away!" he bellowed, tears in his eyes, no longer caring who heard him.

As he started to retrieve his bag, Destiny stepped in between him and the suitcase, holding his arms to prevent him from packing. He tried to move around her but stopped in frustration. Her hand moved to his face. "Not like this." She caressed his cheeks, pleading softly. "Not like this."

The clothes fell from his hands as he dropped his head to her shoulder and wept. Destiny pulled him to herself and stroked his head sweetly, compassionately. He looked at her. She forced a smile as she wiped his tears. "I'm right here." Destiny kissed him gently. "I'm right here." There was a knock on the front door, and she patted his cheek. "All the guests already checked in and are upstairs. Who could that be at this hour?"

"No telling," he replied.

"I'll get it." Destiny kissed him once more, then walked to the front door and peeked through the curtains. Two police officers stood on the front porch. She turned to see Bill standing in his doorway. Destiny opened the door and welcomed the men inside the entryway where they wouldn't be pummeled by the freezing elements that had blown in overnight. "May I help you?"

"We need to speak to Mr. William Ireland."

Bill walked toward them. "I'm Bill Ireland. Is there something I can do for you?"

"Do you know a Justine Aloetti?"

Bill and Destiny exchanged glances, as she took his hand.

"Yes. May I ask what this is about?"

"Did you see Mrs. Aloetti this afternoon?"

Bill hesitated a moment, but finally replied, "Yes, we met to discuss our daughter."

"We will need you to come downtown with us to answer some questions," one of the officers said firmly.

"I'm sorry. I don't understand."

"Mrs. Aloetti was assaulted this afternoon, and she claims you did it."

"*What?*" Bill exclaimed, shaking his head. "When I left her she was sipping expensive vodka and—"

"Daddy?"

Everyone turned to the young girl who was rubbing her eyes and walking toward them. Bill and Destiny moved toward her, but the officer held Bill's arm.

"Sir?"

"Just a minute," he said firmly, as he noted the severity of the officer's demeanor.

Destiny noted it as well. "I'll take care of this. You do what you need to do."

Bill felt overwhelmed. He took a deep breath to calm down before losing his cool in front of two police officers.

"Daddy?" Sydney pulled from Destiny's grip and ran to her father, hugging him tightly.

Bill knelt down and held her by the shoulders. "Daddy has to talk to these officers for a few minutes. You stay here with Destiny."

"I want to go with you," she whined, tired and frustrated.

"Syd. I need you to listen to me. I love you, and I need you to be a big girl right now. Okay?" he said firmly, then smiled.

Sydney continued to rub her eyes but smiled back. "Yessir."

"I love you, Sweetie."

"I love you, too, Daddy." Sydney hugged his neck. Then she took Destiny's hand, and they walked back toward her room.

Destiny looked over her shoulders as Bill put on his coat. "I'm going to clear this up, and I'll be back in a bit," he assured her. "Please be sure to check those numbers we discussed. They are on my dresser. I'm sure you'll find the right one."

Destiny nodded, then watched them walk together out the front door before she turned and headed for Sydney's room.

"Is everything okay?" Sydney asked as she crawled back into bed.

"Of course." Destiny grinned, furrowing her brow. "You know your Daddy knows everybody, and... Well, they just needed to ask him something about one of his friends."

"Did they do something bad?"

Destiny covered her up. "No, Sweetie. Now get some sleep."

"Love you," she murmured, as she closed her eyes.

"Love you too, Sweetie. Now go to sleep."

Destiny closed the door quietly behind her and walked hurriedly to Bill's room. On his dresser was the list he had told her about earlier, with a manila envelope. She took them all to the kitchen, looking over the list of numbers. She took out her phone, dialed his attorney and told him what had transpired. Then she asked him to meet Bill at the police station. Destiny sat perfectly still, nervously chewing on her lip for a moment before dialing Charlie. After several rings the phone was answered.

"Jessie," she gasped as she suddenly burst into tears. "I'm sorry to call so late—"

Chapter Fifty-Six

DALE STOOD by his client's side, in a sports jacket and jeans, not his usual attire for his profession, but the quickest and most comfortable thing he could throw on at eleven o'clock at night in the middle of an ice storm. The pictures set on the table before them were of a beaten and bruised Justine. Bill hadn't spoken a word since they arrived at the police station. He knew the drill. Sadly, he'd just done this a day ago, which was why they were grilling him harder. Dale conferred with his client and then told them his client had nothing else to say. That was right before they arrested him, once again, for assault.

Charlie arrived at the police station only minutes after Dale. In the few minutes Bill had alone with him before they were separated, it was clear what Charlie needed to do. He merely nodded at Bill. That was enough to give him comfort before they handcuffed him and booked him. As he left the station, Charlie made half a dozen quick phone calls, waking up *all* the investigators that he had already secured to help with their investigation of Justine. Each of them was alerted about what had just transpired, and each pledged to work even harder, given the high sense of urgency over the escalating circumstances.

While her husband headed to the police station, Jessie had driven straight to the Kemper House after Destiny's distressed phone call. When she arrived, Lisa was already there. Destiny hadn't called Andy since he had an early morning appointment, but texted him, asking him to call her as soon as he woke, stressing it was urgent. When Jessie arrived, she found Destiny and her colorful friend in the kitchen drinking hot tea. The three women sat up until four o'clock in the morning, drinking tea and discussing everything that was happening and what to do about it. Their plans made, Jessie and Lisa helped Destiny prepare breakfast for their guests.

After everyone had eaten, they helped her do the breakfast dishes. Sydney woke after everything was cleaned up and dragged into the kitchen, still looking like she could use another few hours' sleep.

"What's everyone doing here?" Sydney rubbed her eyes.

"What? We can't just come to visit you?" Lisa asked.

Sydney hugged Lisa and her Aunt Jessie. "How's Peanut?"

"He misses you," Jessie replied, looking up at Destiny. "In fact, I thought if you wanted to stay with us for a few days, you could go riding, providing the weather cooperates."

"Really?" She turned to Destiny. "Where's Daddy?"

"He had to go out, Sweetie," she forced a reassuring smile before cutting her eyes at Jessie.

"Again?" she whined.

"I'll tell you what. Why don't you go and pack a bag and let me worry about your dad? I'm sure it will be okay." Destiny quickly changed the subject. "You hungry?"

"I'll take care of that." Jessie grabbed her niece, turned her around and faced her toward her room. "Get dressed and pack a bag for three days, just in case."

Sydney was suddenly wide awake as she rushed down the hallway.

"Thank you," Destiny smiled. "I'll keep you posted as soon as I know something."

"You'd better. Just remember," Jessie added, as she pulled her jacket back on, "old Charlie may think he's the brains of this operation, but he's got nothin' on me." She winked. "Call your brother and see if he can pull any strings without getting in trouble and just put those results off for one more day." Then she turned to Lisa. "You got this?"

Lisa smiled wryly. "Absolutely."

Jessie turned back to Destiny. "Are you gonna be okay, Honey?"

Destiny hesitated, then nodded.

Jessie tapped her on the chin. "We're not gonna let anything happen to any of you." They all turned as Sydney skipped into the room. "Especially this little munchkin here," she added, hugging the girl to her side. "You ready?"

"Absolutamentee!" Sydney beamed, eager to check on her pony.

"Is that even a word?" Lisa asked.

"Apparently it is now." Jessie steered the young girl toward the back door.

Sydney broke free to hug Lisa one more time, then to hug Destiny. "Tell Daddy I love him, okay?"

"Absolutamentee!" Destiny replied, to laughter.

After they had walked out the door, Lisa clapped her hands together once. "We have a lot to do in a short amount of time, so I suggest we get moving." Lisa smacked her friend on the butt. "Do you think we should call Owen?"

"That idiot? Forget it. He was already on the defense team's witness list, remember."

Lisa wagged her forefinger. "Forgiveness is a virtue."

"So is character, of which he has none."

Lisa took her friend's arm. "You call your attorney, and I'll call my office. I have a very important spa appointment to schedule."

Chapter Fifty-Seven

THEY HAD RELEASED Justine immediately after her police interview. Though she had no broken bones, she was markedly bruised. Uri had hit her before, but never like this. He had been so angry when he saw the two glasses of vodka that he didn't even give her a chance to explain— more pointedly, an opportunity to think up an explanation. Uri had slapped her harder than he ever had, and then he shoved her into the bar, before calling her a whore as he stormed out. Thankfully, Uri didn't notice her secondary cell phone on the table beside the drinks, or it would have been all over.

How could he possibly have known where she was, and why hadn't he called to announce his arrival? Uri was extremely jealous, so Justine figured he must have had her followed. She immediately called Consuelo and told him to stay away for awhile. After composing herself, she went into her ensuite and saw herself in the mirror. She looked like hell, and yet, as she stared at her reflection, she constructed the conclusion to her little web of lies. Her husband may have just handed her daughter over to them on a silver platter.

She immediately called the police and sobbed through her best performance in years. She smoked a cigarette and had another glass of vodka until the doorman announced them. She broke the glass on the table, made a little cut on her hand and waited for them to arrive. They were very considerate and compassionate, especially the nurses at the hospital. They listened empathetically to her weave a tale of mistreatment that began just after she and Bill married. Terrified of him, she'd had to flee without her daughter for fear of him. Everything was now documented for admissibility in court. Better yet, for her coming emotional profession to Uri. How else would one explain abandoning a child so many years before?

Her phone rang during her police interview, and she saw it was Consuelo. She texted him that she would call him later and quickly turned the phone off. Uri called five minutes later, on her other phone, saying he was sorry, and that he went back to the suite, and she wasn't there. She told him she was at the doctor, simply to milk the sympathy, but said she'd be back soon, and he could make it up to her in person. He offered to have her picked up, but she promised she would get a cab.

When they released her, she turned on the phone that she kept separate for her *own* personal use. No one ever wants her husband scrolling through her personal phone numbers, right? You never know what he might find. Better to spend a little extra and keep that part of your life separate, or, at least, that's the way Justine saw it. And so far, it had worked blissfully. The two lives had never met, and she fully intended to keep it that way. Justine also planned on keeping Consuelo on a leash while enjoying her high society life in Venice. When she got full custody of

Sydney, and she was certain that would happen now, she would simply ship the little girl off to boarding school. Justine had already been checking into one in Rome, which was far enough away that she wouldn't be bothered by the tedious day-to-day issues so that she could still enjoy her life while she was young. Besides, Justine wanted the best for her daughter, and she'd heard that this one was the best.

Consuelo wasn't answering his phone, which was mildly irritating. The only two men she'd talked to today had treated her badly, and she desperately wanted to hear Connie's sweet voice, telling her how much he loved her and what he wanted to do to her later. Of course, Justine wasn't sure what she'd be up to, considering how sore she was, not to mention quite bruised, and a little tired from the pain medication they gave her. Before leaving, Justine called for a cab and asked them to pick her up within twenty minutes of her release, which they did. She paid the hospital with a check from her personal bank account in the States, one that Uri didn't know she had, once again to assure there was no paper trail. Then, as she walked out of the hospital, she threw the paperwork they had given her into the trashcan.

The driver glanced back occasionally at her in the rearview mirror, which only annoyed her. The last time he looked back, Justine stared hatefully into the mirror at him, and he never looked back again. She would never have gone out in public like this if she hadn't had a good reason. And right now, it was a means to an end. Before getting out of the car, she draped the long gray scarf over her face, as she had done when she left. No need for those around her to see how visibly disfigured she was. Between that and the sunglasses, no one was the wiser.

Uri was waiting for her in her suite. Housekeeping had

already cleaned up the spilled vodka, the glass, and the blood. When Uri saw his wife's bandaged arm, he burst into tears. He had been in such a rage that he didn't even remember breaking the glass that cut her. She walked past him, distant and unaccepting of his apologies until it suited her. Justine acted offended that he had punished her before she was able to explain that she was entertaining someone who was helping her to buy a particular sailboat that he had been wanting. She made a mental note to find the elusive salesperson before the end of her trip, to validate her story if needed. Uri begged and cajoled until she finally, tearfully accepted his apology.

Justine had considered telling him about Sydney, but wouldn't—not quite yet. She had already paid a private investigator to follow Bill and his little tramp. And since the investigator had someone on the inside at the laboratory in his pocket, the results would indeed come back in her favor. But since she didn't like leaving anything to chance, she would wait until her investigator had the results in his hand to break the news to Uri of his long lost daughter.

Uri was beside himself trying to please her, offering to call room service to order in lobster thermidor for a late night dinner, her favorite, with a fresh berry trifle for dessert. She was too sore and tired, so he was more than happy to take her to bed, although make-up sex was definitely out of the question, with the level of pain she still professed. He promised her a day of pampering at the spa to relieve her sore muscles and make her feel brand new. Justine accepted his offer—*only* if he promised her a shopping spree, and *only* if she was feeling better, of course. Uri, as always, promised her anything she wanted. He could always take care of business tomorrow night. After a day at the spa, she was *always* in a better mood and usually more compliant.

Most nights Justine slept in a separate bedroom since Uri's snoring was like a freight train going through a tunnel, but tonight, with her pain meds, she slept through with no problem. When she awoke in the morning, Uri was already gone, probably working out in the gym downstairs. She pulled her other cell phone from between the mattresses and called Consuelo again. Damn. He still wasn't answering. Where the hell was he? He was there for her, not the other way around. She called her private investigator, this call going to voicemail as well. She checked the time again. It was after ten. She called room service and ordered a specialty smoothie.

Not having any success with her other phone calls, Justine called the hotel spa, but all their appointments for that day were completely booked. Telling them she was in the penthouse didn't pull any weight since they were down a person as well. Did she want to schedule one for tomorrow? Justine emphatically told them no; that was unacceptable and unprofessional, and the manager would be hearing from her. She slammed the phone down to emphasize her point. A moment later her phone rang. It was her investigator informing her of Bill's arrest. They would arraign him Monday the morning. Justine told him to see what he could do to expedite the lab results. Then she instructed him to keep her posted.

Room service arrived a few minutes later with her smoothie. Justine was in such a good mood she'd forgotten how bruised she was until the waiter looked aghast at seeing her face. She gave him an annoyed glare and signed his ticket without giving him a tip before slamming the door in his face. Then she lay on the sofa, propped her feet up and sipped on her smoothie. It was almost as good as Consuelo's. Feeling a little more refreshed she dialed his number again. When it went to voice mail, again she left him a less loving message than she had before, laid back and finished her smoothie. Justine closed her eyes. How humiliating it must have been for Bill—being arrested in front of his daughter and his little whore and all his paying guests. She smiled to herself. Yes, everything was falling into place quite nicely.

Chapter Fifty-Eight

WHEN THEY RELEASED Bill on bail, (again), Monday morning, Charlie picked him up and took him straight to the farm. Sydney ran into his arms, the simple gesture bringing tears to his eyes. Jessie assured him they had discussed everything with Destiny. Under the circumstances, Destiny thought it best Bill not return to the Kemper House at least for a couple of days. There was no media coverage this time, which was a relief. And Destiny and Sandy had everything under control. Bill was concerned that she was through with him, especially when she didn't answer his calls. But Jessie assured him the women had talked for a long time about the circumstances in which they found themselves. She told him just to leave Destiny alone for a couple of days to run his business until they knew what would happen next.

That would allow Bill to have a day to recuperate, and for he and Charlie to discuss what would happen next. He had to admit he was more than a little annoyed that Charlie was being so cryptic. Charlie assured Bill that his contacts would be in touch with him soon on all fronts, and they could proceed from there. They encouraged him to get some rest because he was going to need his strength over the next few days. Bill said he hadn't slept at all the night before, but felt fine. However, once he lay on the bed, just for a few minutes—to relax he said—he slept straight through until the next morning.

When Bill finally woke, he insisted that he needed to go back to Kemper House, even though Charlie and Jessie encouraged him not to. When he argued, they reminded him how badly it went the last time he failed to listen to the advice his attorney had given him. So he sulked, and then went riding with his daughter.

Meanwhile, Destiny had risen early, fed the guests, checked them out and had the rooms' linens flipped. Andy called her with the not so great news. He had been unable to delay the results. Then he told her something he considered a little odd. One of the senior lab techs was handling the results, and more specifically, guarding the results. Which was out of the ordinary, since they were just regular paternity test lab screenings. Destiny filled him in briefly on the arrest and Bill's subsequent release, and they promised to talk later that day. Then she called her attorney to request a meeting with the DA's office later that day.

Lisa called Destiny and asked if she was available about one o'clock that afternoon to meet her at her spa for a massage. Since Sandy had promised to stay through the evening, she told Lisa the time was perfect. She made another phone call to Jessie, inquiring if she wanted to meet them as well. Her excitement was apparent. It was a date. She just had a few phone calls to make first, and then she would be meeting them.

Then Destiny called Bill, who was riding with Sydney. He promised to talk for as long as they had good reception.

"By the way, we found your phone. The one you lost during the storm."

"It's supposed to be waterproof."

"Yeah, well, I don't think it's horse-proof," he laughed. "That's how we found it. Peanut stepped on it."

"I somehow doubt the warranty covers 'stepped on by horse.'"

After a brief silence, Bill asked, "Are you okay?"

"Yeah, I am," Destiny replied.

"Are *we* okay?"

"Absolutamentee!"

"What?"

Destiny laughed. "Ask your daughter. That's her word." She hesitated a beat, then asked, "Do you remember the first time we met?"

"How can I forget? You were hitting on my brother."

"Whatever. Look, I mean…"

Bill furrowed his brow. "You obviously have something to ask me, so just ask me. I won't lie to you."

"Your face," she began. "You looked like you'd been in a fight."

Bill chuckled. "You know that massive, gaudy desk in the hallway?"

"Yeah?"

"Well, there ya' go. She and I had a run-in very early one morning."

Destiny chuckled.

"Hey, it may be funny now, but it hurt like he—" he began, then looked over at his daughter. "—like heck." Bill rubbed his nose at the reminder. "My nose will never be the same."

"I like your nose."

Bill sighed, glancing over at his daughter again as she rode her pony proudly. "I miss you."

"What, you didn't have some guy named Bubba keeping you company in the slammer?"

"That's not funny."

"Maybe a little," Destiny teased. "Okay, maybe not much. I'm sorry. That was in poor taste."

"Am I going to see you today?"

"I don't know. I have some things I have to do, and then I have to meet with my attorney."

"Your attorney?"

"Yeah, long story. Hey, I have to go," she sighed, as a call came through on her phone.

"I love you." But she was already gone.

"I knew it!" Sydney exclaimed.

"Knew what?"

"That you two liked each other," Sydney smiled smugly.

"Really?" Bill wrinkled his lips. "So... How do you feel about that?"

"I'm cool with it. I told Destiny that, too, when she asked me."

Bill smiled a crooked smile. "You're cool with it, huh."

"Yup."

"I'm glad you're cool with it, Sweetie because I *really* like her. Actually... I'm in love with her, and I want to ask her to marry me. Are you cool with that, too?"

"Yup," she added, nonchalantly.

"Good." Bill breathed in the crisp morning air. "Good." He smiled to himself as they crested the next hill, before disappearing into the morning mist.

Reconcilliation

Chapter Fifty-Nine

JUSTINE HAD BEEN ecstatic when Consuelo texted her that he wanted to meet. His phone had been acting up, so she'd have to communicate by text until he could get it fixed. She texted back that she'd forgive him if she could see him. Uri was in town, so they'd have to be discreet. He promised her a day of pampering and an afternoon spent in bed. Even better, he'd set up a spa day at one of the most exclusive and celebrated salons in Austin—and in just two hours! Uri had disappeared again, most likely shopping for jewelry to help *ensure* he would get laid later that night. So she left him a note that she was doing a day at the spa and would meet him for dinner sometime around seven. That would give Consuelo and her plenty of time.

Justine took a cab, only because she didn't want any record of her travels at the hotel. She even changed cabs twice, to assure no one was following her. When she finally arrived, she was greeted by a long legged lovely wearing a low-cut dress that showed off her firm, ample bosom. Justine knew it was a spa of the highest caliber when an attendant met her with fresh cucumber water and immediately showed her to her private room. She undressed, lay face-down on one of the heated tables, under a warm polyester blanket and waited for Connie and her massage, both her phones on the table in front of her chest. Soon, the door opened, and a pair of slender feminine legs entered, a butterfly tattoo on one ankle. She usually preferred to be worked on by a masseur, rather than a masseuse, but sometimes she actually enjoyed women, especially when she and Consuelo were getting couples' massages. She found it kind of erotic. The door opened again, and another set of legs walked in, then another. She lifted up on the table, not concerned at all with covering up her breasts.

"Who the hell are you?" she asked the three women in white robes.

"Is this her?" Jessie asked.

"Yup," Destiny said. "This is her."

"I recognize you." Justine glared at Destiny. "What the hell are you doing here?"

Lisa smiled and sat down in one of three chairs that had been strategically placed against the wall so that Justine would have to face them. "You can just refer to us as the three amigos," she replied, a handful of files and a phone in her lap.

"I'm waiting for someone." Justine lay back down. "I think you are in the wrong room."

Lisa dialed the phone and Justine's phone rang. Justine lifted up again, looking at the number on her phone and saw it was Consuelo's number. Lisa hung up.

"How did you get that?" Justine asked, staring at the phone in the woman's hand.

"I think you need to stop talking and start listening," Jessie stated flatly.

"I think I'm going to call the manager and put an end to this right now."

Lisa raised her hand. "That would be me."

Justine sat up, holding the blanket around her and sliding from the table.

Jessie walked to the door and stood in front of it.

On the massage table, Lisa opened one of the files and laid out several pictures of Justine and Consuelo together, in and out of bed. They were explicit enough that Destiny had blushed when she first saw them. Lisa pointed at one in particular. "That's my favorite," she smiled, tilting her head. "Although, for the life of me I can't figure out how he—well, never mind. You get the gist of it."

Justine was shaken, but only for a moment. "These are nothing."

"Really? Then I guess the set that we have waiting at the hotel for your husband won't bother him at all. Maybe he'd even like to try some of these positions," She looked back at the pictures. "Oh, my! I mean, if he could. Somehow I don't think he's as agile as, what's his name? Consuelo?"

"What have you done with Consuelo?"

Lisa laughed. "We haven't done anything with Connie, is it? In fact, you just missed him. We had a nice little chat."

"Where is he?"

"By now, probably on a flight back to Milan, with his tail tucked between his legs," Lisa smiled slyly. "Nice body, by the way. Not bad to look at, only that's not all you were doing, was it Justine?"

Justine glared at her.

"Actually, he's quite the affable young man. By the way, Connie told us to keep the phone. I mean, I don't think he needs it anymore. Do you? In fact, I don't think he cares if he ever hears from you again. Especially after we explained the situation to him."

"Situation?"

"That we were going to send the same pictures to his wife. Those and several others that we happened upon, only it wasn't *you* in all the *other* photos," she added, almost empathetically. "There were two, or was it three other women?" she asked dramatically, holding out another handful of pictures for Justine to see.

Justine glanced at the first one in Lisa's hand and crossed her arms. She refused to take the pictures. Lisa shrugged and placed them on top of the others.

Jessie and Destiny looked perplexed as well.

"Three, I think," Destiny said.

"Yeah, I think it was three," Jessie agreed.

Lisa continued. "You see; *he* was more concerned about *his* prenup than you seem to be. He's not about to blow his *millions*, is it?"

Jessie interjected. "*Tens* of millions."

"Yes, his tens, of millions, on a piece of ass. Or should I say, several pieces," she added, dramatically.

Justine stared at her hatefully.

"Oh, I can see the wheels-a-turning. You're pissed," Lisa said smugly. "I can tell. But you know what? You're not quite as smart as you think you are. You see, we've had people following your PI since you put a tail on Bill," Lisa said sarcastically. "You knew you couldn't find any dirt on him, so you had to manufacture it. Well, dearie, you just hit a dead-end."

"Oh, *really*," Justine replied, trying to sound self-assured.

"Yeah. Really. See, we have an affidavit by the lab guy," she said, holding up another file. "The one you paid five thousand dollars to doctor the lab results. He's ready to sing to save himself from jail time." Lisa crossed her arms. "So, you see, we've traced the lab guy to your guy, and your guy to you, and you to Consuelo. It's all a matter of connecting the dots."

Justine clenched her teeth in anger.

"Oh, and there's something else. Our *other* investigators, the ones we have in *Italy?* They struck gold, as well. It seems that *your* prenup *also* has a few stipulations. Besides the infidelity clause, it had a ten-year deadline on a having a kid, or lose millions. So, it made sense that you set your sights on Bill's kid."

"She's Uri's daughter."

"No, she's not," Lisa said. "I've got the results right here." She held up a third file and tossed it on top of the pictures. Nonchalantly, she picked up another file. "Oh, and look, here's yet *another* one by *another* investigator—a medical file. Let's see what this one says." Lisa opened it, feigning surprise. "Why, you recently had an implant removed." She turned to Destiny and then to Jessie. "Did you know that they can implant you to keep you from getting pregnant now?"

Destiny shook her head.

Jessie shook her head as well. "Damned if I've ever heard of such a thing."

Lisa grabbed Justine's upper arm, where a tattoo hid the incision. Justine jerked her arm from Lisa's grip.

"I'll bet your husband would so love to hear why, after all those years of trying, and all those tests he took, you still couldn't have kids. What would he say if he found out that you had an implant to ensure that you couldn't get pregnant? Not just once, but three times?"

"He'd never believe you."

"Certified medical records don't lie," Lisa said. "Oh, and don't forget Exhibits E, F and G. Those would be the records from *all* the spas you visited in the States *and* France *and* Germany… That would be from investigators *number four, five and six*. You remember—those trips you took when you told your husband you were going to meet with your own personal physician."

"How could you possibly know that?" Justine snapped.

"Let's just say that some of your house staff aren't very fond of how you treat them. Maybe if you treated them better or even paid them better, they might keep your secrets a little closer to the vest."

Lisa turned to the women. "Did I leave anything out?"

Destiny took her gum out of her mouth and waved her hand, as though in high school. "The charges against Bill?"

Lisa turned back to Justine, her smile gone. "Yes. And here's what happens next: you go to the police and tell them that you falsified the report against Bill."

"I can't do that," she said, angrily. "They'd never believe me."

"They believed you once. Make them *un*-believe you."

"How am I supposed to do that?"

Lisa leaned toward an intimidated Justine. "Don't care. You seem to think you're pretty good at BS-ing people. You'll figure something out." She picked up all the files on the table except the pictures. "I'll call my man at the hotel and tell him not to deliver those pictures to your husband... *yet*. And as for the rest of these records? Once we have confirmation that you have dropped the charges against Bill, and the case doesn't go to trial, then we'll drop these into the shredder."

"How do I know you won't send them anyway? What guarantees can you give me?"

Lisa looked at the other women. "None. You're just going to have to take our word for it. Woman to woman," she said, smartly. "Oh, and if you think you're going to try and outsmart us by not getting the charges dropped, then know that we have someone tailing your husband right now, as well as someone tailing you. And they stay with you, even when you go back home until you make those charges go away. Oh, and the petition for joint custody— that goes away as well. Plus," Lisa added, just for insurance, "you never, *ever* contact Bill or *his* daughter again."

"She's my daughter!" Justine exclaimed.

"Oh, that's right. And shouldn't you be paying child support?" Lisa looked at the other women who eagerly nodded. Lisa turned back to Justine. "Maybe we should get Bill to seek to amend the divorce decree and ask for child support since you obviously can afford it. Oh, but, wait... That would mean," Lisa said, looking at the assembled women, playing at astonishment. "That would mean Uri would know you have a nine-year-old daughter! You want to explain that one?"

Justine swallowed hard.

Lisa looked at the other women and smiled. "I think that's it, right, Ladies?"

The women nodded.

"What about the pictures?"

Lisa put all her files back into her large shoulder bag. "Oh, you can keep the photos. We've got plenty more where those came from. You can turn them into wallets, frame 'em, hell, you can put 'em on your Christmas cards, for all we care. We've got the negatives. We don't need 'em."

Destiny stood, and Lisa moved toward Jessie.

"Who *are* you people?"

"I told you. We're the three amigos," Lisa smiled. "Oh, and Justine, this is us being nice. Cross us, and you'll find out just how dangerous *we* can be." As they walked to the door, Lisa turned. "Oh, and Justine, if you think we're bluffing, ask yourself why your husband made an unscheduled trip to the States and how he knew exactly where to find you. Food for thought," she said flatly.

The women walked from the room together, leaving Justine there alone, shaking angrily. She gritted her teeth and swiped all the pictures to the floor. She clenched her fists and screamed fiercely. A moment later, she looked around at the photos on the floor and then scurried to gather all of them, shoving them into her purse before anyone else walked in.

Chapter Sixty

THE CONFERENCE ROOM WAS SIMPLE, functional. There was nothing ostentatious about it. Nothing showy that proved tax dollars recklessly spent. The conference table was large enough to seat twelve, which was perfect for this meeting because there were twelve present.

Destiny had asked for the meeting, so her attorney was present. Lisa and Jessie were allowed in as they were considered part of the legal team—a stretch, but considering what they brought to the table, the Assistant District Attorney allowed it. Then there was the prosecuting attorney and three of his legal team—two of them there out of sheer morbid curiosity. And lastly, Winston was there with his legal team, which rounded out the table.

Destiny had already spoken to the Assistant DA about a face-to-face meeting with Winston. "It's never been done, before," she had said, then added, "but, what the hell." Destiny's attorney didn't argue with her on this one; once she presented to him what she had. In fact, he applauded her for her bravery.

The Assistant DA, dressed in a slimming blue suit, over

a pin-striped blouse, a non-intimidating smile on her face, looked at Destiny. "This is your meeting. We're here in an unofficial capacity. So you go first."

Destiny drew in a deep breath for courage and then exhaled. "I'm not dropping my civil lawsuit, but I'm willing to settle for five million in damages, simply to keep this from going back and forth any longer. I'll settle based on the following conditions," she began.

Winston leaned back in his chair, clasped his hands behind his head and smirked, scoffing before she had even started.

"Number one," she began. "All proceeds are put into a fund that's used exclusively for programs that help victims of rape and sexual assault." No one said a word, so she continued. "Second, Winston drops the lawsuit against Mr. Ireland for assault."

"There's no lawsuit," his attorney interjected.

"Yet," she stated. "You and I know that he's probably already asked for one, and that goes away. Now."

Winston leaned forward onto his arms, chuckling to himself.

Destiny's eyes moved from each attorney back to Winston, who lowered his head, still chuckling to himself, before looking back up at her, very pleased with himself.

"Number three: In a perfect world Winston would serve the maximum for every charge of rape, but, if he serves, at least, three years for every rape that he's committed—"

"What is this? Law and Order? Why is she doing all the talking?" his attorney asked.

"It's her meeting," she reiterated. "We're *all* here because we were invited. Unofficial, remember?"

"This is crap, and you know it," his lawyer said to the

Assistant District Attorney. He stood, followed by the defense team.

"So, what did you get all dressed up for, Fred? Why did you come? To pontificate?"

"Sheer morbid curiosity," the attorney replied.

"Then, sit down," the Assistant DA said firmly, confidently. "Please. Just pretend like this is mediation or better yet, allocution that's not in front of the media."

"We're leaving," Winston's lead attorney said.

"Fine. We'll see you Tuesday when the grand jury convenes to hear your client's case. Based on the preponderance of evidence against him, he *will* be indicted."

"We'll see about that," Winston's lawyer retorted.

Jessie slid a file across the table to him.

"What is this?"

No one said anything as Winston's attorney looked down at the file. His team stood around him expectantly. He glanced at the Assistant District Attorney before opening it. Everyone on his side of the table including Winston, leaned around him, peering at what he held in his hands. The color from his face drained, and he stood there with his mouth agape. He glanced across the table at Destiny, then the District Attorney, before sitting back down, followed by Winston's other attorneys.

"Where'd you get these?" he asked, looking face to face on the opposite side of the table.

Jessie shrugged and smiled wryly.

"Anything else?" his attorney asked.

Winston suddenly sat upright. "What?" he argued. "I'm not agreeing to any of this."

"One year for each case," his attorney stated, holding his hand in front of Winston to silence him.

"No," Winston snapped angrily, as he stood and stared at his lawyer. "Those are sealed records. They can't use any of that against me!" he screamed in a rage. Then he projected his tirade at the Assistant District Attorney. "None of it is admissible," he smiled smugly. Only, the fear shone in his eyes.

"We might consider two. Unofficially," the Assistant DA said, holding firm. "And that *includes* the ones that we now know about in Oklahoma City, Seattle, and Chicago. By the time we go to trial, who knows how many more we'll find."

"This is BS! I won't plea out on these, these false accusations!" Winston yelled at the Assistant DA, before turning back to his attorney. "I pay you to do what *I* tell you to do."

"No, Mr. Sawyer. You pay me to put up the best defense."

Destiny sat quietly, watching him hang himself. Lisa and Jessie sat on either side of her, holding her hands.

"Bob, I," Winston began.

His attorney turned to him. "'Winston, please sit down and *shut up*," he said, visibly shaken. He turned back to the Assistant DA. "May we have the room for a few minutes so that I can confer with my client?"

She nodded, then rose with everyone from her office and headed for the door. Destiny, Lisa, and Jessie stood up. Destiny began to turn but then she stopped and looked back across at Winston, surrounded by his legal team. He glanced at her, if only for a moment, but at that moment, she saw the rage in his eyes. His rage quickly turned to confusion when he saw the defiance in her eyes. The victory. The relief.

Destiny smiled as she walked from the room with Jessie and Lisa. As the door closed behind them, they could hear Winston yelling and arguing.

"I don't know how you ladies did this, but, thank you," the Assistant DA said, shaking their hands, one by one.

"It was all her," Destiny said, pointing at Jessie. "She's a retired US Marshall."

"Twenty-five years," Jessie said, shaking his hand. "That's where me and Charlie met. A match made in hell," she quipped. "God love him. We're a good team. In twenty-five years, you meet a lot of people, and you make a lot of friends."

"And a lot of enemies," she observed.

"That too," Jessie raised an eyebrow. "But there's a lot of people out there that don't mind helping you out when you're in a pinch."

"Well, if you ever want to do a little investigating for the DA's office, just let me know," she said. "Ten confirmed women. That's phenomenal," she added, turning to her team. "With all our resources, we only knew about four. Who knew how far back this went. The Assistant DA shook her head.

One of the female members of her team grimaced. "Yeah, sadly, some schools have become hunting grounds for rapists, and they don't investigate rapes and sexual assaults reported on campus as well as they could or even *should*. Or they *could* have stopped him there."

The Assistant District Attorney added, "Now we understand why he moved states every couple of years. He was trying to stay ahead of the charges. How'd you find the two women who disappeared?"

"Remember, I was in the business of *helping* people disappear. They weren't really that hard to find," Jessie said.

"Yeah, wait until he realizes that even if he settled with them for millions to disappear a subpoena usurps his legal agreement."

"I'd give anything to be a fly on the wall right now," Lisa said.

The door opened, and one of Winston's legal team stepped out. "We're ready."

The Assistant DA turned to Destiny. "You ready?"

Destiny pursed her lips and shook her head. "I don't need to. I did what I came to do." She turned to her friends. "He knows that I stood my ground. That's all I care about. As long as dropping the charges against Bill and preventing any civil suit against him are part of the deal, I don't much care about all the rest. I know you'll do what you know is right," she said, looking the Assistant District Attorney in the eyes.

"You're a brave woman," she said once more, shaking Destiny's hand before leading her team back into the room.

Destiny looked at her friends and smiled. "Thank you both so much," she said, taking their hands. "I couldn't have done this without you."

"We're so proud of you." Lisa hugged her. "You stood up to him."

"Yeah, but I was shaking like a leaf."

"Me, too," Jessie said. "It was cold in there."

Destiny grabbed Jessie and hugged her tight. "You were amazing," she said. "Thank you from the bottom of my heart."

"You are family," Jessie smiled.

"Not quite yet," Destiny reminded her.

Jessie winked at her. "You will be, Sweetheart, if we have to beat it into him."

They all laughed. Then Destiny turned to Lisa. "Thank you."

"Are you kidding? This is the most fun I've had all

week." Lisa took her best friend's hand. "Where to now?" she asked. "I feel like I could take on the world!"

Destiny smiled at each of them. "If it's okay with you, I'd like to go see my family now."

Lisa took one of Destiny's arms and Jessie the other, as they smiled at one another.

Jessie started walking first, pulling the others behind her. "Come on, Girls. Let's go home."

Chapter Sixty-One

CHRISTMAS MORNING CAME, and the Kemper House was about to be alive with warmth and laughter, though not from paying guests. Bill never booked anyone on Christmas Eve, so that he and Sydney could celebrate Christmas without attending to patrons. Yet, this morning, many of the rooms were filled. Jessie and Charlie had the biggest room with the nicest bathroom. Lisa and Andy and Bill's mother each had their own rooms. Destiny slept in her tiny room, with the door locked firmly.

Sydney long ago stopped believing in Santa, having one morning caught her father placing a new bike by the tree when she got up for a drink of water. The tree was grand enough that passersby on the street could see it, the colored lights shimmering against several clear glass ornaments, new additions to the tree, mixed in with the ones that Sydney and Bill had previously placed there.

Destiny shuffled to her small bathroom after her alarm went off at four o'clock. She brushed her teeth and dressed, and slowly made her way downstairs. She could hear Bill and Sydney already in the kitchen, banging around as they retrieved pots and pans to prepare a full Christmas morning breakfast for their special guests. The moment that Destiny arrived at the bottom step, she could see the fire roaring in the fireplace in the center of the wall in the library. It was so warm and welcoming. Several stockings hung on the mantle filled with an assortment of goodies. There was one for Bill, one for Sydney and they had added one for her. Her hand moved over the felt material, tracing it, bringing a small smile to her face.

As she turned, a glimmer caught her eye, and she slowly moved toward the tree. Something was different, so she stepped closer to investigate. As she drew nearer, she saw additional ornaments that weren't there before. Destiny leaned closer, and suddenly her heart raced, and her eyes began to fill with tears. Her eyes traveled from ornament to ornament, her hand delicately handling each one. She heard the door swing open from the kitchen, and she turned her head. Bill and Sydney were standing there, looking at her. Her hand continued to follow her eyes all around the tree until she had found almost two dozen ornaments they had added. When she turned back, they were suddenly beside her.

"How?" she managed to say weakly, as tears rolled down her face.

"It was Sydney's idea."

Destiny looked at Sydney, who was looking up at her, confused. "I didn't mean to make you cry."

"No, Sweetie. This is a good cry." Destiny knelt beside her, hugging her, and wiping her tears. Then she turned back to the tree, pointing at the orb that was closest to them. "This was the picture we took when Rhett first learned how to walk." She smiled and turned back to Sydney. "How did you get these?"

"That would be Lisa and Andy." Bill put his hands on his daughter's shoulders.

"They are beautiful." Destiny sniffed. "Absolutely beautiful."

"I thought you should have pictures of your family to see, especially at Christmas."

"Oh, Honey, they are perfect."

"Did you find them all?" Bill asked.

"How many are there?"

"Twenty-four." Sydney beamed. "Aunt Jessie helped me make them when I was staying with her."

"Here, you can help me count them to make sure we've found them all."

Destiny and Sydney counted them as they walked around the tree. "I counted twenty-three."

"Then there's one more."

Destiny and Sydney looked through the tree again, where they finally found one hidden deep within the branches. Destiny reached in, carefully unhooking it so that she could get a better look. As she drew it nearer, she stopped. Inside was sand, a picture of Bill and her at Sydney's birthday party, plus two novelty wedding rings, hooked together. Destiny looked up. Immediately Bill knelt before her. Sydney giggled and danced in place. Destiny's hands flew to her mouth as she gasped. He took her left hand and looked up at her as he slid a simple ring with a simple stone setting onto her finger.

"I always believed in destiny, but I never thought I'd find my Destiny by chance. I love you, Destiny, and I want to spend the rest of my life getting to know you and making new memories. Showing you just how much you mean to me." He looked to Sydney and back to Destiny and smiled. "To us."

Tears rolled down her cheeks as she sniffed again. She nodded her head.

"Yes!" Sydney screamed as she jumped into her dad's arms, knocking him over.

They all laughed as he crawled back up and stood beside Destiny. He took her hands in his and pulled her to him, kissing her gently. When they parted, she lowered her head, and he kissed the tip of her nose. Sydney wriggled her way between them, and they included her in the hug.

"We have a breakfast to cook," Bill said, dragging them into the kitchen.

Three hours later, when it was ready to serve, Sydney took a wooden spoon and a pot and banged on its bottom, walking up and down the stairwell, noisily announcing it was time to eat. Slowly, everyone woke and reluctantly left their warm beds in their complimentary bedrooms, yawning and stretching, still in pajamas, making their way downstairs.

"Merry Christmas!" Sydney said to each one as they arrived at the bottom step.

"Merry Christmas," they each said in return, some followed by hugs or pats on Sydney's head.

They arrived to a feast of fried ham, biscuits and gravy, German fried potatoes, scrambled eggs and fresh fruit. They all sat down in front of place cards that Sydney had personally created for each of them. Destiny poured each guest their choice of milk, juice or coffee before handing Lisa a teabag for her small teapot of hot water.

Bill looked around the table as he sat. Without a word, he held out his hands to Destiny and to Sydney, who sat on either side of him until everyone was holding hands. He had to catch himself from the emotions he was feeling, but he mouthed a beautiful prayer, thanking God for the blessings of those seated around him.

Destiny looked around the table and smiled. As she slowly closed her eyes, for the first time in a really long time, she thanked God for the good *and* the bad. For it had all brought her to where she was now. And she knew now, that all the times she was alone, that He had never actually left her at all.

And for the first time in a really, really long time, she had peace.

Epilogue

IT WAS A COMING TOGETHER of family and friends, with food and fellowship for all. There were bounce houses and games and stages for bands who had donated their time for the benefit. There were tears and triumphs. It was an incredible celebration of life, and everyone was invited.

It was the fourth time Destiny had been to California since the accident, seven years ago. And the fear that once kept her away was no longer there. The desire to simply stay away was gone. They drove through the city in a rented mini-van, since they were now a family of five. Bill knew the streets well, as this was now their fourth trip to the OneLegacy event. Every March since the year after they were married, they traveled here, incorporating visits to the parks and the sites into what was meant for something else.

When they arrived at their destination, Bill turned to her, took her hand and smiled. "Ready?"

Destiny smiled in return and slid from her seat, before moving to the back side of the mini-van, to unstrap her two-year-old son. "William Rhett Ireland," she said, shaking her head; Cheerios, and cookies all over his face, his body, and his car seat. "You're a mess." Destiny brushed off what she could from his front, and strategically she straddled him across her hip.

Sydney emerged from the back, bringing with her two small backpacks, one for each of her siblings, to carry for the short hike to the location of the actual ceremony. Sydney stood at Destiny's side, now almost as tall as her step-mother, and still growing. Her features were softer now, and to her father's dismay, she wore, albeit light, makeup. Her hair even had a streak of red in it, thanks to her Auntie Lisa, as she now called her. Sydney reached over and brushed the Cheerios from her brother's bottom and back. She tickled him, and he wriggled in Destiny's arms.

Bill unleashed his four-year-old daughter from the other car seat, her mass of dark curls tickling his nose. He tried to find a comfortable position in which to hold her, but found it difficult, as she hadn't stopped wriggling since he had picked her up. She reached up and held his face in between her small hands and pulled it to her so that she could give him Eskimo kisses. "I wuv you, Daddy," she beamed.

"I wuv you, too, Sweetie," he said, balancing her as she danced in his arms while he tried to close the door.

They walked as a family to the ceremony site, greeting people they recognized along the way. Michelle, one of the volunteers they remembered from past visits, welcomed them by the stage, hugging each of them as they arrived.

"There's someone I think you should meet." Michelle motioned for them to come with her.

Destiny nudged Bill with her shoulder, since her arms

were otherwise occupied, and the whole family began to follow her. There was a small crowd of families close to a bounce house that was filled with young children. Isabelle wriggled with excitement in her father's arms until he set her on the ground. He glanced at Sydney, who rolled her eyes, then followed her little sister who was headed straight for the bounce houses.

Michele walked up to a young red-headed girl and tapped her on the shoulder. "Evelyn. Here's the lady that you wanted to meet."

The young freckled-faced girl turned and smiled. "Are you the lady who wrote me?" she asked, looking into Destiny's eyes.

Destiny felt her body go limp, but somehow she managed to stay standing. She turned to Bill and then handed their son to him before turning back to the young girl. She had to be close to Sydney's age. Tentatively Destiny approached her.

The girl held out her hand. "I'm Evelyn."

"Destiny," she murmured, taking Evelyn's hand.

"You wrote me about your son's donation." Evelyn was soft-spoken, almost whispering. "I got his heart."

Destiny's eyes filled with tears as she stepped closer. She slowly reached her hands out again and Evelyn placed hers in them. "Can I—," she asked, her voice breaking. "Can I hug you?"

Evelyn's eyes filled with tears. "I actually was hoping I could hug *you*." She stepped toward her quickly and then wrapped herself around Destiny.

Within moments, all eyes around them were filled with tears as they watched the emotional meeting.

Destiny held Evelyn tightly as the young girl cried softly against her chest. "Thank you," she kept saying again and again. She held Evelyn carefully, rocking her gently. "No, thank you!" she cried.

And for a brief second in time, a glimpse of a moment, a breath of her life, she held her son in her arms again, felt his heart beating against hers once more.

And all was right with the world.

LOVE Destiny?

Reviews are the lifeblood of any author, so if you enjoyed Destiny by chance, I would really appreciate if you have a few minutes to give a review on the site from which you downloaded the book... it only takes a moment!

And if you loved Destiny, sharing is caring, right? At the time of publishing, the Kindle eBook version of Destiny is only $2.99, so why not share Destiny's heart-warming story with a friend?

I've also included a preview of *Letters from Becca* in a few pages... Keep reading!

Get Involved

Join my newsletter and be notified of future releases and new books:

www.margaretfergusonbooks.com/subscribe

Like my Facebook page:

www.facebook.com/margaretfergusonbooks

An important note about sexual assault

If you are struggling with the trauma of sexual assault or know someone who is or has, I pray that you will remember Deuteronomy 31:8: "He will never leave you or forsake you. Do not be afraid; do not be discouraged."

I know that I in no way can even begin to convey the horror of rape and sexual assault. I pray that if even one person is touched by Destiny's story and her courage, then I have made a difference.

If you are a victim, please speak up... if not for yourself, for the next victim. Courage comes in many forms... may you find the courage you need to stand up to your abuser...

ALWAYS report rape and sexual assault... there is ALWAYS a safe place to go.

Call: **911** or **877-995-5247** from anywhere in the United States

https://www.safehelpline.org/about-rainn

Things that just can't go without saying...

Thanks Armando Villareal for self-defense lessons for Destiny when she needed them.

To Dana Nelson, Assistant District Attorney for Travis County. Thanks for your time and your patience with all my questions. It helped to make my story more real and more true to life. (I hope!)

Rhett Curtis Hering is the real name of a beautiful young man whose life was cut too short in a tragic accident December 28, 2015. His mother is one of my Facebook friends, and it was through her heartfelt story of loss and the incredible memories that she shared on Facebook that I got to know her and her son. It seemed so very appropriate that Destiny's son's name was changed in memory of her precious son. Lorna, I can't imagine your pain. I pray that God gives you and your family some semblance of peace in small and big ways, every day.

The young girl who received Rhett's heart is named after our Grandma, Evelyn Whited.

Oh, and as a side note, Lisa, was in part fashioned after my sister, Tommie. She's strong and sassy and definitely eclectic. And as a tribute to my sis, whose natural hair color I haven't seen in twenty-five years, she has multi-colored hair!

The full name of the main character Bill is William Bryan Ireland; a combination of a great, great grandfather's name on my mother's side, and a shout out to my husband, Bryan.

Bryan, I love you... thanks for hanging in there again! Now let's go write the next New York Times bestseller!

Acknowledgments

First and foremost, I must thank Kat Adair, who has not only been *the* force in creating my website, my newsletters, laying out all the e-books and paperbacks. She's been an amazing inspiration. She's incredibly talented, **AND** amazingly patient. Not only am I not always (or should I say, *ever*,) the most technically savvy, (how many times did you have to run my computer by remote because I messed something up?), but she has an incredible eye for mistakes. Even after I, my editors, my husband, the grandkids, the dog, everyone has seen the manuscript, she can be formatting and glance at a page and find a mistake. When I'm ready to put the works out that you are reading, she's going above and beyond to assure that everything is perfect, to assure that it's professionally done, so that I shine. But she's the one who shines. She's incredibly talented and I'm lucky to have her. (So are you, Bobby.) She's been a great blessing and an even better friend. Love and appreciate you, Kat…

Secondly, I must thank, Bobby, Kat's other half, who has been a true force and a great friend in helping—first in pushing me, then encouraging me, then supporting me as I pursue my dreams of being a published author. Not only has he missed his own deadlines, to see that I hit a target date, but he's given up endless hours coaching me on marketing. Not to mention giving up his better half to work on my novels, putting himself second. You have been incredibly selfless in this, and I can't begin to repay you for your sacrifices and your encouragement. I have the utmost respect for you and for your talent as a writer. You are a true friend and I love ya (Points in heaven, my man… points in heaven!)

I especially want to thank my editors, Marcia and Cathy. Cathy and Marcia came on-board, on *Letters from Becca* and I feel my books are cleaner and stronger because of their keen eye. You are both very talented, and I appreciate you beyond measure.

Alex, you have been amazingly patient when working on my graphic art. You are a dream! I can talk you through what I want and you meet my vision every time, taking bits and pieces of pictures and ideas and actually creating art for my books! You are so talented, and I appreciate you more than words can express!

Letters from Becca

Prologue - July 5, 1948

THE SOFT HUES of the morning embraced the two small children as they played on the rocky banks of the Pedernales River. The small girl, her white dress tattered and yellowed with time, cautiously slid her feet across the massive smooth stone in the cool water. The young boy, his faded blue oversized overalls rolled up unevenly to his knees, walked quickly over the smaller stones in the falls just a foot below where she attempted her crossing. It was a race to see who could get across first. A small mixed-breed pup whimpered and bounced on the banks, unsure of the bubbling water running past.

The young girl, seeing the boy was ahead, quickened the pace, her tiny feet splashing as she ran the rest of the way. He met the challenge, rushing faster to find sure footing in the clear water.

"C'mon Taffy," he called over his shoulder. The puppy bravely jumped in and scampered behind him, scattering minnows and tadpoles in every direction.

The young girl had arrived just moments before him, perching on the stony banks on the opposite side. The rock escarpment was still cool, not yet warmed by the day's sun. The young boy jumped his last step to the stone just below the ledge on which she stood. He looked up to her and smiled.

"You win *this* time, Becca," he said, leaving the challenge hanging in the air for their trip back. He picked up a stone and chucked it into the flowing waters as Taffy shook the water from his ragged coat.

Becca brushed back her matted, golden trusses. She was a year younger than him, and almost six inches shorter. Her momma told her she was born too early and was a miracle in these parts, seeing as there was only one doctor within thirty miles, and he arrived five minutes after she had pushed her out. Her momma told her she'd always be small and that she was lucky to be alive. Becca looked at him and smiled triumphantly. "You can't beat me, John. I'm too fast!"

"What are you looking so smug about?" he asked her.

"You're bigger than me, and you can't even keep up," she retorted proudly.

"Hrrmmpphh," he growled and climbed the small ledge to where Becca stood.

"You're awful sassy for being so little," he chided.

She smiled at him. He nudged her with his shoulder as a smile crept onto his lips. Taffy jumped up, pawing at his pant leg, whimpering and whining to be picked up.

The wind blew silently around them until it reached the trees just beyond the rocks, making itself known in the rustling of the leaves dried from the three-month drought. But the wind carried another sound, and the children stopped suddenly and turned to each other. It was a terrifyingly familiar sound. They both raced back across the river, not caring who arrived first, the puppy splashing on their heels. They raced toward the old weatherworn house on a small hill but stopped suddenly beside, then stepped behind, a set of massive hundred-year-old oak trees that obscured their view.

John peeked around the corner, then turned back, out of breath. "Stay here," he instructed.

Becca nodded, kneeling beside him.

The louder his father yelled, the more intense the crying became. John turned to Becca, but only for a moment. Her hands flew to her ears as she hugged herself tighter into a ball, crouched against the grooved wood of the ancient oaks. He turned away, resolute, then took a deep breath and ran the last twenty feet to the window. He ducked beside the house, its paint peeling and flaking under his fingertips as he cautiously touched the green sill. He carefully peered in. The warm wind blew the sheer curtains through the open window, reminding him of his mother's laundry drying on the line out back. Had the wind been blowing the other direction, John would have smelled his father's approach.

He ducked out of sight as the tall, unshaven man stood just feet away, his sharp tongue attacking the waif of a woman he dragged with him. She, like her daughter, wore clothes that were at least two sizes too big. She cringed before him, her shoulders stooped in defeat under his barrage of obscenities. John cringed as his father struck her, flat-palmed in the face, sending her flying to the floor. John's fists slowly clenched in anger. How many times had he felt that same wrath, the same unprovoked rage? He called her a *'lazy cow,'* among other things, belittling her repeatedly. He pulled her up by the arm just to slap her again, letting her go so she would receive the full impact of the fall.

John gasped out loud, causing his father to turn his direction. John, realizing his mistake, put himself flat against the wall. The man slowly walked toward the window; John's only saving grace the large table inside by the window that prevented his father from seeing him.

"Is that you, Johnny?" came the frighteningly familiar voice. "You come on in here, boy," he said angrily, looking both directions, but not seeing anything from his vantage point.

John heard his father walking across the wooden floor, the sound mixed with the sobs of the beaten woman. He ran as fast as possible to the tree, then wrapped himself around Becca. They huddled behind the oaks, hoping the three towering trees that had grown from one trunk were enough to hide their presence. They heard hinge springs squeal from stretching and then the screen door slam shut on the front porch. Becca stayed silent and immobile under his body.

"Where are you, Johnny?" the man called out, slurring his words.

"Be quiet," John whispered. "He can't see us here."

"Johnny, you'd better be doin' your chores, boy," he ranted. "You'd better be doin' your chores," he repeated, more to himself, wiping the sweat from his brow. After looking around for almost a minute and satisfied that he had been mistaken, he walked back to the door and swung it open so hard it hit the front porch window sill before slamming shut behind him. John felt Becca sobbing beneath him, her small body trembling with fear. He moved to peek around the tree, but Becca grabbed his arm and pulled him tighter to her.

"Please don't leave me," she pleaded. "Don't ever leave me."

"Shh," he said, "I'm right here, Becca. I'm not going anywhere." He held her close, rocking her gently. "I'm not going anywhere."

August 13, 1951

Taffy chased John and Becca around the old oak and pecan trees in the expansive barnyard, toward the chicken coop and then into the red barn. Most days his father's pickup truck would be parked by the old milking barn. But this evening it was gone, usually signifying an early departure to work or to the local tavern, which always meant that they could play unhindered, without fear of being accosted randomly—at least until he returned. His father had become more violent in the past few years, having even broken John's arm once by twisting it too hard when he didn't close the door to the chicken coop.

Becca's mom bore weekly evidence of his drunken tirades. He would make excuses for his behavior, usually saying work was so hard to find that he was frustrated. John didn't know how his dad held a job as often as he drank, but what did he know? He was only eleven. Last night the screams were louder, the hitting more violent. They had not been the victims of his anger that night. They had only escaped it because Becca's mom was the first person he saw when he arrived home, the first person to question where he had been. The first person to call him a liar.

Becca stopped, out of breath just inside the door to the old milking area. The barn that used to house dozens of cattle at one time and bring income to Becca's grandparents now sat empty, except for a few bales of hay and the nests of their laying hens. It used to be a working farm with milking cows, egg-laying chickens and hogs raised for slaughter. After Becca's grandfather died, her mother (with the help of her older brother), sold off some of the land and most of the milk cows to pay off the mortgage on the property. Becca's Uncle Ben made sure they had enough cows and chickens to bring their mother a reasonable income. It helped that Becca's grandmother and her mother were seamstresses and regularly sewed for a few of the wealthy German townsfolk of Fredericksburg.

Becca's father had worked in one of the many local orchards since arriving in the area in 1936. He was in charge of planting and maintaining the peach trees, since he was knowledgeable, having worked in other orchards prior to that. Becca's father was a handsome man, six-foot-one with dark hair and dark eyes. She didn't remember him, but her mother kept a picture of him in her jewelry box. He wasn't of German descent like her mother's family, but having been around the culture all his life, his parents made sure he learned the language. His father, Becca's grandfather, had moved there from San Antonio when the town was chartered to work on the railroad joining Fredericksburg to San Antonio. Becca's father never admitted to Mexican blood, but he had a darker complexion and spoke with just a hint of an accent. Although the Mexicans had settled here once, it was German country now.

Becca's mother used to tell her the story of how they met, of falling in love with her father. Louis Martin was his name, though there were rumors that his real name was Luis Martinez. Since no one ever saw a birth certificate, they called him Louis, nevertheless. It was a romantic tale, or at least it was to Becca. Her mother had been delivering three new dresses to the boutique in town when her car broke down next to the orchard. Louis had been checking the fruit on the trees by the road when he saw her and offered assistance. Her mother told Becca it was love at first sight. He drove her to town in his truck, then brought back one of his friends who was a mechanic to help get hers started again.

Louis made sure he was at that same place every day so

that he would see her when she passed by with deliveries. He wooed her for months, until her parents conceded and allowed them to be married. Becca would learn much later from her mother's sister, her Aunt Betty, that the tale was far less romantic. Sometimes it's better to leave children with their dreams of reality, even if they weren't true, versus spoiling their fantasy of it. She would never know her father because he died within a year of her birth from acute respiratory failure caused by pesticide poisoning, though no one would admit that was the reason until years later.

Becca climbed through the stanchions separating the feeding troughs and through the tall narrow windows above and hung out of them as though she were going to fly. John caught up with her, grabbing her from behind.

"Careful!" he yelled.

"You worry too much," she said, allowing him to pull her back in. Taffy yelped and whined because he couldn't reach them. "I'm not a baby," she whined.

"No, you're not," he agreed. "But if anything happens to you, *I'll* get in trouble," he explained.

Becca climbed back into the trough, ran to the end and leaned into the cattle stalls. "Last one to the house is a rotten egg!" she challenged, climbing the rungs that held the cows' necks in place and jumping onto the concrete barn floor.

John dropped into the trough from the windowsill, swung across the wood stall beams and raced after her, Taffy on his heels. He caught her at the barn door and tugged her back so as to pull ahead of her. They raced together, laughing as they turned the corner to the house. Then they stopped.

The noise was a clap or more like a slap. Even Taffy stopped at the suddenness of it. They looked at each other, then slowly walked toward the house. The sun was setting in their eyes, so there was nothing but glare before them. The glare and the mist of the dirt they had kicked up floated in the air, shimmering in the setting light. They walked slowly at first, and then faster when they saw the body crumpled in the doorway. At the porch steps, Becca screamed out loud, "No!"

John grabbed her, trying to hold her back, but he couldn't. She kicked and screamed and cried until he finally released her, and she fell at her mother's side. He stared at the gun on the porch by her body and for a moment contemplated taking it. For a moment he contemplated using it. His father had killed her, as sure as if he'd pulled the trigger himself. He turned Becca around and hugged her tight.

"Who's going to take care of me now?" she sobbed. "Who's going to take care of me now?"

"I'll take care of you, Becca," he promised. "I will."

September 7, 1951

Betty looked around the house, one last time. For the past three weeks, she had gone through her sister's belongings in their childhood home. She had to sort what she wanted, what she would save for Becca, and determine the ultimate destination of the rest. Her sister had lived at home since before their parents had both died, having been their caretaker when they both became ill. None of her family had ever indulged in fine trinkets, so most of her possessions had been pictures and a few pieces of fine jewelry that had been their grandmother's. That and a few random pieces of second-hand furniture was all that they had acquired through the years.

John's father hadn't shown up that first night of her death. Or the next. Or the next. He had run his truck off the road after overindulging at the tavern that evening, having driven straight into the woods at the curve instead of turning. One of the local farmers found him three days later, disoriented and bleeding, wandering down a country road. The Good Samaritan took him into Fredericksburg to the doctor—the same doctor who had declared Becca's mother dead. When they told him what had happened, he broke down and cried. Then he was arrested.

Those summoned to the scene were all witness to the brutality of his abuse just the night before her death. Her face and body were swollen and bruised, obviously not a result of her gunshot wound to the chest. But without a witness or anyone to press charges, he was released a few days later. John's father insisted that the property and all the belongings were rightfully his because he and Becca's mother had eloped. But his protest fell on deaf ears, since he failed to produce a marriage certificate. He and John were asked to leave the premises within thirty days of her death. And for the next thirty days, Becca's Uncle Jimmy was waiting with a rifle to intimidate John's father every time he came to collect his belongings.

Betty and her husband Jimmy were childless, but not by choice. They were in good health, mid-thirties, and Becca's only living relatives, so they willingly took her in. They didn't even question whether to take responsibility for their niece. They couldn't bear to see her go into the foster care system. Betty looked out the window for Becca and spied her in the distance, sitting by the river. Becca had hardly spoken since her aunt and uncle's arrival. They stayed with her to help her sort through her mother's possessions and to take her to their home. Betty knew her niece would be forever scarred with the memories of what she had endured at her childhood home.

Becca sat on the short, wooden fishing pier over the river, stirring the water with her toes, her hands full of daisies from her mother's garden. One by one she pulled the petals from the flowers and dropped them into the moving water. She didn't hear her name being called. She could hear nothing except the rhythm of the water running over the ledge just a few feet away. She stared numbly into it, feeling too tired for a ten-year-old.

Three weeks has passed since her mother's death, but it felt like yesterday. Becca would never be able to erase that memory. Ever. Her Aunt Betty told her she should forgive John's father. "God wills it," she had said. But how could she? Becca swore she'd never forgive him for what he did to her mother—for beating her, for berating her, for driving her to suicide. She looked down into the clear waters. She could see the rich green moss dancing on the pebbles at the bottom of the shallow river that flowed beneath the pier. Becca didn't hear or feel John walking up on the dock behind her. He sat by her, hanging his legs off the pier, his feet dipping into the cool water next to hers.

"We're about to leave." John glanced over at her, wincing with the sun in his eyes. He looked down at the petals she was dropping, watching them float away. "I hate leaving you," he said softly. "It's always been us, taking care of each other."

Becca didn't move, didn't speak, or even acknowledge his presence.

He drew in a deep breath then exhaled. "I guess I'll see you later, Becca." But before he could stand up, she reached over and took his hand. He looked in her direction and saw a tear sliding down her face. She leaned on his shoulder without speaking. He smiled in understanding. They sat there together in silence.

The silence was broken only by the gruff voice of his father. "Johnny, get in the truck." The man who had seemed so threatening before suddenly didn't seem as threatening now.

John didn't move.

"Boy, did you hear me? I said, get in the truck! Now!" he repeated, his voice raised.

Becca turned to him and gave him a sad smile. "You have to go," she said, her voice barely a whisper.

John nodded sadly. He released her hand and stood up. "It's gonna be okay, Becca. I promise."

Becca nodded, trying to maintain her smile.

Slowly John turned and walked the short distance to the old pickup truck with the newly dented hood, which was filled with the few things they rightfully owned. Betty gave them John's furniture but refused to give him the other pieces she didn't want. He deserved nothing from her family that he hadn't already taken. John's father grabbed him by the shoulder and shoved him toward the truck. John nodded a silent goodbye to Betty and Jimmy before crawling into the cab. His father climbed into the driver's side and slammed his door, hoping that the action would emphasize his disdain for the family. John looked out the window and watched Becca disappear in the dust from the road as his father drove them away, taking him from the only people he truly loved.

September 22, 2000

JOHN PICKED UP HIS PACE. Thanks to his age and a few old football and war injuries, that pace wasn't what it used to be. His doctor had firmly instructed him to get more exercise. "Envision yourself working toward a purpose, or a goal," the doctor had encouraged him. That motivation didn't work at first. There was no place in particular he wanted to go. Then it happened. The Schultze sisters, Moira and Gerta, had just moved into the house on the corner. Since meeting him the day they arrived, the sisters had seemingly rescheduled their daily walks around his. The first time—and perhaps the second—might have seemed a coincidence. But for the better part of a month he ran into them daily. Now he moved with a purpose. Running away.

He envisioned them at the windows; one with spyglasses, alerting the other that he was coming. He even tried changing his route, but somehow they always appeared. In their former lives, they must have been spies and somehow figured out how to implant tracking devices on his person. It's not that they were overly annoying. They were very nice, even cordial. It's just that John liked his privacy. He kept to himself. His twin daughters urged him constantly to get out more. If it weren't for his kids' insistence and the doctor's orders, he'd never leave the house.

John was the only "single" man of his age within three blocks, except for Old Man Humphrey, as the kids in the neighborhood called him. Old Man Humphrey, who had lived at the other corner of his street all of his seventy-six years, was rarely seen. His grass would sometimes go unmowed for months at a time. And just when the neighborhood would start speculating as to whether he was decomposing inside, he would emerge to put out the trash (once a month) or to drive to the store (less often). Most of the other residents in the older community were either families or older couples that had been married forty plus years. It was a quiet neighborhood. Everyone left everyone else alone. John liked it like that.

He rounded the corner on his block, having gone a long way in a different direction to avoid the sisters. He smiled to himself, having outwitted the Schultze sisters today, but knowing that by tomorrow, they would have somehow figured out his new route. He arrived at his mailbox at the exact time as Van, his mail carrier. He smiled and nodded cordially, thanking him as Van handed him the mail. Then he made one vital mistake. He stopped to talk. Van asked him about his girls and grandkids, so he, in turn, asked about Van's. They chatted for a few minutes, then before he stepped away, Van tipped his hat and smiled.

"Good morning, ladies."

John cringed at the words. Darn it! *So close.*

Van smiled and winked at John, and for a moment, he wondered if Van was in on it and was deliberately sent to distract him until they arrived. Then Van, thanks to his excuse of work, said goodbye.

John turned and forced a smile over his frustrated face.

"Good morning, John," Gerta giggled.

John nodded. "Good morning, ladies."

"Oh, John," Moira beamed. "No sense in being so formal with us."

John stepped backward, toward his house.

"Did you have a nice walk?" Moira asked, keeping up with him.

Gerta smiled. "I'm so surprised we ran into you here this morning."

"But we're glad we did," Moira added quickly.

"Me, too," he lied through his smile.

"We were just on our way to the market. I was going to do some baking this afternoon and thought I'd make you something special," Moira said.

"Because you're always just so nice to us," Gerta added.

"That's really not necessary," John replied.

"Oh, but we *want to*," said Gerta, stepping closer.

"What's your favorite dessert?" Moira asked.

"Um, er," he stammered. "I'm a borderline diabetic. My doctor says I have to watch my sugar and carb intake."

Both their faces fell at once.

"But thank you for your kind offer," he added, cornered against his front door.

"Well," Moira said with a sigh, "we'll just have to find some other way to show you how much we appreciate you."

"Really," John insisted, "you ladies do way too much for me already." He was on a roll now. "Why, just seeing you every day gives me such pleasure."

They both smiled simultaneously. "You're just too kind, John," Moira added.

John slowly opened his door and stepped inside, feeling safer with just the screen between them. "I hate to go, ladies, but I have to finish something I was working on," he said, struggling for something better to say, but falling short.

"Goodbye, John," Gerta giggled.

"See you tomorrow, then," Moira said with a confident smile.

John tried not to cringe, but maintained his smile until they turned and walked away. He closed the door and shook his head. Slowly, he smiled. He had to give them an "A" for effort. He walked to his desk in the hallway and set down the mail to look for his reading glasses. He turned with a start when Patches, his ten-year-old golden tabby cat jumped onto the desk beside him, sending his mail flying in every direction.

John reached down and began gathering the pieces of mail and putting them back onto the desk, then smiled and petted his only friend as she purred and rubbed against him, vying for his attention. He picked up his cat, reading glasses, and mail, and headed for the kitchen where the light was much better. He could care less about reading any of it. It was mostly bills or the annoying junk mail he never opened.

The only piece he would have cared about was still on the floor, under his desk, amidst the dust and cobwebs to be forgotten. For now.

Also available on e-book and in
paperback

Meeting Melissa

Letters from Becca

**The Missionary: Book One of the Rogue Warrior
Series**